The PHOENIX INITIATIVE: FIRST MISSIONS

BOOK SIX OF THE PHOENIX INITIATIVE

Edited by Chris Kennedy
& Mark Wandrey

Seventh Seal Press
Coinjock, NC

Copyright © 2023 by Chris Kennedy & Mark Wandrey.

All rights reserved. No part of this publication may be reproduced, distributed or transmitted in any form or by any means, including photocopying, recording, or other electronic or mechanical methods, without the prior written permission of the publisher, except in the case of brief quotations embodied in critical reviews and certain other noncommercial uses permitted by copyright law.

Chris Kennedy/Seventh Seal Press
1097 Waterlily Rd.
Coinjock, NC 27923
https://chriskennedypublishing.com/

Publisher's Note: This is a work of fiction. Names, characters, places, and incidents are a product of the author's imagination. Locales and public names are sometimes used for atmospheric purposes. Any resemblance to actual people, living or dead, or to businesses, companies, events, institutions, or locales is completely coincidental.

Cover Art by Ricky Ryan. Cover Design by Brenda Mihalko

The stories and articles contained herein have never been previously published. They are copyrighted as follows:

HONEY BADGERED by Kacey Ezell and H. Y. Gregor © 2023 by Kacey Ezell and H. Y. Gregor
OSHIAN'S TWO by David Shadoin © 2023 by David Shadoin
JAGGED EDGES by Marisa Wolf © 2023 by Marisa Wolf
THE REAPER'S SCYTHE by Kevin Ikenberry © 2023 by Kevin Ikenberry
OPSHA OPS by Mike Jack Stoumbos © 2023 by Mike Jack Stoumbos
BUFF ORPINGTON AND THE SINISTER SCIENTIST BUNNIES by Casey Moores © 2023 by Casey Moores
DUCK ME by Melissa Olthoff © 2023 by Melissa Olthoff
SAFARI by Dan Bridgwater © 2023 by Dan Bridgwater
SOMETHING BEAUTIFUL by Chris Kennedy © 2023 by Chris Kennedy
SUB ROSA INFILTRATION COMPANY by John M. Olsen © 2023 by John M. Olsen
HOGAN'S ZEROS by Nick Steverson © 2023 by Nick Steverson
SUGAR FOOT by David Alan Jones © 2023 by David Alan Jones
THE BATTLE OF BRONZER HILL by Benjamin Tyler Smith © 2023 by Benjamin Tyler Smith
TRAINING MISSION by Kim M. Schoeffel © 2023 by Kim M. Schoeffel
REDEMPTION ARC by Jon R. Osborne © 2023 by Jon R. Osborne
IN THE BLACK by Charli Cox © 2023 by Charli Cox
CHIP by Mark Wandrey © 2023 by Mark Wandrey

Title/Chris Kennedy & Mark Wandrey -- 1st ed.
ISBN 978-1648557804

Contents

Foreword 4
Honey Badgered by Kacey Ezell and H. Y. Gregor 5
Oshian's Two by David Shadoin 43
Jagged Edges by Marisa Wolf 75
The Reaper's Scythe by Kevin Ikenberry 113
Opsha Ops by Mike Jack Stoumbos 145
Buff Orpington And The Sinister Scientist Bunnies by Casey Moores 183
Duck Me by Melissa Olthoff 223
Safari by Dan Bridgwater 259
Something Beautiful by Chris Kennedy 293
Sub Rosa Infiltration Company by John M. Olsen . 327
Hogan's Zeros by Nick Steverson 363
Sugar Foot by David Alan Jones 397
The Battle of Bronzer Hill by Benjamin Tyler Smith 435
Training Mission by Kim M. Schoeffel 475
Redemption Arc by Jon R. Osborne 501
In The Black by Charli Cox 541
Chip by Mark Wandrey 581

* * * * *

Foreword

In an effort to build up the mercenary forces in preparation for the war he knows is to come, Nigel Shirazi has proclaimed the Phoenix Initiative. He's twisted some arms at Binnig, and they have agreed to offer low-rate financing for the latest Mk 8 CASPers, as well as some of the earlier models they still have in stock.

The government of Earth has also chimed in to help. In their effort to repatriate the tens of thousands of aliens stranded on Earth after the Omega War (of which there are still thousands, including some from nearly every merc race), the Federation has offered incentives to help get some of the aliens off Earth by incorporating them into the new start-up mercenary companies (100,000 credits a piece, plus 9.9% loans for purchasing military hardware to get companies started).

A diverse group of startups, including a number of non-conventional ones and ones that originated on some of the colony worlds, have all just taken their first missions. These are some of their stories.

Honey Badgered by Kacey Ezell and H. Y. Gregor

Tejas

"Showing atmospheric penetration velocity on your drop pod. Good luck, Tejas," Volanta's voice crackled through the pod's speakers as the planet's magnetic field distorted their EM transmissions. Tejas let out a sigh of irritation and wished, not for the first time, that her Theela Financial contact had a proper quintessential communications node.

"I'm a Hunter, I don't need luck," she replied absently. She wasn't trying to be rude, but Volanta wasn't going to tell her anything she didn't already know, and the viewscreen showed a cloud layer coming up fast to envelop her drop pod. When she emerged, she wanted to see the terrain below as soon as possible.

"Tejas…" Even with the static, Tejas could hear the warning note in Volanta's tone. "Remember your mission parameters."

"I'm a Hunter," Tejas repeated, slowly, as if speaking to a tiny kit. "I remember everything."

"Yes, but you're a *solitary* Hunter, and that makes you vulnerable—"

"I assure you, controller," Tejas cut in, letting her voice go hard. "No one knows that better than I." Then she cut the connection.

For the most part, she liked Volanta. Theela had a reputation for hiring competent individuals, and Volanta met that criterion in spades.

But if there was one thing that Tejas didn't need, it was a reminder that she was solitary. Companionless. Alone.

"Subira, you can't leave me."

"I don't have a choice, kitten—" Another wracking cough interrupted, sending spasms ricocheting through Subira's once-muscular, wasted frame. "Believe me, it's not by choice."

The mewl of distress rose up from deep inside Tejas's chest and whispered out into the humid Azure night. She put her head down and shoved it up under Subira's chin, desperate to share scents with the woman who'd been her other half since she was a tiny kita.

Subira's long fingers came down on Tejas's neck and stroked in long, slow strokes from skull to tail, just as she'd done night after night when Tejas was young and fretful.

"I love you," Subira whispered.

"I love you," Tejas wailed. "Please don't leave. Please keep fighting."

"Kitten, I've fought as long as I can. The nanites just aren't having any effect on this infection. We've got the best docs in the galaxy here on Azure and they've tried everything they know. It's just... not working. I'm tired."

"But I need you!"

"I'll always be with you, Kitten. You're so strong. I need you to be strong now, for me. All right? Promise me. Promise me you won't go feral. Take the time to heal but find a new partner to watch your back. I won't rest easy unless I know you're safe."

"Subira, I don't want another partner! I need you!"

"You'll always have me, little love."

"Subira! Subira..."

Tejas snarled, pushed the memory to the back of her mind, and ripped her attention back to the viewscreen. The white blankness shredded into wisps and dissipated as the pod punched through the bottom of the cloud ceiling. The terrain of this unnamed dirtball spread out in all directions as the pod arrowed toward the drop coordinates.

Tejas flicked a claw to toggle off the autopilot and wrapped the pads of her fingers around the pod's control yoke. Flying by hand wasn't strictly necessary, but it might help keep her mind on her current mission, instead of venturing into memories that really needed to stay locked up in the box she'd created for them in her mind.

She nosed the pod over to pick up more speed and took a moment to look around and get her bearings. As usual, Volanta's high-level intel—or maybe Theela's intel, in reality—was quite good. On her right, the patchy light of this system's star glinted off the waves of the ocean that covered two-thirds of the dirtball. According to the intel report, the ocean wasn't actually water. There was some water mixed in, but most of the planet's liquid was some kind of highly corrosive acid that was apparently quite rare in the galaxy.

Unique, in fact, at least among known planetary bodies. Theela's report had a note that they'd consulted the Cartography Guild records to confirm that fact. No other known planet, moon, or asteroid, habitable or uninhabitable, had oceans of that same composition. And therein lay the problem: the stuff was so unique, no one had studied it enough to know how to use it. Or to counteract it.

Which was why when a Wathayat consortium transport full of physical red diamonds crashed directly into that ocean, certain players in the galactic community got *very* interested in the substance. It was apparently so corrosive and deadly that conventional search and recovery technologies were useless. Wathayat had spent a fortune trying to get the tattered remnants of the Science and Engineering Guilds to come up with a solution to no avail. Meanwhile, their investors continued breathing down their necks about the lost cargo, which apparently represented a significant portion of the consortium's wealth in these turbulent times. Wathayat had done fairly well during the last war, but red diamonds were always considered a safe investment.

Unless they sat at the bottom of a corrosive ocean for too long.

Tejas pulled her nose up to level out her dive and began to skim across the undulating seaside terrain below her. Up ahead, a break in the cloud cover sent a shaft of sunlight slanting down over a series of bright white, regular shapes with right angles standing out of the orange and yellow native vegetation.

"That must be the settlement," Tejas said. She'd taken to murmuring out loud to herself, though she refused to think about why. "The report said that Wathayat hired a Human merc company through Karma, and Humans do love their squares and rectangles." She tilted the yoke to bank slowly in that direction. The drop pod didn't really have proper wings, just little stabilization winglets, so it responded sluggishly, but there was *some* directional control. She arced down in a wide curve to flare and land the pod behind a series of dunes that shielded her LZ from the settlement. Though it wasn't easy with the pod's sluggish controls, Tejas managed to set down relatively softly on the shifting sand that fronted the corrosive ocean. She could see the high tide line created by the dirtball's small, even dirtballier moon, and it sat several lengths away, so she felt secure that her pod should be safe enough to use for extraction later.

One last check of the pod's instruments to make sure the atmosphere and pressure were suited to her physiology, and Tejas popped the seal on her pod's canopy. The breeze that rushed in smelled faintly astringent, like the citrus fruit that Subira had loved to eat.

Tejas wrinkled her nose and leapt up out of her pod's seat. For just a moment, she reveled in the sensation of moving, stretching, using her muscles after crouching in one spot for so long in the drop pod. The pads of her fingers and toes sank into the fine, gritty sand of the beach. Almost idly, she scooped up a pinch and rubbed it between her forefinger and opposable thumb. It felt like a standard silicon-heavy mineral mix, but she was no expert. She dropped the grains and stood up on her hind legs, brushing her fingertips over the pockets, sheaths, and holsters affixed to her combat harness.

Not that I'm allowed to combat *anything on this mission*, she thought. The thought was cynical, but not quite sour. The idea of sinking her claws into a struggling victim excited her as much as it always did, but she knew that without a companion, she was vulnerable. Vulnerable to a sneak attack, vulnerable to the darkness of her own rage. Subira had made her promise not to go feral, and so she wouldn't. But that meant she had to stay in control.

And violence, while an essential part of her nature, was entirely too seductive right now.

To turn her mind from *that* delicious path, Tejas took a deep breath and used her pinplants to open up her quintessential comm line with Volanta.

"*Tejas?*"

"I'm safely dirtside," she said. "Checking Q-comms."

"*I have you loud and clear, but I'm about to enter planetary shadow. I don't know if this receiver you rigged will work quite right while I'm shadowed.*"

"How long?"

"*A few hours at most.*"

Tejas smirked. "I should have no trouble."

"*Tejas…*" Volanta drew out her name with that warning note she'd used earlier.

"What?"

"*Please, be careful. Stay in your quintessence. You're only hunting information on this one, remember?*"

"I am a Hunter. I told you; we do not forget."

"*No, I know. It's just... Theela is very aware of the trust your clan placed in us by allowing us to work with you. With no comp—*"

"You must be entering shadow, controller. You are breaking up. Disconnecting now."

Volanta's transmission wasn't breaking up at all, but Tejas was tired of talking to her. She was tired of the controller's incessant *worry* over her.

She was a Hunter. She would be fine.

Even without her companion.

Tejas balled her hands into fists and flexed her fingertips so that her claws extended enough to dig into the pad of her palm. Not enough to rip and tear, just enough that she felt four pinches on either side. A tiny pinprick of pain to bring her back to equilibrium and focus.

The contract. Find a way in, remain unseen. See what data the Wathayat's mercs have gathered. If they really have figured out a way to get into the ocean, steal the information and get out. A second-season kit could do this.

With that little pep talk, Tejas pulled her cloak of quintessence around her and bounded her way up the side of the dune that hid her drop pod from the Human camp. Judging by the whiff she got at the top of the dune, she shouldn't have much trouble finding the place on the ground. These Humans didn't appear to care about their scent signatures much. She could just follow her nose.

* * *

Gye

The Alpha Strike Warriors prided themselves on being the fastest, toughest, and meanest mercs working for the Wathayat Consortium. Gye'Flieg hadn't seen any evidence to support the first two. It was only his first mission with the Human merc company, and so far their trip had been painfully boring compared to the life of adventure and riches Gye had expected.

No, there hadn't been any chances for the mercs to prove whether they were the fastest or toughest. But if the Alpha Strike Warriors weren't the meanest, Gye never wanted to work with Humans again.

He sidled into the rudimentary server room they'd set up on their arrival to the desolate wasteland that was Agnes Cordera, his slate clutched to his chest. Two or three of the Humans looked up at his entrance, but they dismissed him once they realized he wasn't the commander. *Just the Cochkala. Nothing worth worrying about.* They weren't even trying to look busy.

It probably means they're relaxed. A good sign. And now they had good reason to be. There were no signs of rival mercs closing in on the Wathayat crash they'd been hired to track down, and Gye had finally finished his terrestrial report. They'd retrieve the cache of red diamonds on the missing ship and be collecting their bounty in no time.

All thanks to Gye.

They'll thank me now that I've earned my keep.

Gye made his way toward an open console next to Tommy, one of the youngest members of the company. Tommy bared his teeth as he approached. Gye instinctively looked over the merc's shoulder before his gaze snapped back to Tommy's face. Humans didn't have tails, but knowing that never stopped Gye from looking for the prehensile fifth limb to try and interpret their emotions.

The Alpha Strike Warriors had taken him on because of his specialties in cartography and planetology, but he'd spent just as much time studying the Humans as he had the acidic quality of the strange ocean here. He looked carefully at Tommy's face.

Humans had short, even teeth. There was nothing at all menacing about them. Early in the voyage, Gye had hypothesized that this expression wasn't usually a challenge. The theory had been proven right time and again—the Humans smiled at each other all the time, especially when they were joking or happy. It was... friendly. Gye's nose twitched as he tried to mimic the expression.

"How was target practice?" Gye asked, trying to sound casual.

He hated that he'd missed a chance to practice *again*. They'd issued him a laser pistol, but Gye hadn't gotten much time to use it. The commander had been clear he was supposed to be focused on his part of the mission. His skill set was unique, after all. None of the other mercs could calculate just how long their CASPers could avoid detrimental corrosion in the acidic ocean, or how long it would take for them to reach the wreck.

"Not bad." Tommy's grin widened. "Any other mercs are in for a big surprise if they get it into their heads to go after that wreck. So, you got those numbers all crunched?"

Gye's tail flicked once in excitement at the question. Some of the Humans went out of their way to pretend he didn't exist. That would change once he provided the key to getting the diamonds. He tightened his grip on his slate.

"Yes, I've completed proofs on all of my equations. My report is nearly complete and then I can present my findings on the diamonds' exact coordinates and the best extraction method," Gye said.

Tommy's fingers started to drum on top of the desk. The motion drew Gye's eye at once—he shook himself when he realized what he'd done. It still wasn't a tail. He swallowed and continued. The merc had asked for the information, after all. The red diamonds were the whole reason they were here. "The ship crashed at the edge of the continental shelf just fifteen kilometers from the shore. It's extremely fortunate it hasn't tipped off the edge into the abyssal plain, but the sooner we're able to retrieve the cargo, the better. Because of the acidic content in the Alpha Strike Gulf—"

"The *what?*" Tommy interrupted, leaning forward now.

"The Alpha Strike Gulf." Gye's tail drooped. "That's what I named the ocean. It's on the map I sent to everyone. I thought…"

Gye had been one of the first to study the qualities of the strange acidic waters on Agnes Cordera. And the Alpha Strike Warriors would be the ones diving to recover the cache. He thought they'd be pleased he'd taken the initiative to name it after the new merc company. Gye had even been preparing the petition to send to the Cartography Guild to make it official.

"Very cool." Tommy glanced sidelong at Steven, a one-eared Human with teeth as yellow as any Cochkala's.

"Sounds like the Cochkala's figured everything out. Makes you wonder why Wathayat bothered to send the rest of us," Steven drawled.

Gye's tail swished to one side. *No, you're with Humans. Your Humans. You have to speak their language now.* He showed his teeth in a Human smile.

"Naturally everyone has a very important role to play," Gye said. That was the most important part of a team. After being shunted from department to department for years at the Cartography Guild, it was what Gye had been most looking forward to when he'd joined the merc company. Camaraderie.

A low buzzing sound filled the server room. Gye's ears twitched, trying to pinpoint the location of the signal.

"Damned environmental sensor's on the fritz again," a merc named Derek growled. He was one of the few men actually working.

Gye squinted at the holographic projection over Derek's desk. Satisfaction swept over him as he realized what Derek was looking at: one of Gye's maps of the continental shelf where the Wathayat ship had crashed.

"You're actually reading that?" Steven asked Derek. Gye's gaze flicked between the two mercs. Steven's eyes rolled, and he laughed when the other man nodded.

"It's the job, unless you're too hopped up on fumes to remember," Derek said, "and if you—"

A blaring siren cut through the gently buzzing alarm. Gye jolted out of his seat at the sound. His slate slipped from his grasp, bouncing once before crashing to the floor. A projection flared to life from the console on the center table. Boots thudded down the hall outside the server room, shaking the floor and adding to the cacophonous alarm.

"*Fuck.*" Derek grabbed his laser rifle. He looked around wildly and his gaze locked onto Gye. "You got that data backed up, Cochkala?"

"Yes I—" Gye's eyes dropped to the spot beneath a desk where his slate had fallen. Backup? Yes, of course he'd backed up the data. "Yes, I have it!"

"Good. Now stay here!"

"Yes, sir, I…" Gye's hand strayed to the laser pistol at his hip. What was going on? "*Alone?*"

"Steven!" Derek barked as the mercs rushed for the exit. He grabbed the lapel of Steven's uniform and jerked him back into the room. "Stay with him."

"You can't be serious," Steven sputtered. Derek stomped out into the hall without replying. The door swung shut on the nearly empty server room.

"Th—" The word stuck in Gye's throat. *Maybe if I'd practiced shooting, they wouldn't have left me here.* The thought terrified him.

Steven bobbed on the balls of his feet, hefting his laser rifle in one hand and glaring at Gye.

"Thanks," Gye managed the word this time.

"Fuck this." Steven reached for the door handle.

"Wait, Steven—" Gye's chest constricted, forcing the air from his lungs. Was he being abandoned?

"Just stay here!" Steven bared his teeth before he ran out the door. The Human expression was anything but friendly.

* * *

Tejas

Though the sand gave way under her feet as she ran, Tejas continued to enjoy the bunch and pull of her muscles as she darted across the beach. The burn of exertion and the heat in her breath wasn't the same as feeling her claws shredding flesh, but it provided a small release to the screaming tension that wreathed her every thought since—

No. Better not to think of that. Focus on the heat of the sand between my pads, the astringent sting of the wind in my nostrils. The glint of the sunlight on... wait, is that movement?

She stopped, holding herself motionless while the sand shifted around her, spilling over top of all four of her feet while she flicked her ears and raised her nose to the sky.

A high whine caught at the edge of her awareness, grating along the insides of her ears. So high as to be inaudible to Humans, she could barely catch it herself. *A vehicle? But whose?* A thread of deep musk joining the acid sting of the ocean in her nose… but far away. Upwind of her. Upwind of the settlement. Careless…

Unless they just don't *care. So either the Humans know they are coming, or they know that Humans are noseblind. Interesting.*

She directed a thought through her pinplants to open up the Q-comm channel with Volanta, but got no response. Tejas wrinkled her nose again in annoyance. A proper Q-comm suite wouldn't have had issue with planetary shadow, but she'd had to retrofit Volanta's setup as best she could, and there were limits to what she could do without the proper Hunter-made components. For the next couple of hours, she was on her own.

But then, she was always on her own now.

Tejas's mind flinched from that thought. She sniffed at the air again, drawing in that intriguing thread of deep musk. It tasted like old fur and rich organic decay, nothing like what you'd expect on this near-sterile planet. Curiosity teased at her, seducing her mind with the promise of a puzzle to be uncovered.

No. I heard Volanta's incessant warnings. Stick to the mission. Don't step out of parameters. I need this contract to go well, otherwise Dama will never let me work again unless I choose another companion and I—

That thought was even worse.

Tejas scrubbed the back of her hand over her nose, trying to rub out the tantalizing mystery the scents presented, and re-seated the protective goggles over her eyes.

Whoever is coming is on the other side of the settlement anyway. If I hurry, I should get there just before they do. I suppose I'll find out what they're doing then.

With that thought, she dropped back down to all fours and bolted for the settlement with all the speed and intensity of a Hunter giving chase.

It still took longer than she expected to arrive. The settlement—or temporary camp, as it clearly was from close up—had looked much closer from her vantage point aloft. Fortunately, she'd broken off from her dead sprint after the first few moments and settled into an easy lope that left her no more than pleasantly winded when she slowed to a stop outside the sagging fabric fence of the camp's perimeter.

She lifted her head and took another whiff, trying to gauge the progress of the mystery visitors. They weren't here, but they were close. That was all she could tell over the miasma of the Human camp. Whoever these mercs were, hygiene did not appear to be their focus.

Which made it all the worse when she slipped past the fabric perimeter and made her way to the central building only to find the perfect access point: an overfilled waste recycler. Tejas huffed out her breath as quietly as possible and spared a moment for her clean, shiny coat of night-dark fur. Then she steeled her stomach and leapt up on top of the overflowing pile of garbage, touching down lightly on a crumpled piece of thin polymer that reeked of rot and stale fat before launching herself upward again. She stretched out her arms, claws extended from her fingerpads and just barely caught the metal edge of the grease-slick and slimy garbage chute.

Tejas swallowed hard and pulled herself up and into the stinking passageway. It wasn't a large opening—maybe half a meter square—and it sloped sharply down toward the bin on the outside. She badly wanted to keep from touching the walls, but that didn't seem to be an option, so she gave a mental shrug and began to climb. With her limbs extended, she could easily anchor herself with her claws in the metal seams that ringed the chute, and before long, she'd arrived at an overhead trapdoor.

She listened but heard nothing. Unfortunately, her current circumstances significantly compromised her olfactory sense, so she moved with slow, deliberate caution as she lifted the trapdoor and peered out into a darkened room.

Once again, the food scents assailed her. This time, though, the scent of fresh meat and the green things that Humans liked overlaid the sticky sweetness of decay.

Kitchen, she decided, having learned the word from her seasons of life with Subira. *And still none too clean. But I bet it's got a sink!*

Perhaps it wasn't the wisest course, but Tejas decided that she didn't care. Maybe these Human mercenaries didn't understand olfactory signatures and operations security, but *she* certainly did! And it would do her no good to be invisible if she stank to high orbit. She had a feeling that in her current state, even a Human would smell her coming.

She pushed up out of the garbage chute and found herself on a flat metal counter that ran the length of the wall. Careful to step lightly, lest she leave footprints, Tejas made her way along the counter to where a large sink stood at the far end. Slowly, so as to make as little noise as possible, she pushed the lever to start the flow of water—she confirmed it was *actual* water with a sniff—and eased herself beneath its flow.

Ordinarily, she didn't love being wet, but Tejas had to admit that it was a relief when the stink started to lessen. She recognized a small dispenser of liquid soap like what Subira used to use to clean her eating tools. When she touched the pump, it gave her some resistance and then shot a plug of solidified soap down into the sink before releasing a stream of thick, blue-green liquid.

Never been used? Why am I not surprised? I guess they just throw everything down that chute I decided to climb. Great idea, Tejas. Super smart. Please never do that *again.*

With the help of the soap, she managed a decent job of cleaning the worst of the stench from her pads and fur. When she was finished, she turned off the water with a snap of her wrist and shook herself mostly dry. Her harness was still wet, but there wasn't much she could do about it. At least it no longer smelled like rotten food.

Tejas jumped down from the sink to the polymer floor that Humans loved to use in these modular buildings of theirs and took stock. She'd been in temporary camps like this one before, and they tended to follow a similar plan. Vehicle and large equipment storage bays on the ground floor, living and working quarters on the second. Thus the long chute she'd had to climb to get in. But now what?

What I really need is a server room of some kind. If they're collecting or processing information about the location of the wreck and how to get to it, that would be where they are storing it. If I can get in and access their systems, I should be able to relay anything of interest to Volanta when she comes out of Dirtball's shadow. And Humans like to protect their server rooms, so I'm guessing it's toward the center of the buildi—

A long, low buzzing sound split the air overhead. At first, Tejas thought it might be an incoming aerial vehicle, but the sound wasn't quite right. She eased over to the double swinging doors and peered out just in time to see half a dozen male Humans in light power armor—not CASPers, but just their garrison wear—come sauntering down the hallway, laughing and joking and shoving each other the way the males were wont to do.

Couldn't be an attack alarm, then, she thought, stepping back and letting the door slowly swing fully closed again as she listened to them pass. *Not with them looking as relaxed as they do. But they're coming from the center of the building. I wonder where they were?*

Tejas waited until their noise indicated they'd gone past and then slipped through the swinging door into the hallway. She stayed cloaked, of course, and walked quadrupedally, her belly held low to the floor in order to give her the best chance of dodging an unexpected attack.

Or seizing an unexpected opportunity.

She followed the hallway until it dead-ended into a crossing hallway, and then she followed *that* toward the center of the building—at least according to her directional sense. A sense that was apparently pretty good because she found herself in a room staring at a magnetically locked door and no way in.

Well, clearly there is *a way in*. She sat down on the floor and began to wash her face. The faint soapy taste of her fur made her grimace, but the repetitive action always helped her think. *I just have to figure it out. What was it Esthik used to say? "Watch, and find a way."*

She'd been watching—and washing—for several moments when the answer presented itself. Without warning, the low buzzing alarm she'd noticed before cut off, and a shrill klaxon split the air instead.

With the back of her hand halfway to her mouth, she watched as the red light above the door abruptly flashed green, and a sudden hiss of air heralded the opening of the locked door.

"Wait, Steven—"

"Just stay here!"

Tejas barely registered the Human's anger-edged words as he pushed the door wide enough to accommodate his power-armored self. She darted quickly between his legs as he strode out and ducked to one side as the door closed behind him. It closed with a heavy thunk and the accompanying click of the mag lock reengaging. A low, buzzing machine hum rose all around her, punctuated by something that sounded suspiciously like a terrified sob.

She'd found the server room.

And it was occupied.

Watch, and find a way.

Tejas backed herself up against the nearest corner, her eyes riveted to the trembling form of what looked like a very frightened, very alone Cochkala.

* * *

Gye

The door to the hall snapped shut on Steven's heels with a resolute thunk. Gye stared blankly ahead. His heart thundered in his chest, the sound nearly as loud as the siren still shrieking through the halls.

An alarm Gye had never heard before, but it didn't take a genius to know that something was very, very wrong.

What the FUCK just happened?

Gye's tail drooped to the floor. He didn't know whether he was more angry or shocked, but he was absolutely terrified.

Alone.

What was going on?

But it was obvious enough, and he knew he shouldn't be surprised. Word about the red diamonds was bound to get out sooner or later. Agnus Cordera was a void-blasted, inhospitable planet, but the job was too tempting. It had only been a matter of time before more mercs came sniffing around.

Weren't you just complaining that the job was boring?

Gye shook himself and looked around the room, trying to orient and focus through the raging sirens. *Focus. There's a procedure. Focus.*

He stumbled to the nearest console and started fumbling with the system files… planetary data… personnel files… *there*. Security. Gye opened the camera feed and flipped through them one at a time. Members of Alpha Strike Warriors storming through the halls, some gearing up in power armor, others already dressed and on patrol. Gye swallowed his guilt. He should be helping—he *wanted* to help.

His relief at being left in the server room—even alone—was pathetic.

Alarms. Gye tapped through the commands until he found the right system. The siren cut off all at once, but Gye's brain still rattled around in his head as an aftereffect of the noise.

Frantic activity on the Tri-V drew his attention back to the camera feed. Two mercs raced from the compound's front gate, disappearing into the main entrance. Several towering figures, heavily armed and outfitted in power armor, stalked after the Humans. Gye's insides turned to water.

Besquith.

He found the inner hall feed in time to see the two mercs barring the main doors and setting the security locks.

Click—another hall, and the Besquith were already inside. *Click*—a human in armor being dragged down the hall, dark stains trailing the floor behind him. *Click*—three more Besquith walking down an otherwise empty hall.

The hall leading right to the server room.

Fuck. The Human curse had never felt more appropriate. Gye's fingers flew across the console's controls. He closed the camera feeds and opened the server database, initiating an override protocol to delete all the research files he'd uploaded. The Alpha Strike Warriors were supposed to be the fastest, toughest, and meanest... no Besquith could stand up to them. That's what Tommy and Steven would say.

Better safe than sorry. If they survived this, and the Besquith got to the diamonds first, Gye was as good as outcast—again. It would be even worse than getting kicked around the Cartography Guild.

Gye glanced over his shoulder at the door to the hall, regretting that he'd closed the camera feeds. The progress bar on the Tri-V moved at a glacial pace. *Come on, come on…*

Those Besquith would be here any second. Maybe with friends. Gye needed to run—or preferably hide, if he could find somewhere safe. But he had to make sure the data was wiped first. He had to keep up his part of the deal.

Gye's ears swiveled toward the hall. Were those footsteps? The Besquith had to be close… The progress bar indicated the file deletion was barely half complete. He leaned down to pick up his fallen slate. He would have the only remaining copy of the data they needed, but he could wipe the slate if it came to that, too. Worst-case scenario, he'd have to replicate his work. It was better than letting the Besquith get to the cache first.

His heart fell into his stomach as he considered the now slightly dented slate in his hands. Derek had asked about a backup drive. Apprehension flickered around the corners of Gye's already racing mind. He'd locked the backup drive in the safe next door.

Was the progress bar even still moving? Gye slipped the slate into his satchel and secured the bag's straps with shaking fingers. *Focus.* Backup drive. Safe first.

He wasn't helping anybody by sitting around staring at the Tri-V.

Gye shot a backward glance at the hall door before darting to the adjacent storage facility. It took his eyes a moment to adjust to the semi-darkness of the smaller room. He wiped a forehand across his face, then scratched his ears as he made his way to the safe. He always got itchy when he was nervous—this was another thing entirely. Sweat dampened his fur and slicked his hands. He *wished* he was nervous.

A shadow in the corner shifted. Gye froze, his gaze sweeping the room. The server room's lights switched on.

"It's almost too easy," a deep voice grated through a translator. Gye's heart leapt in his chest, and he dropped to the floor with a whimper, smashing his elbow against a shelf as he flopped down. He was partially concealed behind a metal shelving unit.

In all his panic, he'd forgotten there was another entrance into the storage unit. Heavy footfalls thumped through the room, getting closer and closer. The Besquith had found him.

Fear coiled around Gye's chest with vicelike intensity. He couldn't breathe. He couldn't *think*. Blood pounded in his temples. More footsteps.

How many were there? Gye managed a single, shuddering breath, and forced himself to crawl a few lengths forward. If he summoned enough courage to peek out around the shelf, he'd be able to see the door to the server room from his position.

All I have is this tiny laser pistol.

"What's in the safe, little Humans?" the Besquith growled.

Gye's tail flicked up indignantly, almost reaching the top of the shelf he was hiding behind. *Humans?* The completely irrational annoyance broke Gye from his paralysis, and he lifted himself into a crouch.

Run. Hide. In that order.

Gye slipped around the shelves, keeping low. He winced at every scuff of his boots on the cheap flooring. Grumbling laughter filled the room with menace, setting Gye's fur on end.

It was too much. He jumped up and bolted for the door to the main server room. He didn't dare look back at the Besquith. Adrenaline pulsed through his body with all the skittering panic and single-minded focus of a prey animal on the run. Gye slammed into the door, stumbled across the threshold. He threw himself back against the door and fumbled with the locks.

The door rattled on its hinges as the Besquith threw its weight at the barrier. Gye yelped and backed away from the door. He scrabbled for a radio on the table.

"Uhm, mayday, mayday." Gye's voice cracked as the pounding from the storage room got louder. The door wouldn't hold up against a fully equipped Besquith for long. "Mayday, help, this is Gye'Flieg. I'm in the server room and—"

The Besquith bellowed. Gye started and dropped beneath the table, clutching the radio to his chest.

"I'm in the server room, and the Besquith are here!" The words were shouts, now. Angry ones. No point in trying to pretend he wasn't in here with the enemy pounding down the door.

Gye was trapped. As good as dead, unless someone from his team decided his neck was worth saving.

"I'm the only one with the coordinates," he screamed, straining his vocal chords in a vain attempt to be heard over the Besquith. "And *where the hell is Steven?*"

Silence on the radio.

It was worse than static. At least then he might have believed there was a problem with the comm system.

The door splintered open. The Besquith stormed across the threshold—all teeth and menace. Gye's grip on the radio went slack, and the comm device fell to the floor with a clatter. The Besquith turned at the sound, and its eyes narrowed when it saw Gye. A razor-sharp smile split its face.

Where the hell is Steven?

Gye's entire body shook from head to toe, but he found himself clambering to his feet. His tail shot straight up, bristling with his indignation and terror. The Besquith's smile widened, and there was no mistaking the meaning behind the expression.

I'm going to die.

The Besquith advanced.

Gye grabbed the laser pistol on his belt.

* * *

Tejas

The Cochkala raised a tiny laser pistol in a shaking forehand. Admiration bloomed within Tejas's chest as the Besquith's growling laugh rumbled through the room.

"What are you going to do with that little toy?" The Besquith's voice sounded like so much grinding metal overlaid with the translator's words. Even so, the insulting sneer came through loud and clear, and Tejas found herself suppressing a growl of her own.

The Besquith stalked slowly toward the trembling Cochkala, who backed into one of the room's buzzing server racks, making the whole thing rattle in its protective cage. The Cochkala let out a tiny noise, but kept that ridiculous pistol raised. Tejas flicked her gaze to his face, and saw something harden in the alien's eyes. Almost as if... he'd decided to go out fighting?

"Keep fighting, Subira."

"I can't fight anymore..."

Tejas shoved the memory away and was airborne before she realized she was making the jump. She extended her claws and landed perfectly atop the Besquith's curved spinal hump. Before the snarling alien could do more than flinch at the sudden weight on his back, Tejas lunged to the side and dragged all five of her back right claws across the small vulnerable spot beneath the Besquith's chin, where their main artery ran close under their famously tough skin and fur.

Tough, but no match for a Hunter's claws.

Blood fountained forth, spraying the Cochkala from toes to crown as the Besquith's legs crumpled. Tejas let her quintessence go with a sigh as she rode the body to the floor, then looked up at the stunned being in front of her.

"There are more coming," she said, twitching her ears as they caught the sounds of running feet and growled commands. "Find a table and get under it. But hide."

Behind her, the door beeped, then slammed open. Tejas whirled, pulling her quintessence back around her just in time to see a squad of

Besquith move in. The largest, lead Besquith carried a dismembered Human torso with a security badge hanging from the shredded power armor.

Steven, I suppose. Or one of his fellows. Smart of them to realize they'd need his badge to get in here. Who sent them, I wonder? Not... that I care. She realized this last as red joy began to spike through her veins. She breathed in the metallic scent of the Besquith's blood and let her lips stretch in a Human-style smile.

It felt so *good* to rend. To kill.

It felt *right*. Right in a way nothing had felt right since she watched Subira's eyes go flat and lifeless.

A subliminal snarl trickled forth from between her lips, causing the lead Besquith to pause in his advance into the room.

Something pulled at the corner of Tejas's mind. Some responsibility, some promise—but the savage heat of carnage called to her, and its siren song would not be resisted any longer.

"Volanta," she murmured, toggling on her Q-comms and calling in the blind. "Change of plans. I'm going loud."

"*Going lo—wait! Tejas! Wai—*"

Tejas cut the connection again with a thought and released any pretense of self-control. With a yowl loud enough to cut through the servers' buzz, she leapt out of her quintessence, appearing in midair just before raking her foreclaws across the lead Besquith's vulnerable eye sockets. He screamed and reached up to slap at her, but she was already gone. She re-cloaked herself and let Dirtball's gravity take her to the floor, where she rolled between the Besquith's feet and pulled out one of her knives. Two quick slashes to the backs of his ankles and knees, and he was down, still screaming, writhing and blind as his fellows frantically opened fire in the close confines of the server room.

Someone hit the lights with their laser bolt, causing a power surge that knocked out the other lights. Darkness slammed down over them all. With a thought, Tejas retracted her day-goggles and continued her dance. She slashed and leapt, hamstringing another one of the Besquith here, removing the forehands of one there. Once taking a rifle from loose, trembling digits and spinning it around to fire it back into the open, panting mouth of the terrified attacker. The coppery tang of Besquith blood filled the room, filled her nostrils, her mouth. Red joy and savage grief wrapped her up in their embrace, protecting her from feeling anything but lust for more blood, more pain, more flesh rending beneath her claws.

She dodged another laser bolt and flipped herself to her hands, then sprang up to dig her claws into the inner thigh of one of the remaining Besquith. Like many bipedal species, they carried their reproductive organs low on their torsos, close to the junction of their legs. The layer of powered armor there didn't cause her much trouble, she merely flipped her knife under the seam, twisted, and popped it free. Then she jabbed the same knife into the vulnerable flesh beneath, sending another high, piercing scream into the close metallic darkness of the server room.

There. Another heart beat to her left. Rapid and thready and scared. Someone started laughing as she leapt again, knives out, claws out, eyes and nose and ears trained on that terrified pulse.

A body under her pads, impacted with a slap.

Something swished over her head. She ducked. The laughter continued.

Jab. *Squish.*

Knife into flesh. Claws into flesh. Screams joining the laughter.

It's me. It's me, I'm the one laughing…

Wet, thick ripping. Gurgle stifling the scream. Falling...

Tejas kept laughing as she rode this body to the floor as well.

* * *

Gye

So that's what they mean when they say critical wounds 'spurt.'

The thought bounced around Gye's mind like a ricochet as blood arced through the air. He threw his arms up, but his instincts were too slow—blood splattered him from head to toe, its coppery tang suffusing the air. Even more spurted from the snarling Besquith's neck, cutting its last threat off mid-growl.

Tremors wracked Gye's body. He clasped the laser pistol with both hands now, but his arms were shaking so wildly he knew he'd never get off a clean shot. The tiny red dot from the laser sight bounced around too fast to follow. His knees trembled violently, and it was all he could do to keep standing—let alone move away from the dying alien and its unseen attacker.

The once-warm, sticky blood cooled and congealed almost at once. The tacky substance covered his pants and boots, coated his fur, his uniform. His *face*. It pooled on the floor. The server room's grim, dingy lighting reflected off the dark surface.

He'd never seen someone die before, let alone like *this*.

The Besquith fell to its knees, then crashed forward. The noise was enough to shake Gye from his horrified trance. He jumped back, boots skittering in the dark blood, and fell against a shelf. His elbow bashed against a console. He hissed in pain as shocks of nervous pain shot up his arm.

"There are more coming."

Gye's ears twitched toward the voice. He ran a hand over his eyes to clear some of the blood caked on his face, then squinted back at the Besquith's now-still form. A Depik with fur black as night crouched on the back.

"Find a table and get under it. But hide." Her vivid orange eyes blinked up at him once before the door behind her beeped, then slammed open. The Depik's attention snapped to the disturbance with preternatural speed.

More Besquith. One of them hauled a body across the threshold. *No. Not a body.* Gye bit back a terrified squeak.

A body *part.* Or most of a body. Or—Gye's brain hyper focused on the dead Human's black hair, and the long scar where an ear should be. It was Steven.

The Depik flickered out of sight. Gye was alone again. He tightened his grip on the laser pistol as the Besquith began to fall before his eyes.

No. Not alone.

A Besquith roared out in agony. Gye's tail twitched once. This Depik was fierce.

Maybe there was still a chance. Steven was dead—but if the Depik could take on the Besquith, maybe the rest of the Alpha Strike Warriors had survived.

Hide. The Depik told you to hide. Everything in Gye's mind screamed at him to do it. A table, a shelf, a closet—anything. *Hide, hide, hide.* He closed his eyes and swallowed against the lump of dread in his throat. It would be so easy to hide. But this Depik was fighting the Besquith— and she was doing it alone. To help *him.*

There was definitely a chance the other mercs were still alive. His legs carried him back across the server room before he realized he'd made the decision. He still had a job to do.

Gye's boots slipped on the cheap tile floor, leaving smears of Besquith blood behind him. *Hiding might not have been an option after all.* He almost laughed at the absurd thought. He grabbed the handle into the storage room and yanked the door open. Blood pounded in his ears as he burst across the threshold and into the dimly lit room.

Blasts of laser fire rang out from the adjacent space. More screaming, and the crashing of falling shelves and breaking furniture joined the rapport of the firefight.

Gye hesitated. *I could go back.* But go back and do what, exactly? He was only a Cochkala—the only Cochkala in a Human merc company that hadn't even bothered to properly equip him.

He turned back. The safe was right where he'd left it—*don't be stupid, of course it is*—had that only been a few moments earlier? He reached it in three quick strides and put his eye against the optical reader. The scanner verified his identity with a quick flash, and the locking mechanism whirred to life.

There was a soft click, indicating the lock had disengaged. Gye wiped his hand on his uniform pants. They only came away even more filthy.

Blood. Its sticky tackiness matted his fur and tainted the air with its metallic tang. Blood *everywhere*. But the data was still on the backup slate whether he got blood on it or not. He grabbed the slate and tucked it into his bag. *At least I did one thing right.*

Gye's gaze flickered between the storage room's two exits. More screaming echoed from the main server room. He clutched his bag against his chest in one hand, the laser pistol in the other.

He hesitated too long. The server room door slammed open, revealing a hulking Besquith. An amused growl floated across the distance between them.

"Uhm. Help?" Gye's words were barely audible to his own ears, let alone loud enough to reach the murderous Depik in the adjacent room. Besides, if this Besquith had made it through the carnage, the assassin was still busy dancing with death on her own.

Gye took several side steps toward the hall door, keeping the Besquith in his line of vision at all times. Sweat slicked the hand holding his gun. The Besquith chuckled and propped its laser rifle against its shoulder. The alien advanced at a leisurely pace. It looked almost *relaxed*. Gye's tail flicked back and forth with frenetic energy—panic, dismay.

The hall door was almost in reach, but the Besquith's huge strides had already closed the distance. Gye grabbed for the handle. *Locked.* He cursed and jabbed at the locking mechanism.

The floor shook under the alien's heavy footfalls. It lunged.

For once, Gye's instincts didn't fail him. He raised the laser pistol and fired. The first bolt flew wide. The Besquith snarled, rage glittering in its eyes, and shifted its grip on the rifle it carried.

A soft growl tickled the back of Gye's throat. He fired again, striking the Besquith's shoulder. Dropping his grip on his satchel, he grasped the pistol in both hands. He fired again, missed. Took two steps closer, hardly trusting his own daring.

What was the point of letting that Depik fight for him if he just gave up here?

His hands steadied with each shot as adrenaline pulsed through his body. Gye squeezed the trigger again and again, and bolts smashed into the Besquith's face with increasing accuracy. The scents of seared flesh and singed fur mingled with the coppery tang of blood hanging in the air.

I've come this far.

The Besquith's snarling rage faded to a high-pitched keening. The rifle dropped from the alien's grip as it reeled back from Gye's attack. Gye hardly noticed. His lips curled back, baring his teeth. He fired until the Besquith dropped to the floor, unmoving.

The sudden silence that filled the room was deafening. Gye lowered the pistol, hardly daring to believe the Besquith was dead.

I did that.

I did that?

He'd killed a Besquith. Gye took several steadying breaths and backed away from the body. Time to go. A quick inspection confirmed that both slates were safely tucked into his bag. He re-secured the straps and wrapped an arm protectively around it.

A strangled cry carried from the server room—and Gye found himself edging around the Besquith's body, following the sound of the cries. He crouched by the door and peered around the corner, holding his breath.

The room was carnage made flesh. Bodies of fallen Besquith lay beneath tables, or else slumped over console desks. One hulking foe remained, but Gye didn't like the Besquith's chances. The alien bellowed a final protest before Gye's eyes. It was dead before it hit the floor.

Gye took in the rest of the room. It was over—for now. The Depik was in here somewhere, even if he still couldn't see her. He cleared his throat.

"Hey!" His throat tightened on the word, but he pushed past it. He rose from his crouch and eased into the room, still clutching the satchel to his chest.

It was either the bravest thing he'd ever done, or the stupidest. He slipped the laser pistol back into its holster on his belt and lifted his hand, palm out, toward the last dead Besquith. "Hey, it's over. Come with me!"

The Depik flickered back into view. No longer night black, her fur was coated in even more Besquith blood than Gye's was. Gye took another step forward. Knowing full well it might be the last thing he ever did, Gye extended his hand toward the killer.

The Depik blinked. Her orange eyes burned with an ecstasy so intense it was almost feral.

"Please, stop. They're dead. You did it. You killed them, but more are on their way. Come with me. We have to get out of here!"

This Depik had just saved his life—he wouldn't leave without her.

* * *

Tejas

Rip. *Squelch.* Spin.
Leap. *Strike.*
Red and black ecstasy shivered under her skin. She flowed like blood in the darkness, blood on the floor. Blood spraying outward from slashed arteries and punctured membranes...

Metallic copper coated her tongue, filled her nostrils. Fire pulsed within her muscles, smoldering like a looming orgasm as she teetered on the ragged edge of breath—

"—with me!"

With you. I will always be with you.

Tejas spun toward this new sound, claws and knives at the ready. Her blood-tacky pads stuck momentarily on the carnage-covered floor, slowing her down enough to blink.

And stare.

The Cochkala, terror in his eyes, drying blood coating his face. His hand raised, still shaking like it had when he pointed his puny laser pistol at the first Besquith. Raised and empty.

Beckoning.

"Please, stop. They're dead. You did it. You killed them, but more are on their way. Come with me. We have to get out of here!"

"Go," Tejas growled, the word low and guttural.

"N-not without you. Please. You saved me and I can't… I won't just leave you."

Don't leave me!

I will never leave you, Kitten.

"You… won't…"

"I won't," he said, his voice firming up. "But you have to come with me now, because there are more Besquith on the way, and while I'm sure you could take them, I'm not sure *I* would survive long enough for you to kill them all single handedly so can we just please *go!*"

"What is your name?"

"My—my name? Gye. Um. Gye'Flieg… I don't know why I told you that."

"Gye. I greet you. I am Tejas."

"Is this where you welcome me to our negotiation?"

Tejas sucked in a deep breath and focused on Gye's frantic eyes. It helped her push the red and black savagery further to the edges of her brain. She swallowed, then swiped her knife on a clean-ish patch of fur before sheathing it.

"You said you will not leave me," she said, refusing to sound tentative, even though her entire being quaked to hear his answer.

"I... I won't."

"Then there is nothing to negotiate. You are mine, and I am yours."

Gye blinked, and his confusion was clear, even with his alien features. "So can we go?"

Tejas flicked her ears. "I must complete my mission first."

"What mission?"

"I am to learn the location of the Wathayat wreck and how to access it."

Gye swallowed hard. "Um... I may know those things."

Now it was Tejas's turn to blink in surprise. "You?"

"Yes. Um. That's what I was doing here. Wathayat hired me to map the crash site and analyze the ocean's content to figure out how to get to the wreck for salvage. I was... part of a merc company. Or I thought I was, anyway." His shoulders drooped, and even though it remained dark, Gye looked down at the floor in obvious sadness.

"They left you," Tejas said, thinking of the mercs she'd seen laughing and sauntering away from the server room. Of the lone merc running after the alarm. "When they were supposed to protect you."

"Yes."

She leapt, heedless of the bloody mess they'd both become. Gye flinched, but some instinct must have warned him, because he held up his forelimbs to catch her.

"You are mine," Tejas repeated. "And I am yours. You will not leave me. Nor will I leave you. But if you know those things, we may leave together—" She broke off, her ears twitching. "Later."

"*Later?*" Gye's voice wasn't quite a shriek, but it wasn't far off. Tejas rammed her bloody head against his neck in an attempt to comfort him. "Why can't we go *now?*"

"Because I just heard the door to the building being forced open. I suspect more Besquith are coming to look for their packmates. On my way into the camp, I saw a rather large group of them. More than accounted for here."

"Oh."

"But," she said, nuzzling under his ear harder. It may not comfort him, but it comforted *her*, and she'd figure out how to soothe him soon enough. "I think we shall be safe enough here for a few moments if we lock the door and make sure the torso is inside."

"Steven's... *torso*..." Gye's words suddenly sounded weak and strangled.

"Yes. It has his access badge attached to what remains of his armor. It's how this group got in."

"Oh. I... see."

"Can you? See, I mean? I have excellent dark vision. Do you?"

"I... have these implants..."

"Good enough. Can you move the bodies away from the door while I make a call?"

"A call? Sure but..."

"I will explain in a moment. I will explain everything, but let me save us first, all right? You saved me. Let me return the favor."

Gye looked like he wanted to say more, but he simply closed his mouth and ducked his head in what she assumed was a gesture of assent. She rubbed her head along his jawline one more time and leapt down from his arms.

Immediately, she missed the scent, the feel of him. She swallowed hard against the need to return and toggled her pinplants on instead.

"Volanta."

"*TEJAS! Oh chaos and entropy!* Where are you? *I thought you'd gone fer—*"

"Not now. I have what I came for, but I need an extract. There is a company of Besquith currently looting the remains of the Human camp. I am holed up with the sole survivor of the company in the server room in their central building. Second floor."

"*I have a team on the way. But they're not going to be able to cut through a whole company of Besquith to get to you. Can you make your way out for a rendezvous? I'll send you coordinates.*"

Tejas bared her teeth in a Human-style grin and looked up at Gye. "Oh, we certainly can."

"*Tejas… use stealth. For the love of little atoms Do. Not. Engage. If you go feral, there's no way to bring you back, Tejas. Your Dama was very clear on this.*"

"I have already engaged," Tejas said, slow blinking as she imagined Volanta's expression. "And I did go feral… for a moment. But you are wrong. I came back because…" She paused, turning to watch Gye's surprisingly liquid, beautiful movements as he used his prehensile tail to help him clear the Besquith body parts from the door.

"*Because? Tejas? Hunter, you cut out. Confirm that you are all right?*"

"I am perfect," Tejas said. "Because my Companion saved me."

* * * * *

Kacey Ezell Bio

Kacey Ezell was born in South Dakota in 1977. Her parents joined the US Air Force in 1984, and she grew up around the world on various military bases. When she was seven, her mother gave her a copy of Anne McCaffrey's Dragondrums, and shortly thereafter, Kacey decided that she wanted to be a dragonrider when she grew up. In 1999, she followed her parents into the "family business" and graduated from the United States Air Force Academy before going to pilot training. As dragons were in short supply at the time, she reasoned that flying aircraft was the next best thing. She earned her wings in 2001 and has over 2500 hours in the UH-1N and Mi-17 helicopters.

From the time she was a small child, Kacey made up stories to tell her friends and family. In 2009, while deployed to Iraq, she wrote the military-themed supernatural story "Light," which was accepted for publication in the Baen Books anthology Citizens. She was asked to consult on John Ringo's 2015 novel Strands of Sorrow and wrote the cover story for the Black Tide Rising anthology set in Ringo's zombie apocalypse universe. That story, "Not in Vain," was selected for inclusion in the "Year's Best Military SF and Adventure Fiction" anthology produced by Baen Books.

Kacey writes science fiction, fantasy, horror, noir, romance… she writes fiction. She lives with her husband, two daughters, and two cats.

* * * * *

H. Y. Gregor Bio

H.Y. Gregor was born in Portland, Oregon, but will always call the mountains of Colorado home. She has a bachelor's in political science but managed to narrowly avoid law school and now happily uses her background to create intricate, colorful backdrops for her favorite work writing speculative fiction of all flavors.

A long-time lover of all things magic, her first love will always be fantasy, but she hopes her Four Horsemen debut is the start of a great multi-genre career. Her short fiction has appeared in Particular Passages 4: The South Wing, Animal Magica Volume 2, and her debut novel Stonewhisper released from Eldros Legacy Press in June 2023.

Find her at hygregor.com for free short stories and updates, or on Facebook at H.Y. Gregor – Author.

# # # # #

Oshian's Two by David Shadoin

"Lay out the ropes here and here. No, not like a Lumar, Yogi. Like you have some damn sense," Dah'nee called out to the seven-foot purple fur giant around the backside of the vault. She had no idea why they called him Yogi, but the Humans had some sort of inside joke going that they had not exactly explained. Nicknames didn't exactly make sense to Dah'nee's HecSha social instincts, but no one had ever accused Humans of being logical. "And make sure they are good and tight. We can't have this trap springing haphazardly." Dah'nee took another look around at the stack of red diamonds.

"Dah'nee, what should we do with these tubes?" This from Wahite, a grayish black Zuul. Or was that Peenk. She could never tell them apart. The Zuul stalked around the pile headed toward where the Oogar stood. She was not quite sure where the Triplets of Zuul had come from, but Dah'nee was not about to get picky with who was on the team. She was just thankful to be off Earth, courtesy of the Oshian Break Retrieval Company.

"Line them up with the vents on the back wall. Thanks, Peenk."

The Zuul stared at her and grunted, "I'm Oraanj." He locked Dah'nee's gaze for only a moment longer before a small smirk crossed his face and he did as directed. The commander of Oshian's, Jimmy Utah, had assured her he had assembled the best there was to offer for their unit. Dah'nee knew better. Utah had slim pickings after signing up for the Phoenix Initiative.

"That's Peenk over there." A brownish gray Zuul that must be Wahite pointed with more of the tubes as she dragged them in. She indicated a behemoth of a Zuul that was white with black-tipped ears and stood almost shoulder to shoulder with Yogi, helping lay out the ropes. Dah'nee found herself half-wishing she had taken the Humans up on their offer to tag the Triplets. They were not related by any means that any of them knew about, but they applied and were hired as a trio. Thus, the nickname. The Humans in the company were oddly delighted by giving all of them nicknames.

Once the Triplets and Yogi finished the set-up, Dah'nee cleared them out of the vault and swept around the back wall. There she found Utah, Sergeant Nathan Hardison, and Sophie Ford. Hardison made wild gestures while careening through his explanation to the commanding officer, his half-moon glasses precariously perched on the bridge of his crooked nose.

"Once we have access to the ventilation system and the inside of the vault, it's just a simple move to switch the air flow at the right times to guide the objects through to our collection point."

"Simple. Right." Sophie's eyebrows rose while staring at the screens. "Are you understanding this, Jimmy?"

"Are you not?" Utah's smirk briefly touched his golden-brown eyes.

"Hardy, it might be simple to you, but can you speed up the theatrics?"

Hardison finished touching a few more strings of code on the screen before turning to Dah'nee.

"All set, are we?"

"Affirmative, Sergeant."

"Call me Hardy, or Nathan, or Nate… it's truly awkward to carry a rank." Dah'nee locked gazes with Utah, who shrugged his shoulders. "All right folks, hang on to your butts." Hardison's fingers tapped the screen quickly and finished with a dramatic flair. A video feed inside the dummy vault popped up on another screen nearby as air rushed through the fake ventilation system he had built above them. The group stared at the screen as the ropes slowly started moving toward the tubes, dragging different piles of the fake diamonds with them. Dah'nee's eyes narrowed. If Hardison pulled this off…

The pile had barely reached the tube when rushing wind sounds died down as one diamond entered the tubes and immediately fell back out.

The screen he studied began to blare at him. His face visibly fell. "No, no, no, no, NO!"

"Well look at it this way. You got a diamond into the tube this time. That's progress." Ford patted Hardison on the back as she walked away. Hardison hung his head. Utah also reached up and patted him. Dah'nee could not understand this Human interaction in the face of failure. Clearly, he needed to be prodded to work better. Just as she was about to supply an alternative remark, a tawny-white feathered face popped up in place of the video of the vault.

"Commander, Dah'nee. I need you on the bridge. We have our first assignment." Volanta, the bossy Buma who served as their administrator and communications expert. She was also their contact to their benefactor, Theela Financial.

"Keep working on it, Hardy. The idea has merit." Utah nodded to Dah'nee and strode off.

"Run the variables with limited amounts of air. It looks like there's too much of it trying to circulate and you can't really build up back pressure in the vault." Dah'nee nodded to the perplexed Human and followed her commander, heading for the bridge.

The Oshian Company may not have had the best crew, but at least they had been able to pick up a halfway decent ship. Rechristened *The Usual Suspect*, they had bought it on the cheap from a bankrupt Zuul mercenary company. The black and gold plated hull had come outfitted with all the standard gadgets and defenses, but Volanta had secured some after-market upgrades for their specialized mission. Rush-T, a blue-streaked white Maki pilot and Dah'nee's customary partner, provided the company with a dropship he "acquired" on his last job. Utah never wanted to know the details of that particular job, but Dah'nee was pretty sure the dropship's previous owner had not approved of the change of ownership.

The labyrinth of corridors had taken a few weeks to get used to as they travelled from the outer edges of Karma's gravitational orbit to a system Theela had wanted them camping in. Dah'nee still found herself getting lost from time to time and discovering parts of the ship she had yet to explore. As they moved, Dah'nee would catch glimpses of the yellowish green star in the distant reaches of the system. She caught herself staring at her own reflection, noting how the black stripe that ran from her skull down the center of her throat had started to fade between her eyes. Either she was getting old, or the mileage was taking its toll. For just a moment, her mind got lost remembering her bygone years of roaming Bartertown, listening to rumors of high value asset contracts, and plotting the subsequent procurement of said assets before, and daringly after, the mercenary companies arrived. That was before she and the Maki had landed on Earth as refugees, fleeing the Veetanho. Her shoulder caught a sharp edge of the next doorframe, rattling her from her reverie. She tapped her pistol in its hip holster as she realized she was falling behind, and Dah'nee refocused on the boots of the Human floating in front of her.

The commander never had any issues traveling from one end to the other, so there was no chance Dah'nee would get lost today, despite Hardison's research bay being located as far away from the bridge as it could be on the only perpendicular deck. It still took them the better part of twenty minutes to reach the forward location where the bridge was located. Inside the bridge, they found Rush-T floating from panel to panel, plugging in a route as he aroused the dormant systems of the ship for departure. Volanta rested near the bow-facing glass, her golden eyes following the Maki's movements as if she could learn how to helm the ship.

The *Suspect* started to rumble from its slumber before Utah asked the question on their minds. "Volanta, I trust your travels have turned up a contract Theela wants us to take?"

Theela Financial, their enigmatic benefactor. Somehow, they had convinced Jimmy Utah, through Volanta, to form this mercenary retrieval company and take advantage of the Phoenix Initiative for startup costs. Dah'nee gained information on Theela through the illicit circles she used to run in, before they had sent her and Rush-T a formal job offer. A banking company based on the Sidaran home planet of Bracken, they seemed to have their talons in many pots. The most commonly whispered rumor was that they had bankrolled the herculean effort in saving the Depik race. Whether the rest of the Galactic Union was thankful for that proved to be a point of much debate.

The other rumors ranged from their support and use of well-established mercenary companies to take down the grotesque immoral underbelly of the Milky Way to a silent trade war with the Wathayat Trading Consortium. Dah'nee and Rush-T spent many hours discussing getting in bed with a potential major player that had the reach Theela had. Ultimately, Volanta laid out the logic of joining the crew, and that, coupled with Utah's innate, charismatic trustworthiness, convinced them both to put their skills to use in this new lucrative, legal-ish way.

The beings in this room were the only ones aware of Theela's role... or Volanta's. The rest of the team assumed she was a hire from Karma to assist them in getting contracts they wanted.

"My travels were cut a bit short. Theela has found an opportunity to score at the expense of their dear friends in the Wathayat. It seems a shipment of red diamonds crashed in an ocean on Agnus Cordera *right here in this very system*. Wathayat contracted a Human mercenary company to retrieve the shipment, but they ran into problems. Two, to be precise. First, the oceans on Cordera are vast and acidic. Most outfits are not equipped for this type of venture. Second, a group of Besquith showed up and annihilated the Human company, presumably because they're going after the diamonds themselves."

"So, what does Theela have that allows us to think we solve those two problems and pull this job off?" Dah'nee let her hesitation to accept this death-wish of a contract into her tone.

Volanta turned her golden gaze on Dah'nee like a starship's defensive array taking aim. "Theela already has an operative on the ground, who is currently in possession of the necessary key to finding and accessing the crash site. Your mission is to retrieve our operative and the key, and then do what we formed you to do: retrieve the diamonds."

"Did the operative pass you any information that could help us prepare?" Rush-T finally spoke up from his perch near the navigation panel, his bifurcated white tail anchoring him near the ceiling.

"No. Only that she was in possession of the Wathayat's asset and needed extract. She was planted with the Human company to gather intel and find the asset. As we speak, she's alone with a host of Besquith hunting her so they can find the information they need to retrieve the diamonds. What is that Human adage? Time is of the essence." Volanta glanced at Utah. Dah'nee noted that Rush-T had also shifted his attention to their commander. It was decision time.

"Well. We can't leave an operative in the field at the very least. Dah'nee. Rush-T." He looked at both in turn. "Ideas?"

They looked at each other and smirked. Utah's reluctant acceptance meant they needed to solve the retrieval and extraction.

The Maki beat Dah'nee to the punch. "What if we run a Magician's Apprentice with a swinging Picnic Basket?"

Dah'nee considered the cons. "Yogi is good but not that smart. How about the Fenced Grimm Attraction? Utah and the Triplets will just have to find some black paint."

"Too conspicuous and what's the out if the Besquith don't buy it? And where are we going to get a Flatar and Tortantula in time?" Rush-T's eyes glanced around the deck, searching for an answer.

"What about a Merchant's Penchant for Disaster?" Dah'nee's pupils narrowed in surprise, matching Rush-T's bushy brows. Only Volanta kept her cool. Apparently, Commander Utah had been studying.

"The scheme has merit." Dah'nee peered at her partner.

"Hardy would need to fix his variables and add a remote trigger." Rush-T nodded in agreement.

"We don't have a clear extraction route, but we have time to solve that." Dah'nee returned her attention to Utah. "Well, Commander, you have your first con. Give the order."

"Rush, we're a go. Get us there by the shortest route possible."

"Look outside, Commander. I set us on course when you hit the deck."

Sure enough, they were barreling toward the star and the orbit that contained a haul unlike any they had ever seen.

* * *

The journey proved boring. Hardison continued to work the kinks from his new extraction device. Sophie and the last Human, Eliot Parker, gathered materials from around the ship to prep the CASPers for the data they would have to retrieve. The Triplets kept busy training on weapons and teaching Yogi some of the gambling games customary to Zuul. Yogi showed off a surprising knack for stealth by disappearing around the ship for long stretches, reappearing at mealtimes or just before Dah'nee would get some much-needed target practice on the range. The Oogar, Dah'nee noted, carried a calm demeanor, counter to their reputation from the battlefield. He said very little, offered tips on her aim, but otherwise appeared ready for the mission.

Their Buma handler mainly spent her time on the bridge working with Rush-T to learn how to control the ship if things went wrong or hiding in her private ship she had docked on the side. Dah'nee assumed she was providing updates to their client from her private communications channel.

The Humans, however, skittered around like lost Altar. When not consumed with their own labors, Dah'nee and Utah fielded rapid-fire questions from all three. Dah'nee built a mission brief, complete with every question she had been asked, and presented it hours before they entered orbit. The target planet, Agnus Cordera, was an oceanic planet with small continents of alternately barren desert and humid forested area. They had very little data on the surface as the planet was mostly uninhabited and was only used as a stopover point for trading freighters needing resupply. This meant there were very few structures and little civilization on the planet. It also meant that once they got into orbit, any waiting mercenary ships would know exactly where they were.

"The plan is to take the *Suspect* into low orbit, release our dropship for the initial team, consisting of Rush-T, the Triplets, Sophie, Yogi, and Commander Utah, and try to keep the dropship off any radar or system scans. I will helm the *Suspect* at this point." Dah'nee eyed the group as she explained the scheme she and the Maki had pored over. Utah blanched a bit at realizing he was going to play a pivotal part in the first phase.

"Upon leaving orbit, I will stand off at near maximum communications distance to avoid conflict with the Besquith ship. The rescue team will land near one of the abandoned resupply stations and split up from there. Yogi and the Triplets will masquerade as merchants with a security guard to distract the nearest Besquith team." Yogi remained stoic as ever at this news but Wahite, or maybe Oraanj, scrunched his nose in discomfort at the prospect of being that close to the nightmarish mercenaries.

Rush-T continued where Dah'nee had left off. "Commander Utah and Sophie will try to make contact once we are sure we can avoid any frequency scanners and jammers. Once we find and retrieve the asset and the necessary information they control, they will radio back the information to the *Suspect* for Eliot, Hardison, and Volanta to update the CASPers. This will start phase two." The Maki touched the giant screen showing the brief, and it updated with the pertinent information. "I will rendezvous with the *Suspect* on a second low orbit pass to pick up the gear we need for the diamond extraction. The retrieval team will consist of Commander Utah, Eliot, Sophie, and the operative. That should leave one spare mech suit in case one breaks. Sophie, as the smallest of the three of Humans, be ready for a tight fit." Sophie grimaced at the prospect of sharing her CASPer with this unknown agent.

"Once aboard the crashed transport, they will load up the red diamonds, make their way back to the surface, and get retrieved by our overworked pilot to return to the *Suspect*." Dah'nee gave a small bow to her partner. "Then we make our way as direct as we can, to the nearest stargate and jump out of here."

Eliot raised his hand. "One question. What happens if the Besquith don't buy that an Oogar travelling with three Zuul are actually merchants?"

"Well, Mr. Parker, you should make sure the weapons on these suits you Humans like to parade around in are functional after you make the armor upgrades." Rush-T shared a wicked grin with the group. "All of these pieces must land in their exact places. No mistakes. No misses. If you want out of this job, this is your last opportunity." Several pairs of eyes glanced around the room to see if there were any takers and to gauge the commander's reaction. No one spoke up or walked out.

"Do we have merchant's gear that fits Yogi?" one of the Triplets piped up.

"Sounds like the 'ayes' have it," Utah jumped in. "Stop sitting around and let's get to work."

* * *

"Prepare to drop in one minute." Rush-T called out to his first delivery. "Keep your paws and tails inside the vehicle unless you mean to depart."

Exactly one minute later, he opened the drop door. A light flashed indicating the two Humans had departed the aircraft. Exactly seven minutes later, he maneuvered to a landing pad outside of a warehouse that had seen better days. The jungle had begun to reclaim the concrete and shattered panes of glass as it found more space to grow. The pad had a few chunks missing, requiring the Maki to be precise in his placement. Once he shut down, he swung himself out of his seat to join his remaining passengers in unloading their wares.

"No, you pull, and I will push."

"No, *you* pull, and *I* will push."

Two of the Triplets growled at each other and were struggling to take a heavier chest off the dropship. Yogi lifted two trunks, glared at the two Zuul, and kept working. The last of the Triplets appeared to be taking stock of the crates already removed. Rush-T approached the ongoing argument and hopped on the crate.

"Why not turn sideways and you can both carry it out?" His advice was met with bewilderment and then understanding.

"See, Oraanj. Now we look like idiots in front of the Maki."

"That was your fault, Peenk. You are an idiot."

"I swear, Oraanj, if I wasn't holding this trunk…"

"Then you had best be holding another trunk and pulling it off my ship." Rush-T's patience ran out quickly on the best of days. "Focus on the job." Both Zuul stared at him, eyes wide, and carried it, along with him, off the ship. He waited until they were clear of the cargo door to jump to Yogi's shoulder as he passed.

"How you doing, big guy?" Rush-T let a grin spread halfway across his face for the Oogar. He liked Yogi. No-nonsense types like him were hard to come by in the Maki's usual line of work. Quiet and professional, much like Dah'nee until she got a real hair-brained scheme going.

"Work goes. Zuul argue. Yogi keep working. Little pilot try to be Flatar?" It was the most words Rush-T had heard the Oogar speak since he joined the company. His basso growl put the Zuul's own pitch on notice. The Maki's smile faltered as he realized he had no idea if Yogi was joking or even knew how to joke. Worse was the fact that the Oogar spoke in a low tone—rather than yelling like most Oogar—which really threw him.

"Ha! The Flatar only wish they had teamed with Oogar instead of those insane monstrosities with legs." He said it with false bravado.

"I only poke fun, little pilot. I would not warn you. I just rip your limbs off when mad." An involuntary shiver passed down Rush-T's spine. He believed every word. An Oogar with a sense of humor just seemed... unfair.

"I have nothing for that. Glad you're on our side for now. Just keep an eye on the Triplets for me. They act just smart enough to get us in trouble." Yogi nodded while sparing a glance at the three Zuul outside the ship. He reached to grab the last crate they would carry, the one with all their quick don armor, which was the Maki's cue to take his leave. He leaped onto the deck of the ship, using his bifurcated tail to keep his balance and soften the landing before returning to the cockpit. He leaned against the compartment doorframe, shut the cargo door once they were clear, and started his timer before he returned to flight.

* * *

"Suspect, *Away Team. Do we have updated coordinates for the target?*" Utah's voice crackled over the comms systems on the bridge of the *Suspect.*

"Away Team, this is the *Suspect*. Radar returns show the operative a klick ahead of you and moving. I've been unable to raise her on comms. It may just be her comms aren't set for the ship." Volanta's smooth tone responded from the console up in front of Dah'nee. "Make sure to go in quiet when you do catch up to her. I can't imagine she isn't a little skittish from evading the Besquith."

"Roger that. Wilco."

Dah'nee tapped a button on the screen in front of her with her claw. "Shrike Team, this is the *Suspect*. Tell me you have good news."

"Suspect, *we have started our route. If the communication nerd's intel is correct, we should intercept the lead hunting party in ten minutes,*" grunted one of the Triplets. Dah'nee found herself wondering what the word "nerd" meant in the original Zuul tongue. The only thing they could do on the bridge was sit and wait for information or action. After a tense hour, Dah'nee noticed light glinting off something closer to the planet.

"Volanta? Tell me that we haven't been discovered."

"Dah'nee, we haven't been discovered. There's been no chatter and no signals to detect. Why the sudden cold feet?" Volanta's head swiveled where she sat to stare at the HecSha.

"Call it a feeling. We knew we'd be risking this ship out here. That feeling is haunting me currently." Dah'nee's eyes shifted on either side of her head, a vain attempt to see what had caused the light to shift.

"And your feelings are rarely wrong. I know." The Buma's gaze returned to her station. "It seems the commander is still struggling to keep up with our operative. Let me try bouncing the signal through my rig to reach her." She tapped a few buttons and picked up her comm piece. "Tejas, this is Volanta broadcasting in the blind. We need you to slow your pace. Our retrieval team is en route."

"*Greetings again, Volanta. There are too many threats for us to slow down. Tell your team to speed up,*" purred a voice over the bridge speakers. Dah'nee's brilles collapsed into place almost on instinct giving her a smoky-eyed, glazed look.

Volanta pointedly ignored her.

"Greetings Hunter. Good to hear your voice. Please tell me you've kept a lid on your emotions."

"*Volanta, I have not gone feral again. We are here and safe without extra bodies.*" The Hunter sounded only slightly disappointed.

Dah'nee enabled her own comms. "Rush-T, I need you in support of Away Team immediately. The parameters have changed."

* * *

Rush-T parked the dropship at the coordinates Dah'nee provided. He loaded his assault rifle, locked the controls, and stepped out. After about ten minutes, he wondered if he had landed in the correct location. Then something rustled the brush off to his left.

"Commander? Hunter? Hurry up, we're sitting ducks out here." The Maki moved a little closer to the brush. His instincts warned him only a second too late.

A low rumbling preceded the heavy musk of the nightmarish being that burst from a hidden spot to his right. Rush-T could only register the gnashing teeth and hate-filled dark eyes before clawed paws grabbed his rifle. The Besquith mercenary forced his first few shots into the dirt before swiping at him with its free paw. Rush-T let go of the rifle with one hand and leaned away from the swipe. For a few seconds, he was sure he had dodged it. Then the searing pain kicked in. One of the claws had nicked his shoulder.

His attacker pressed the advantage and pinned him against the dirt with his own rifle. Its breath reminded the Maki of decay and mass graves. He would just be one more addition to whatever clung to the fangs of the being bearing down on him. His heart beat its final tune, his ragged breathing failing to support his muscles before they would finally give out to the weight.

The massive killer paused suddenly, not removing its weight but not pressing its advantage. Rush-T then had to blink as a hot liquid stung his eyes. He tasted a copper tang as he struggled to hold the monstrous mercenary off. And then it was over. There was no more struggle. He was stuck under the body but could not see.

"Rush-T! Hey, are you all right?" Commander Utah's voice came from his left.

"I will be if you get this thing off of me," he grunted out. The Maki heard grunting as Utah and Sophie removed the dead Besquith. His hands now free, he wiped his face and eyes clear. Finally able to see, he noted a dripping hole in the bottom of his opponent's jaw. His hands were covered in that same sticky mess. He was willing to bet, it was the hot liquid all around his eyes and cheeks as well. This was not the plan. "Thanks for the save at least. Tell me you found the Hunter."

"This was not our handiwork," Sophie waved at the corpse. "And did you say Hunter? As in, Depik? Deadliest furballs in the galaxy?" All three of them looked around as if they were moments from death. Rush-T saw a flash of fur back near where he had originally investigated the brush.

A voice that made their hairs stand on end answered from behind. "Why yes, I believe that's exactly what the pilot said. Don't look so surprised, Human commander. I'm the operative you seek. This is the asset you seek." A petrified Cochkala stepped out just as a night-black Hunter coated in drying blood flashed into view. "Welcome to our negotiation."

* * *

Dah'nee watched on as the Human Eliot directed Nathan and Volanta through the final steps of the upgrades to the CASPers. The combat suits would be extra heavy, but the Wathayat science agent had promised his information was solid. It was one of the few times the Cochkala seemed sure of himself. That and when he had passed the coordinates for the downed freighter. Otherwise, he proved barely put together. Poor thing probably had no clue what he had been dropped into when the Wathayat put him in play.

Theela Financial, and therefore Dah'nee, were more than willing to take advantage of their misstep.

"Eliot, you've got ten minutes to finish and get in position. We're on approach to rendezvous with the dropship!" she called out.

"Yes, ma'am! We'll be ready in two shakes of a lamb's tail." Eliot dropped his face shield into place as his arc welder powered up.

Dah'nee's talons clacked against the metal grates as she approached the sergeant. "Hardy, were you able to solve our extraction problem?"

"I spent some time on it. I think I have some left-over parts from a job I was on in Argentina. They should work for this."

* * *

Rush-T landed on the shore closest to their target. They had considered dropping them straight in to save some time, but no one was quite willing to say they trusted the Cochkala's proposed upgrades. As Commander Utah put it, "Maybe it's best we just dip our toes in first and see how it holds?"

They unloaded four of the five CASPers and divvied up personnel between them. Rush-T found himself riding with Sophie. Next to them, Utah was loading up with the Wathayat agent. "Hey, buddy. If you and I are going to be crowded in this clunky piece of death trap, then I need to know your name."

The Cochkala flinched slightly at the commander's presence. "G-Gye'Flieg," he stammered out.

"Well, Gye, welcome aboard, not that you had much choice. Just don't touch anything, a'ight?"

Next to them, Hardy looked as petrified as the Cochkala. He had the distinct pleasure of being paired with the Hunter, Tejas. She barely spared him a glance as she rested in his seat. She just looked over at Gye, blinking slowly. Hardy didn't seem inclined to bother her, and continued to ensure the CASPer was secured and ready for the dive.

The Hunter had spoken very little since saving the Maki, other than some terse conversations with Volanta and hushed words to Gye. It didn't help that both the operative and asset were caked in Besquith blood. Tejas took time to clean herself while they flew to their meet up with the *Suspect*, but no one could shake the sense that she found a distinct, grotesque pleasure in this task.

"All right, cowboys, let's mount up. We are burning daylight." Eliot, the only one riding solo, drove his CASPer out in front of the group.

"Must be nice not having to share a cockpit," Sophie intoned over the short-wave radios. Eliot's mech waved a hand in acknowledgement as he neared the water's edge. Everyone stopped what they were doing to watch. Only Gye, of all beings, seemed uninterested in the results. Some of the race's legendary cockiness could still be found in the scientist after all.

Eliot stepped into the water. There was a bit of minor hissing as some unprotected materials burned away, leaving trails of gas bubbles, but overall, the suit's feet held. He took another step in, his hatch still open in case he needed a quick getaway. More hissing but no warning tones reached the ears of the onlookers. Several more steps, and the waves lapped just below the front facing opening. The upgrades seemed to be holding. Now to find out if Binnig's glass was as good as they claimed. Eliot closed his hatch.

"Hang on," Utah's command came over the radio. "Let me finish mounting up so I can pull you out if it doesn't hold." He and Gye got extremely close and comfortable before closing their own hatch and striding out behind Eliot's CASPer. Rush-T could only stare on at this moment of truth. Eliot was not only putting his fate in the hands of a Wathayat agent, but he had machined the upgrades. Once Utah was in position to assist, Eliot marched forward, submerging the mech completely.

Bubbles hit the surface but nothing signaled catastrophe. "*Systems are green, no signs of leaks,*" Eliot's voice broke the silent waiting on the beach. "*We've got limited air unless the freighter somehow maintained pockets. Sync your watches, ladies and jellybeans, it's show time.*"

Hardy clambered up into his mech and took his seat after a brief and nervous glance at the furry embodiment of death who he now had as a copilot. Soon, their hatch closed.

Rush-T needed no extra encouragement. He used his tail to swing himself up into the cockpit next to Ford, who closed their hatch behind them. He tried to make himself comfortable for the descent. "Giddy-up I guess," Sophie muttered before battening down their hatch.

They had barely taken a step when the whole machine rocked forward as if hit in the back and a warning tone sounded. Rush-T glanced out to see the Hardy's mech taking a few shots. "We're under attack."

Sophie turned to engage as she slowly moved toward the ocean. Emerging from the trees, the Besquith search party pressed the attack. She fired off a few rounds of the machine gun before it sputtered and clicked.

"*Disengage! Get in the water!*" Utah's voice called out over the comms channel.

Next to them, Hardy had gotten his mech moving and mostly submerged. Rush-T looped around his pilot to check the warnings and damage.

"Ammo feed is jammed! Oxygen filtration also got hit. According to the computer, we should still be good to submerge."

"Or die trying," responded Ford. So, she turned and ran to embrace a crashing wave.

* * *

"*We were attacked by the scout party. They know we're here. The dropship might be compromised as is the last CASPer. We will be too deep to reach you soon. Good luck,* Suspect." Utah's voice echoed around the empty bridge while Dah'nee and Volanta stared at each other.

"You don't think…" Volanta started but could not finish.

"Shrike team, do you copy?" Dah'nee took control of the comms.

Silence reigned on the net.

"Shrike Team. Do. You. Copy?"

Static.

Dah'nee hissed a curse in her native tongue. "Volanta, we've lost four heavies who were somewhat decent at their jobs. Our escape route was compromised. The subsurface team might be compromised as well. Get in your ship, contact our benefactor, and get us out of here." She bustled around the consoles, setting up all the stations to respond appropriately.

"And what exactly are you planning to do? One-gun blaze of glory against a whole company of Besquith?" Volanta's feathers ruffled at her frustration.

"Of course not, you worry-wart. I have a plan." She tapped the side of her flattened skull. "It just so happens the plan stops at escape the planet. Maybe I can figure something out, or maybe I rely on you to solve that piece for me. So, stop your hopping and squawking and get us an away team." Volanta threw her one last insulted glance as she floated off the bridge.

For a financial company dealing in information, they sure do like to have sticky fingers on operations, Dah'nee thought, then mentally kicked herself. She could not afford her mind wandering too far away from the current situation. She had to buy time for Volanta to get clear, draw another ship's undivided attention, escape to the surface, steal the loot they came here for, and somehow get all of this madness under control. *Nothing to it for a HecSha, right?*

After several minutes of bouncing between consoles and getting the calculations right, she fired up the main drives. The *Suspect* made an arcing turn back toward the planet. A chime sounded. The second stage of navigation began.

"Volanta, how much time until you are ready to depart?" Dah'nee reached out over the ship's intercoms.

"A bit impatient, are we? What are you, a hatchling? I'm almost there. Then it'll take me a few minutes to get it fired up." The Buma's voice came over breathy. "It's not my fault you parked me halfway to the center of the galaxy."

"You have ten minutes before the Besquith ship finds out where we are," Dah'nee replied.

The *Suspect* sped toward the planet's orbit, no longer trying to remain undetected with the automated defenses primed and radar hot. Dah'nee double-checked her calculations and pulled herself across the bridge toward her escape pod. She took one last look at the bridge. They had not had her long, but it seemed unfitting to lose their ship on the first mission. The cost of doing mercenary business. *The Usual Suspect* pinged at that moment as it signaled a radar sweep. They had been discovered.

Exactly eight minutes later, as Dah'nee had timed it, she launched her pod toward the planet as their craft brushed low orbit for a final pass before careening out to space, a planned atmospheric skip that allowed it to maintain speed and force any would-be pursuers to pause. As her pod cleared the bay, she came face to face with the hulking mass of tonnage as the Besquith drove toward *Suspect*. She also saw the Buma's tiny vessel hovering in the shadow of *Suspect*, waiting to fly behind their enemy to avoid detection. Only a minute later, Dah'nee was greeted with a gratifying display of firepower.

It reminded Dah'nee of the human mythical creature that their current "initiative" was named after. As the Besquith hulk loomed close enough to board, the automated defenses sprang their trap. The sky glowed for several minutes as the *Suspect* fought for a crew that was no longer on board. The perfect decoy. Drones, missiles, lasers and flares emptied out of the metal mass that carried them. Dah'nee felt a pang at the haphazard waste of the armaments. It would do some damage but not enough to cripple or even wound its pursuer.

However, it drew out the offensive capabilities of the opponent, as it lined up its shots and patiently tracked its prey. *The Usual Suspect* took a pounding even its previous Zuul owners would have shuddered at. But she kept pressing on. Seconds later, now well clear of the planet and in no danger of crashing down with its exit velocity, the engines turned off, another planned ploy. The boarding ships left the Besquith cruiser as flames finally engulfed Dah'nee's view. There would be no tracking pointed toward her and the team, no further death from above. *The Suspect* gave its last protecting her crew. It was up to Dah'nee to use the time she had bought wisely.

* * *

The dive team found the crashed hulk of the Wathayat freighter on the edge of a shelf, precariously balanced over a deeper portion of the ocean. Sophie and Rush-T walked over to the edge and looked out into the darkening green abyss.

"You couldn't have given us a bit of warning, Gye?" Rush-T's impatience bit through the radios.

"*Well, I may have not accounted for the seabed drift. I swear it wasn't here before.*" Gye's tinny answer only served to draw a look that Sophie and Rush-T shared. A warning sounded, startling both occupants. Their oxygen level was getting low.

"As much as we like sight-seeing, Sophie and I would prefer not to suffocate in a toxic ocean. Can we find an air pocket or sealed compartment ASAP?" the Maki called out to the group.

The crew searched the hull for an opening near where Gye had indicated the vault of diamonds were stored. Most of this part of the freighter remained sealed. Utah guided his CASPer toward a pair of bay doors. They stood facing the latch, presumably letting Gye do his thing. The bay doors irised open, and the whole crew stepped in. A light rumble indicated the bay closing behind them and a dull roar started as the acid water was vacated.

Once the chamber was sufficiently drained, lights popped on, providing assistance to the CASPers' lights. Eliot tested the lack of water by opening his CASPer. He put gloves on to climb out and flashed them toward the rest of the group. Rush-T noted that with minimal contact, they had already developed holes. The warning was received. Everyone climbed out quickly, touching as few of the outside panels as necessary before alighting on the ground. Gye and Hardy needed a bit of help getting out, but once the whole crew was assembled, the Cochkala started to work on the next set of doors.

Utah barked out at the group, "Once our friend here gets us in, everyone has their assignments. Split up and find what you need. You should have all been briefed on where Gye'Flieg here thinks your tasks are located. Radio out if you need help." Rush-T found himself nodding in compliance despite himself. Tejas licked her paw in response, clearly unfazed. She kept glancing at the Cochkala though, one of the few times the Maki caught an expression of concern or care. Volanta had warned them that the Hunter had gone feral once already. There was no telling what might set her off again.

The doors clicked, hissed, and slid apart. Gye stepped aside with a wave of his paw, indicating everyone should go through. Eliot and Hardy took an immediate right. Gye, after a few moments of hesitation and one final silent desperate glance at Tejas, followed them. The remainder headed left for the last known location of the loot they were here to nab. Winding through corridor after corridor of metal, barely finding a flat surface, they traversed toward their objective. Utah and Sophie broke out personal lights in the areas where the on-board lighting flickered and failed. Rush-T noted several doors toward the outer hull that showed greenish tinted water. It was best to not squander time here.

They arrived at the cargo area, where an exact replica of the training vault they had on the *Suspect* sat. Rush-T raised a brow at this surprise, Utah and Sophie both audibly gasped.

"Well, I guess we know why Volanta got us that vault now," Utah managed to get out. "All right, Sophie, do that voodoo that you do. Get us in. Rush-T, provide her cover and help. Tejas, help me find the hookups Hardy needs on this end." He moved as soon as he was done giving orders.

Sophie pulled out her slate while Rush-T got into position. She jacked in at the vault door. "Hardy, have you got the codes I need?"

"*Working on it. We couldn't get to the bridge, but Gye found us a maintenance console that's taking a little longer to bypass into the ship's main servers. Give me one minute.*" The answer was faint with static but without the bridge comm's console, they were lucky to hear him at all. Sophie kept tapping away at her slate. Apparently, she figured she could use the time. "*All right, I've got them when you're ready.*"

"First one is coming up shortly… and… send it." Sophie's fingers paused while she listened to Hardy's answer. Rush-T understood only some of it and dedicated his time to find good cover and get his rifle ready. He chose a spot where he could hang from some exposed ceiling ducts and perched just out of sight in the shadows of the room. Sophie and Hardy continued their exchange through several strings of code. Then Sophie declared, "Looks like the last one and then you can set your paths."

As she finished, there was an audible metallic click within the vault door. Two panels popped out and swung open. The Maki could see two old-school combination locks hiding in the recesses.

"Rush, I can't do these simultaneously by myself. Can you provide a hand? Or tail?" She reached in and grabbed a second ear bud and placed her slate between the two locks.

"Of course. I suspect we regret not bringing the drills?" Rush-T clambered down from his perch.

"If that's the case, next time you can plan the vault entry, and I'll fly the cargo." She didn't even look up from her slate as she set the parameters she was listening to.

"I'm only pulling your tail, or whatever you Humans pull." He backed up against the vault door, keeping his rifle pointed at the entrance to the bay while one-half of his bifurcated tail found the dial.

"On my mark, spin at the one-for-thirty pace. Left, right, left based on the looks of it. In three, two, one, mark." Rush-T spun his dial ever so slowly, glancing back only to ensure he was matching pace with Sophie. She marked something down and kept turning, her eyes glazed as she listened to the archaic lock mechanism buried deep within the door. Rush-T heard footsteps just as Sophie told him to change direction. He raised the rifle but kept his finger off the trigger.

"Hunter. Commander. If you wouldn't mind not stomping around like a herd of elephants while I listen to the faintest of clicks, I would greatly appreciate it," Sophie growled quietly.

"I do not think an elephant to be near as graceful as a Hunter." Tejas's voice drifted from somewhere off to Rush-T's right hand. Sure enough, the graceful assassin appeared there on all fours, staring at them both. The whole reveal startled the Maki, but he did not let his tail lose control on the dial. Tejas let out an audible sniff before grooming herself. "Hmmph. Maybe you are a professional."

Commander Utah came around the corner of the vault a lot more quietly than he had been previously and took a position of watch as well. They switched directions on the dials one more time.

"Stop!" Sophie directed. Rush-T held completely still as she pulled her hand away, then he removed his tail as carefully as possible. She pulled her extra earpiece out and grabbed the handle on the vault. "Commander, mind giving me a hand?"

Utah stepped up to the door and they both pulled, revealing a room of red diamonds on the inside. Rush-T's eyes went wide and even the Hunter sat up to get a good view of the sparkling loot. But they had no time to waste.

"Get these loaded in bags. Rush-T, you have the door still." Utah threw a couple of duffle bags into the piles and the Hunter and two Humans began to load up. Soon, they had lines of duffle bags set against the back wall. All three stepped out. "Hardy, spin 'em up. It's time to go." Utah waited.

Silence.

The Hunter stood on her hind legs and stared at the open bay door.

"Hardy, come in. Gye? Eliot?"

Into view stepped Eliot, with one of the Triplets, Oraanj, holding a laser rifle to his back.

"Thank you for delivering us the rightful property of the Wathayat. Now, no one else needs to die. I just want the diamonds," he growled to the group. The Maki felt the Hunter flinch next to him, preparing to strike. "Don't even consider pulling quintessence, assassin. I will end the flesh bag here and follow it up by killing the rest before you get to me. Then you'll have to fight your way out alone."

That last sentence seemed to provoke the Hunter. Rush-T could feel the blood rage radiating from her. She took a step, staring down the Zuul.

A shot rang out in the bay. Eliot collapsed. Another shot followed, ricocheting off the walls before Sophie stumbled into the vault, closing the door behind her.

Utah dove sideways, behind some crates near the wall. Rush-T followed suit on his side. The Hunter disappeared. A third shot echoed in the chamber, followed by a thump of a body hitting the floor. Rush-T chanced a glance. Tejas had revealed herself just in front of the dead Zuul.

In the door stood the familiar flat head and black stripe of his Hec-Sha partner, pistol raised and her yellow eyes focused.

* * *

Dah'nee's CASPer was hissing in a way she did not enjoy as she arrived at the sunken spacecraft.

"Away Team, I need an entry point."

"*Gye says to use the southern bay. He can get you in without flooding the other CASPers,*" Hardy responded on comms. "*Eliot has disappeared after stuffing us in a closet. We heard a loud creaking noise, and he went to investigate. We haven't seen him since.*"

"I'll keep an eye out for him," she assured them. "Just stay hidden until I tell you to come back to the CASPers."

"*No problem, boss.*" That must have been the Cochkala. Dah'nee didn't immediately recognize the voice.

Once she was in the chamber and drained, she clambered out and worked her way through the maze of corridors based on what the Wathayat scientist had told them. As she approached the cargo bay, she heard one of the Triplets say, "Then you'll have to fight your way out alone."

Dah'nee drew her pistol and stepped around the corner, bringing the door into view. Eliot stood at gunpoint in front of the Triplet that went by Oraanj. Before she could raise it and declare herself with advantage, a shot was fired, and Eliot dropped. Dah'nee raced forward, not willing to risk a miss. A second shot followed. Dah'nee lined up her shot and pulled the trigger from near point blank in the back of the Zuul's skull. He dropped to the ground on top of the Human. In front of her, Tejas revealed herself, bloodlust clear on her face.

"Hunter, calm. I am not your enemy."

"I will kill you for taking what was rightfully mine. He killed my companion."

"The Cochkala? He and Hardy were alive last I checked. I need you to calm yourself before I move from here." Dah'nee kept her eyes locked on the penetrating gaze of the deadly assassin in front of her. She saw inquiry there and disbelief.

"Gye'Flieg, come in. Are you there?" the Hunter called over her comms.

"*Yes, I'm here Hunter. What's going on down there?*" Relief flooded the gaze of Tejas, but she stilled the remainder of her expression.

"Nothing you need to worry about."

Behind the Hunter, Utah was desperately trying to get the door open. Dah'nee's partner, Rush-T now engaged at the door as well. "Sophie, come in. We need the combination to get you out."

"*It's… too… late.*" Sophie's ragged words filled their ears with her pain. "*Hardy… start the… start the… start the extract.*"

"Belay that order, Hardy. Sophie, we need to open the door. Where's the last number?" Utah left the handle and stared at the notes next to the slate.

"*Not that simple, Jimmy,*" came the gasping answer. "*Once the... door shut... aaagh... the whole security system reset. I'm... on borrowed time... Complete... the mission.*" She hissed again in pain.

"Goddammit Sophie." Utah pounded once more on the door and his head hit the metal as he gave in to the inevitable. Dah'nee could only look on in silence.

"Hit it, Hardison," she finally stated.

"*Thanks... Jimmy. See you... on the... flip side.*"

A rushing sound filled the vents around them as the vault was depressurized, which turned to a clanging sound as the bags of diamonds were sucked up into them and transported to the CASPer bay. After the rush of air, a new groaning metal sound filled their ears as the ship shuddered and settled.

"Gye? Hardison? What was that?" Dah'nee inquired of their brainiacs.

"*That was the sound of the ship shifting. We* are *on a shelf, after all,*" Gye came back with utmost certainty but lacking any significant notable concern.

"As in, we might be going over the edge?" Rush-T this time, his concern very clear in his tone.

"*Why yes, that is a distinct possibility.*" Gye really needed to learn a better bedside manner.

The commander still stood staring at the vault door. Dah'nee approached him, putting her hand on his shoulder. "Commander Utah, we have to go now. Grieve when we are all safe."

He looked at her with a distant stare but nodded his understanding. After one last glance at the vault and Eliot's body, he moved toward their exit.

The crew made their way back, swiftly but careful to keep their guns up and ready. No more surprises. Dah'nee took the time to explain what happened to the *Suspect* and how she had arrived at the dropship. They met back up with Hardison and Gye before loading up the diamonds and clambering into three of the CASPers. Rush-T declared two of them inoperable for the sea. Acid had eaten through essential systems. The last one was the one Dah'nee had brought down. They would only have one shot.

Rush-T loaded into Dah'nee's CASPer. Once they cleared the bays and started their ascent, the ocean began to bubble as debris kicked up. They could hear a distant whine of metal clinging to life just before the back end of the crashed ship split and fell off the shelf. Dah'nee heard Rush-T's audible sigh of relief but decided not to remind him of their current fatal circumstances. She opted to tell the rest what they had missed, instead.

"We hadn't heard from the Triplets or Yogi. I thought they were all dead until I saw Peenk here."

"*You mean Oraanj, right? The Zuul you shot?*" Utah interrupted her.

"I mean whichever one it was. Hopefully, Volanta has gotten her message out." Dah'nee met her partner's gaze. The hissing she had heard on the way down hit a volume that interrupted thought. She drove the CASPer to go faster, and the other two tried to match speed.

They made landfall near the dropship just as Rush-T pointed out the hissing was coming from their hatch. Green liquid pooled in the base of the feet and slowly released in the sand, indicating a leak. They attempted to push their hatch open, but it was sealed.

"Grab an arc welder. We need to get out of here." Dah'nee called to the group after they had all parked on the dropship and dismounted.

"Yogi will free you," responded the purple behemoth that stepped out from behind the dropship. He lumbered over to the mech, grabbed the two points of the hatch and hauled it off, nearly tipping the whole CASPer.

"Are you a sight for sore eyes, big fella." Utah clapped him on the back. Dah'nee and Rush-T climbed down, now free of their cage.

Another shadow appeared. One of the Triplets stepped out from the same spot Yogi had come from.

Tejas was at his throat in a heartbeat.

"Steady Hunter, I am not Oraanj," he growled but remained still.

"Yogi?" Dah'nee turned to the Oogar.

"Wahite growl truth. Peenk died when Besquith not believe us. Oraanj agreed to help. Used data found on ship to find you. Wahite and I escaped after battle. He good Zuul." Yogi walked over to Tejas and Wahite. "Nice Hunter let him be now?"

Tejas simply stared at the Oogar. Dah'nee could not be sure if she was sizing up Yogi as her next kill or just simply surprised at how much he said. Either way, she backed down.

"The abandoned station you landed us at is only a few klicks from here. We can take the dropship, hide it, and hole up there. It's our best chance of survival." Wahite met Dah'nee's eyes. Commander Utah also looked at her.

"What do you think?" he asked. She weighed all the options they had.

"I think we've got enough diamonds to buy a new ship and supplies if we can sneak around unnoticed. I think we've managed a heist that should have been impossible. I think we owe it to our fallen to survive this filthball of a planet and leave the Besquith to rule over their failure. We wait until nightfall, and we move." Dah'nee glanced around before settling on the commander. "Is that all right with you, sir?"

"Dah'nee, it's always been your show. I'm in."

"I'm in," Rush-T chimed in as well. The rest of the crew echoed the sentiment.

"The scheme has merit." Dah'nee let a small grin reveal her serrated teeth. "Let's make it happen."

* * * * *

David Shadoin Bio

David "Shady" Shadoin is a troublemaking, corn-fed Nebraska boy the United States Air Force managed to turn into a somewhat decent pilot of whirly birds. An avid reader from a young age, literally the picture definition of 'book worm' in Webster's, he has always found inspiration in listening to rock music while reading Fantasy and Sci Fi novels and drinking single malt scotch. This love of written adventure set up Shady to moonlight as an author trying to find a good outlet for creative ideas that start with nothing more than a misplaced pop culture reference and some DnD dungeons.

For more Shady dealings, visit www.davidshadoin.com/home.

# # # # #

Jagged Edges by Marisa Wolf

Far Earth Orbit

"Pass."

"You can't pass on every candidate, Jan." Nick Braker spun a stylus through his fingers, his tone idle.

"You spend three hours underneath a dead Goka, see how excited you are to bring one on board."

"Twenty-seven." Taleena spun over the table, the bulk of her attention on the mess of spare parts hanging together in her small elSha hands.

"That's worse. You see how that's worse, right?" Jan spread her arms wide and threw her head backward, floating from the table. "It takes one of us to veto, and I'm vetoing."

"You've vetoed everyone so far." Nick tossed the stylus toward her, and Jan snagged it while twisting back toward her chair.

"In my defense, we've fought a lot of aliens in shitty circumstances over the years." She hooked her feet into the back of her chair and spun the stylus.

"Well in not your defense, we need to pick at least a few to qualify for all these bonuses that *you* suggested we go for."

"Running a Goltar warship is expensive," she muttered.

Taleena whipped her tail and motored past Jan, making grabby hands. Jan gave her the stylus, and the elSha dug it into her ball of scrap. Nick protested but craned his neck to watch what his partner in tech-meddling was up to.

Jan rolled her eyes and flapped a hand toward her brother. "Who's next?"

Dave Colby, commander of Colby's Killers for a Human record-setting hundred-plus years, flipped the display through a series of dossiers featuring various aliens that had been stranded on Earth after the Veetanho occupation. Jan scrubbed her hands through her short blond hair and frowned over each one.

"Nick's not wrong." Dave tapped his fingers against the table, flipping between two files. "We can't veto all of them if we want the money. We're already qualifying on a technicality."

"The Killers are still on the rolls, but time in grade, inactivity, and loss of members allows us to re-form and qualify for new company bonuses." Taleena didn't lift her gaze from her latest project, but her voice piped cheerfully through her modified translator. "As long as we meet all the requirements."

"And the *Mighty Wave* is expensive," Nick said, echoing Jan with all of Taleena's cheer.

"Why aren't there elSha scattered across Earth?" Jan knew her tone was sulky but didn't modulate it. "I like ours."

"I like my Humans too, but they probably signed on to smarter contracts." Taleena tossed Nick's stylus—now noticeably shorter—back to him.

"Smarter? We have a better set up than most mercenary companies—especially the new ones."

"*One big battlecruiser, yes.*" Their former dropship pilot and current Captain, Jeff Payton, interjected agreeably over comms. "*And six dropships, no CASPers, and a stated mission to, I quote, 'Handle the weird stuff.'*"

"I believe I said tricky." Dave smiled, the expression brief. "And there's an order of CASPers en route."

"Ideally we can bring them in on the same shipment as our new members and save on fuel." Jan sighed and let herself float. "Can't believe they wouldn't open a closer orbit for us."

"Goltar warships make them nervous." Taleena swam closer and hooked her tail through Jan's abandoned chair back, still focused on her contraption. "Maybe they don't believe you're really you."

"Half the time I don't believe we're really us." Nick examined his shortened stylus, grumbled, and tucked it into one of his many pockets. "So we're gonna what, take one of those dropships to the planet and interview these sets of aliens?"

"Lumar or Maki." Dave tilted his head back to regard the floating woman. "We never had much in the way of those to fight."

"Fine." Jan resolutely kept her face to the curve of ship above the table. "Lumar or Maki. How bad could they be?"

* * *

Not bad… but certainly not great. The seven Lumar hadn't been snatched up by another newly formed company because they were, without a doubt, the meanest, slovenliest, laziest Lumar that had ever gone out into the galaxy.

Jan would have vetoed them at first sight if the Maki hadn't been somehow even worse, the lemur-like creatures gone to seed on Human snack food and all things fermented. The reek that accompanied them had been an immediate red flag, and the resulting brief interview had made zero improvements. She'd floated the idea of heading back to the *Mighty Wave* and calling it a bad show, but Nick had shrugged and said, "We've already spent the fuel, might as well be thorough."

Which was sensible enough from a financial standpoint. So instead of going home, she sat in the back of the rented conference room in the Houston starport—and if that hadn't gotten seedier and uglier since her day she didn't know seedy and ugly—and glared at nothing in particular.

The largest and ugliest of the Lumar grunted, which seemed to be the extent of his conversational abilities and shrugged. It was an elaborate motion given the extra arms and made Jan's gut squirm.

"Do you plan on staying on Earth long?"

Grunt.

"How do you plan to get off world?"

Grunt.

"What've you been doing to keep yourself occupied down here?"

"Veetanho."

It was the first recognizable word in a handful of minutes, and unwillingly Jan dropped her gaze down to Nick and Big Mean's interview.

"What about Veetanho?"

Big Mean's mouth stretched wide in a snarl or a smile or some unholy combination of the two. Jan thought fondly of the three-muzzled shooter Taneeko had made for her and swallowed back her yearning.

"Hunt."

"You're… hunting Veetanho left on Earth?" Nick's voice had retained its neutral professionalism throughout the frustrating exchange, but now his tone shifted pitch. "Didn't think there were any left."

"Less now. Earth big."

"So I've heard."

That appeared to snag Big Mean's interest, because the Lumar crossed his lower arms and leaned forward a fraction of an inch. "You Earth."

"Was." Nick shrugged, the motion less rippling with fewer extremities. "Hundred years ago, or so."

The Lumar's face moved, a wave of expressions Jan had no capacity to parse, and low noises passed through the other six. "Old Human."

"We didn't have much of a choice on that one." Nick tapped the table between them, maybe about to change the subject, and Jan failed to bite back the words bubbling out of her.

"The Veetanho fucked us over and handed us off to their SI overlord, who experimented on us and kept us fighting all his other lab rats for a century. Wouldn't have been a good investment if that dickface had let us die of old age too soon."

Big Mean leaned his head forward as she spoke, and another susurrus of sound passed through the Lumar. "Not understand all."

Fair, "dickface" probably didn't translate into other languages, especially with aliens who may or may not have—Jan cut the unhelpful line of thought off, given Big Mean continued speaking. "Enough. Experiments bad. Is humanshit."

"It is," Nick interjected before Jan could continue her rant. To be fair, Jan had lost the momentum at the bitterness in the Lumar's bearing. The translator did them no favors, inflectionless and flat, but even she couldn't miss the tension and the scowl across seven humanoid faces. Maybe she was wrong, but in that moment, she was sure she understood them—and that they understood the Killers perhaps more than she'd expected.

"Now? Fight SI?"

"We'll take contracts, same as any mercenary company. But we asked the broker on Karma to get us the really tough contracts."

"Which?" Big Mean crossed his upper arms and leaned so far back his chair creaked in protest.

"Which broker? The Lyon. Human, he used to have a—"

"Lyon." A chorus of grunts. "Good Human."

"Good bar," a slightly smaller Lumar added, opening and closing his fists in some pattern Jan couldn't decipher.

Big Mean flicked his fingers, and Nick must have taken that as a signal to continue, as he leaned back in turn. "We asked for those kinds of contracts, because that SI is going to come back, and we intend to be ready."

So many fists crashed into the table between them Jan registered it as sudden thunder before her brain caught up. She blinked but didn't flinch—though it took another blink to realize her hand had wrapped itself around her holstered weapon. The Lumar didn't seem to notice, all intent on Nick.

"Ready fight."

"Yes, Garg. We intend to find a way to get SI's down to their component parts, sink those parts into various black holes, broken hyperspace drives, and stars going nova, then piss all over what's left."

"Piss." Big Mean—Garg, Jan corrected herself—lifted and slammed two of his fists against the table. Jan hoped no one came in after their designated time to check for damage, then dismissed it as unlikely. The conference room had seen worse. "Yes. Lumar piss too."

That was a biological confirmation she didn't need.

"We piss SI. Veetanho. All the humanshit who treat wrong."

"You want to sign on to Colby's Killers, then?"

"Try. Broken Bomb do one contract with Killers. See." Garg grunted, a deeper sound than his earlier noises. In perfect unison, each Lumar clapped one clenched fist to their chest.

That had been the plan proposed in setting up the meeting—a trial period or shakedown contract. Enough to qualify them for the incentives and still leave wiggle room to part ways if it wasn't a match. No harm no foul.

She refused to believe she actually wanted it to work out. Time under Dunamis, the SI that had, until very recently, run the Mercenary Guild and farmed the Veetanho out as its creepy rabid proxies, had beaten the habit of optimism out of her decades ago.

Having her own warship and a growing company of pissed off asskickers though… maybe that would help.

* * *

There were twenty-two Lumar. Nick cocked his head, and Garg shrugged with all his arms. "Lumar look same. Humans count bad."

After a glance to ensure Jan nodded, Nick adjusted the percentage they'd agreed to before the Lumar loaded onto the dropship and sent the contracts to all interested parties.

The second largest of the Lumar, Jooj, chortled and slapped Nick hard on the back. When Nick didn't stagger forward, the group of them hooted in what Jan took as approval.

"All right, enough fucking around. Unless you've got another squad lurking in the corridors, we've got to get going before we miss our window." Jan pointed and was pleasantly surprised when they fell in and marched to the ship in quick order. She'd half expected the big meatheads to ignore her and focus on Nick, but it seemed they'd listened when he'd introduced her and her role. Or they didn't have an issue with a woman bossing them around. Or they didn't understand that she *was* a woman—she'd never heard of a female Lumar, and for all she knew they hatched out of eggs. Or sprang from each other's heads, fully formed.

She really had to stop thinking about their reproductive cycles. Enough nightmare fodder already bounced through her skull; she didn't need to add alien mating habits to the soup.

The comms delay to *Mighty Wave* measured in bare seconds, so she pinged home while everyone got sorted in the crew compartment.

"*CASPers are getting shipped direct,*" the captain replied cheerily. "*Favor from the incentive board for such a helpful airlift off Earth.*" Jeff Payton was having way too much fun for her current mood.

"Did you try to get anything else out of them? Given they thought they had a third less Lumar?"

"*Turns out Earth is still Earth. 'Files were meant to be a starting place, not the whole picture, do your own research, yadda blahdadee.' We're going to hold a while longer to get our shipment, you sure you don't want to do some sightseeing?*"

A shudder twitched all the nerves across her back, and Jan forced her shoulders back to halt the involuntary motion. "Didn't so much as step outside the starport, thank you much, and no need to change that."

There was nothing outside the starport for her. Who would she even talk to? Her references had been backward-looking a century ago, and now…

Earth was a nice theory. Better than Battle World. She was glad it existed still.

She didn't need to put her eyes on it.

They hit their window with minimal exchanges with the control tower, and she navigated the dropship on autopilot, trusting Nick to brief the Lumar. Nick had been their tech genius for a long stretch of time, and the addition of the elSha to their mismatched crew had both encouraged his creativity and freed him up to do other things.

Bright side: now they had other things to do.

Not bright side: she really missed shooting things.

Time for introspection wasn't especially her favorite either. On approach to the *Mighty Wave*, she made a point to execute the docking maneuver textbook perfect to keep her brain occupied. No one noticed, but she knew. That was enough.

Until they stepped onto their ship and Reen swam anxiously toward them through the bay.

"XO needed in CIC." His tail ruddered behind him as he spoke. The first of their elSha partners tended to be a shade or two off from calm and collected at all times, but the mods to his translator carried his nerves loud and clear.

"Welcome to the *Mighty Wave*, Broken Bomb." She tossed it over her shoulder as she marched off in her thick magnetic boots, but at least she remembered to say it. Professional, that was her.

Reen kept pace, his little lizard body fishtailing through the corridors, but after the first turn he curled a hand into the sleeve of her jumpsuit and let her momentum carry him.

"It's not the Lumar that's got your toots in a twist—what's going on?"

He didn't give so much as a humoring tongue flick to acknowledge her attempt to throw his translator. Jan steeled herself for the issue. "We have to leave for Karma immediately."

"The CASPers won't be ready for—"

"I didn't hear the message, but your brother is at alert, and Payton is getting us ready for the course."

"Reen." She held her pace and tapped his tiny hand. "It's probably a contract opportunity."

"Why the haste then? What if it's Dunamis? What if it's time to—and we're not ready—and what if—"

His anxiety spiked her heartrate, but this wasn't her first go-round. She took a steadying breath, released her boots to swing around a curve to the next crossing, and landed with a reassuring thunk.

"Did Dave go very still and pale?"

"No, but he's—"

"Did he dig his hand into the base of his skull and push really hard?"

The question paused Reen mid-word, and after a moment he shook his body all over like a small, lizardy dog. "No."

"It's not Dunamis. It's probably a contract, and he's gone battle ready." Jan's pulse returned to its regular beat, though the small bones in her fingers ached to wrap around the butt of a large projectile weapon.

"We can't wait for the CASPers," Dave said the moment Jan and her trailing elSha entered the CIC. "We're en route to Karma soon as Payton gives the all clear."

"Don't put the enormous battlecruiser into energy saving mode if you need it with zero notice," Payton muttered, though the captain's tone indicated focus, not stress.

"The message?" Jan asked, falling automatically into ready position.

"Routed to your console. I want to hear what you think."

She regarded her brother for a long moment as she crossed the CIC. Her assessment to Reen had been correct—he was alert but not on edge, which made the caginess suspect but not worrying. Curiosity held her urge for a snappy comment, and she dialed up the message.

"Colby's Killers, this is the Lyon. I have an opportunity your experience is uniquely suited to. Interesting contract, details to be discussed at the Den. Soonest is best—it won't last."

Reen rotated to Jan's other shoulder to regard their CO. "That's normal correspondence. What's got your toots in a twist?"

Jan bit back her smile and cocked her head inquiringly at her brother, who went through a series of expressions so quickly only their uncommonly long sibling relationship allowed her to catch the nuance. Confusion, flicker of smile, exasperation, accusing look at Jan, realization, empathetic understanding, commander face.

"I don't like that he wasn't clear what the contract entails, and that we have to go in person to get it despite what else we might have on deck. 'It won't last' says to me less that there will be other companies that want in, and more that whatever it is we're being sent for is under direct threat of destruction."

"And we've still got to get there." Jan pressed her nails into the palm of her right hand and considered. "So, he's balancing protecting whatever the objective is with a need for secrecy."

"And encryption clearly can't be trusted, so it's not like we can call for backup." Dave didn't frown, but she heard it in his voice.

"It's not like we *would* call for backup." Jan shrugged and powered down her console. "Nothing we can do until we get to Karma—wanna meet the new temps?"

Reen kicked free of her and angled toward the door. "I'm going to tell Taleena to pause on her plans for the CASPers and will update our contact at Binnig. Hopefully they'll be able to meet us at Karma."

"Let them know the Lyon'll cover the difference." Jan forced a grin. "He loves when we do that."

"Pretty sure he charged you some of the Horde's drinks last time we were at the Den to get back at you for pretending there was a tab."

"Us, Reen. He charged *us*."

"Nice try, Human." Returned to his normal level of not entirely calm, the elSha slipped out of the CIC, and Jan let her grin drop.

"Walk with me," Dave said as he strode to the hall, his pace brisk as though he weren't wearing heavy magnetic boots. Jan waved to Payton and followed, matching her stride to her brother's before they reached the first turn.

"Why didn't you let Reen hear the message? He was worried it was way worse than an urgent contract."

"I assumed he'd hear it and worry more—"

"He thought it was *Dunamis*."

"Oh." Dave was quiet for a handful of moments. "That would be worse."

"We're all broken in our own way, Dave. You can't protect anyone from their own feelings."

"He's calmer when you're on board." Dave Colby, near unflappable founder and sole commander of Colby's Killers for all its hundred-plus years of action, was nonplussed. For two entire steps, and then his expression cleared. "I didn't think he'd jump to it being the SI. I suppose I have it in my head that when Dunamis resurfaces, there won't be any question that it's him." He cleared his throat.

"That's not really Dunamis' style off Battle World, it seems." She lifted a shoulder and kept her gaze locked in front of them. "He's been a bit more subtle out in the wider galaxy."

"Shit, Jan." He scrubbed a hand over his close-cut hair and increased his pace. "It's not Dunamis, is it? The Lyon... he wouldn't bring us in blind."

The laugh bubbled out of her throat before she could decide to stop it. "Fuck if I know. But your explanation is more plausible. Urgent contract, someone under the gun. Besides, we kicked Dunamis' coded excuse for an ass last time. So what if it's him? We'll bust him up again and Sansar'll be pissed she missed it."

He snorted but didn't argue. The SIs were a problem, and they hadn't seen the last of Dunamis. That would be a future issue, though. For now, their ship was clear of his tendrils and traps, Battle World was abandoned many jumps across the galaxy, and the Lyon had finally found a job worthy of their time and absurd amount of expertise.

Jan repeated that to herself twice more before they reached the section of the ship Nick was meant to be settling the Lumar into. The silence struck her, and she locked her boots down against the *Mighty Wave's* decking.

"Where are they?"

"Nick?" Dave toggled comms rather than answering. After a moment, a panel flew off the wall further down the corridor, and a small elSha head emerged.

"Why're you up here? There were so many more Lumar, they wanted to stay together—Nick brought them two floors down." Speeko, the smallest of their elSha, flipped to orient to their direction and flicked out her tongue.

"We didn't get that message." If Jan's foot hadn't been magnetically locked to the floor, she would have tapped it to show her mood.

As it was, Speeko recognized enough to visibly start. "Oh! No! No no no, that's my fault. Hold on!" She ducked back into the wall of the ship and no more than ten seconds later both their comms buzzed.

"You coming?"

"We're moving in five."

"Speeko," Dave said with audible patience. "What're you doing in there?"

Jan tapped acknowledgement to their captain and a quick "hold please" to Nick, and after a moment the edge of an elSha snout tipped around the edge of the wall's opening. "I set something up and was practicing with it?"

"You want to get more specific?"

"Do I have to?"

"Better if you do. Otherwise, I'll send Taleena down to ask." There was no smile in Dave's voice, but Jan noted the easing of tension along his spine. He wasn't angry—their elSha partners were more often than not up to experiments and tinkering best not to question too closely—but he hadn't delivered an idle threat either. The elSha didn't have the same measure of respect for the hierarchy of the Killers as trained mercenaries, but Taleena understood maximum efficiency, and she was not shy about enforcing her preferences on her fellows.

"I was interested in what the Lumar might have to say. But they're not staying here. But instead of just dismantling my system, I thought

I should try some tweaks. But it was better than I thought. But I didn't think anyone would be down here—but I'm sorry that—"

"Got it." He cut across the rapidly building waterfall of worry. "You were going to listen in on our new members, then practiced blanketing frequencies and blocking comms, is that right?"

"No no no... well. A little."

"What have we said about eavesdropping?"

"But I don't!" More of her face emerged, enough to turn two wide eyes in their direction. Jan held an attentive rest and kept her face blank. "They're not members, not yet, they're trial! I wanted to see what they were thinking, and I have a passive translator that will just feed bursts to me because that's not against the rules; it's just smart, to know what people are thinking who are on the ship that we don't know!"

When had she frowned? Jan smoothed her face back to neutral and waited for her brother's reaction. The silence held too long, and pressure itched along the back of her neck. Jan cleared her throat. Speeko's wide eyes snapped to her, and Jan held out a hand.

Slowly, reluctance clear in every stiff movement of the usually limber elSha body, Speeko pushed out of the wall and crossed the distance between them.

"Speeko," she said, more softly than she'd intended. "You know we wouldn't bring anyone onto *Mighty Wave* we couldn't trust."

"Lumar have pinplants," the elSha muttered, a slight shudder running from her head to the tip of her tail. "Dunamis can overwrite them."

"I didn't want anyone else on board either." The truth in those words burned in the back of her mouth, but she swallowed and pushed onward. "We checked them out. Do you know when they decided to come along with *us*?"

Speeko shook her empty hand, a small negation.

"When they heard that we'd been fucked over by the Veetanho, and by Dunamis. I think they have some experience with getting fucked over."

"But the Lumar are so big." She shivered again, floating close enough to anchor herself against Jan's outstretched hand.

"You remember where we came from. Big, small, didn't matter to Dunamis. It probably happens to Lumar just as much out here as it did to us back there."

"That's some entropic shit." The elSha flicked her tongue, as though surprised by her own language. "*Huge* entropic shit."

"It sure as shit is, Speeko. So our fight's not with them."

The pause didn't itch down her spine this time, and after a few breaths the elSha spread her hands wide. She grabbed back onto Jan and her hotstick before anything floated too far, and then gave a human-style nod for good measure.

"So, you want to come with us to introduce yourself, and tell us about this jamming frequency? We didn't even notice comms falling off."

Speeko launched into a discussion so technical Jan resolved to connect her back with Nick and added it to her list of things to do—right after figuring out what had just turned her brother into a silent cardboard version of himself.

* * *

Time got away from her in their transit to Karma. There were training simulations to run, spooked elSha to soothe, levels of plans to make if something at Karma was hinky, and then suddenly they were docked at the massive space station in the Crapti region of the Jesc arm of the entropic galaxy.

Payton waved them off—a Goltar ship in the vicinity, crewed by actual Goltar, wanted to have an argument about their possession of the ship. He'd had more than enough practice fending these off at this point and had the right names to drop. They didn't need to stay for it, though she did mutter the need for an all-points message board on the GalNet as they exited the CIC.

The captain's lips quirked, but he was too much a professional to grin while exchanging words with the Goltar. Somehow their translators seemed to pick that up as "smug" when the aliens were already up in arms. A mystery.

Garg and his second, Jooj, waited at the airlock, and Dave motioned for them to fall in. Nick had fallen into an invention-off with Taleena and Taneeko, and Reen had decided to stay back, so the four of them made their way through Karma to the Lyon's Den.

"Maybe we need therapy."

Jan missed a step and glared at her brother. The last thing she wanted to do was trip her way through Karma. Some idiot alien would take it as her making fun of the way they walked, and it would be a whole thing, and she didn't have the patience for it.

Nor the firepower, though she'd begun to covet Jooj's incendiary blasting sidearm. She hauled her thoughts back into place and doubled her glare. "What now?"

"The Killers. Maybe we all need therapy. We went through…" He cleared his throat, his eyes forward as they tromped through crowded corridors. "A long time on Battle World hasn't left us entirely normal."

"What the fuck is normal, Dave?" The burning sensation crawled up her throat again.

"It's not going into panic mode in the guts of the *Mighty Wave* because we have new people on board. Or because a message came in. Or a troop of Lumar got moved two floors to have more room to spread out."

Had Dave been in panic mode about that? Or did he think she'd been?

"We were in hyperspace two damn weeks, Dave. We could have talked this out then."

"There might be actual therapists on Karma to—"

"To what? Make us feel better about what happened? We've been at loose ends too long. We need to get back in the action. Let's kill a bunch of dickheads, and we'll feel right as rain."

Usually, her brother was the master of compartmentalization. She couldn't begin to figure what had broken one of those boxes open for them to be having this conversation.

"Jan—"

"Listen to woman." In the din of their surroundings, Jan had to guess which Lumar had spoken—Jooj, probably. He seemed the most fascinated that she had as much authority as Dave, though all the Lumar listened to her just as well as anyone else. She'd served with worse mercs.

"Right? Thank you. Kill aliens, get paid. It's why we got into this."

"Jan."

"Do you think this will hurt us in the field?"

"No, I think we'll lock in the second we're back out there." Dave made a cutting motion, closer to his body than usual to keep from getting into an Oogar's personal space. The enormous bear-like creature glared at him regardless, but she figured that was just its face.

"Good enough. Oh look, we're here." They weren't, but she increased her pace, using her smaller profile to dodge between traffic. She didn't get stabbed or shot or yelled at, and then she was in front of two vaguely familiar Lumar.

"Drink or business?" The one on the left shifted slightly at her approach, and the one on the right spoke.

"Both. The Lyon sent for us."

"Colby's Killers." This time the one on the left spoke, and the one on the right straightened as Dave caught up to her.

"That's us," Dave said with a grin that struck Jan as natural. Had he been testing her? Did he want *her* to go to some alien therapist? They'd been out on the float too long, familiarizing themselves with the Lyon, the Mercenary Guild, the current state of the galaxy. They should have been taking contracts all along.

The financial incentives for the Phoenix Initiative were worth the delay, but they were well-honed weapons. Sitting on the sidelines did their edges no favors.

Both Lyon's Den Lumar stiffened as Garg and Jooj joined them, and when no one said anything, Dave nodded with his chin. "They're with us."

"Broken Bomb," Jooj grunted.

"Lyon's Pride."

Garg tapped his fist to his chest, and the Lyon's Den Lumar to her left ran through the rules. No drawing weapons, take fights outside, contracts negotiable but drinks aren't. Jooj and Garg gave every evidence of listening, made a point of examining the doorway that differentiated the "outside" fights were to be taken to, and nodded in harmony. The Lumar waved them through, gazes fixed on their fellow four-armed towering aliens.

Jan told them to find seats and veered off for the bar. The loud music washed over her, almost familiar. Well, the Lyon and Lyoness were basically the only Humans remotely contemporaneous to the Killers, so no surprise they'd be familiar with…

Was that Bad Reputation? She started to hum along, then realized it was subtly off. Pitch, words… catchy, a cover from someone with the perfect growl in their voice for the song. She bopped her head along and edged into a clear spot at the long bar in the back of the room.

"Glad you're here." The voice was too well known for her to reach for her weapon, and she kept her hands flat on the bar. "I've already got you a table and a round set up."

"Good to see you, Mari," Jan replied, tilting her head to take in the Lyoness. The other Human woman, shorter and dark haired but bright eyed despite her own hell of a story, gestured to the side, and they moved between well-spaced tables close enough to talk over the music and general hubbub of a crowd of aliens scattered across a large bar.

"Everything ok with Sera and Pura?" Jan had realized, halfway through hyperspace, that perhaps that had been why the Lyon needed them so urgently. His daughter had not chosen a safe life, becoming some sort of companion to one of the murder kitties, and maybe he trusted the Killers—or their experience—enough to call for aid.

"They're doing well. Visiting a mining station somewhere out in the wilds." Mari smiled—quick and faint, but genuine enough to settle at least one of Jan's worries. "And your assorted pack of killers and never-do-wells?"

"Fine." They curved around a table overflowing with XenSha, and Jan rolled her eyes. "As far as that goes. Dave suggested therapy."

"Oh?"

Jan reminded herself that Mari had spent far too many decades in a Veetanho hellhole. Not the same shit as her own, but close enough. "Just now, on the walk in. Crazy, right?"

"Talking to someone isn't a bad idea. Finding someone who would get it, though…"

"That's what I would have said, if he'd bothered to bring it up in the endless hours we spent in hyperspace."

"Maybe he's deciding how he feels about it?" Mari glanced at Jan, then motioned her ahead between a table of NapSha and Pushtal.

"I don't know. I think we all need to get to shooting things again."

"I'm fairly sure that opportunity is coming up fast." Mari paused and touched the tips of her fingers to Jan's elbow. "Hopefully one of these times you visit we can actually sit and catch up. I'm happy to talk to you any time. Maybe it'll help both of us." She pointed ahead, where Joel Lyons, the Lyon himself, leaned against a table populated by her brother and temporary Lumar compatriots.

"In the meantime, duty roars."

"Cute."

Mari laughed and patted her shoulder, then waved to her husband before turning back toward the bar.

As promised, drinks were in fact waiting, and Jan nabbed hers before making a proper hello. She liked showing respect to the fine beverages on hand, and perhaps some part of her wanted to prolong the moment before she had to know whatever it was that came next.

"Glad you're making new friends." The Lyon chuckled, and the Lumar looked at each other, then back at him. To be fair, Jan wasn't sure whether he was talking to Human or alien either—probably both, she decided, and took a generous swallow.

"Took your advice and got hooked into the Phoenix Initiative, and we're pleased that put us in line with the Broken Bomb." Dave tilted his glass to Garg, who very unsurprisingly grunted in reply.

"Broken Bomb, is it." The Lyon wrapped his hands around his glass and made a low sound in his throat. "I do like a good explosion."

Jooj grunted this time, and the Lyon nodded seriously, as though he'd taken some other level of meaning from it. Maybe he had. Jan took a third drink for luck and clunked her mug against the table.

"So, what's the what, Joel?" She echoed his pose on the other side of Dave, leaning her elbow on the wood-adjacent material between them. "Not that we don't love leaving our very expensive order of CASPers behind to visit with you."

"Ah." He spread his hands flat. "About that. I don't think you'll be here long enough to accept the order."

"Because?"

"You know how the Phoenix Initiative goes. Any number of new companies heading out to deep space, better trained than your day, but still not entirely ready for what's out there."

"With better contracts than we got that first go-round, I hope." Dave's voice deepened, not quite a warning. Their broker, back in the day of what was now referred to as the Alpha Contracts, had not had humanity's best interest in mind. They'd hoped for better from the Lyon.

"Better, but not safe. Had a crew ship out not too long ago—the Alpha Strike Warriors—for what should have been a simple garrison.

They had a good mix of old vets and decent newbies, solid enough that Wathayat approved their bid. They went comms dark, long enough that a new contract came in. I upgraded the company this time—still new, but with a heavier backing."

Jan wanted to ask who the heavy was, Joel or some other power, but figured that would come up if it were relevant. Rather, she figured that she'd make it relevant, but after he got the introductory goodies out of the way.

"They're off the board too. Contract is still open, but I can't throw just anyone after them."

"Third time's not the charm?" Jan hadn't meant to ask it, and Dave shot her a Look. She drained the rest of her drink instead of engaging.

"That, and we don't have eyes on the situation. Been hearing a lot about companies going missing, and after what you all went through, I didn't want to blindly add to that kind of equation."

A laser-sharp shock pierced her gut, and Jan forced herself to put her empty mug down with great care. It didn't clatter or thump, and she was absurdly proud of it. "You think they're being taken?"

"I want to make sure that isn't the case. Considering the scope and focus of the contract, I couldn't think of another company that would feel as strongly about it—and be as well prepared to take it down, if necessary."

"It's definitely the weird stuff." Dave had his "locked in" face on, and Jan was sure she wasn't the only one who saw it. The Lyon nodded, took a handheld display out of his pocket, and slid it toward the Killers' lead siblings. "Read it over. I'll send another round, but if you don't have any questions, I'd recommend you get moving in the next hour."

"You're storing our CASPers," Jan said without looking up from the details in front of her. "Nominal fee. Maybe take it out of your percentage."

"You get back with these two companies, I'll waive handling and storage entirely."

"Done and done, Lyon. We'll take care of it."

Someone had to.

* * *

"Does the ship fly differently when it's flooded?" Payton turned toward the four floating elSha over their table—several had stayed on Karma to greet their CASPers, and the rest were deep in the bowels of the ship continuing their respective projects.

Garg raised a hand with a question-grunt, and Speeko pivoted toward him. "This was a Goltar ship, and they're aquatic-based, so *Mighty Wave* has the option to operate full of water or air, depending on the preferences of the crew." The Lumar seemed to understand better when one of the elSha explained—perhaps something to do with the modifications the clever little lizards had done to their translators. Speeko reoriented to the captain and continued with confidence. "Yes. Not much—a different rate of spin, a wobble on the distal axis on the fifteenth revolution—"

"Why?" Reen asked, which seemed the more important question.

"We hit emergence as a full Goltar ship. Being floaty means we can make excuses about not going video to talk to whoever we find on the other side."

"Most races are going to step more cautiously around a Goltar warship." Dave nodded. "We go in hot, they won't look for the subtlety."

"Oh, oh, can I guess the subtlety?" Taleena waggled her tail and floated off to the far end of the conference room.

"No." Briggs, one of the sergeants they'd picked up over the endless years on Battle World, frowned in the ferocious manner that he only used for those few entities he was fond of. "Given it was probably your idea."

"Sport spoiler."

Jan laced her fingers together on her lap and pressed them tight to keep from smiling. The seven Humans around the table were the longest surviving members of Colby's Killers, four of whom had found their way into the company along the way on Battle World. She would trust them with her life—and had, more times than she could count. And given they were jumping into some measure of the unknown, they were the people she most wanted around the table.

The Lumar she was still on the fence about, but it wasn't right to ask them to risk their lives without any representation in the planning. The Killers had lived that life, and weren't about to perpetuate such bullshit now that they were free.

Dave sketched out the various suggestions, and each of the Humans and both of the Lumar weighed in. The elSha wiggles above them got more and more noticeable, and finally Jan held up a hand.

"Taleena?"

"Speeko had an *excellent* idea regarding the seas of acid that take up most of Agnus Cordero." The chief enforcer of the elSha swam her way toward Jan. "And Reen has a lovely device that will make the most of it. We'll have to tweak once we have confirmation on the actual chemical composition, but it should be short work."

"I have all the mechanical—"

"Reen." Dave smiled at their fix-it-er, who rolled in understanding. "You can tell me about it after the meeting, but you know it's going to go over all our heads."

"I want to see!" Nick interjected, because of course he did.

"In the meantime—can you make the ship fly like she's flooded?" Dave ran through each of their tech issues, point by point, and by the time they exited hyperspace, they had seven plans—though they each knew none was likely to survive actual contact with whatever they found on the other side.

* * *

Jan kicked her feet at her console and beamed at the voice-only transmission. They'd emerged into a crappy system to find their target planet and a metric fuckton of Besquith. When their course made clear they were en route, the Besquith had actually sent a message—apparently not everyone jumped at the chance to take on a Goltar battlecruiser.

The werewolf monsters had an enormous ship, of a kind she'd never encountered because all of her Besquith-encounters had been face to face, as nature had absolutely never intended. Payton had to man the actual command of the ship, so she got comms, and to be fair that was a complete delight. Even if they kept demanding to see her face. Given her lack of tentacles, she reiterated her talking point.

"When my ship is properly flooded, it makes visual communications with terrestrial lifeforms disconcerting. I will not engage other than in this method."

"*We are on official contract, and will attack if you encroach upon it on the planet.*"

"I do not enjoy repeating myself." She laced her hands behind her neck and stretched, nowhere near as annoyed as her tone. "We are in pursuit of a group of Human fugitives, and have all the authorizations necessary. I don't care what you're doing on Agnus Cordero, but we will take the justice we are due." Jan wished she could spin her chair, but instead she made her tone extra stuffy. They'd had more than their fair share of encounters with Goltar, and it served her well in her current impersonation.

"*You may not approach the planet—*"

"We are not asking permission. The *Mighty Wave* has taken out larger ships than yours. Attack if you are done with your lives." She cut the transmission and laughed until the captain turned around.

"If you're done having fun, you've got to get to your pod." Payton grinned and shot her a thumbs up. "We'll keep them guessing here, but I want to shed you all before they decide to move."

"No motion from the *Usual Suspect*?" Jan released her belt and stood, steadying herself against the return of gravity as they accelerated.

"Best we can tell the Besquith might be making repairs, but nothing's reading hot to us—if it comes to a dogfight out here, they won't be part of it. But we don't know how many are on board, only that there's at least one dropship still docked to it."

"So, zero to a hundred?"

"Zero to fifty, let's say. Now get. You're not messing up my finely crafted trajectory."

"Aye, Captain!" Jan left the CIC at a run.

* * *

The pod skimmed the bare surface of *The Usual Suspect*, and Taleena ran her tongue under her eyes in satisfaction. "Lock in three." A small clunk followed, and she eased back from the controls. "And we're on. If the schematics were accurate, we can bore in here without stirring a single fur or line of drool."

"I don't think they walk around drooling all the time." Jan shrugged and arranged her werewolf killer more comfortably against her suit. "I mean, all the time I ever saw them, but those were very particular circumstances."

"Yeah, we'll have somewhere between ten and thirty minutes before we get to those same particular circumstances, if by circumstances you mean 'when we fight them.'" Nick pulled down their hatch and applied one of the elSha hotsticks to the plating of the ship they'd latched onto.

"Besquith drool." Garg agreed, his arms folded close to his body to maximize their limited space.

"If everything went smoothly, the other Killers should be a lock in five." Taleena pushed upward and added her hotstick on the other side of the open circle between pod and ship. An elSha hotstick, Jan had learned against her will, was an upgraded, mini version of a welding arc, intensely hotter and more precise than the Human version.

"Also!" Taleena twisted to glare at Nick, though her hotstick didn't so much as twitch. "You are not to cut off any Besquith arms and use them as weapons."

"Whoa whoa whoa, Leena. Taneeko agreed that was a necessary act with the KzSha. And besides I would never." He focused on his cuts, but Jan didn't have to see his mouth twitching to know there was going to be more. "Besides, KzSha have sword arms, which are cool and useful in puncturing other KzSha, who are sadly laser deflecting. Besquith don't have cool sword arms."

Garg peered up at Nick, an expression very like a grin spreading across his face.

Jan counted the beats, got to three, and could almost have mouthed along as Nick added, "Their teeth are pretty damn awesome though. Imagine what I could do with a set of Besquith jaws?"

"Keep them in your room like a trophy until Speeko takes them and tosses them in an incinerator?" Jan asked sweetly.

"I knew it was her!" Nick carefully removed a section of hull plating and moved to his next section.

"It was me, dumbass. But I promised Speeko she could swipe from your rooms the next time you kept something gross."

"Who says there'll be a—oh fine. I'll just work out a better lock on my door." He grumbled to himself a little longer, then removed another section of plating. "Also, eventually we're going to need to take a different approach to boarding enemy ships. Someone's going to catch on to this."

"Hey, last time it was airlocks, not cutting through hull plating. And it wouldn't work if this ship hadn't already taken a beating or two with its Zuul owners before these Oshians bought it second hand."

Having the Lyon as a friend meant they got excellent intel. Detailed schematics on *The Usual Suspect* along with its combat history, possible landing points for the first and second mercenary groups, thorough postulations and a litany of wild guesses as to the absolutely insane acid on the planet. They'd probably need to get their own researcher on board at some point, Jan decided. Even if they couldn't match the Lyon's information gathering operation, at least someone who knew the current state of the galaxy. Someone who could tell them things like "what kind of Besquith ship is that brooding over their target" in real time.

Though maybe it was better not to know, given it wouldn't change what they had to do.

Colby's Killers. It was in the name.

Taleena wormed through, and after giving her time to get clear, Nick kept cutting and Jan pushed up to join him. The time it took them to make something big enough for them and Garg to get through would also give Taleena and the other elSha the space they needed to get to their respective control nodes. The more blinding and confusing done to their enemy before they engaged, the better.

Before they boarded the ship, Jan spared a thought for the *Mighty Wave* out there doing flashy flying to distract the larger Besquith ship from noticing their recently claimed prize going dark. If it came to an exchange of the big guns, she knew the *Mighty Wave* would triumph, but the goal was to avoid direct blows for as long as possible. Payton was up for it, she reminded herself, then let it go.

There was there. Her issue was here. She shoved up into the ship ahead of Nick and Garg, and by the time she reached Taleena's marker—a dash of green for go—her thoughts locked into each next moment.

Stalk the halls with her small, handheld, chemical laser pistol—twenty shots to take out the enemy.

Ease around corner. See Besquith. Shoot Besquith in the eye. Nineteen shots.

Stalk. Ease. Shoot. Repeat.

Ten shots.

A flicker of motion and she dropped, spun—registered the explosion. Close but not about her.

Stalk. Ease—

The floor disappeared from under her and something wrapped around her leg and *yanked*.

She pointed the pistol down, between her legs. Fired.

Besquith weren't as laser resistant as KzSha, but this one, armored, wasn't presenting its vulnerable eyes. Claws shredded through her suit. Fired. Fired. Fired.

Six shots.

Pain radiated through her calf, but it wasn't her thigh, wasn't an artery. She fired again, one-handed, grabbed the knife from her hip, and when the Besquith yanked again, its claws reaching higher, she rode the momentum and folded down her body.

The Besquith had used a small tube, barely broader than her, and it didn't have the room to twist and turn she did. Something tore, something pulled, and Jan ignored it. She followed the motion down, knife down, and found the joint between its head and neck.

Dig in knife. Fire into the hole.

Gaping jaws. Fire there too.

Two shots.

The Besquith did not go limp in death, and she couldn't trust it wouldn't burst back into motion. She fired the last shots into each of its finally revealed eyes.

And floated for a second or a minute or a day.

Three more explosions.

Right, Jan. Untangle the claws. Put pressure on the bleeding. Jam in nanites. Find your people.

* * *

She woke up on the *Mighty Wave*, which meant she had no choice but to listen as Nick shared, in great detail, how Garg had found her after merrily exploding half the ship, Taleena had bandaged her, and she'd rode back in Dave's pod on a heap of broken Besquith bodies.

Probably better she didn't remember it herself.

They'd only lost three. Four, she corrected herself, because the Lumar counted. Still, not a bad exchange for some thirty Besquith currently rotting in one of their dropships. They'd done worse for less.

Dave strode into medical too late to save her from Nick, but soon enough that sitting up still made her wince. She waved off his concern—the nanites would finish any moment—and demanded, "Well?"

"Braker, you were supposed to debrief her." Her brother raised his eyebrows, though the corner of his mouth twitched upward.

"Just got to the part where she snuggled into her nest of corpses, sir." Nick saluted, formal in a way he never was, and Jan heroically didn't strangle either of them.

"And *now* is the part where you tell me what's next, boys. We still on target?"

"We are. Payton's got us in a further orbit as a 'concession' to the Besquith. We've negotiated three dropships, each to a point the Besquith helpfully suggested might hold our fugitives." Dave grinned and spread his arms. "Over/under on ambushes?"

"Nah, they'll take out one dropship, blame it on the renegade Humans we're after. The other two will be areas as far away from the action as possible." Nick shook his head rapidly. "Bad bet."

"Taleena got a fair amount from *The Usual Suspect's* comms. She used Speeko's eavesdrop/jammer device to keep the main Besquith force blissfully unaware of the ship's change of prospects." Dave crossed his arms, still amused. Before she could prod him, he continued, "There's a little circle of death planetside. Three-mile radius. Besquith keep dropping dead. But they don't see *any*thing."

It took Jan a moment. In her defense, she'd definitely almost died an hour or so ago. "One of the groups had one of those Cheshire cats, didn't it?"

"Someone's still alive and present on Agnus Cordero."

"And we have a drop point." Jan beamed. "I should go unconscious more often."

"I'd rather you didn't," Dave said mildly, and Nick tipped his hand back and forth in an "ehhh" gesture.

"I'm flying delivery one."

"Good. Lizzy wants delivery two, and I already told her yes. Payton's pissed he can't take one." The *Mighty Wave* was some consolation prize for their former dropship pilot. "Get cleared and get to your dropship."

* * *

Lizzy Bell, a hotshot pilot who'd hotshotted her way to Battle World fifty years ago, took a small number of Besquith corpses and a larger number of elSha, and aimed for the circle of death where the invisible assassin had to be based.

Had to be, or they were throwing their elSha to the wind, but Jan had faith.

Jan also had most of the rest of the dead Besquith, and a slightly more dangerous route—she was aiming for the distinctly Human temporary buildings that no doubt held a fair amount of Besquith and the most likely ambush.

Jeremy Blake had the third dropship, with a token corpse or two, and a string of densely vegetated islands to fly over. Second most likely location of ambush, but Blake had been flying for seventy years and could handle it.

The three dropships fell away from the *Mighty Wave* one after another, and took their individual routes to the planet, giving the Besquith ship a wide berth.

Jan flew her designated route, whistling off-key. If she were looking for suspect Humans, she'd have to get a lot lower, opening her to a well-disguised ambush that the Besquith could convincingly deny.

But she didn't actually have to go low. Only low enough to ensure her cargo was still recognizable when it landed.

"Briggs? Bell's on approach for her drop. How's it looking?"

"Better than it smells, Colby."

Belatedly, Jan realized someone had to have hosed her off after her nap on dead furry monsters. Unsure which part of the thought was worse, she filed it away for never, and signaled Briggs. "Commence Airdrop: How I Learned to Stop Worrying and Love the Bomb."

"That movie was old before you were born."

"Barely!"

"Fire in the hold! Or corpses. Whatever."

Jan opened the cargo hold and Briggs and his boys tossed out corpse after corpse. Not the most glamorous of duties—they all wished they'd had their ordered CASPers and could be jumping out to rain death rather than the dead—but excellent cover for the elSha dropping planetside in their rigged gear. They'd be hidden in Besquith corpses, keeping the living from noticing them.

If any of their target mercenaries remained—and the strong presence of the Besquith indicated they did—she hoped they appreciated their personalized delivery. Four elSha, in tiny almost-CASPers, with modified flamethrowers they could fill with Agnus Cordero's fancy acid... When was the last time she got presents that nice?

Besides the *Mighty Wave*, though that was less a present and more a repayment.

"*All clear.*"

"Taking us home!"

Three missiles shot into the air, but she'd already curved away and up. She didn't bother to shoot back, because she couldn't risk further marring the merchandise before the Besquith went out to see what they'd won.

She broke orbit and warned everyone to strap in for higher-G, and a moment later the comms pinged to a blanket signal—the werewolves were yelling at everyone about the body parts they'd apparently identified. Payton, bless him, responded in kind, so she got to watch while she arrowed for the *Mighty Wave*. Space might get a little hot soon, figuratively speaking.

"*You got us. We lied. Now stand down or we'll blow up your ship and blast you from orbit for good measure. In whichever order we feel like.*" Payton sounded like he was having as much fun as she was.

"*You can't engage the planet from orbit—*"

"*Fun fact.*" Jan huffed a laugh when the transmission flickered and resolved with video. "*I can do whatever the fuck I want. I'm a Human in possession of a Goltar battlecruiser, so you should assume laws aren't really something I care about.*"

Silence held for thirty long seconds. Despite the pressure of their acceleration, Jan cackled through every single one of them.

"*We're going to retrieve what we're here to get. You stand down, we leave, you carry on your business. No one else has to die,*" Payton declared.

"You took our ship. We will answer."

"You're answering right now, and frankly it's boring. Ship's ours. We'll take the other stuff, and we'll go. What happens in the middle is up to you." Payton's face vanished, and Jan committed to the fanciest flying she could manage, in case there were any pissed off alien wolves on her trail.

* * *

It wasn't entirely smooth. The remaining mercs—a Depik, a Cochkala, a HecSha, an Oogar, a Zuul, two Humans, and a Maki (it sounded like a terrible joke but she couldn't make a punchline)—had to fight their way out to Blake's dropship, which had gone to ground on an island jungle. Garg and the Lumar on board with Blake had been a huge value add, and the pilot hadn't stopped raving about them.

When the survivors stumbled onto the *Mighty Wave* with double their combined bodyweight in red diamonds, Dave immediately offered them membership in Colby's Killers.

"We'll get *The Usual Suspect* fixed up, maybe start a fleet." Dave's enthusiasm, always infectious, seemed likely to carry the day, but Jan told everyone to think about it until business was complete on Karma.

Garg and Broken Bomb accepted before they entered hyperspace. Tejas and Gye, the Hunter/Cochkala pair, signed on before they emerged in the Crapti region. Before they docked at Karma, the remaining Oshians agreed to a temporary contract akin to the Lumar's first agreement.

They walked in a weirdly assembled group through the weirdly populated corridors of Karma, and as they approached the Lyon's Den, Jan tapped her brother's arm while their elSha gabbled about the improvements Taneeko had made to their CASPers.

"We don't need therapy." She met his eyes briefly, then focused ahead. "We need to kick ass all around the galaxy and make sure the kind of shit that happened to us doesn't happen to anyone else. As long as that's pressing and we're doing it, we'll hold together. Once we fuck Dunamis up and *win*? Then we can take the time to heal."

Dave grinned. "You're saying for now we might be broken, but we're goddamn effective."

"Exactly. So let all those broken little pieces stab the shit out of everyone who needs stabbing."

"Colby's Killers. Making the galaxy better one gory stabbing at a time."

"It needs work. We'll find our tagline eventually."

After a drink or ten. They could afford it.

* * * * *

Marisa Wolf Bio

Marisa Wolf is a second-generation nerd who started writing genre stories at six. At least one was good enough to be laminated, and she's been chasing that high ever since. Over the years she's taught middle school, been headbutted by an alligator, earned a black belt in Tae Kwon Do, and finally decided to finish all the half-started stories in her head.

She writes SFF throughout multiple corners of the genre, including military science fiction and space opera as a core author in the bestselling Four Horseman Universe (*Assassin, Hunter*, and *Ally* with Kacey Ezell, *Night Song* with Mark Wandrey, *The Lyons' Pride* and *World Enders* with Chris Kennedy, and a co-edited anthology with Kacey Ezell, *Negotiation*), urban fantasy in Hit World (with *The Valkyries Initiative*), and video and table-top gaming in tie-in stories.

Marisa is currently based in Texas, though she lives in an RV with her husband and their two absurd rescue dogs, so it's anyone's guess where in the country she is. More at www.marisawolf.net.

# # # # #

The Reaper's Scythe by Kevin Ikenberry

Benes

3Terke-A
Jesc Region

"*One minute!*" Benes heard the company's first sergeant growl over the channel. The dropship's rear personnel and equipment ramp opened, and the frigid air howled and filled the cylindrical space. Benes dialed down the ambient volume with a twist of his left thumb. Like everyone else in the Blasters, the sheer cosmic nature of the brand-new Mk 8 CASPers had awed him. He'd qualified in Mk 5s and operated Mk 6s for the bulk of his time as a member of Force 25 and knew his old commander, Colonel Ibson, wouldn't want him or his new company to be reliant on the technology to save them.

"You might have the best weapons in the galaxy, but they matter shit if you ain't got a brain, Benes. Use that and you'll make it."

Benes smiled at the memory and blinked it away. Three years since Victoria Bravo—the second time around. He'd lost his friends, his wife, and what he'd thought was his chance to amount to anything on the field. After being nearly eradicated, he didn't begrudge Tara Mason for disbanding Force 25. There wasn't any other choice, really. They, like him, had nothing left to give. He'd returned to Earth believing neither Mason, nor any of the survivors of Force 25, would keep up the fight. Mercenary companies didn't survive after the kind of beating Force 25 had taken. From what he learned later, they hadn't, but Tara Mason had some fight left in her after all.

Tara Mason was there at Scylla on the shoulder of Jessica Francis, and again during the initial attack at Kleve. When the dust settled, she was listed as missing in action and presumed dead. He'd watched the newsprogs and seen Guild Master Hak-Chet's speech from the comfort of a well-worn recliner at his Florida beach house. By the time the speech was over, he was standing in his living room staring at the Tri-V thinking he had to get back into the fight. The first commercial break in the coverage gave him what he needed. Nigel Shirazi's face filled the screen with an urgent request. The Mercenary Guild needed new companies. There were investors lined up around the world ready to bring new units to bear across the galaxy to remove the stain of the Crusaders and restore the Mercenary Guild to prominence. Opportunities abounded. New equipment. New sponsors. Experience almost ensured command. What better way to continue the fight?

Two weeks later, he was standing in front of seventeen men and women, all experienced combat veterans and qualified CASPer drivers. He'd easily done the paperwork and recruiting through his network of friends. The financing came from a benefactor named Hashimoto on Hokkaido in the Nippon Trading Conglomerate. Their guild paperwork had been filed and accepted, and after an initial conference call to establish their chain of command, Benes had reported to a former military base south of Sapporo to meet his brand-new company.

* * *

Two Weeks Earlier...

Chitose Intergalactic Spaceport, Earth

"We ain't many," First Sergeant Jerald Hornsby had said in his East Texas twang, "but we've got sixteen qualified operators. When Mister Hashimoto gets us the logistical base we need, we'll rise to the top real quick and bring in the best of the best to fill the ranks. For now, this about all we got."

"It's not much, Top," he'd replied with a wry grin.

"Better than a bunch of shavetails, sir," Hornsby had replied.

But there wasn't time to establish the logistical base or recruit additional forces of any type. All they had were two out of work Midderall pilots and a rickety dropship they'd bolt to a Yamato Holdings ThrustCore and depart immediately for the Terke system. He didn't even have a chance to speak with Hashimoto until they'd departed the airfield.

"Colonel Benes, a pleasure to make your acquaintance." Hashimoto nodded at the screen with an almost ceremonial bow. He hadn't bothered to take the twenty-minute train ride from Sapporo after all. "Your mission is very simple. When you get to the Terke system, the third planet, 3Terke-A, has a research station near its South Pole investigating helium-3 deposits. The research station belongs to me and has been taken hostage by a company of mercenaries calling themselves the Red Wolves. I have no more information on them than that, though my team is working to provide some intelligence. You're going in blind. With the Peacemaker Guild rebuilding, there is no choice but to take back what is mine. I regret I do not have the intelligence necessary to help you plan an assault, but you must retake the station at all costs. Collateral damage is not an issue. Eliminate the threat without regard to the facility. It's abandoned. Are we clear?"

"Yes, sir," Benes replied. "Retake the station at all costs has a much higher standard fee."

"Excuse me?" Hashimoto looked as if he'd swallowed his wallet.

Benes grinned. "You are this company's benefactor, but any one of my people could walk away from this and make twice the credits with another organization. This isn't a milk run, so it's going to require adequate compensation."

Hashimoto appeared to consult something out of view. "What are you proposing, Colonel Benes?"

"Bonus of ten thousand credits a man over the base pay to survivors. Anyone who dies gets five thousand for their next of kin. If they have none, it goes to a community fund."

"Agreed," Hashimoto replied curtly. "I will be waiting for confirmation. Safe travels."

That was easy, Benes thought. *What's so important about this research station?*

The connection clicked off and he gave the deployment order. In under two minutes, they secured the Mk 8 CASPers into the dropship and lifted off. For the next ten minutes, he reviewed the equipment status updates and saw they'd have plenty of work to do during their 170-hour hyperspace transition. Benes caught the change in lighting as they reached orbit and approached the waiting ThrustCore. Docking took a couple of minutes, but they jumped for Terke before he'd even unclasped his harness.

What's the godsdamned hurry?

* * *

Benes

3Terke-A

"*Thirty seconds!*"

Hornsby's voice cut through the memory and brought him back to the present. He cued the Mk 8's systems and set the radars and sensor suites to HALD. "Maintain laser comms; the whole place is jammed all over the spectrum. No comms. No info. So, keep your lasers engaged at all times. Ramp ready. First section on the line!"

Benes stepped forward. A commander led from the front. There were no exceptions. "All right, Blasters, just like we briefed. Get to the ground, establish security, and we move out. Alpha section is with me. Bravo follows Top. Anything with a weapon in your sights is a target. Lock your lasers on, and I'll see you on the objective."

He paused at the edge of the ramp. The frozen southern pole region of 3Terke-A didn't surprise him, but he turned up the CASPer's temperature controls slightly. When the drop light turned green, Benes dove the Mk 8 into the bright, clear sky. He settled into a stable flight position, checked that all eighteen CASPers had left the drop ship, then used the CASPer's sensors to scan the terrain below.

Benes winced. The electromagnetic spectrum was a mess. Everything from an ancient VLF radio to state-of-the-art CASPer information networks would be worthless.

Focus on what you can see.

Buildings and vehicles showed up in his scan. As he fell toward the target, the images clarified and near the research station he saw numerous skiffs and tanks moving around—

The tanks are moving sideways. That's—

"Heads up, Blasters, we have Xiq'tal on the objectives." He laughed. "The Red Wolves are actually crabs. Who's up for seafood?"

There were several whoops and calls over the unit's radio channel. He couldn't identify who it was, and then the laughter froze in his throat. Several points of light flickered to life and long, tree-like stalks rose toward them at frightening speed. His caution and warning system alerted at the same time he flinched to the right and avoided the first one.

//SAM Launch. SAM Launch.//

No shit!

"Smoke in the air! Break, break, break!" Benes over-rotated and the CASPer tumbled out of control.

Shit! Shit! Shit!

"*Evasive action!*" he heard Hornsby growl. "*Bravo section, take the left.*"

Benes tapped his jumpjet pedals and rolled the CASPer onto its belly. They were much lower now, maybe three thousand meters to go. Benes re-oriented his sensors and found the surface-to-air missile batteries flanking the major building complex. He targeted them and sent the information to his team as the primary targets. There were ten or twelve Xiq'tal scurrying around between the buildings to the right. They'd be the secondary targets for Alpha section. He sent the information and saw two of the CASPer icons were black.

Two thousand meters.

"Alpha, Hughes and Siers are dead. Use their debris as cover," Benes ordered.

The SAM warning tones chimed again. This time, Benes and the others were ready. Three missiles streaked into their formation. Benes sighted his MAC on the first and fired three quick rounds. One clipped the missile and spun it out of control, and it detonated harmlessly to Benes's far right. The other two missiles never stood a chance as the entirety of Bravo team fired on them.

One thousand meters.

"Spread out and open fire!" Benes called as he swung his MAC toward two Xiq'tal skittering in the open and loosed a barrage at them. One stumbled forward, detaching a severed leg as it did. The other raised a cannon of some type and fired. The burst passed harmlessly over Benes's head.

Five hundred meters.

Three hundred meters.

WHOOOMP!

The HALD chute deployed and as soon as the drogue jerked his CASPer to a feet-down position, Benes stomped on the jump pedals, cut the chute, and fell the last hundred meters or so to the frozen ground.

"Alpha, form on me. Let's ride!"

* * *

Hornsby

Hornsby barely felt the CASPer's feet touch the ice before he jumped high and forward to the cover of an outbuilding. At the apex of his leap, there were two Xiq'tal on the left at a few hundred meters. They turned his way and fired. He saw an icon drop off his heads-up display.

"Piatt's down. No life signs," he called to Colonel Benes.

Benes didn't respond, nor did Hornsby expect him to. The colonel merely needed to know who was alive, and who was not. Three Blasters hadn't made the landing; sixteen percent of their combat power was gone before they even started the fight.

"Let's go, Bravo. On the bounce!" Hornsby growled into his headset. He moved right, around the building, in three quick steps. Compared to his old Mk 6, the new Mk 8 was incredibly agile and lethally fast. At the edge of the building, Hornsby brought up a hand cannon with the CASPer's right hand and a combat axe with his left. A Xiq'tal charged from the left, slamming a pincer down at him. Hornsby sidestepped and knocked the glancing blow aside with the axe, fired the hand cannon toward the alien's eyes, and spun toward the creature. As he turned, he swung the axe toward the center of the Xiq'tal's facial structure and felt the weapon slam into the thick armored plating. He brought the hand cannon up from under the alien's mouth and fired a long burst.

The Xiq'tal squealed, flinched backward, and swung at Hornsby with a pincer. He jumped straight up and angled the CASPer to land on the Xiq'tal's upper shell. As he did, two more aliens rapidly approached, firing some type of beam weapon.

"Valens! Holly! Keep this one engaged. I've got two moving on the left," Hornsby called. "Adamson. You, Watson, and Black hold down the left side of the position from the corner of the building. Walker and Brooks, get up to the roof and lay down suppressive fire. I need eyes on the rest of the Xiq'tal now!"

Hornsby leapt off the Xiq'tal and used the axe to slash one of its back legs. It screeched and turned, and he knew the combat veterans behind him would put it down. He angled the Mk 8 toward the building where Walker and Brooks now stood. They fired their MACs in a steady rhythm at the two approaching Xiq'tal, pulling them farther to the right and away from Adamson and the others.

"Once they reach your kill box, Adamson, let 'em have it."

"*Aye, Top,*" the Scotsman replied. "*Standin' by.*"

Hornsby backed away from the edge of the roof and peered to the east-southeast. Decayed Human remains littered the ground between the Blaster elements. Scorch marks and impact craters suggested a quick, ferocious battle had taken place.

This place wasn't abandoned. Goddamn crabs.

Alpha section moved behind several large earthmover vehicles for cover. A massive explosion, followed by a couple of less powerful secondary detonations, signaled the end of one surface-to-air battery.

To the north, tucked against the bulk of a rocky, snow-covered mound, were three additional buildings where the station's crews ate and slept. All three appeared secure, with steel shutters covering the windows. The possibility of survivors meant they'd have to secure the SAM sites so the dropship could land. They'd have to clear the field of Xiq'tal first.

Hornsby scanned the entire station and his stomach roiled. Four Xiq'tal skittered out of a hangar to the west carrying large rocket launcher pods.

"*Crabs to the west with spikes.*" He heard Walker call the spot report before he could. Working with real combat veterans was something he'd missed. Like many of the others, credits had lured him back into the cockpit and the chance to make things right again. He'd lost a cousin to the Crusaders and their self-righteous fervor. He'd died on Kleve at the hands of a MinSha queen, paralyzed by his pinplants, or so they'd said. Hashimoto had ensured all the Blasters had encrypted connections, secured pinplants, and the best weapons. All they had to do was fight.

"*Here we come!*" Adamson yelped.

Hornsby heard the concentrated ambush on the two nearest Xiq'tal behind him. It was over in less than thirty seconds. Three down, at least nine to go.

"*More at the hangar, Top,*" Walker called again. "*That's their rally point.*"

"Which means that's our target, Bravo." Hornsby tapped his controls and set waypoints. "We're gonna bound our way there like we're grunts, people. Provide covering fire, get up, find cover, get down. Ain't pretty, but that's the way it is. Adamson, take your section first. We'll cover you from here. Valens and Holly, fall in on me as we go. Acknowledge."

All of them acknowledged with clicks of their radio buttons. *They all think they're pilots.* Hornsby grinned. *Some things'll never change, huh?*

"Go, Adamson!" Hornsby said. He moved to the edge of the roof. Three dead Xiq'tal littered the ground below them, leaking eerie-colored bodily fluids across the snow. The bodies steamed, and he was glad he couldn't smell them inside his CASPer. He brought his MAC up and aimed at the Xiq'tal in the distance. Given their armor, they wouldn't really feel the effects. Harassment was the key. "Go for their eyes and mouths. Keep them annoyed and unfocused."

"*Set!*" Adamson called from their covered position behind some sheds. Hornsby identified a low, concrete structure to the north.

"Waypoint's up. Follow me!" He stomped his jump pedals and leapt from the roof. It took two jumps to get there, and he slammed to the ground and put his back against the wall as the others arrived. Brooks brought up the rear. As he descended, a rocket impacted the CASPer's center of mass, knocking him from the sky.

Dammit.

"We're set, Adamson. Go!" he said and moved out from the structure's edge to provide cover. "Get some fire on the roof of this thing!"

"*On it, Top!*" Valens called through increasing chatter; her voice was easy to pick out as the others worked the problem together.

Hornsby let them talk and concentrated on distracting the Xiq'tal. There were now six of them moving toward his forces. With three aliens already down, his team now faced the bulk of the enemy's strength.

If there aren't more than a dozen, that is. Maybe I shoulda picked the right side. Dumbass.

"*Fuckin' hell,*" Brooks said, grunting and wheezing over the radio. Hornsby looked and saw the CASPer struggling to its feet. "That hurts."

"Get back with the formation so we can move, Brooks."

"*Copy.*" Brooks groaned. "*Armor's pretty stout, Top. Thought I was a goner.*"

You ain't dead yet, Hillbilly.

Hornsby grinned to himself and kept firing. The Xiq'tal squawked and screeched in the distance. Confused and annoyed, they appeared to lash out at each other. It was time to up the ante.

"Adamson? K-bombs. Now!" he ordered. "My team, let's go!"

* * *

Benes

Benes moved forward to one of two parallel rows of earthmoving equipment parked outside the first of the three main buildings. His HUD identified the building as the mining operations complex. There was no evidence of a mine in the barren hillside that he could see. Large rolling doors suggested the mine entrance was inside, perhaps even under the three-story building itself. As he moved around the front of a large dump truck, Benes caught sight of three Xiq'tal moving toward his team. The last one lingered in front of the central building as if guarding it.

They've got hostages. Benes bit the inside of his cheek. *No, we don't know that. But if it looks like a duck and quacks like a duck…*

Assumptions in a fight were necessary, but often misguided. Enemy actions could be a feint, an outright lie, or maybe the Xiq'tal didn't feel like fighting. There was no immediate answer and Benes knew the first rule of combat—stay focused on the mission and the people.

Haven't seen a live Human yet. We're down three CASPers and Brooks's condition is yellow. We've killed a quarter of the Xiq'tal we've seen, though.

The thought did little to calm his rising anxiety. Something was missing. Something wasn't right, and what they were facing made little sense. The Xiq'tal were a good choice to hold the surface, but there had to be more to this mission.

Who else is here and where the hell are they?

"*Sir?*" Jameson called. The female medic's voice was oddly quiet. "*Got some remains over here. Injuries aren't consistent with Xiq'tal or their weapons.*"

Benes squinted. "What?"

"*Sir, these Humans weren't killed by the Xiq'tal,*" Jameson said. "*No blunt force trauma. Lots of bite and claw marks and scattershot wounds. Spread distance between the wounds suggests Besquith. Matches up with the other marks and lacerations.*"

"Say again?" Benes said and then clamped his mouth shut. "We haven't seen any Besquith. It's the Xiq'tal, right?"

"*No, sir,*" Jameson said. "*The Xiq'tal don't do this kind of thing. There's something else going on here.*"

No shit.

Benes leaned out from behind the equipment again and saw the Xiq'tal in the distant waving its forelegs in the air and stomping back and forth. From his early mercenary education, the Xiq'tal often moved their pincers when agitated and aggressive—waving them back and forth. This particular one, though, wasn't waving both pincers. One was being waved and the other seemed to be pointing. Benes followed where the alien was pointing, toward the hill above the operations buildings. Benes saw nothing in the snow and ice at first glance. Then a flat surface appeared. Benes tweaked his CASPer's sensors to focus on the site.

"Jammers," Benes said. "Top, I've got a jammer emplacement on the hill above the operations buildings. Change in mission: move toward my position and hold things here. Do not, I say again, *do not* press the attack against the Xiq'tal."

"*Standby, sir.*"

Benes released the transmit button and a dialog box for a private conversation appeared. Benes selected it with his eyes.

"Top? I've got a Xiq'tal pointing at that jammer emplacement," Benes explained. "Jameson says the Human corpses on the field show wounds consistent with a Besquith attack."

Hornsby was silent for a few seconds. "*You're thinking the Xiq'tal are trying to communicate; given the jammer field?*"

"I do. I think the high terrain is impassable to them," Benes said. "I'm taking Alpha up there to disable it."

"*Copy, sir. Bravo moving to your position now.*"

"Time to press the attack, folks," Benes called to Alpha team. "We've got a jammer on the high ground above. I want Cheung and Alphonso with me on this side moving around the right in case that Xiq'tal opens fire. Morrison, Strickland, and Jameson head out to the left, around the lines of vehicles. If the Xiq'tal charges us, hit it. We'll max jump up the terrain and get the jammer. Copy?"

"*Affirm, sir,*" Morrison replied in his stiff, Canadian accent. "*Moving.*"

The three CASPers sprinted down the line of vehicles, paused at the large scraper at the end of the row, and shot between it and the earth mover next to it. He let them get into position as he looked again at the advancing enemy. The first two Xiq'tal had formed up and were creeping toward the center of the vehicle park. In the distance, the third remained near the central building.

"Cheung, get to the left side of this truck. Alphonso, once I say go, you follow me with Cheung in the rear. Got it?"

"*Yes, sir,*" both drivers responded in unison.

"On me." Benes readied the MAC and the hand cannon in his right hand. "Now!"

He moved out from the cover of the truck and oriented his MAC on the first Xiq'tal, now only twenty meters away, but he did not fire. The Xiq'tal's weapon came up. Being so close, their size and appearance unnerved him. When it didn't fire, he ran toward the hill. Icons on his heads-up display showed Cheung and Alphonso were right behind him. Experience took over, and he turned toward the hill and ran the Mk 8 as fast as he dared across the icy ground. He closed the distance to the base of the hills quickly.

"Max jump," Benes called. "Ready. Ready. Now!"

The Mk 8 shot up the side of the hill and landed roughly halfway to the jammer's location. As he got the CASPer's feet under it again, Benes jumped again, sighted his MAC on the target, and fired six quick shots. He saw the rounds impact the antenna complex and the emitter's power level fluctuated for a moment but came back. "Mark my impact points and fire!"

The snow around the jammer site erupted with dozens of impacts. Benes ran toward the site and brandished one of the CASPer's hand cannons. Fifty meters from the site, he opened fire at the complex. The first burst appeared to penetrate what looked like an antenna shroud. It toppled and revealed the antenna itself. Benes fired again and flinched as four Besquith popped up from spider holes and returned fire to repel the attack.

Benes brought his cannon to bear on the closest Besquith as it shouldered a familiar-looking rocket launcher and pointed it in their direction. His cannon rounds found their mark as the Besquith activated the firing mechanism on what they called the CASPer-killer and shot Alphonso's CASPer in the chest. Alphonso went down, and the remaining three Besquith came up out of their holes and charged. Benes targeted two of them with his MAC and took them down quickly. The third closed the distance to Cheung, who took it down with a burst of his hand cannon.

"Give me security, Cheung. Taking out the jammer."

"*Copy.*"

Benes leapt forward and centered his MAC on the emitter. He clenched his fist and drove twelve rounds through the equipment sheltered in the snow. As he descended, his communications system opened up. Without the jamming, every frequency their systems could hear came to life. After a click and burst of static, a deep, gravelly voice called:

"*Human forces, this is Tchgnur of the Endless Current. We are not your enemy.*"

Benes blinked. There was nothing in their intelligence or mission planning sets about any Endless Current. Their target was the Red Wolves.

What in the hell is going on?

"Tchgnur, this is Colonel Ed Benes of the Blasters. You're the Xiq'tal on the field, correct?"

"*Affirmative, Colonel Benes. The Red Wolves are our common foe,*" Tchgnur said. "*We are—*"

Static exploded over the channel for a split-second before his commset automatically silenced it. Another jammer icon appeared in his heads-up display from the operations buildings below. Benes frowned. They'd have to get closer to the Xiq'tal, and potential danger if his hunch was wrong...

Benes heard the private channel tone. "Go, Top."

"*I've got the crab in my sights, sir. You want me to take it down?*" Hornsby growled.

Benes turned his back on the destroyed jammer and walked downhill. "You caught that transmission, right?"

"*We can't trust it.*"

Maybe, Benes thought, but didn't say aloud. Instead, he said, "I'm not quite sure what it is but something—"

A flurry of rounds impacted the back of his CASPer.

"Contact!" he yelled instinctively and spun to fire at more Besquith that had erupted from under the destroyed jammer emplacement. He counted six, seven, ten Besquith with assault rifles diving into prepared positions. Benes saw a large outcropping of rock to their right. "Cheung! Follow me!"

"*Moving*—" There was a hiss of static and Benes saw the icon for Cheung's CASPer turn from green to black. His left arm vibrated as a Besquith rocket tore his hand cannon away. He sprinted and tapped the jumpjet pedals, vaulting himself in a face-first dive for cover. As the CASPer crashed into the snow, he tried to roll and move closer to the rocks at the same time. Rounds from Besquith cannons slammed into the CASPer's legs. The left one buckled and alarms sounded in his ears as the CASPer fell backward into the rocks. A loud bang followed by scraping shook Benes as the mech slid down the rocks to sit upright, useless.

A new sound buzzed in his ears. He glanced at the caution and warning indicator and frowned. LOS LOCK. Line-of-sight laser communications were down. MAC INOP. The magnetic accelerator cannon was inoperable. The radio wouldn't reach his troops because of the jamming. His laser transceiver couldn't see the rest of his unit on the plains below the hill. They did not know if he was alive or dead. Unless he could stand the CASPer up and reacquire the network, he was unarmed and alone.

Benes thought of the Human remains across the lower battlefield and shuddered. No one wanted to die in the jaws of a Besquith.

But he might not have a choice.

* * *

Hornsby

"I've lost the boss," Hornsby growled. "I've got locator data, but no comms. We need to get line of sight on him now!"

"Top? We've got four Xiq'tal moving out of the hangars toward us. They're not firing," Valens said. *"They're moving pretty fast."*

"They have weapons pointed our direction?"

"Roger that," Valens said. *"Holly and I can provide covering fire."*

Tactics were a commander's job in his old non-commissioned officer's mind, but he knew the score. With Benes down, the tactics fell to him with a big exception. His job was to always look after the men and women of the Blasters even when the mission requirements came first. In this case, they needed to support the boss and let the situation around them develop. The plan formed quickly, and he had to clear his throat to avoid laughing.

"Okay, let's do that. Valens and Holly are gonna lay down a little covering fire while we move back along those parked earth movers. Adamson and Watson? You're the second element. When you reach that first vehicle, get under cover and lay down fire so Valens and Holly can join up. How copy so far?"

"Get to the first vehicles and come up screaming," Adamson replied in his brogue. *"We got it, Top."*

"Black and Stirling are next. Then Brooks and me. We'll set up in the line and be ready to pass the rest of you. We'll get to the far end, regroup, and then we'll head up the hill. Any questions?" The channel was silent, and Hornsby allowed the smile to form on his face. There was nothing like working with true professionals. "Let's do it."

"Firing!" Valens called. Hornsby heard the hand cannons rattle, but he didn't turn to see the result. Instead, he took three steps and moved the Mk 8 into a run. Brooks, despite the damage to the cockpit section of his Mk 8, was right at Hornsby's side.

"On me, Brooks," Hornsby growled. "Stay to the right and don't jump."

"*Copy, Top,*" Brooks replied.

"*Set one,*" Adamson called. "*Let's go, Valens!*"

"*Moving,*" Valens replied. "*On the bounce, Holly!*"

"Don't jump!" Hornsby stumbled the Mk 8 around as the two CASPers leapt into the air and made themselves wide open targets for the Xiq'tal. He waited for the missiles and CASPer-killers to streak through the sky, but nothing happened. The two CASPers descended and landed near Adamson and Watson.

"*Set three!*" Black called. "*Bring it on!*"

They continued to move in an orderly, ripple-like fashion toward the line of vehicles. Hornsby turned and sighted in on two large dump trucks. He lit them with a targeting laser. "That's our point, Brooks."

"*We're gonna be exposed out there, Top,*" Brooks replied. "*It's out front of the line.*"

Hornsby turned a corner of his mouth under. "Well, then cover me. I'll go first."

Before Brooks could respond, Hornsby ran forward then stomped on his jump pedals. As he arced through the sky, he saw the lone Xiq'tal had moved from its position outside the operations buildings toward the south. The damned thing appeared to be climbing the hill toward Benes. As soon as he realized that, his laser chimed. "You've got company coming, Boss!"

The system chimed at the same time he descended. He tapped the transmit button again, but nothing happened. He looked up in time to see the doors open on the operations center. For a brief second, he hoped for reinforcements despite knowing better. When two squads of Besquith charged out and raced in his direction, Hornsby realized they were in trouble. Distracted, he landed much harder than he intended and almost rolled to a stop behind an earth mover. "Go, Brooks!"

Brooks raced forward and leapt into the air. Two missiles streaked up and struck the CASPer, which detonated in a wide fireball. Brooks's status icon faded to black. Hornsby heard the rest of them move and settle behind him.

"Valens! I need you and Holly at my position, now! Adamson, move everyone to the end of this line of vehicles. We've got Besquith on the objective moving our way and one of those damned Xiq'tal is headed after the boss. We've gotta move, but stay on the ground. Repeat, stay on the godsdamned ground!"

"*Here we come, Top,*" Valens called. They hadn't really set up squads or platoons, and the young female from Texas had his eye. She was special. "*Coming in from your left rear on the sweep. Orient right.*"

Hornsby smiled. "Copy, Valens. Bring it in." He stepped to the right side of the earth mover and brought his hand cannons to bear on the charging Besquith. With two long bursts, he made three of them dive for the snow. Two more broke off toward the vehicles on his far left and toward the charging CASPers. "You've got company, Valens."

"*Knocking them down now,*" she replied. He didn't see the Besquith go down, but the survivors roared as one.

We've got their attention now. Time to pull them in the rest of the way.

He felt the ground thrum as the two CASPers joined his position. He turned to them. "Nice work, you two."

"*All in a day's work.*" Holly laughed. "*The Xiq'tal are moving faster with the Besquith engaged. They're firing on them.*"

"*Top, I've got everyone set over here. Orders?*" Adamson asked.

"The crabs are firing on the Besquith?" Hornsby asked. "You're sure?"

"*Affirm, Top. And—*"

A massive explosion on the far side of the earth mover cut off Valens's words. Besquith howled, and the chatter of small arms and laser fire erupted.

"*I'll get eyes on it!*"

Hornsby considered telling her to stay put, but he let the young driver go. She raced toward a small group of shipping containers between them and the Xiq'tal. Several Besquith appeared to fire at her, but she was too fast in the brand-new Mk 8. Hornsby saw her slide to a stop behind the containers.

"*The Xiq'tal are launching something like K-bombs into the Besquith, Top,*" Valens said. "*What do you want me to—*"

He saw the Xiq'tal appear to the left of Valens's position. He brought up his MAC and sighted it on the alien and fired without thinking. Six rounds bounced off the Xiq'tal's thick shell. It sighted in on him and lowered a rocket launcher in his direction. Two more Xiq'tal scurried into position behind the first with their weapons oriented toward him. They crept forward; weapons leveled as they moved in for the kill.

This is how it ends, huh?

* * *

Benes

The first Besquith appeared to his right and Benes dispatched it with a burst from his hand cannon. He tried to ascertain his exact position and the height of the cliff behind him but could not. Without access to the network, there was little he could do except react to what he could see.

Which ain't much.

If the high ground behind him was easily traversable, the Besquith would scramble above him, orient their weapons downward, and end him quickly. If they came around from the left, synchronized with an attack from the right, his one remaining hand cannon wouldn't be enough, and they'd get him that way. He had four K-bombs left, but they wouldn't be good for anything but keep him from getting eaten by the damned wolf-things. All in all, it wasn't where he wanted to be.

In the distance, a CASPer appeared above the artificial horizon created by the high ground. His system chimed with a network connection, and he heard Hornsby yelp, "*You've got company coming, Boss!*"

"No shit," Benes said and reached again for the magnetic accelerator cannon's control panel. If by some miracle he could re-wire it enough to work, he would at least have two weapons—one for each avenue of approach. Movement on the right caught his eye. Another Besquith. He brought up the hand cannon and fired. His ammunition status light flickered from green to yellow.

Take it easy. Don't use fifty rounds when ten will do.

Benes laughed. "Damn you, Ibson."

The ground moved under his collapsed CASPer. He felt it again. And again. Something heavy was approaching, but he couldn't see anything in front of him except the rocky horizon of the hilltop.

SCREE!

WHAP!

Benes heard rounds from the right side as Besquith fired. Several muted impacts along the CASPer's arm ricocheted away. More impacted the central section over his head and chest, but the improved armor of the Mk 8 kept him protected, as Binnig had advertised. He raised the hand cannon and waited until the first Besquith charged around the rocks. He fired and separated the alien's head from its neck. Dark blood sprayed across the snow. Benes kept firing as a second, and a third, Besquith appeared.

Again, the ground under him trembled. Benes reloaded the hand cannon and saw his icon flicker from yellow to red. The tremors were closer together now, and stronger. As they gained an almost steady rhythm, Benes smiled. Earth movers made the same type of noise. Hornsby and the others were on their way.

Two things happened at once and froze Benes in place. The first was the realization that his troops all fought in CASPers and wouldn't need an earth mover of any type to move across the battlefield. Their mechs easily adapted to any environment, even in the harsh, frigid landscape around them.

Of course, so did the Xiq'tal marching toward him with its weapons focused on the center of his CASPer.

Damn.

* * *

Hornsby

"*Top, more Besquith from the buildings to the north!*" Holly called. "*They're headed for the end of this row.*"

Before Hornsby could respond, he heard Adamson. "*We got 'em, Top. When they're in range, we'll be there.*"

Hornsby stared at the Xiq'tal for a moment. They looked over him, toward the attacking Besquith, and skittered to engage the new threat. He shook his head. *What the fuck is going on?*

The next instant, he knew the priority had changed. "Valens? You and Holly get ready to move and take out the jammer on that roof. Do you see it?"

"*Got it, Top. Its emissions anyway. Target locked,*" Valens replied. "*What about the Xiq'tal?*"

"They ain't firing on us." Hornsby chuckled. "That whole enemy of my enemy is my friend shit, I reckon. Get ready to move."

He moved back down the line of vehicles toward Adamson and the others. He jogged the CASPer toward them and approached the edge of the loose perimeter. "What are you guys doing? We know where the fucking enemy is! Go get them!"

"*What about the crabs?*" Stirling asked.

"You let me worry about them," Hornsby growled. "Adamson? You and Watson go on my count. We'll be on your six."

"*Aye, Top,*" Adamson replied. "*We're ready.*"

"Three, two, one, now!" Hornsby called. "Valens! You're up."

"*Moving!*" she replied.

They ran toward the operations buildings and a dozen heavily armed Besquith. Another six remained on their left flank, but their attention was on the Xiq'tal charging their position. Their rear exposed, Hornsby sighted his MAC on the Besquith and fired. Stirling and Black joined his party, and the six aliens fell quickly.

"*Let's go, you bastards!*" Adamson yelled, and the channel filled with hoots and screams as the remaining CASPers charged into the Besquith, their weapons blazing. Without breaking stride, they cut down the attacking squad.

Hornsby grinned like a child inside his CASPer. Seldom did technology reach its potential, like the Mk 8s had in combat. There were no more Besquith between them and the buildings. He saw Valens and

Holly leap into the air on a max jump trajectory. As they descended, he saw both of them fire their MACs. In seconds, the jammer was offline and communications were restored.

"*—forces this is Tchgnur of the Endless Current. Please respond.*"

"Tchgnur, this is First Sergeant Hornsby of the Blasters. I hear you," Hornsby replied. "State your intentions."

"*We were contracted to clear this facility of the Red Wolves. They stated they were contracted to hold it at all costs. The Besquith killed our commander on landing. We have remained in the hangar for three days and are short on provisions. What are your intentions?*"

Hornsby chewed on the inside of his lip. "We had a similar contract with an Earth organization to take back this facility."

"*The Nippon Trading Conglomerate?*" Tchgnur asked. "*They contracted us as well. I believe they may have contracted the Red Wolves as well.*"

What? A goddammed insurance scheme? Hornsby managed to not blurt the question over the radio. "That's affirmative. Seems like we have a situation. The Wolves won't discuss?"

"*Negative. We tried until they jammed our transceivers. There are more Besquith massing behind those rolling doors on the middle building,*" Tchgnur replied. "*We will fight at your side, First Sergeant. Will you do the same?*"

Why not?

"Affirmative, Tchgnur. We have a truce under the guidance of Mercenary Guild regulations, such as they are. Let's clear this facility," Hornsby replied. "Do you have contact with the Xiq'tal on the mountain above? My commander is up there and in need of assistance."

"*Negative,*" Tchgnur replied. "*The situation there appears grim as well.*"

Hornsby was unable to respond as his CASPer chimed with multiple missile warnings. The door of the operations building rolled open and more Besquith than he could count erupted through the opening in a last-ditch attack.

"Hit 'em, Blasters!"

Hornsby leapt into the air and aimed his MAC into the charging pack. His comm unit chimed. He could see Benes's CASPer on the network, but there was no active connection. "Clear the threat so we can get to the boss. Stirling, deploy a comm drone!"

"*On it, Top!*" Stirling replied. A CASPer-launched drone would enable them to route communications over terrain restricted areas. Their only prayer of talking to Benes was to get something in the air and pray the Besquith didn't take it down. "*Launch. Network in thirty seconds.*"

Hornsby grunted. "Copy."

Thirty seconds is a long time to—

"*We'll get the boss, Top,*" Valens said. "*Cover us while we move.*"

Hornsby grinned and opened a private channel to the young mercenary as he descended below the terrain line again. "We survive this, Valens, and you might just make lieutenant."

"*You'll put in a good word for me?*" she replied with a laugh. "*Moving!*"

"There's a Xiq'tal up there, too," Hornsby said. "Don't shoot it. We don't want to piss off our new friends, okay?"

* * *

Benes

The Xiq'tal swung a claw toward him. Unable to move, Benes closed his eyes and waited for the impact. When nothing happened, he opened his eyes and saw the Xiq'tal stepping over him and fighting a squad of Besquith at close range. He raised the hand cannon but couldn't fire without fear of hitting the Xiq'tal.

Are we allies? Benes blinked the thought away. He raised the cannon again and squeezed off a burst at the Besquith but hit nothing. He tried again and the cannon emptied. The reload option was black on his HUD. For a moment, he considered the K-bombs, but again, the concern with taking out the friendly Xiq'tal outweighed the risk. A glance at his heads-up display confirmed it was cold enough outside to freeze his skin in a matter of minutes. While his gatorskin haptics were good at thermal regulation, they weren't *that* good. Still, he could activate the hood and if the gloves and feet held, they'd work for a short period, and he could avoid hypothermia.

The Xiq'tal weapon thumped repeatedly, but the Besquith were still coming. He had to do something. He activated the release and the front of the CASPer opened. Bitterly cold air prickled his skin as he extricated himself from the cockpit. Benes pulled the collar of the gatorskin suit and deployed the hood. Pulling it tight around his head might look funny to an observer, but the warming effect was immediate. He drew his pistol from the holster slung across his chest and stepped away from the CASPer and toward the Xiq'tal. Benes kept close to the exposed rocks he'd fallen against and crawled up about a meter to find a decent firing position. He pulled himself up, lowered the weapon, and tried not to piss himself.

Two dozen Besquith were charging toward them. The Xiq'tal stepped forward, almost took off Benes's shoulder, and opened fire. Benes willed himself to find a target, aim for the center of its chest, and open fire. His first shot got the attention of multiple Besquith. He saw their eyes widen as they realized he was an undoubtedly softer target than the Xiq'tal. Three of them charged, and he opened fire again. They were wearing body armor, and his first shots did nothing. Benes aimed higher, for the center of their long faces, and tried again. The first went down. Then the second. He aimed for the third as it leapt straight toward him. He fired once, and time slowed so much he almost saw the bullet spinning as it raced harmlessly over the Besquith's head. Its dark eyes fixated on him, and the wide, long mouth salivated. He saw endless rows of teeth as he tried to aim again.

A shadow crossed his vision. The Besquith's eyes lifted. A blur of movement crashed down and Benes saw the Besquith impaled by a Xiq'tal claw, pinned into the rocks and snow.

Sonuva—

His earpiece chimed with connection alerts as he rejoined the network. He heard Valens shout, *"Sir! Get back to your CASPer. We've got this!"*

Benes saw two CASPers jump to the top of the ridge, their weapons blazing. Moving back to his CASPer sounded good in theory, but there was nothing he could do there. Pressed against the rocks, Benes looked up at the Xiq'tal standing off to his side as if it was guarding him. He tapped his earpiece twice and opened the frequencies as much as he could.

"Xiq'tal forces, this is Colonel Benes. Concur that the Besquith are our common enemies. Let's take them out." He paused. "Top? Clear those buildings and search for survivors."

"We're clearing them now. No survivors," Hornsby reported. *"No helium-3, either. The Endless Current had the same contract. I'm guessing Hashimoto used the Red Wolves to kill everyone and then called in two rival companies to destroy the complex while they fought each other. The jammers were all stamped Nippon Trade Conglomerate. We were about to buy a farm, sir."*

Benes clenched his jaw and forced himself to relax. "But we didn't."

"Colonel Benes, this is Tchgnur of the Endless Current. Our leadership is dead and I assumed command. Our company affairs dictate a senior Xiq'tal take command. Of our survivors, none is senior enough. We must surrender ourselves and our Zuul flight crews."

Benes listened carefully and, sensing an opportunity, smiled. "Tchgnur, I will not accept your surrender. However, if your company's standard operations procedures as written mean you disband the company, I'll hire all of you right now. Payments might be deferred a bit until we confront our friends at the NTC, but we could integrate our companies under the Blasters. We could use your firepower, and you could use our leadership. We'd be pretty strong together. And did you say Zuul flight crews?"

"Yes, sir. Our dropships are en route with supplies. I believe we can accept your offer, but we will need to verify there are no Mercenary Guild procedures which negate that possibility. We will need GalNet access to ensure this is the case," Tchgnur said. *"That said, this facility could be used as a base of operations as well. Under the stipulations of our contract, the Nippon Trade Conglomerate forfeited any rights to the base, so collateral damage wasn't an issue. Everything here belongs to... us."*

Benes nodded. He'd read the same thing in his contract, and Hashimoto had said collateral damage wasn't an issue. Benes sighed as he realized he'd fallen for the oldest con job in the Mercenary Guild: doing someone else's dirty work for them and not following the money. There wasn't any helium-3 or likely anything of value on the planet. Benes realized his error and his face flushed.

You dumbass. He imagined his father saying with his raspy voice and a rueful smile on his face. *The reaper's scythe, what does its cutting is avarice. Want too much and you're easy prey for death. You got greedy, too.*

Don't do this shit again.

Hornsby chuckled and broke his thoughts. *"Deal here went south, so they purge it and destroy everything with a couple of new mercenary companies who don't know any better. Jam the shit out of everything and let us all kill each other while they get their credits back. Greedy bastards."*

"I concur. They wanted this place gone and they hired three brand new companies to ensure everyone was dead and the base was destroyed." Benes felt his anger rise at both the situation and himself. He'd fix both or die trying. "We'll let them think that for now. If the Gate Master, or anyone else, gets interested, we'll deal with that when it happens."

He paused as the plan crystalized in his mind. "Top? Let's recall our dropship and secure this base for operations," Benes said. "We'll set a chain of command with Tchgnur as a lieutenant over the Xiq'tal forces. We'll need a senior CASPer driver, too."

"Lieutenant *Valens, sir,*" Hornsby said. *"She earned it."*

"Very well." Benes grinned. "Once we're set here, I'll call the Haulers for emergency resupply and transport. They'll keep their word. One of these days, we'll pay a visit to the Nippon Trade Conglomerate. Maybe we can drag a Peacemaker along with us by then."

Hornsby added, *"We have thirty days provisions, plus what was left here for the Human crews. The Besquith hardly touched it all. Should be a fine start, sir."*

"Colonel Benes?" Tchgnur asked. *"Our ship, the Beggar's Reef, remains in geosynchronous orbit. We brought everything from Earth when we deployed. We can sign it over to the company as well, but I recommend the company reform*

something new. Our units are all known by the NTC and would draw attention—especially if we were expected to die here."

"Tchgnur has a point, sir," Hornsby said. "*We can't be who we were. At least until we figure out a way to skin this cat and form a new company. There's not enough heraldry to make it matter.*"

This might just end up being a good day after all.

"We'll get there when we get there, Top," Benes said. Through the CASPer's cameras, he saw the local star setting over the western horizon. The temperature fell quickly, and it would soon become inhospitable. For the first time, he noticed a collection of tools which had been dumped from a shipping crate across the snow. As a boy traveling with his family across the various fields of North America, he'd seen thousands of them. Used more than a few, too. Farming was hard work when harvest time came. Inspiration struck.

Ibson might even approve. He knew his father would.

He tapped his radio. "All stations on this network, this is Colonel Benes in command. Gather in the hangar on the west side of the compound in fifteen mikes. We have some dirty work to do and make this ours, but that comes with the territory. Welcome to the Reapers."

* * * * *

Kevin Ikenberry Bio

Kevin Ikenberry is a life-long space geek and retired Army officer. As an adult, he managed the U.S. Space Camp program and served in space operations before Space Force was a thing. He's an international bestselling science fiction author and renowned writing instructor which is pretty cool because he never imagined being either one of those – he still wants to be an astronaut. Kevin's debut novel, *Sleeper Protocol*, was hailed by *Publishers Weekly* as "an emotionally powerful debut." His twenty-five novels science fiction novels include *The Crossing, Vendetta Protocol, Eminence Protocol, Runs In The Family, Peacemaker, Honor The Threat, Stand or Fall, Fields of Fire,* and *Harbinger*. He is core author of the mega-bestselling Four Horsemen Universe, with more than a dozen novels spawned by *Peacemaker*. Kevin is an Active Member of the International Association of Science Fiction and Fantasy Authors, International Thriller Writers, and SIGMA – the science fiction think tank. Kevin continues to work with space every day and lives in Colorado with his family.

# # # # #

OpSha Ops by Mike Jack Stoumbos

Two quick zaps accompanied the prongs of long-range tasers. The charged needles pierced the uniforms and dug through fur into flesh.

Both guards involuntarily clenched their jaws, seized at the elbows and knees, then fell onto the hard clay. The charge stopped a few seconds after they were unconscious, but they never had a chance to recognize their assailants.

Four pairs of quick, quiet feet scampered past the downed guards, one pausing just long enough to pluck the fired shockers from their chests and fish a key card out of a pocket.

The exterior personnel door was practically flush with the wall, the seams and scanner well hidden. A quick swipe of the card opened the door, letting out a wash of diffuse light from an overhead LED strip—due to prefab design for the more universal visual species. Even as they entered, illumination would have revealed little about their identities, even if their onlookers weren't opSha.

All four intruders wore sleek, dark suits as well as gloves on their hands and feet to minimize trace evidence. They resembled the size and shape of the guards taken down, except for the bulbous extensions around their jaws—air filters—held tightly under the same elastic fabric that covered the whole face. The opaque fabric shielded substandard eyes. Only their ears were free to the night air, so they could fan and re-angle and hear everything they needed.

They silently confirmed no alarms had been sounded and no other obstacles lay in earshot. The one at the rear closed the door behind them; the one in front adjusted a device in the ear. Then, as a unit, they darted deeper into the complex and the maze of corridors, taking the most efficient route to their quarry, where large crates had been delivered earlier that day.

Emblazoned on the crates, in colors they could hardly perceive and languages they couldn't read, were the words "Phoenix Initiative."

* * *

Niirama only opened her eyes when the transport came to a complete stop. Although most members of the opSha species had terrible eyesight and relied much more on their ears, some instinct prompted her to squeeze her eyelids shut until the world around her was no longer in motion, and her inner ear and guts could feel some evidence of solid ground below.

The reptilian HecSha piloting the rig had done a fine job, even when dodging the dense, gnarled trees on their way to the landing platform.

Niirama just wasn't used to space travel yet, having lived most of her life on solid ground—or at least the piles of debris littering solid ground.

"We shouldn't have any trouble with this gravity," an older, grayer opSha sitting beside her casually observed as he unbelted. Her uncle Ruumil was not fazed by interstellar travel and easily walked forward to check in with the pilot.

Niirama wondered if his nanite-altered perceptions assisted in the transitions to zero gravity or various thrust intensities, or if his lower sensitivities were a result of old injuries. With one missing ear, hairless scarring covering a quarter of his head, and dark goggles completely blocking out his eyes, Ruumil stood out among any crowd of opSha.

The other passengers might not have been as comfortable as Ruumil, but none seemed as disoriented as Niirama felt. As soon as she unclipped and tried to stand, she nearly fell onto the floor.

The touch on her shoulder and the scent identified the Cochkala before he spoke. "You okay?" Kreski asked.

Niirama grimaced, further annoyed that Kreski—who matched her youth and inexperience—seemed to be handling the transition better than she.

"I'm fine," she grumbled, and willed herself to push past any dizziness or nausea. She no longer felt disoriented when driving her modified mech, so she could adjust to flight. Perhaps if transports could also translate motion and visuals into sound for her...

"Kreski," Ruumil called back from the cockpit, "get suited up, and be ready here for any needed demonstration." Still facing the screens, the old opSha delegated duties to the rest of the landing party.

Kreski refrained from voicing his smug satisfaction, knowing Niirama would prefer they swap places. He didn't manage to contain his tail, which spoke volumes, even if no one else on the ship understood them. The young Cochkala hustled to the hatch in the floor and down into the cargo bay, where Niirama could hear him ready his mech.

The task lists for the two Zuparti and the one other opSha were dual purposed to both demonstrate professionalism to potential clients and be ready in case of any "funny business."

Both Niirama and Ruumil—in fact, most of their company—had experienced more than their share of attempts to swindle, extort, or simply outright steal during the formation of Revilo Defense. They knew better than to look like easy prey to anyone, including prospective clients.

Ruumil had saved Niirama for last, which might've been an intentional courtesy to allow her to regain her bearings, but only for a few more seconds. "Let's go," he said, helping her to her feet. "We don't want to keep clients waiting."

The exterior hatch was already sliding open, so Niirama willed herself upright and followed.

Ruumil exuded excitement and determination as he descended the shuttle's ladder, his simian hands well equipped for climbing.

Niirama had her misgivings about making the long journey to this planet without a guarantee, not just because she would have preferred to stay on familiar ground. These were exacerbated by the fact that no one from the nearby compound had come out to greet them. "You do remember that they already turned us down."

"No, not at all," Ruumil said. "They purchased our design schematics. They only *initially* declined the offer of installation and demonstration. Clearly, the job was too big for them, and they now need our assistance. Come along." Ruumil led Niirama toward the compound's wall, where his modified eyes and goggles must have picked out an entrance.

The hard-packed clay didn't show any immediate evidence of footprints or a path, and no one stood outside the base. Niirama used a handheld scanner to confirm a door.

"Remember," Ruumil said, "we're here to project confidence. That's what inspires larger sales and returning customers."

Niirama swallowed her next objection. It wouldn't do her any good to argue with Ruumil; besides, she hoped he was right, and that Revilo Defense could add a success story to their still tiny reputation. Even better if they could be known as helpful companions to the Phoenix Initiative. Although only built and sold to Humans as part of the Initiative, the fact that CASPers could be had so cheaply now meant that a number had been bought to sell on the black market. For the first time in history, it was possible to get them off Earth. For a price.

"Maybe you could get further if you offered them your ocular nanite formula," Niirama said, but Ruumil began clicking his tongue to get her to stop before she'd finished the sentence.

She found her uncle's paranoia amusing, but, again, not worth fighting about. They were too far away to be in earshot of anyone Niirama couldn't pick up on her scanner. Besides, she firmly believed they should spread the word; Ruumil's nanite manipulation was just another asset, untapped wealth and opportunity for their group, even if the old scientist insisted the formula *wasn't ready*.

They halted at the wall and the presumed entryway that stayed closed. It was a little wider than the two side-by-side and not much taller than Niirama, but it had no apparent control panel or keypad.

"Hello?" she asked, loudly and clearly enough to be understood across interstellar deviations of dialect.

Her ears flapped from side to side, but she caught nothing other than the wildlife in the trees and the sounds from their own ship.

Ruumil started to say, "Maybe we went to the wrong—"

"Stay where you are!" an unpleasant, nasally voice shouted through a speaker that popped out of the ground. "We have you surrounded and are prepared to sonic."

"What?" Ruumil demanded, twisting frantically to spy the source of the threat.

A second voice, a little lower pitched, came out of the same speaker. "You're in our crosshairs and in no position to demand ransom. Tell your partners to return the cargo, and no one gets hurt."

Niirama had raised both hands, but she didn't tremble in her reply. "You seem to have mistaken us for someone else. We are representatives of Revilo Defense."

She took a breath, during which no weapons, cages, or noxious gasses assaulted either her or Ruumil. The door, however, remained closed, so she added, "We are here to help."

"How do we know that?" the nasally one asked quietly.

The deeper voice rephrased, "How can we know you are who you say you are?"

"Well, for starters," Ruumil cut in, "you could take my voiceprint. My name is Ruumil, and I spoke with someone named Tiimuna. Certainly, a professional operation like yours has records of this, yes?"

Niirama was quite familiar with her uncle's judgmental and irked tone, having been on the receiving end of it many times.

A click briefly paused conversation. Then—presumably after debate on the other side, nasally said, "Dreadfully sorry! We—"

The deeper, calmer voice overtook the babbling. "By your voiceprint, we have verified that you are Ruumil, representative of Revilo Defense." A pressure seal was released, and the door hissed open. All told, the door frame was wider than Niirama's arm span, ample for soundproofing as well as protection against the elements—common in prefab structures.

When the voice next spoke, Niirama heard it over the speakers a moment before a severely muted version traveled over the open air. "Come in."

Niirama took one step forward, then Ruumil caught her by the shoulder.

"According to our protocol," Ruumil said, "I am bound to inform you that we did not come here alone, our ship is nearby, and fitted with appropriate defensive capabilities as well as skilled operatives who would not hesitate to retrieve us, should we be prevented from making our scheduled communication or rendezvous."

Ruumil sounded as if he were reading from a script. Niirama was sure she'd never heard said script, but after this reception, she considered it a good tactic on Ruumil's part. She hoped to remember what he said or to think on her feet as quickly if in the situation again.

The more nasally of the greeters stammered like a Zuparti in reply. "Of-of course! We meant no disrespect—just we—"

"You have our word." The deeper, calmer one, whom Niirama guessed was Tiimuna, seemed more composed with each sentence. "We will operate peacefully and professionally, and you'll be free to leave if either party finds the arrangement not to their liking."

"Unless threatened," the nasally one added, before being shushed.

Niirama laughed at the irony. "Same to you."

Ruumil gritted his teeth but gave no reprimand.

Tiimuna said, "Agreed. Please follow the chimes so you don't get lost."

Niirama was pretty sure she could follow the voice reverberating through the corridors, but after a few steps took her to a multidirectional fork in the interior structure, she was glad to have the guide. The chimes acted like directional floor lights in a structure designed for visual species—only, this time, Niirama didn't have to think about them. Directional sound seemed to be instinctive.

The complex interior also didn't have much light to irritate her eyes. There were some gray or blue diffuse glowing strips, but nothing that overwhelmed her low-light-attuned eyes or created buzzing sounds to interfere with her ears. Ladder rungs frequently led up or down to new passages. The angles of ascent of the many tubes seemed oddly organic to Niirama without being a hodgepodge of slapped together salvage, like her childhood home. The whole interior benefited from strictly planned architecture, but it appealed to an instinct or genetic memory, which inexorably assured her this was an opSha home.

Ruumil broke the spell before they arrived. He reached up to adjust his goggles and grumbled, "Too dark in here."

After a hard left and a soft right, the chimes pointed them up one of the angled chutes, which Niirama had hoped to climb.

She reached out to grab the rung, but was interrupted by another being, climbing quickly from below.

"Excuse me," the local opSha hissed, pushing past at a speed that would have bulldozed Niirama off the rungs had she occupied the ladder.

Then, this opSha suddenly halted, gripping a rung with one hand and letting the rest of her body swivel upward from the momentum. She landed upside down, facing Niirama. One hand hovered at her hip, ready to draw a weapon. "New recruits?" she asked.

Ruumil puffed out his chest. "Representatives from Revilo Defense, here to train this company in installation and use of—"

"Revilo Defense?" she repeated. Her words came out in harsh whispers, as if she'd repeatedly strained her vocal cords or was conditioned to keep her voice low. "So you were the ones at the perimeter?"

"Yes!" Ruumil huffed in frustration. "But after the welcome we've received—"

"No, there's no need to leave," she said, clearly anticipating his next comment. "You're wanting to go to the control room to speak with Tiimuna. I'm going there too. I'll lead you."

"Wait!" Niirama blurted. "Why is everyone so…?" But she faltered under the withering gaze of this fast-climbing whisperer. She had never met an opSha who could so easily visually intimidate.

"They did not tell you of the theft?" the whisperer asked.

"They accused *us* of being the thieves and demanded we return cargo," Ruumil said. "I can assure you we just arrived and have nothing of yours to return."

"No. You wouldn't—not if you're from Revilo Defense." She seemed to contemplate for a moment, then said, "I'm Caavendir. This way."

They had to go up two levels, both very short levels, separated by less than 1.5 meters, according to Human standard, with a short stretch of lateral corridor between them. Caavendir cleared these gaps too quickly for Niirama to even watch, let alone keep up, climbing faster than Niirama could run at a full sprint.

Here, Niirama thought, she was looking at a real opSha. Caavendir, this whispering climber, lived among her own species and had opportunities to excel at her natural strengths. Niirama, on the other hand, had largely endured a world controlled by species who kept everything brightly lit and relatively flat.

Fortunately, she wasn't winded by the time she emerged into the control room *and* had beaten Ruumil there by a good margin.

Caavendir had already begun a conversation with an opSha at a central console, of which Niirama only caught a few words.

Caavendir was saying, "—tell me they were still coming—" but abruptly cut off to stand still, her ears cupped in Niirama's direction.

The opSha at the center console instead let his ears fan wide as he hummed something Niirama found friendly but didn't recognize enough to respond to. Possibly sensing Niirama's confusion, he said, "Greetings! I am Tiimuna," finally confirming a match between the deeper voice they'd heard and the name. "I arranged the consultation."

He was probably the largest of the five opSha in that domed upper room, all of whom stared at Niirama—or, more accurately, intently listened in her direction. They made low glottal clicks and twitched their ears to fully take in her appearance. Niirama reciprocated without realizing.

In most environments, she refrained from using the more finely tuned echolocation on other sentient beings, for fear of breaching protocol or making them uncomfortable. Now that her hosts had established the social norm, Niirama didn't hold herself back on listening to anything, organic or technology.

As someone whose engineering expertise involved rigging mismatched scraps of salvage, Niirama could certainly appreciate the planned and easy layout of the space. Consoles were set up with textured input pads and an array of directional speakers rather than purely visual screens. Instead of chairs, there were ergonomic rungs and perches to support stretching or squatting.

Throughout her scan, part of Niirama's attention remained on Tiimuna. In the low light, she had no concept of his fur's color, but she keyed into patterns. Without light to distract her, Niirama identified which exposed sections were fluffy and which were short and sleek; she found herself disappointed that his entire torso was shielded by clothing, but there was still much to appreciate. The curve of his ears, the obvious strength of his arms, the fullness of his voice—poorly replicated by the front door speaker.

"Weren't there two of you?" Tiimuna asked, which confused Niirama, until Ruumil appeared behind her.

"That's right," he said. "Two representatives here now. The rest of our armed, trained team remained with the transport. Now, perhaps you can tell us what's going on."

Niirama pivoted from Tiimuna to Ruumil and back again. Of everything she could observe, Ruumil was the one who most stood out, who least belonged.

The nasally one, whose posture and tone was far less inviting, identified himself with a single nervous note. He hopped off his perch and scurried to Tiimuna's side, partially concealing himself with the larger opSha's frame. Without even attempting to whisper, he said, "Maybe we should delay, until we are better able to employ their aid." Niirama found the remark so sniveling that it could have been a question.

"No, Baandalin," Tiimuna told the nasally one. "This might present an ideal opportunity."

Tiimuna chirped at Caavendir who responded in kind—maybe agreeing about the *opportunity*. Then he gestured at his guests, or somehow managed to send his voice more directly at them. "Ruumil, and—um—"

"Niirama," Ruumil said before Niirama had caught on.

"Yes, Niirama," the local opSha said. "I apologize for our poor reception. We are still interested in contracting as clients. Although, perhaps, we will have to enlist your services in a different way than previously planned." The more Tiimuna spoke, the more composure he gained. "Would you say you also take on retrieval jobs?"

* * *

According to their advertisements, Revilo Defense handled a wide range of services, from security system installation, to engineering and repair of broken structures. They trained not just guards but standing armies and ready militias. According to rumors—gleefully fueled by the Revilo Defenses outreach team—the amount of aid they could render went far beyond what appeared in their catalogs. They were not a mercenary company, and not in direct competition according to the commerce authorities and an audit by the Mercenary Guild. However, someone like Tiimuna would know they were capable of more direct measures for helping small groups protect their interests. Their mission statement, translated into several languages, said Revilo Defense would provide aid to physically weaker and smaller species who struggled to defend themselves.

Colonies of weaker species had also heard that this new company had combat-ready ships and deployable mechs, at least one of which had been altered to translate all visual cues into sounds for the savvy opSha warrior.

In truth, Revilo Defense was in its infancy, and Niirama knew it. In fact, she was the one and only opSha CASPer driver in their company. Sure, she would puff up with pride and say that they were far more prepared than this opSha operation, but she wasn't as confident when they followed Tiimuna out of the control room and into a garage.

The garage was laid out least like an opSha habitat. It was a universal delivery and storage location, assuming species operated on flat ground and constant gravity.

It was also mostly empty, as if it were waiting to be stocked, or just been cleaned out. Other than some basic loading and scanning equipment which had been shoved against one wall, there was a single open crate. Niirama had to squint to see the phrase "Phoenix Initiative" stamped into the side in multiple languages, including phonetic Zuparti.

Niirama could hear the servos in Ruumil's goggles changing the zoom and focus. "The CASPers are the stolen cargo, aren't they?"

Baandalin blurted his distress—not words, but clear enough emotion to confirm Ruumil's suspicion. There were a few other opSha either in the garage or a doorway who'd paused in their tasks to listen, but all seemed to simultaneously droop when admitting their recent loss.

Ruumil paced out a rectangular section of the metal floor which must've had an outline for another cargo crate that Niirama could not see. "This is where you held the black market Phoenix Initiative CASPers, isn't it?" he asked. "That is what you want us to help retrieve."

"It's true," Tiimuna said. Caavendir and Baandalin each nodded. "We didn't think that on a mostly opSha-occupied planet we would need more protections than we already had."

"Incidentally," Ruumil said, "protections are exactly what we could have provided if you'd contracted with us sooner. Then we could have installed defensive measures in advance, instead of arriving a day after they were needed."

"Ruumil!" Niirama whispered, even though everyone could hear her.

Tiimuna didn't outright reject Ruumil's commentary, but he explained, "We thought that between the Phoenix Initiative manuals and Revilo Defense's blueprints for modified CASPer sensory mechanisms, we could figure out the rest."

"That was foolish," Caavendir said, which Niirama thought was aimed at Tiimuna, rather than her and Ruumil.

"So, when it turned out to be harder than you thought," Ruumil continued, filling in the gap, "you contacted us for further consultation and assistance with the installation and programming." He didn't sound cruel about it, but Ruumil was certainly pleased with himself, satisfied that he had predicted this fledgling company's challenge.

Niirama couldn't help but empathize with the locals. The process of turning a highly visual mobile weaponry like a CASPer into something that could be refitted for echolocation had been a challenge even when a multi-species team of engineers had tried to tackle the task for her. Even then, Niirama remembered the difficulty of learning to drive based on the auditory signals.

"But, before we arrived..." Niirama began, helping Tiimuna to continue the explanation.

"Last night, our arsenal was stolen."

"It makes some sense," Ruumil said. "After all, why pay for CASPers when you can just steal them?"

Niirama couldn't disagree with Ruumil, but she wouldn't have assumed it in an all-opSha location.

"They didn't get all of them!" Baandalin suddenly said, small squeaks accompanying his speech. "I was—Well, a team of us was trying to install the audio-conversion program in the lab, and, even though we hadn't worked it out, we left the CASPer back there with all of the schematics, when they…" Baandalin must have realized he was babbling, for he ground to a halt under Ruumil's stare.

"How exactly did you get robbed?" Ruumil asked. "You're in an enclosed complex. I didn't see any holes in the walls, and I've smelled no evidence of blood or smoke."

"It was a stealth operation," Caavendir said. "Whoever did it knew how to break in through the personnel doors and get into the garage."

"Well, forgive my skepticism, but it can't be as simple as that." Ruumil walked to the open crate and tested the door, demonstrating that he needed to expend a great deal of energy before it began to swing. "We've moved CASPers before. CASPers, their charging stations, any additional fuel or ammunition—that's too heavy and difficult to casually haul. Clearly, someone would have seen it and tried to stop it." He faced Baandalin. "Possibly even a crew of scientists working in the lab."

Baandalin literally hid behind Tiimuna, with a level of familiarity that struck Niirama as a sibling relationship, with Tiimuna as a leader and Baandalin's expertise much quieter and relying on a measure of safety. Tiimuna said, "This was clearly a professional job. They incapacitated the standing watch outside, and then knocked out everyone on shift in the garage—mostly our tech team, not even scouts or the drivers-in-training—with gas."

"What about hauling sleds?" Niirama asked. Perhaps, in this environment, they would use something more like a forklift than a hover sled, but either way, hauling machinery was loud. "Anyone not on duty should have heard it and come running, right?"

The opSha glanced between each other, their ears fanning more than their heads turning.

"We keep the interior doors closed so we can't idly listen to each other. It would be…"

"It's not appropriate," Ruumil said, leaning toward Niirama. "Sound barriers to them are like sight barriers to most other species."

"Yes." Tiimuna sounded embarrassed, but maybe more on Niirama's behalf than for himself. "We didn't think it an issue, with guards and the layout of our tunnels." He pointed up the ramp to a much larger set of doors, which Niirama was sure she could have recognized from outside had she seen them. "This garage door can *only* be opened from the inside, so someone would need a key card to go through a personnel door to get in here, in order to unlock and haul out our CASPers."

"Not your CASPers anymore." Ruumil had folded his arms across his chest, a visual indicator that he would not be swayed by sympathy. Which might be lost on opSha.

Niirama did empathize, knowing the difficulty of going through their own grass-roots process of starting Revilo Defense not too long ago. Granted, she considered her and Ruumil's startup circumstances much more harrowing than an opSha-only base on a lush moon with clean air and no Pushtal slave drivers. She was aware that the Phoenix Initiative had made CASPers available on the black market, but that hadn't necessarily made them affordable.

Ruumil asked, "How exactly *were* you planning to pay *us*?"

This shut Tiimuna up. He and Baandalin each flicked an ear toward the other, but neither tried to click nor chirp covertly with Ruumil and Niirama right in front of them, surrounded by open space that should have been filled with their purchased cargo. Caavendir's ears darted between all other parties in the garage.

Baandalin said, "Well, we… weren't—not directly or-or upfront. We–"

"Was this a scam?" The question could have been a sincere accusation, but Ruumil said it almost mockingly, the auditory equivalent of a smirk. "Did you have a method for faking credits in your account? Maybe you thought we'd get out of the system and not notice, or not come back to settle the debt? Or maybe you thought you could steal from us!" Ruumil let out a laugh. "What might you try to lift from our ship, credits or information—or maybe our CASPers? I wouldn't pay to see that, but I'd be entertained by the effort."

It was true; Revilo Defense's light ship was much better defended than this whole opSha base. Perhaps Tiimuna and Caavendir hadn't assumed Ruumil and Niirama would arrive with reinforcements. Niirama couldn't be sure what they assumed, but she ascertained based on heart rate and breathing patterns that Caavendir was growing offended and Tiimuna was feeling ashamed.

Niirama could also tell when Ruumil was forcing a laugh or putting on a show. He couldn't convince those who knew him well.

"You must have had a plan," Niirama said, with a tone she hoped was stern but without the mockery. "What was it?" They fidgeted again. "You're already in trouble. If you want us to help you get out of it, you'll answer the question—or we'll leave." It was the kind of threat Niirama was willing to follow through with, and it seemed to hit its mark.

"We thought maybe we could get you to help us first, and then we'd figure out the rest later," Tiimuna said, but hastened to add, "but with the intention of paying you what you're owed, as soon as we're able to."

"Yes! With a percentage of our first job," Baandalin added.

"Or as many as it takes," Tiimuna said.

Ruumil scowled. "Assuming you *survive* long enough to do so."

No one answered, so Ruumil opted to initiate the next reasonable course of action. "Let's go."

Ruumil was halfway out of the garage before Niirama had managed, "Hey."

Instead of halting, Ruumil hastened his stride, forcing Niirama to jog to catch up.

"Ruumil, we can't just walk away."

"Given our lack of contractual commitments or gunpoint capture, yes, we can. Make that *fly* away," he said after a moment.

"No, Ruumil, these are our—"

Ruumil stopped so abruptly that Niirama bonked her shoulder into him and had to spin on her heel to keep from toppling over.

Ruumil had barely moved. "Yes?" he prompted, with a tone that urged her to choose her words carefully—or maybe dared her to finish the outburst with the phrase "our people."

Niirama took the less confrontational path, knowing how Ruumil felt about segregation of species. Her upbringing on Haven and her time with Revilo Defense had in many ways instilled the sentiment in her as well, but the species association bubbled to the surface just the same. After taking a breath and enduring a stern glare from behind her uncle's black goggles, Niirama tried a different tactic.

"They are our responsibility," she said.

Ruumil reacted—more subtly, but his stance shifted and the furless creases in his scarred forehead softened.

She knew she'd hit another vulnerable spot, the kind he couldn't easily dismiss, even if he was about to question the claim. "Our mission is to aid in the safety and military preparedness of people struggling to defend themselves. We can make good on that promise here."

"It's not a promise; it's our offer, provided good business sense and payment," Ruumil said. "They can't afford our services."

"But we can make another arrangement—a payment plan, a publicity exchange—"

Ruumil gave one sharp, derisive hoot. "They can't pay us if they get killed, and we don't want to be known for helping send underprepared units to their deaths. Failures do not help us advertise."

"Success stories do," Niirama said. "If our adaptive technology really is so good, why not take the opportunity to demonstrate it to them?"

Ruumil hesitated long enough for Niirama to make another move.

She spun and kept her composure when she saw that everyone else in the garage had all moved closer and cupped their ears to hear every word. These local opSha could travel in near silence when they wanted to, even though they stood in plain sight.

"Tiimuna," Niirama called, "are you competent?"

"What?"

Niirama wondered if she'd chosen the wrong word, but she'd already committed. Placing her fists on her hips like a pontificating Zuparti, she repeated, "Are you competent? Can you lead this crew, learn the CASPers, take assignments, and not get killed? Can you really make this worthwhile for Revilo Defense, or are we wasting our time?"

She pressed her tongue to the roof of her mouth to keep from babbling. It was up to Tiimuna now.

Baandalin made clicking sounds, and Caavendir tugged at her ears. But Tiimuna declared, "We're up to the task. You help us to get back our mechs and adapt them for audio driving, and we'll make sure you get paid."

"With interest," Ruumil said.

Tiimuna hesitated only a moment before agreeing, "With interest."

Baandalin scurried beside Tiimuna and began to whisper something too quickly for Niirama to track, but the frantic protests inspired Tiimuna to lock in further. "And with collateral."

Several opSha made noises that Niirama instinctually registered as confusion and protest, even without any words she recognized. Caavendir refrained, but she seemed to be the only local who maintained composure.

Tiimuna said, "If we cannot repay you in credits, you'll own this complex."

"Tiimuna!" Baandalin exclaimed.

"We can't take away your base," Niirama said, surprising herself. "It's your home."

Others joined in with similar echoes, including one forlorn, "It's all we have left."

"Listen, everyone," Tiimuna called, and they fell silent. "If we're not able to reclaim the CASPers and start earning for ourselves, we don't have anything to lose. The truth is we invested almost everything we had in mechs from the Phoenix Initiative. That was already a gamble that we agreed on. If Revilo Defense walks away now, we might lose any chance of getting them back."

Ruumil said, "That sounds fair to me. We'll draw up a contract and make it worth the risk all the way around." A little quieter, he added, "It's what I'd do in your situation." Niirama wondered if that was for her benefit.

Niirama worried they were taking advantage of the already compromised opSha outfit, but she'd already gotten her way in convincing Ruumil to stay.

"That said," Ruumil went on, "all negotiations might be moot. What makes you think they haven't already hightailed off planet by now?"

Tiimuna hummed his satisfaction, as if about to reveal the one winning card he had left. "Because we've managed to track their location."

"You found them?" Caavendir asked, meaning the discovery must've been very recent.

"Yes," Baandalin jumped in, his higher voice causing Niirama to recoil. "We performed thorough scans of the CASPers—even though we had planted trackers on them, it wasn't hard to scan for where they'd been and where they were going."

"But Ruumil is right," Tiimuna said. "Time may be short. We were going to see if we could move in on their camp and disable them. In fact, we were working on a plot to surround them when you arrived and—well, we thought you might be here with a ransom demand."

"That's why it looks so empty in here," Niirama added, then flushed and corrected herself. "Sounds—sounds so empty."

"We sent out stealth scout teams, and once we confirmed their location, our other forces converged on the area."

The fact that he was calling them *forces* might've been a good sign.

"But this is a stroke of luck. You're here with heavy weapons and armor. What better way to scare the thieves into submission and to inspire our troops while we're at it."

Murmurs of agreement surround him.

"Just scare the thieves?" Ruumil asked. "You're not planning to kill them?"

"Well…" Again, ears fanned from one side to the next, and a few glottal clicks of check in an agreement sounded. "This continent is made up of opSha settlements, many of them refugees."

"Refugees who steal and sell to the fastest bidder," Niirama said, but Tiimuna continued.

"We're not looking to exterminate our own people. Besides, if we can show even the thieves a powerful and unified front, they might surrender and join us."

Ruumil opened and shut his mouth a few times. It wasn't too long ago that he had given similar speeches.

"It's true," came Caavendir's whispering agreement. "The operatives who broke in didn't use lethal force."

"That sounds fair," Niirama said, "but if *we* need to protect ourselves—"

"Of course," both Tiimuna and Caavendir said.

Niirama was glad they were on board, but apparently they'd spoken a little too quickly and eagerly for Ruumil's liking. "Very well," he said. "If we're going to do this, it should happen quickly. Let me make some quick notes for our team…" He pulled out his pad. "I'll stay here; Niirama, you and Kreski will assist in the retrieval while I take a look at what they're working with and draw up a quote."

He said it quite casually, as if she might use her mech to haul inert rocks rather than confront an enemy. Perhaps he had grown more confident in her abilities. No sooner had she thought this than Niirama received a notification on her device for a message Ruumil had sent her in the Zuparti language: *Suspicions of inside operative; be wary of Tiimuna; flee if trouble.*

* * *

Niirama was glad to be back in her CASPer. The interior had been modified to the point that the original designer wouldn't even recognize it. In terms of the size and shape, it had been set up for a much smaller being with more sensitive and independently dexterous hands and feet. Revilo Defense had gone beyond the early days of jerryrigged pulley systems and now had multi-sized species adaptations they could be proud of. More importantly, adaptations that they could effectively sell on the open market.

The trickier part of the design was also harder to spot. But when Niirama activated her system's adapted perception, the CASPer began producing finely tuned ultrasonic pulses from all directions, letting her know exactly what the visuals would show to a human—more information than a human's eyes could ever process in real time, she suspected, potentially on par with direct technological interfaces, like a pinplant in the brain. Ruumil still dragged his feet about giving Niirama or Kreski nanites, which is why Niirama marched out of their ship's cargo hold rather than sprinted. She had some acceleration dampeners, and also the benefits of being a small being with less mass and inertia than a human, plus much more room for padding.

Their second CASPer, whose interior was arranged for a Cochkala, stood in front of her, where her sensors could easily take in its exact shape. Over the comm, Kreski asked, "*Ready?*"

Having gone through the pre-deployment check, Niirama said, "Ready."

A bipedal being who was clearly not used to being dwarfed by CASPers gave both machines a wide berth but called out to Niirama. "Can you hear me?"

"Yes, Tiimuna," Niirama said through her speakers, intentionally leaving them loud enough to see if Tiimuna would startle. He only slightly flinched, but Baandalin jumped in alarm from the back of a swift ground transport.

"We'll lead the way and will keep an open channel with you and our base," Tiimuna said. "Please move as quietly as you can."

* * *

Ruumil and Caavendir returned to the command room at the top of the base, just in time to hear reports of the engagement at the enemy camp where they'd tracked the CASPers. "I must say, I'm impressed by how many tasks you managed to adapt. It's not every day I meet opSha transport pilots or computer programmers."

"You flatter us," Caavendir said, keeping one ear toward her console and her hands busy. "You have quite a reputation yourself."

The console's speakers relayed information in audible pulses which Ruumil didn't know enough to fully translate. Still, Tiimuna had already given the *go* order, so Ruumil tried to infer locations and movements, even as he said, "Oh, I can't take all the credit for our modified CASPers. That took several species and troubleshooting."

"Yes, but you operate like a seeing species." Caavendir tapped her own forehead between the eyes and let out a sharp whistle.

Ruumil self-consciously traced his goggles. "That was necessary for adapting to a bad situation."

"Which part? The goggles or the nanites?"

Ruumil did not respond.

"You know, you would have many interested customers if you could bring targeted nanotechnology to make opSha see."

"I fear that's not where my expertise lies."

Caavendir faced the consoles and entered some new information but didn't drop the previous subject. "Why go through the trouble of adapting CASPers for auditory input when you could just make the drivers see instead?"

"Well, it's a little more complicated than—"

"*Command, come in,*" Tiimuna's voice said over the console.

"This is Caavendir," she said. Ruumil moved closer as well to catch every bit of the conversation.

"*They escaped!*" Tiimuna sounded frustrated. "*They must've known we were coming. They left the crate with two CASPers behind for us to track, but, otherwise, all personnel disappeared. We heard some take off on scout vehicles when we arrived, but they were too fast and knew the forest too well for us to follow. We found tunnel entrances underground too narrow for Niirama to take her mech through, and we don't want to send anyone down to get captured.*"

Ruumil leaned toward a microphone. "Tiimuna, can you switch this to a secure channel?"

"*What?*" Tiimuna asked.

"He means can anyone else listen in?" Caavendir translated. "If this is to the whole complex, switch to just us."

Ruumil heard a click. Although the security measures hadn't been confirmed, Ruumil had to risk it in favor of efficiency. "Tiimuna, I believe the thieves have a confederate from your base, someone who tipped them off."

Another voice, Kreski the Cochkala, spoke over the presumed private channel. "*We think so too.*"

Ruumil nodded to himself. "Niirama, are you also listening in?"

Over the comm, the younger opSha cleared her throat and admitted, "*Yes, we were able to follow and stay on the frequency.*"

"Good. Did Tiimuna show any tells when I mentioned the insider?"

"*What?!*" Tiimuna yelled, this time, indignant.

Niirama said, "*No guilt indicators.*"

"Okay, I'll apologize later," Ruumil said. "For now, we need to figure out where they went and their next steps."

"*Unless they already left the planet,*" Niirama said.

"No, why leave two mechs behind if they were already in a position to load and take off?"

"Mass limitations?" Caavendir suggested, but even she didn't sound convinced.

"No." Ruumil tugged at the hairs on his chin while he mused. "They were trying to draw your attention away, and someone knew that they could by leaving CASPers to track. The question is, 'Why?'"

The answer came in the form of a deafening crash and a sudden underfoot earthquake. Ruumil and Caavendir both maintained their balance, thanks to the rungs, but neither was prepared for the screeching sound as a chunk of the outer wall was wrenched aside.

At the next impact, the floor shuddered and slanted underfoot. Ruumil didn't know how many levels down the basement went, but he didn't want to find out by falling the distance—or, worse, how heavy the ceiling might feel.

Caavendir twisted away from the console and emitted a peal of low trills, sending echolocation in all directions. "Let's go," she said, reaching for Ruumil's wrist.

"Hang on—the report!" Ruumil had watched Caavendir's movements enough to operate the comm. "Tiimuna, we are under attack at the base."

"There's no time," Caavendir hissed. "Come on."

The response was distorted, but Tiimuna must've received something, for he replied, "*Say again: they're at the base?*"

"Something's here they couldn't leave without," Ruumil said, "even with the CASPers, they—"

A sonic pulse blared past Ruumil, knocking his hands away from the console, and punching a ring of force into any movable parts of its frame.

Clutching a bruised hand against his chest, Ruumil swiveled to face Caavendir as she adjusted her earpiece with one hand; the other gripped a sonic pistol. "I told you," she said, aiming the sonic weapon at him now, "we don't have time."

Ruumil froze in place, intent on protecting his one good ear and his skeletal structure by not aggravating the saboteur. This meant his shocked open mouth stayed open. He saw no point in giving any melodramatic declarations of "it was you." Even if he couldn't work out every aspect of the how and why, Ruumil's sharp mind quickly grasped the what. The theft had indeed been made possible by an opSha insider, and that insider had been in a position to orchestrate the ruse that left the base defenseless for at least one more acquisition.

"I won't stand in your way," Ruumil said, doing his best not to show frustration for losing Revilo Defense's collateral in the form of what was now a less than operational base.

"Continue that policy, and you'll keep breathing," Caavendir said, then chirped out directions without bothering to visually gesture.

Ruumil had his marching orders, which included staying in front of his captor and playing the dutiful hostage. He also had a guess at the major item of value. Though he hadn't heard it since childhood, an old, colloquial opSha word grunted its way out of his throat, roughly translating to, "Shit."

* * *

"Ruumil! Can you hear me?" Niirama flicked the comm channel to Kreski and the Revilo Defense transport. "I lost signal."

Outside of her CASPer, Tiimuna reacted with as much confusion. The once orderly operatives of the opSha company now appeared to mill aimlessly. Most anxiously waited for new orders while a few continued to investigate the decoy location. Some shouted out questions along with theories and coordinates.

"*Nothing on our end,*" the Zuparti on the Revilo transport ship said. "*Did it sound like they said the base was—*"

"Under attack," Niirama finished. She hadn't heard Ruumil perfectly, but enough had gotten through. "Get in the air and get a visual."

Tiimuna scampered forward to stand in front of Niirama's CASPer, as if she wouldn't be able to hear him from the previous distance. "Niirama," he called, "are you able to—"

If Tiimuna had continued talking, Niirama missed it, because the Zuparti in her transport vessel suddenly yelped with alarm. "*Incoming! Big incoming.*"

Niirama didn't wait for the full report to tell Kreski, "Follow me."

She began to run back the way they'd come, toward her ship, toward the base, knowing that Kreski was most likely at her heels. Inertial thresholds prevented her from taking off like a rocket, but even steady acceleration could garner a lot of speed pretty quickly in a CASPer.

"Revilo transport, what's your situation? Respond."

"*Large ship, just set down by the base. Scanning for weapons.*"

"*Large ship?*" Kreski asked, panting a little even though his suit was doing most of the exerting. "*How large?*"

"*Unknown classification, but heavy freighter capacity.*"

Whatever this rogue unit was, they had covertly stolen CASPers, set an effective misdirect to draw out forces, and now attacked a base—with a large ship.

Ruumil's suspicions of an insider's betrayal carried far more weight—Ruumil, who was inside the base under attack and couldn't be contacted.

Niirama tried to shut down her worries and ordered the crew of their own comparably small ship. "Do not engage. If they attack, evade and escape."

She couldn't ignore the alarm in her own voice. Still, she and Kreski pressed on, running as fast as they could without overtaking the safety parameters installed in their mechs.

"They don't seem interested in us," the Zuparti said over her headset, *"just the opSha base."*

Niirama could imagine fire raining down on the structure—which seemed well constructed enough to thwart many species' attempts to break in, but starships were a class all their own.

Then, over the same channel, Kreski said, "I'm not seeing that kind of firepower. No munitions on any of my scanners."

That was surprising. They couldn't see everything through the trees, but glimpses of the sky ahead didn't reveal the flames or even smoke Niirama associated with heavy explosives. For that matter, she hadn't felt shockwaves or heard distant reports.

The Zuparti on her comm said, *"They tore open the wall. Large hydraulic crane contraction. Then a boarding party went inside, and they're loading the enemy vessel."*

Niirama had her answer. The thieves hadn't taken off because something valuable had remained in the base.

Realistically, however, they could have stayed covert and had done so the night before, but heavy freighters with massive external cranes were exactly *not* covert. Maybe they had planned for more stealth measures, but one factor had changed: the presence of Revilo Defense.

Niirama's fur prickled as she realized Ruumil was the most valuable and time sensitive acquisition. She also knew they wouldn't reach Ruumil in time.

* * *

The door to his room hissed open, but Ruumil wasn't sure whether to lean toward or jerk away from the intruder.

He only knew the door was to his right because that's where it had been when his captors strapped him into the crash couch for safe takeoff on high thrust.

Otherwise, his one ear couldn't intuit direction very well, and his eyes were squeezed as tightly shut as they could be, though not from disorientation or space sickness. Even so, the minimal light was quite painful to his oversensitive optic nerves.

Perhaps *annoyed* was not the best tone to take when held hostage on an enemy vessel, but Ruumil placed little stock in the niceties. "Can I have my goggles back?"

A gruff voice speaking a language Ruumil found familiar made a remark he didn't follow.

Then the whispering Caavendir said, "Intriguing design. If our extrapolations are correct, your modified vision must be astounding."

"Presently, it's painful. My goggles please."

The other being grunted something that reminded Ruumil of gruff mammals he had dealt with before, albeit with a different dialect. Ruumil strained to open one eyelid just a crack. It was a Pushtal—a hulking feline carnivore who might as well have been named *Thug*.

Ruumil would've rolled his eyes had that not placed extra strain.

"You are in no position to make requests," Caavendir said. "However, if you were to help us, I'm sure we could—"

"Yes, yes," Ruumil interrupted, his voice flat and dismissive. "I'm sure you want to know everything about not only our audio-adaptive installation in the CASPers but also my research into nanites for non-human species. I'm well aware that I've been captured and at your mercy, so I'll tell you anything you want to know. It's not like I'll risk torture or death to protect proprietary information. Spare me the dramatic threats, give me back my goggles, and I'll get to work straight away."

Ruumil couldn't see her expression but imagined from the silence that she was disappointed.

The Pushtal unstrapped Ruumil's wrists, and Caavendir placed the goggles in his hands. It took seconds to fit the comfortable frames back into their well-worn creases.

"I'm impressed you are so practical, Ruumil."

"You flatter me." Ruumil got to his feet, testing the thrust gravity and finding it sufficient to walk in without injury. "So, did you plan to bring necessary tools to my cell, or is there a lab I can work in, with or without an ankle chain?"

"I'll take you," Caavendir said without addressing the possibility of chains. The Pushtal remained as well, presumably in case Ruumil decided to risk anyone's well-being. Before she proceeded, however, Caavendir remarked, "I would have thought you'd oppose working with a company like ours."

"Of course, I would. Don't mistake my understanding of the arrangement as happiness. I am perfectly capable of finding you as appalling as the refuse tunnels of a generational ship even while acting as your research tool."

When Ruumil stepped through the doorway, the Pushtal said a message of "welcome" whose proper nouns Ruumil couldn't decipher.

Caavendir translated. "He welcomed you to his ship, the *Devil's Wrench*."

* * *

Niirama jabbed her finger into Tiimuna's chest, causing him to stagger back. "You should have known!"

"I'm sorry," Tiimuna said, and he sounded like he was.

"Don't blame this all on him—it's not his fault!" Baandalin protested. "None of us knew Caavendir would betray us."

"We didn't think anyone would." Tiimuna threw his hands up in exasperation. "We thought with an all-opSha operation we could expect loyalty."

Niirama held back the derisive laugh. "That's ridiculous. Even if you thought that before, how could you still believe it after the first theft?"

Tiimuna gave no response.

Kreski's voice came over a CASPer speaker. "What's more important is figuring out what we'll do next." He remained in his machine while they investigated the wreckage of the base, the lone intimidation factor, daring anyone else to try a third heist. But the enemy ship, and all the thieves, were long gone.

A large section of the outer wall had been wrenched free and flung away, the lower garage doors forced open. Otherwise, there was relatively little damage and much of the base could still be usable.

No one was shocked that Ruumil and Caavendir had disappeared, along with the final CASPer, the in-progress audio-adaptive installation, and several consoles.

"Well, our biologists have confirmed that the enemy crew was not only made up of opSha. At least four other sentient species were present at the decoy site at one time or other."

Niirama groaned. That their outfit had multiple "biologists" but apparently no skilled tacticians bugged her, but not nearly as much as Tiimuna's aim to blame anyone other than opSha.

Kreski said, "That means it was an off-world band. Makes sense with a ship like that."

Niirama hadn't sized the ship herself, and the opSha base wasn't exactly known for recording video footage. From what she'd heard however, she surmised a few things. "That vessel would be way bigger than needed for a few CASPers. In fact, that could be a small score for them. Anyone flying a rig that big would need more to keep it funded."

Despite their shortage of years, Niirama and Kreski each had more experience with selling salvaged and stolen cargo than most.

Kreski said, "This can't be the only place they're hitting."

* * *

The *Devil's Wrench* set down as quietly as it could about fifty klicks away from the Flatar city, where another set of newly delivered Phoenix Initiative CASPers awaited the Pushtal's crew and any smugglers they planned to pick up on this world.

Caavendir hadn't been the chief point of contact with the Flatar inside man. However, she had proven herself on both the opSha job and their new captive science lead that she was given the task of first in-person rendezvous, not far from the appointed landing site.

The pilot confirmed that they were parked on the exact coordinates. This time, they followed an energy beacon buried in the damp soil and hadn't needed to find a clearing between the trees.

In her excitement, Caavendir scurried down the ramp before it had even touched foreign soil and leapt down the last gap.

During this leap, however, a low tone—subsonic for most species—overwhelmed her opSha ears. When she landed, her feet burned through their protective coverings while waves of concentrated electrical energy lanced through her. Caavendir collapsed. As her shoulder hit the moist, highly charged soil, she convulsed, while listening to more devices erupt from the ground to ensnare the heavy freighter.

Caavendir quickly lost consciousness. The ramp never finished lowering behind her.

* * *

From her safe observation point, Niirama chittered happily to herself in appreciation of redundancy.

If the ionizing pulses didn't overtake the freighter, the physical clamps jetting out of the ground would manage to hold it in place. The fact that the ramp froze about a meter off the ground was a good sign that systems inside the vessel had gone inactive.

Niirama leaned toward the Flatar representative, another small-statured mammalian species, who had acted as the liaison with the *Devil's Wrench* and pretended to sell out his people.

"This is just a small taste of what Revilo Defense can do for you," she said.

Between tuned electrical pulses, physical restraints, infrasonic assaults, and a team ready to board, Niirama's interception move appeared effective, even if it had required reinforcements from Revilo Defense to pull off.

Technically, Niirama's plan had been a gambit, based on the theory that the crew of the *Devil's Wrench* would target any species they determined weaker and who had purchased CASPers. She hadn't expected to find the right one so quickly. She also wouldn't publicize the bribes needed to acquire the list of who might have black market Phoenix Initiative CASPers.

She had rehearsed the speech she would give to Ruumil that it was a small price to pay for Revilo Defense's reputation—not to mention Ruumil's safe return.

It didn't take long to confirm that the opSha's stolen CASPers and Revilo Defense's favorite scientist were still inside, undamaged. The older opSha had been knocked unconscious and might wake with some aches, but he would live. She'd have to find out if Ruumil had divulged any pertinent information to these smugglers, but that was a task for another day.

"So," Niirama said, leaning to the other side and her fellow opSha, "after seeing us in action, do you think you might invest in training after all?"

"Absolutely," Tiimuna said. "We are in your debt once again, but we will most certainly pay you back. Although—" He hesitated. "If I can ask one more small favor."

Niirama's pulse quickened in anticipation, or perhaps nervousness. Although she had felt initial attraction for Tiimuna, those feelings evaporated when Ruumil had been captured due in part to Tiimuna's naïveté. But perhaps that conclusion had been too hasty, and Tiimuna was coyly segueing into a question of the more personal nature. Surely, he didn't expect Revilo Defense to provide any services for free.

"Yes?" Niirama asked.

"I wonder if you could refrain from telling anyone about our being swindled and robbed. Reputation is everything, and *OpSha Operations* needs an opportunity to form a positive one."

"*OpSha Operations?*" Niirama asked, not sure whether she should feel relieved or disappointed.

"Yes," Tiimuna said with a chuckle. "When translated into Human English, it abbreviates to sound like '*OpSha Ops.*' What do you think?"

Niirama wrinkled her nose. "I think we can keep your secret for you. No one need ever hear the blundering origin story of OpSha Ops."

* * * * *

Mike Jack Stoumbos Bio

Mike Jack Stoumbos is an author and educator, living with his wife and their parrot in Richmond, VA. He is best known for his space opera novel series *THIS FINE CREW* and as a 1st-place Writers of the Future winner. His work appears in anthologies from Zombies Need Brains, WordFire Press, and Camden Park Press, among others. Mike Jack is the lead editor of WonderBird Press, whose debut anthology, *Murderbirds*, made 1st-day funding and was named a #ProjectWeLove on Kickstarter. Mike Jack teaches writing craft classes for teens and writing habits workshops for emerging authors. You can find him at MikeJackStoumbos.com.

# # # # #

Buff Orpington and the Sinister Scientist Bunnies by Casey Moores

Commodore Alvin Relinquishes Command

Aboard the *Solstice*
Mategir System

Simon was tapping at a tower defense game when the primary door to the *Solstice's* bridge hissed open. He adjusted his goggles to see a tall, thin Human in a green and gray uniform and graying hair stomp in.

The Human Colonel Dean Adams and the Goka Colonel Ch'Vez both rose respectfully. Captain Leischner walked in behind the new Human.

"Colonel Wallace, may I introduce Colonel Dean Adams and Colonel Ch'Vez, the co-commanders of the Badass Blades," Leischner said.

Colonel Adams, a young steely-eyed Human with short, brown hair, shook Colonel Wallace's hand. Simon noted both men's forearms tightened with the grasp. Colonel Ch'Vez' antennae twitched.

"Colonels, this is Colonel Dave Wallace of Wallace's Combat Wombats," Leischner said.

"Well met, Colonel," Colonel Ch'Vez' translator barked.

"Commodore Alvin, at your service," Alvin shouted. Simon couldn't see his red-armored, fellow Flatar friend from that angle, and neither could Colonel Wallace. The Human scanned around before fixing his gaze at his feet. By the surprise on his face, Simon guessed the Human had either never seen a Flatar before or not expected one to be the commodore.

"Commodore, yes of course, and well met," Colonel Wallace said. He looked back up and smiled. "I have to say, *Badass Blades* is a hell of a name. I thought as much when the contract came out."

"Thanks," Adams said. "Human employers appreciate it and most other races translate it to something warrior-esque."

"In Goka, the name translates similar to our previous company's name," Ch'Vez said.

At the sound of a tiny explosion, Simon looked to his slate and found his base was getting overrun by zombies.

"Oh, curses," he said.

"Curses?" Theodore said. "I don't know how you can play that, considering what we went through on Tambu."

"Please," Simon said. "Those were *cyber*-zombies, not proper Human witch doctor zombies. Besides, we handled the ones on Tambu. Saved your girlfriend, saved the station."

"Handled them well enough," Theodore said. "And yes, I *did* save my girlfriend and the whole station."

"Yes, *we* did," Simon said. "It's why Alvin's the commodore. It's also why Mr. Bull started sending us on missions like this. So look at it this way. By playing these strategy games, I'm staying sharp in case it ever happens again."

"Fine. You win. Now shut up so I can listen to the diversion plan."

Simon nodded, but when Theodore looked at the others, he checked his slate. Sadly, the game was over. He turned it off to better pay attention.

"So that's the objective," Colonel Adams concluded. A Tri-V display of an enormous, metal pyramid-shaped building rotated in the center of the bridge. "Our combined CASPer and Goka shock troops will crack their defenses like an egg, while your Wombats hold everything we take. Considering the sheer size of the facility, don't think for a second this will be a cake walk for your troops. The deeper in we drive, the more likely the MinSha are going to organize counterattacks to cut our forces in half. The Badass Blades are going to rely on speed and pure violent aggression. You're the ones who are going to have to employ good, intelligent tactics."

"Understood," Colonel Wallace said. The merc commander paced around the display and chewed his lip.

"Is there something about the setup that bothers you, Colonel?" Adams asked.

"A lot of things, actually," Wallace answered. "Primarily, I'm wondering who *your* contract is with and what your objective is. I realize the terms of our subcontract to you stipulate no requirement on your part to disclose that, but I'd like to know whatever you *can* tell me."

"You don't need to know either." Eric "Patches" Adams stood and glowered at Colonel Wallace. The mean, wiry old Human carried his characteristic pained expression, and he scratched at the back of his neck.

"I understand, as I said," Wallace replied. "But please appreciate this is the Wombats' first contract. Though half of my troops have seen their fair share of action, the other half haven't seen any. Seeing as it's also *your* first contract, I'm looking at substantial risk. I'm not asking you drop trou and show me the goods, I'm simply asking for a quick peek so I can be assured I won't be disappointed in your performance."

"Did you understand any of that?" Theodore asked Simon, leaning in.

"Of course," Simon replied. "The Combat Wombat commander wants assurance the capabilities and statistics listed in the Blades official Merc Guild records are accurate."

"Oh." Theodore nodded and returned his attention to the colonels.

"It may be our first contract," Colonel Ch'Vez said, "but our troops are not merely veterans, they are elite. We have combined the best fighters of the Human Bushido Bandits with my Bladestorm Goka. Both were highly rated before we nearly destroyed each other on Monogatari, and now we have combined to—"

"Wait, I'm sorry, did you say you nearly *destroyed* each other?" Wallace gasped.

"Yeah," Colonel Adams said. "To say our history is complicated would be a great understatement. But we came out fighting the same enemy, and we've been working for the same—"

"Careful, son," Patches said. Conversation ceased as father and son glared at each other.

"Working for the same… who?" Wallace asked.

"Someone's paying our bills, and we're paying yours," Patches said. "You follow these folks in and keep the damn bugs off their backs, got it?"

Theodore nudged Simon.

"Hey, do you think Mr. Patches gets the irony in asking a Human commander to keep bugs off the backs of a Goka assault force?"

"Shut up, Theodore."

"Okay, Colonels," Wallace said. "So it's MinSha on the periphery, XenSha further in?"

"Yes," Adams said. "Though, as we noted, the XenSha are all Science Guild personnel, so when we penetrate deep enough, we don't expect much resistance from the XenSha."

Theodore snickered and slapped Simon's shoulder. "Heh, *penetrate*. Miss Melissa would say 'so to speak' if she was here."

Simon rubbed his shoulder, nodded, and chuckled.

"Got it," Wallace said. "Now can we talk about the insertion?"

"He said *insertion*," Theodore said with another snicker.

"Knock it off, Theo, I'm trying to pay attention!"

Everyone stopped talking and glared at Simon after the outburst. He shrugged and looked innocently at his slate. When the tension faded, he looked up again.

The Tri-V depiction zoomed into the upper atmosphere. Projections of the Badass Blades dropships appeared with CASPer pods falling out.

"HALD," Wallace said while running his hand across his chin. "I figured as much. But what about the Goka? Do they have re-entry pods?"

"Actually, they're the same pods," Colonel Ch'Vez said. The image zoomed inside a pod. A Goka sat on each of the CASPer's shoulders.

"What the... your CASPers come with shoulder-mounted Goka?" Wallace asked.

Simon nudged Theodore. "You must admit, it is pretty badass. And they have blades. Oh, hey, Badass Blades, I get it!"

Everyone stopped to stare at Simon again. He pretended to open his slate again.

"That's fine and wonderful," Wallace said, returning his attention to the projection, "but you know my troops aren't HALD capable, right? It was specified in our company document."

"Yes, it was," Adams said. "Your Phoenix dropships will re-enter in more permissive airspace, fly low level to the objective, drop your CASPers at low altitude, then head to the staging area until the exfil."

"Ah, old school," Wallace said. "And it makes a ton of sense. Those were my major questions. The details can be handled offline."

"Thank you for your time, Colonel," Alvin shouted, though Simon still couldn't see him. "You're dismissed."

The Humans and Goka glanced uncomfortably at each other. Finally, Captain Leischner waved a hand to the door.

"Yes, thank you, Commodore," he said. "If that is all, Colonel Wallace, thank you for coming."

With the meeting concluded, Simon started a new round of Zombie Towers.

As the commander of the Combat Wombats departed, Alvin stepped around to join Simon and Theodore.

"Simon, Theodore, shall we excuse ourselves to discuss our part in all this?" he said.

Simon sighed and turned the slate off again. "Let's."

"Captain Leischner!" Alvin shouted. "The ship is yours."

Leischner looked up from a display with an eyebrow raised. "Uh, yes, sir," he said. Someone mumbled something to Captain Leischner, who shrugged in response.

"Theo, are you okay?" Alvin asked.

At this, Simon noticed Theodore standing still, chest heaving as he gasped for air, and gaze still firmly locked on a depiction of the Badass Blades CASPer with the Goka on its shoulders.

"Theo?" Simon asked. When the green-armored Flatar didn't respond, Simon grabbed his elbow. Theodore jumped.

"What?" Theodore asked with exasperation.

"What's wrong?" Simon asked.

"Alvin, did you say we were going to ride in with the Badass Blades?" Theodore asked.

Simon snapped his head up. He must've missed that part.

"Yes, why?"

"I... I don't think I can do that!" Theodore said. Eyes wide in terror, he scratched at his arms and fidgeted.

"But we want to be at the front of the assault," Alvin said. "In the tradition of Sergeant Alvin York, for whom the Humans named me! Like Buff Orpington would do!"

"But... falling out of the sky from so high up the very air wants to incinerate you?" Theodore said. "No, just no! I can't do it!"

Alvin threw his hands up in exasperation. "But there's no other way! How else are we supposed to get down there?"

"Actually," Simon said. "There is another way."

* * *

Enter the Phoenix

Precariously balanced on Alvin's shoulders, Simon shifted his feet as he wobbled.

"Simon, stop kicking me!" Alvin said. "I knew I should've been on top!"

"Keep it down," Theodore whispered. "Someone will hear us."

Simon looked around in paranoia but didn't see anyone.

"No, no, it's clear. Turn left a little."

The leaning tower of Flatar staggered to the left, lining them straight down the corridor.

"Simon, you're not helping!" Theodore said.

"Oh, yeah, Alvin shut up! I know where we're going, so I'm on top. Right turn."

"I know where we're going," Alvin said. "We're going to the Combat Wombat dropships."

"Quiet! Just because I can't see anyone doesn't mean it's clear."

Underscoring the point, a hatch slid open on the left.

"Shush," Simon said. He straightened and tightened his core. Alvin's grip on his ankles tightened, and the trio stood as tall and stable as they could. Simon kept his eyes straight and pulled the hood forward.

Two Humans, deep in conversation, stepped through the hatch and walked past without giving him a second glance. They soon disappeared around a corner.

"Anyway, Alvin," Simon said. "For a *commodore*, you have surprisingly little idea where anything is. Turn right again."

"A commodore has much greater responsibilities than knowing boring stuff like schematics."

"For the last time, keep it down!" Theodore said. The Flatar stack teetered, and Simon feared the trio might come crashing down. After a few moments of staggering, they settled.

"If we're done arguing," Simon said. "Then what Theodore said. We're about to enter the dropship bay. If we're still bickering and squabbling, we'll get found out. Then, we'll have no choice but to drop in with the Blades."

"Fine with me," Alvin said.

"Alvin, I swear, if you screw this up, I'm gonna rip your—"

"Shush!" Simon said. "Two steps to the left and stop for a second."

This put Simon at the hatch control panel. With a tap, the hatch opened.

"Two steps back to the right, then straight ahead," Simon said.

They walked into the *Solstice's* expansive dropship bay. A couple people glanced their way, but none appeared suspicious. Most Humans and other creatures took it for granted a ship in hyperspace had few security concerns.

Simon snapped his head at a loud bang on his left. A maintenance technician was struggling to remove a panel. He cursed, struck it harder, and then tossed the mallet aside. While reaching for a laser cutter, the man looked toward the Flatar stack. Simon tucked his head back into his hood and searched for the next closest dropship.

"Shuffle two steps left!" he said when they almost ran into a short Human female with dark brown hair. He caught the slightest glimpse of freckles and narrowing brown eyes before they moved past. Simon felt certain she'd seen him. Frantically, he spotted a dropship immediately to their right. The ramp was open. With a few whispered instructions, the trio was inside the Phoenix's cargo hold.

"Down!" Simon whispered as he jumped off Alvin's shoulders. He pulled the coat off as he went and balled it up.

Alvin tumbled off, smacking his face on the floor, while Theodore simply braced himself until Alvin was clear.

"There, the ECE hold!" Simon whispered. He raced to the Emergency Crew Equipment panel and popped it open. "Inside."

The other two rushed in. Simon tossed the balled-up coat in, entered, and pulled the panel shut.

"Hello?" someone said.

In the dim light around the cracks of the panel, the trio glanced at each other and held their breath. He expected the panel to pop open and their whole plan to fall apart, but it never did. The stomp of feet on metal faded out of the cargo hold.

They'd done it.

"Now what?" Alvin asked.

"We wait until the infiltration," Simon replied.

"How long is that?"

"You're the commodore," Theodore said. "How do you not know when emergence is? And the time from emergence to the planet?"

"Silly details like that are for the subordinates!" Alvin said.

The comment triggered a thought. Simon inspected himself and his two companions.

"You mean details like what kind of gear we're bringing along?" Simon said. "We snuck in with just pistols and slates."

"That's all we needed against the cyber zombies on Tambu," Alvin said. "Pistols to kill whatever gets in our way, slates so you and Theodore can do your tech data stealing thing."

"Point of discussion," Theodore said. "On Tambu we also had a whole factory floor death trap to fight the cyber zombies."

"Hey," Alvin said, "did you ever realize 'Cyber Zombies of Tambu' would be a perfect Buff Orpington movie title?"

Metal clanged in the cargo hold again.

"Shush," Simon whispered.

The three held their tongues and stared at each other for a long while. Eventually, Alvin yawned, leaned back, and closed his eyes. It wasn't long before Theodore followed him into slumber.

* * *

Descent of the Phoenix

Phoenix Dropship, Whiskey Two
Planet Rubired

The ship bucked hard, and Simon's head banged off the top of the small compartment.

"Ow!" he shouted.

"Quiet!" Theodore said.

"What's going on?" Simon asked as he rubbed his head.

"Who's the dummy now?" Alvin asked. "It's the assault."

Another buck sent Simon flying into Alvin and the two slammed against a wall.

"Hey, stay off," Alvin said.

Distant pops reverberated through the walls. A great boom was followed by yet another hard buck.

"Yeah, but what's going on?" Simon asked. "Are we taking fire?"

"Duh," Alvin said.

Theodore retched and Alvin noticed his green-armored friend had turned away from them with his hands on his head. The scent of vomit wafted through the stale air and stayed.

Clutching his stomach, Theodore turned back to the others. "I thought we weren't—"

His eyes went wide, he spun, and he retched again.

"Really, Theo?" Alvin asked while clutching his nose and tucking his chin. "And what? Did you think this would be safer?

An earth-rending boom and an angry rumble ran through the ship. The dropship rolled and the Flatar tumbled like they were in a Human washing machine.

The ship bounced hard, bounced again, and thudded to an abrupt stop. The three Flatar were piled up, but at least the dropship was upright.

Simon's ears were ringing. Alvin's foot was pressed against his jaw. Theodore lay face down on the bottom of the pile.

"Simon, you alive?" Alvin asked.

Simon thrust a thumbs up in front of Alvin's face.

On the other side of the panel, there was a whine of servos, the screech of scraping metal, and the stomp of boots.

"Everyone out!" someone yelled.

Simon realized it wasn't his ears ringing, it was the dropship's alarm bell. He stood and popped the panel open to peer out. A herd of CASPers was marching out the back. A tall male Human and a short female Human, both in flight suits and light body armor, stumbled out after the CASPers.

Once the cargo compartment looked clear, the Flatar rushed out down the ramp. As Simon passed by the female pilot, he smacked her leg. "Nice flying, ace!"

Before she could answer, he scurried around the side into the hot, dusty terrain. Thick, spiky bramble grew in clumps to the side and aft of the ship, while tall, waving grass stretched into a field off the nose. An explosion rocked the ship, followed by muffled laser blasts.

"I think whatever shot us down found us already," Alvin said.

A chatter of MACs erupted from the back of the dropship along with more small explosions and chirps of laser fire. Waves of acrid smoke wafted through the air, growing into a thick haze.

"Wait, where are we?" Alvin asked.

Rolling his eyes, Simon opened the navigational app on his slate.

"Oh no, we're *kilometers* from the objective!"

"That can't be right," Alvin said, snatching the slate out of his hands. "Oh no, by the time we get there, the whole offensive is going be over."

"No, it won't," Theodore said.

"Theodore," Alvin said in his standard condescending tone, "unless you can sprint faster than most CASPers while carrying us, it's going to take us at least an hour."

A gray and green CASPer stomped into view along the back of the dropship, arms locked in a grapple with a MinSha. The CASPer crouched, lifted the MinSha as it rose, and repeatedly slammed the giant insect into the side of the ship. The MinSha crunched and juices spurted in every direction.

"Blech," Simon said as MinSha guts splashed across his face. "We gotta get out of here!"

"How?" Alvin asked. "We'll never make it in time."

"I bet it takes us less than five minutes," Theodore said.

"Have you been training for the Intergalactic Olympics without telling us?" Alvin asked.

"No, but I know Phoenix dropships," Theodore said. "Plus, this placard says 'Emergency Crew Evacuation Vehicle.'"

Theodore smiled and yanked the handle. The panel swung down, revealing a strange, compact machine with a line of lift fans.

"What's that?" Alvin asked.

"A hover bike, like the one from Buff Orpington and the Cannibal Chicks of Cancun," Theodore said as he struggled to pull it from the box. "We fire it up and reach the objective in no time."

"Huh, why's it there?" Simon asked.

"It's a recent addition to Human dropship emergency equipment," Theodore said. "After the recent string of disasters, someone thought to give the aircrews a means of getting away from their dropship in a hurry in case something like this happens. It's a tight fit for two Humans, and they weigh it down, but they'll escape, say, charging Besquith. Plenty of room for the three of us."

Simon and Alvin gawked as Theodore wrestled it out. Meanwhile, the firefight ended. The world became eerily silent, though the tension of combat seemed to linger.

"Thanks for the help, by the way," Theodore said. Once clear, he pushed the release buttons and the lift fans folded outward. He twisted a few locks into place, unfolded the handles, and tapped on a slate mounted on the front. The fans spun to life with a soft hum and the bike lifted off the ground.

"Wow, it's quiet," Alvin said.

"They're no good if everyone in a five-mile radius hears them. If the Humans need this, they'd need to be stealthy."

A Human male called out, "Ducky, go grab our gear and prep the ECEV."

"Right… right," a shaky female voice replied.

Boots pounded on metal inside the dropship.

"Quick, put the hatch back on!" Theodore whispered.

Simon threw the metal panel closed and shoved until something clicked.

"Hop on!" Theodore whispered. He hopped onto the front and grabbed the handles. Alvin shoved Simon aside to climb on next, leaving Simon in back. As soon as he climbed on, the sharp acceleration nearly threw him off. Theodore flew them into the tall grass, which left nothing visible save the sky.

* * *

Raining Razors

The trio soared on the hover bike over several ridges until the rolling, grass-covered hills gave way to flat plains. The tall, pyramidal Science Guild facility lay across the expansive field, a monument of civilization in an otherwise savage landscape.

At the base of the pyramid, Simon could barely make out neat lines of MinSha troops lining up for deployment.

"Wait, aren't they supposed to be knee deep in CASPers and Goka by now?" Simon asked.

Alvin looked up and scanned the sky. Simon hadn't thought to look up, but now he did. The large red sun made him squint, but he still couldn't see anything.

"Yeah, they should be."

"No," Theodore said. "The Wombats were supposed to low level in first to draw the MinSha out—which it seems to be doing."

"Are you sure?" Simon said.

"Yeah, you must've missed it while dealing with zombies."

As Theodore spoke, he kept the hover bike pointed straight at the main entrance to the pyramid, which now had several lines of MinSha troops standing in the way. Simon gulped as they rocketed toward the enemy without slowing. Any moment now, they'd be the sole target for hundreds of MinSha.

"See anything yet?" Theodore shouted.

Simon squinted and shifted and stared at the sky but saw nothing. "No!"

A missile screamed past them and blasted a section of the MinSha lines. Several more thundered in behind it. The MinSha scattered into looser skirmish lines and unleashed a torrent of laser fire.

Simon craned his head to see the gray and green Combat Wombat CASPers advancing across the field. They moved slowly, led with their laser shields, and returned fire by squad. Half of the Combat Wombat CASPers moved with grace and solid discipline. The other half stumbled forward, crowded against the more professional looking ones, and fired random, horribly aimed shots.

The MinSha surged forward in dispersed, but perfectly organized lines. Missiles flew, lasers zipped, and explosions spewed smoke and debris all over. One rocket streaked a little too close and Alvin yelped.

"Anything?" Theodore asked. Though his voice wavered, he held the hover bike's speed and course steady.

Looking up once more, Simon still didn't see any falling CASPers, but he did see a faint scintillation, like light reflecting off grains of sand or through a fine mist. They were less than a kilometer from the objective, and it seemed Theodore planned for them to assault the entire MinSha contingent by themselves.

"Theodore, break off!" Simon shouted. "I think the Badass Blades burned up in re-entry, or their dropships got shot down!"

The hover bike swerved so hard Simon couldn't hold on. He flew top over tail toward the oncoming horde of giant, armed insects. Alvin similarly lost contact with the hover bike, but it was probably for the better. Theodore kicked clear of the bike as it dug sideways into the ground. It crashed and rolled, though it remained surprisingly intact.

Simon slammed into a spiky bush. A thousand pinpricks found their way through his armor and pain washed through him.

For what seemed several hours, he stared at the purplish-blue sky and suffered in silence. A shadow drifted across his vision.

"Alvin, Theodore, is that you?" he asked.

As the shadow grew and his eyes adjusted, the image resolved into one of the giant insects from his nightmares. A MinSha stood over him, its rifle trained. Three more joined it.

A black object fell from the sky onto the lead MinSha's back. Curiously, the MinSha's head bounced a few mere millimeters up from its thorax. The head tilted, rolled, and tumbled to the side.

The other three MinSha aimed their rifles at their fallen comrade and riddled the headless body with laser fire. A Goka jumped to the side and the shots reflected off. Another Goka landed left of the cluster and immediately sliced through the nearest MinSha's legs.

The roar of jump jets announced the arrival of a red and black painted CASPer. While the two flanking MinSha fought a losing battle against the two Goka at their feet, the third took a MAC round to the thorax. The entire patrol was dead within seconds. As the last one collapsed, Alvin leaped out from behind a bush and fired his hypervelocity pistol into its head.

"Thanks for the help, guys!" he said. "Simon, you okay?"

More CASPers floated down on cushions of fire, each with a pair of Goka on their shoulders. Each CASPer had "7 Sisters" printed above their canopies.

"I'm not dead," Simon said.

The growing horde of CASPers and Goka landed amidst MinSha lines and unleashed a torrent of missiles, lasers, MAC rounds, and flashing blades. Explosions plumed everywhere.

"Great. Where's Theodore?"

"Here." Their third companion sounded as broken and pitiful as Simon felt. They dug him from another spiky bush. As he looked in even worse condition than Simon, Alvin jabbed a nanite injector into Theodore's hip.

"Aaaahhh!!" he screamed. Simon and Alvin struggled to hold Theodore down until he settled. Gasping and trembling, he asked, "*Now* how do we get there?"

"Commodore Alvin?" a Goka asked. A trio of the shiny black insects scuttled up.

"Who's asking?" Alvin replied.

"Colonel Ch'Vez ordered us to deliver these." The Goka pulled its arms inside its shell and rustled around for a moment before producing a small, leather knapsack.

"Our gear!" Theodore said. The other two Goka produced similar sacks and handed them off. The three Flatar passed the sacks around until Alvin had the red one, Theodore had the green one, and Simon had the blue one.

"We were also ordered to ensure the Chipmunks got inside the facility."

Alvin nodded and stroked his chin while observing the great metal pyramid. "I see. And what is your plan?"

"Under the cover of the ongoing battle, we're to carry you to your insertion point."

Now Alvin straightened and put his hands behind his back.

"Understood. Theodore, assessment?"

"Uh, it'll work better than anything else I can think of?" Theodore replied.

"And Simon," Alvin continued, "do you concur?"

Simon sighed and rolled his eyes. "Yes, *Commodore*, I concur."

"Good. Chipmunks, mount up!"

Simon exchanged an exasperated glance with Theodore as they climbed onto the Goka's backs.

"Riding into glorious combat on the backs of the Galaxy's second-best warriors!" Alvin shouted as their mounts skittered toward the pyramid.

Everywhere Simon looked, the MinSha defense was crumbling under the vicious melee assault of the Badass Blades and the Combat Wombats. The last of the MinSha retreated behind a barricade in front of the entrance to the pyramid.

"Second best?" Alvin's Goka asked. "You can't possibly mean Humans or Veetanho. Are you putting us after Depik or Tortantula?"

"Come on, Depik are a merc's myth," Alvin said. "Invisible feline assassins? Even Human entertainment couldn't dream up something so absurd."

"What about Buff Orpington and the Cuddle Kitties of Death?" Theodore asked.

The Goka mounts cut sideways across the edge of the barricade as a gray and green CASPer launched a double handful of K-bombs at the center. The barricade fell, and a pair of red and black CASPers cut through the MinSha defenders with a large detachment of Goka on their heels.

"So how are we supposed to get into this place?" Alvin asked.

"Don't you guys know?" Alvin's Goka replied.

"Yes, of course," Theodore said. "You really need to pay attention when I'm talking."

Simon adjusted his goggles, as he always did when he explained a plan. However, letting go of the Goka shell proved a horrible idea as the Goka reached a cliff face and scuttled straight up. He swung to one side and nearly fell off.

"Yes, Alvin, remember?" he said. "Hopefully these Goka are taking us to the—"

"But Cuddle Kitties," Alvin said, "as much as I truly adore Jezebel French, has become one of my least favorite in the Buff Orpington franchise."

The sounds of battle receded as they reached the top of the cliff. The ground sloped downward, making Simon wonder if the cliff had been created rather than shaped by natural causes.

"Commodore, with all due respect," his Goka said, "we were discussing something important."

"Yes, we were," Theodore said.

"So who do you consider the greatest warrior race?" the Goka asked.

Theodore groaned in disgust. The slope shallowed and the air turned cool. The noise of battle was gone, replaced by a sound of trickling water.

"Flatar, of course!" Alvin said. "I mean, Tortantula would be nothing without us!"

The Goka slammed to a halt and the three Flatar flew forward. Thankfully, there were no more spiky bushes. Instead, Simon smacked into a painfully solid tree.

"Flatar! We'd been told the legendary Chipmunks are hilarious, but we had no idea! Anyway, we're off to rejoin the assault. As our Humans say, best of luck!"

As the trio of Flatar collected themselves and checked their gear, the Goka skittered away.

"Where the hell are we?" Alvin asked.

Theodore walked to the edge of a small canyon and Simon followed. Below lay a stream in which the water was slick with a lustrous rainbow-colored sludge. Smoldering chunks of porous black rock bobbed along sporadically.

"The facility's toxic waste channels," Theodore said.

"Wait," Alvin said, "don't tell me we're going in through the waste expulsion tubes."

Simon and Theodore looked at each other, shrugged, and followed the canyon toward the Science Guild facility.

"Fine, we won't tell you," Theodore said. "Though, technically, I already told you."

* * *

Mind Fuckery

Alvin squeezed out of the narrow pipe, flopped onto his back, and grumbled incoherently. Noxious sludge dripped from his fur, as it did from Simon and Theodore's.

"That. Was. Disgusting. And not like Buff Orpington and the Secret Society of Savant Squid Surgeons disgusting… no, this was another whole level, like the rumor about Human females and Besquith-level disgusting. Seriously, I feel like I just got f—"

"Alvin, it was the only way," Theodore said. "So shut up, we gotta get moving."

"Why was it the only way?" Alvin asked.

"Because if there was an SI running the facility," Theodore replied, "this carried the lowest probability of detection by an entity which can simultaneously watch every entrance, even in the midst of an assault."

"Wait, who said anything about an SI?" Alvin asked.

Simon wondered the same but decided to let Alvin remain the ignorant one.

Theodore sighed. "It's the primary goal of this mission, to determine if Minerva, the SI that runs the Science Guild, is present in the facility. It's why I have a kill switch in my pack."

"You have a kill switch in your pack? Why didn't I get the kill switch?"

"Because you've demonstrated zero ability to retain any of the details of the mission. It's why Mr. Bull trusted me with the important parts."

Alvin scraped a handful of sludge from his shoulder and flicked it away. "So why are you so enthusiastic about this mission?"

"What do you mean?" Theodore asked. He walked a few steps to a nearby hatchway. "Custodial station is right here. We can clean ourselves off and re-inspect our gear."

"Wait a second, he's right," Simon said as he opened the hatch and stepped in. "You've been a lot more attentive to the details on this mission. Normally, I'm the one who's memorized all the important stuff, but this time you're oddly focused."

Theodore stood under a spigot and pulled a lever. Water sprayed down and washed the sludge off his fur.

"Be honest," Theodore said. "Normally none of us have the slightest clue what we're doing. Like our mission to Gor'Mak where we got stuck in that closet and had to listen to a King Xiq'tal mating for four hours. If anyone had read Nikki's brief, we would've known the layout of the warehouse." His gaze drifted into the distance. "I can still see it sometimes. The sounds, the smells... lurking in the shadows of my mind, waiting to pounce and make me nauseous all over again."

"Thanks for the reminder," Alvin said. "*That* may be the one thing more disgusting than this."

Simon joined Alvin in scraping the sludge off and dumping it over the drain.

"But you know what I mean," Simon said. "Normally, we ignore Nikki's brief and bumble our way through to success by sheer, dumb luck. You know, like Buff Orpington does."

"You take that back!" Theodore said, stepping toward Simon with his fists raised. "He does not."

While Simon slapped at Theodore's weak attacks, Alvin took the opportunity to steal the shower. He closed his eyes, clearly basking in the warm rinse water.

"Fine, Buff Orpington doesn't do that," Simon lied. "But we do, and you know it. Until this mission. You're all about this one, why?"

"If you'd read the brief, you'd know why." Theodore checked his pistols and rinsed his pack off in a sink. "Anyway, let's get cleaned off and get moving. If there *is* an SI in charge, they're probably already on to us."

"Fine, I'm sure we'll figure it out," Simon said.

Simon did his best to be patient, but as the seconds lingered with Alvin standing there under the hot spray, patience waned.

"Okay, Alvin, my turn!"

"One more minute."

Simon stepped up to shove Alvin aside, but his companion's eyes snapped open, and they fell into a slap fight. Sludge and water flew everywhere. Soon, the two were wrestling for the spot.

"Morons," Theodore said.

The warm water turned ice cold and Alvin jumped away.

"Hey jerkwad, you wasted all the hot water," Alvin said.

Simon, dejected but still covered in toxic sludge topped with radioactive chips, stood in the freezing water, and scrubbed for all he was worth.

Shaking his head, Alvin pulled a red T-shirt from his pack and put it on.

"Quiet!" Theodore said.

Though Simon wasn't fully rinsed, Theodore nonetheless cut off the water. Heavy tapping and clanging echoed from the other side of the door. Alvin eased the hatch open. In a flash, he drew a hypervelocity pistol and kicked the hatch wide. He knelt, fired with a loud crack, and shuffled sideways.

Alvin fired again and jumped across the hallway to dodge responsive laser fire. Theodore rushed to the door with a pistol drawn. Though Simon wished he could've cleaned off more, he followed. Theodore stepped through, aimed, and fired. Right on his heels, Simon leaned out, found a MinSha target, and cracked a hypervelocity round through its head. Alvin fired a third time and caught the last one in the abdomen.

Five broken MinSha collapsed to the floor, oozing blue. Explosions, chirps of lasers, and rattles of ballistic weapons echoed down the hallway.

"Come on!" Alvin shouted.

Theodore waved his pistol in the opposite direction. "But we have to… oh, dammit Alvin!"

He and Simon ran after their companion.

The inside of the pyramid was a labyrinth of stairs and hallways, but Alvin sprinted toward the sound of battle.

Turning a corner, the trio found themselves behind about a dozen MinSha fighting to hold a makeshift barricade primarily comprised of a broken door. A thick laser beam flashed overhead, and a series of detonations rocked the barricade. The MinSha stayed low and braced against the attack, but immediately rose and returned fire when it subsided.

Alvin waved a series of unintelligible hand gestures and took aim. Simon knelt, leaned into his shot, and aimed as well. On one of their first missions, Theodore and Simon realized Alvin always shot for the middle of any group of targets. Therefore, Simon and Theodore decided Theodore would shoot to the right and Simon to the left.

The three Flatar fired almost as one. Three MinSha exploded. When half the survivors turned to face the new threat, the trio had taken aim again. Hypervelocity rounds tore through three more MinSha. As another raised its rifle, Alvin screamed and rushed it.

Simon shouted for Alvin to jump aside, but the MinSha's head exploded before it fired.

Past the pile of dead insectoids, a gray and green CASPer charged through the haze, arm blade deployed on one arm and a laser shield on the other. A pair of Goka scuttled at his side, and together they engaged the remaining MinSha.

Across the atrium, another gray and green CASPer crouched in front of the same Human female pilot from the dropship. She locked eyes with Simon and shook her head as if in disbelief.

"Alvin, we're going the wrong way!" Theodore shouted as he pulled Alvin back.

Wide-eyed, Alvin looked at Theodore and smiled.

"Of course, I was just helping the assault. Lead on!"

Theodore shook his head and ran back the way they'd come. As Theodore ran up and down stairwells, left and right at intersections, Simon tried to determine a pattern but couldn't. He realized they were slowly working upwards, got a vague notion they were moving further into the center, and knew for a fact they'd quickly gotten far from the battle.

They only encountered more MinSha twice. They met a pair head on, but easily dispatched them. The next time, he spotted a patrol of six down a hallway, but they were gone before the Flatar could shoot. After that, they only caught quick glimpses of XenSha technicians running away.

Theodore led them through unobstructed passageways and stairwells until finally pausing at one particular hatch. He listened while spinning a wheel to open it. It swung inward and opened onto a metal walkway, one of an expansive network of parallel walkways. They were suspended a dozen meters above an expansive room, like a low-ceilinged warehouse.

The room was filled with thousands of aliens of all races. Each was suspended in a harness and wore a shiny metal helmet with a dozen wires raising to the ceiling.

"Oh no, more cyber zombies!" Alvin said.

"Which explains your passion over this mission, Theodore," Simon said.

"Oh yeah, because your Cochkala girlfriend got cyber-zombied," Alvin said.

"Shut up, Alvin!" Theodore replied.

"How does that even work?" Alvin asked. "I mean, like physiologically. How do your pieces parts—"

"They just do, okay? Thank you very much, but the pieces parts fit fine."

"Fellas, could we drop Theo's sex life and focus on the mission, please?"

"No argument here," Theodore said.

Alvin innocently threw his hands up.

If Simon had longer arms, he could've reached out and grabbed the wires. A screen was mounted from the ceiling wherever the wires connected.

Peering into one screen, Simon saw a small crab-like creature wandering through a city. At first, he thought it was a Xiq'tal and the revolting memories of Gor'Mak returned. However, he looked down to the helmeted creature below and recognized it was an Otoo, much smaller than Xiq'tal but with more arms. In fact, each alien's race was matched by the avatar on the screen, though the appearance and equipment varied wildly.

The longer he watched the Otoo's screen, the more he got the sense the creature was trying to perform a series of tasks in some digital world.

"They're playing video games?" Alvin asked. "All this, our assault on a Science Guild facility, our harrowing drop straight into combat with MinSha, our trip through the disgusting waste tubes, all so we can find a massive Science Guild *gaming* facility? I thought this was a cyber zombie factory."

"In a way, it is," Theodore said. While Alvin stared at the screens, Simon noticed his green-shirted friend was scanning the walkways for something else. "For whatever purpose, they've taken over these beings' minds. Cyber zombie or no, the Science Guild is still up to its standard old mind fuckery."

"Do they know they're in a game?" Simon asked. "I mean, did they volunteer… or do they ever wake up?"

"When has the Science Guild ever taken volunteers? I doubt they know they're in a game, but who knows?"

"Hey guys!" Alvin said in exasperation. "What if *we're* in a game? What if all these missions are simulations, like—"

"Shut up, Alvin," Theodore said. "This isn't Buff Orpington and the Talented Technicians of Trojan's Tacticians. We're not going to suddenly learn we're in a simulation."

"Yeah, that's absurd," Simon said, though doubt crept in. He pinched himself for good measure.

A soft clang echoed from the opposite end of the walkway. Three walkways over, an albino XenSha in an immaculate white lab coat had opened a hatch and walked in from the other side. Tentacles waving in a hypnotic pattern, it alternated its attention between the screens, the creatures below, and its slate.

Theodore waved his hands down and put a finger to his lips. Slowly and cautiously, he stepped along the walkway to line up with the XenSha.

A K'kng huffed and shuffled. Simon glanced at it to ensure it wasn't waking. When he looked back at the XenSha, the XenSha was looking at *him*.

"Stop!" Theodore shouted with his pistol raised.

Tentacles flailing, the XenSha ignored him, and took off running.

"We're late!" it screamed.

"Back!" Alvin shouted. "Head him off at the pass!"

Simon ran back along the walkway to parallel the XenSha's course. When he returned to the hallway, the XenSha was clearing its own hatch and turning to run. He aimed his pistol and repeated Theodore's call to stop, with a similar lack of success.

"We're too late!" it repeated as it ran.

"Follow him!" Theodore said.

Simon in the lead, the trio sprinted after the white XenSha as fast as their legs could carry them. The XenSha disappeared around a corner, but Simon found it again heading up a flight of stairs. He leaped atop the railing, jumped onto a wire mesh fence in the middle, and scampered up the side faster than the XenSha could climb. From the rattle of metal below, Simon knew his companions were keeping up.

In this manner, Simon closed to within half a stairwell by the time the XenSha reached a door at the top. When it pushed through, Simon was only a meter behind it. A bright white light flashed, blinding Simon.

His body went numb as the light turned to darkness.

* * *

Up the XenSha Hole

Simon blinked and let his eyes adjust. He tried to rub his eyes, but his wrists wouldn't budge.

"Welcome back, Subject Five Six Four Two One Seven," the albino XenSha said. "You're coming to just in time to witness my cunning trap."

The XenSha waved his hands across a row of slates. He watched a line of screens hanging from the ceiling which showed CASPers and Goka flooding unopposed through the facility. There weren't any MinSha on any of the screens, though every so often he spotted a XenSha firing a pistol and running away. From the looks of it, the Badass Blades and Combat Wombats had essentially won.

Two well-armed XenSha stood on either side of the room, their attention focused on Simon. Beyond them, transparent but dimmed windows sloped around the edges of the room. Simon concluded they must be at the pinnacle of the pyramid.

As Simon struggled with his restraints to no avail, he racked his mind for a brilliant plan to escape his bonds.

What would Buff Orpington do?

Naturally, the dashing hero would have a means of picking his restraints cleverly hidden in the cuffs of his shirt. Simon did not have cuffs, much less lock picks hidden in them.

Can I chew my way through the restraints?

It wasn't a classic Buff Orpington move, but it should be do-able for a Flatar. However, he realized he couldn't move his neck either. Worse, he had one of those shiny helmets on his head.

Quick! What else would Buff Orpington do?

In Buff Orpington and the Evil Penguin Doctor, Buff cleverly talked his way out of his predicament.

"And you are?" Simon asked.

"Not that it matters to you, but I am Klidek Rashkip, the director of this facility." The XenSha continued to wave his hands at the screens as he spoke. Simon noted every time he waved a hand, a door either opened or closed.

He's trying to direct the movements of the Blades and Wombats.

"Why does it not matter to me?" Simon asked.

"Because you've failed," Director Rashkip said. "Your presumptive rescue will soon be crushed by my hordes of test subjects. You've done nothing more than provide me with *more* test subjects. Humans and Goka alike will be truly interesting. Humans are well-known for their adaptability, but also for their blind faith in believing whatever they see. I can play with that to no end. Meanwhile, the Goka are remarkably resilient, but I'll get some wonderful data from testing the bounds of that resilience."

"You can control them?" Simon asked. "Like cyber zombies?"

"Of course," the director said. "I can make them think or do anything I want. Like swarm your attacking force, casualties be damned."

Just like the attack on Tambu. What is it with the Science Guild and cyber zombies?

Out of the corner of Simon's vision, something thrashed and metal rattled.

"I'll kill you before you do," Theodore growled.

"I appreciate the spirit, new test subject, but even if you could do so, I wouldn't advise it. The survival of this facility is tied to my vital statistics. Kill me and you'll have a nuclear meltdown on your hands."

Nuclear meltdown if he dies, really? This whole situation feels so much like a Buff Orpington plot.

"Evil like yours never triumphs!" Theodore shouted. "You're destined to lose!"

Even Theodore's dialogue felt like something out of a Buff Orpington script.

Buff would keep him talking. Distract the evil mastermind from springing his trap until Buff found a way out.

"Did Minerva set that up?" Simon asked.

The XenSha froze.

"Where did you hear that name?"

"Oh, everyone knows about Minerva. In fact, we were sent here to destroy Minerva."

The director's head twitched, and he returned to gesturing at the screens.

"Imbecile. That's not possible. But even if you could, Minerva is not here. Hasn't been here for quite some time, in fact." The XenSha's eyes darted around in what looked to be fear. "Though I remain Minerva's faithful servant and will preserve this research facility until my master returns. To which end, I'm almost ready. Soon, I'll eviscerate your friends. Then, your reality will be whatever I want it to be."

An idea worthy of Buff Orpington appeared in Simon's head.

"How do you know Minerva didn't already do that to *you*?" Simon asked.

The XenSha's ministrations slowed, and the tentacles drooped. "What?"

"How do you know *you're* not in a simulation? One run by Minerva? How would you know?"

The director dropped his hands and turned to glare. Simon could see doubt joining the fear in the XenSha's eyes.

"Absurd." The XenSha straightened and returned his attention yet again to the screens. "And stop stalling. Let me defeat these interlopers, then I'll finish converting you two."

Two?

Simon strained to look off to his sides. He could barely make out Theodore to his left but couldn't see anything to his right.

Boom!

Smoke and debris burst into the room.

Crack!

One of the armed XenSha dropped. The other raised his laser rifle and fired lances of light at some unseen targets.

"Missed, sucker!" Alvin shouted.

Crack!

The other armed XenSha was torn off the floor and thrown against the far wall.

The director took two rapid steps toward the first dead guard.

"Don't try it," Alvin said.

There was a hiss and a clank to the left. Theodore sprang to his feet and rushed to one of the control consoles. With another hiss and clank, the shiny dome lifted from Simon's head. His restraints sprang apart and Simon was free.

"Good job, Alvin!"

"I know, right? It's the first time that being last worked out for me."

Simon moved next to Theodore, who tapped and swiped at the row of slates.

"Help me, Simon! We need to figure out how to release all those poor test subjects!"

Staring at the screens, Simon didn't have the slightest clue how to control anything. Theodore hit every icon he could find, but all he did was randomly open and close doors throughout the facility. Scanning the row of slates, Simon noticed something curious *wasn't* there.

"Maybe this big, red button?" Simon asked.

Theodore stopped. On the center pedestal, between the two middle slates, was a big, red button. It reminded Simon of the ubiquitous button from nearly every Buff Orpington movie.

"There's no way to know what that does," Theodore said.

"Then, by all means, hit it," Director Rashkip said snidely.

"Don't do it," Alvin said. "If he wants you to hit it, it's obviously some kind of trick!"

"Unless that's what he wants me to think," Simon said. He hit the button.

All the screens went blank, followed a moment later by the message, "Emergency Simulation Shutdown."

The screens flashed again, now displaying the bays where the test subjects had stood wired into their endless fantasies. The helmets lifted and the various beings blinked, shifted, and looked around. Most shuddered in confusion or fear, though some had expressions of growing rage.

"Huh, that was surprisingly easy," Theodore said. "And it's all too convenient, kind of like a Buff Orpington Tri-V."

"It was, wasn't it?" Simon said. "Kind of makes you wonder if we're actually in a simulation ourselves, doesn't it?"

"Maybe it is," Director Rashkip said with a sneer.

"How can we know for sure?" Theodore asked with a gulp, his eyes wide.

"I got this!" Alvin yelled.

Crack!

The director staggered back and clutched his chest. Blood soaked into the white lab coat around the edges of his fingers.

"Alvin, no!" Theodore shouted.

"What, why?" Alvin asked. "If this is a simulation, he's the boss. We win the boss battle, we win the game, right?"

Klaxons blared and red lights flashed.

"Facility destruction sequence activated. Total nuclear meltdown will occur in three hundred seconds. All personnel evacuate. Facility destruction sequence activated. Total nuclear meltdown will occur in two-hundred ninety-five seconds..."

"Because that," Theodore said. "Duck me."

"Duck?" Alvin asked.

"Shoshanna doesn't like swearing."

"In fairness to Alvin, I thought he was bluffing," Simon said.

"That doesn't help," Theodore said. "But more importantly, this place is a labyrinth! How are we gonna make it out?"

Simon grabbed Alvin's hypervelocity pistol and shot the nearest window. It didn't shatter, but the shot did smash a hole. Wind whistled in and loose debris swirled into the air.

"Out and down the side!" Simon shouted as he broke out a larger hole.

Simon and Alvin pushed Theodore through the hole and then climbed out after him. Theodore tumbled down the sharp slope, screaming curses as he went. Alvin deftly ran down without any problem, whereas Simon fell into a middle ground. He'd keep his footing for a few steps, slide or roll for a bit, and then find his footing again.

Below, chaos reigned as beings of all race and size, MinSha and XenSha included, flooded out of the pyramid. Goka, red and black Badass Blades CASPers, and green and gray Combat Wombat CASPers did their best to funnel and corral the mass, but it was a losing battle.

Alvin, Simon, and Theodore rushed down the side. Once clear, they ran to where they'd left the hover bike and found it was still flyable. They flew to the nearest Combat Wombat dropship and hurried aboard. The Human female pilot who'd crashed the dropship earlier tugged at another Human's arm and shouted.

"I told you! I told you it was there when I did the preflight! I told you I saw three chipmunks… Flatar, *whatever*!"

Simon shrugged an apology and found a spot to strap in.

* * *

Debrief

The three Flatar were stacked up again, this time at the door to Bull's office. They had their ears pressed against the door to hear the conversation between Patches and Bull.

"Are you fucking kidding me, Bull? Again?" Patches asked.

"Wish I was, but are you really surprised?" the gruff man replied. "This whole Phoenix Initiative, as necessary and well intentioned as it may be, is still the perfect opportunity for our SI friends or any other nefarious entities to resume their age old dirty tricks on unsuspecting new units. I'm not saying all the new startup companies are getting targeted, but some sure as shit are. I'll bet your ass the Silverhawks are the canary in the coal mine, and they were a veteran company. We'll need to find out what happened there, sooner rather than later."

"Okay, but if you're saying there's gonna be more than one asshole out there trying to stick it to Phoenix startups, are you planning to just stick more fingers in the dike until you're soaked?"

"And they say *my* analogies are too off color," Bull replied. "But yes. With all the rebuilt companies and contacts at my disposal, we'll play our best whack-a-mole as intel rolls in. That said, are you ready to report on the fucktard op?"

"Why's he reporting on that?" Alvin asked. "It was our op!"

"Maybe he had his own mission?" Theodore offered.

"Well, there was no sign of Minerva, as you predicted," Patches said.

Alvin shifted so much, Simon wavered while holding on, causing Theodore to stagger back a step.

"I knew it!" Alvin said. "He sent the crusty old man in on the same mission! Move me closer again, Theodore! What are you doing back there?"

Alvin leaned hard for the door. Simon tried to hold him back, but the weight shift was too much for Theodore. All three crashed against the door and tumbled into a heap.

"Think he heard us?" Alvin asked as he rubbed his head.

The door swung inward.

"Apologies, Commodore, I shouldn't have started the debrief without you," Bull said. He waved a hand to invite them inside. "Please."

"Who's that?" Patches said, turning and scratching he back of his neck. "Oh yeah, your distraction team."

"We're not the—" Alvin said until another wave of Bull's hand cut him off.

"My primary team," Bull said. "For whom the assault was a distraction and you were the backup."

Something about Bull's tone sounded funny, but Alvin was placated, so Simon let it go.

"Oh yeah, my bad," Patches said.

"Commodore Alvin, please report," Bull said.

Alvin straightened to his full height, ran a hand through his fur, and turned to Theodore.

"Theo, report."

"Yes, of course. Mister Bull, first, there was no sign of any SI. In fact, the director of the facility seemed somewhat perturbed and disoriented by Minerva's absence. Second, we directly witnessed neurological experiments on a wide range of species. It seemed to be the primary purpose of the facility. The Badass Blades and Combat Wombats collected the survivors, Arronax is assessing them now."

"Excellent work," Bull said. "Were you able to download their research data?"

Theodore shuffled and shot a death glare at Alvin.

"No, sir. Al—uh, a self-destruct sequence was activated before we could access the facility's data."

"Really?" Bull said with a raised eyebrow. "Any idea why?"

"No, sir!" Alvin said a little too loudly while returning Theodore's death glare.

Bull nodded and turned toward Patches.

"How about my backup plan?"

"Yeah, what do you take me for? I got the research files."

The large bald man moved back to his desk and sat.

"Great to hear. Commodore, I've already got another quick mission for you and your companions. A simple message delivery. Beyond that, brace yourselves. Based on a few of the first Phoenix Initiative contracts, we might have our work cut out for us in the near future."

* * * * *

Casey Moores Bio

Casey Moores was a USAF rescue/special ops C-130 pilot for over 17 years—airdropping, air refueling, and flying into tiny, blacked-out, dirt airstrips in bad places using night vision goggles. He's been to *those* places and done *those* things with *those* people. Now he lives a quieter life, translating those experiences into military science fiction, fantasy, alternate history, and post-apocalyptic fiction. With seven novels and over twenty published short stories, his biggest challenge is focusing on any one genre. Or focusing on anything at all, really.

Casey is the winner of the Imaginarium Imadjinn Awards Best Historical Fiction for *Witch Hunt*, a story about monster-hunting marines in the Civil War from Three Ravens Publishing's JTF-13 series. The prequel story, "Blood Sacrifice," was published in the Helicon award-winning *JTF-13 Legends* anthology.

For Chris Kennedy Publishing, he's written in the Four Horsemen universe with numerous novels and short stories, primarily about Bull and his black ops rescue company. He also has a novel, *The Guilted Cage*, set in the Fallen World universe at his alma mater, the Air Force Academy, as well as short stories in the Fallen World and Salvage System universes.

Finally, he has numerous stories out in his Deathmage War fantasy series, two of which—"A Quaint Pastime" and "The Unwanted Legion"—were finalists in the annual FantaSci fantasy story contest.

He's recently begun a near-future military science fiction series with Bill Fawcett.

A Colorado native and Air Force Academy graduate, he's now semi-retired in New Mexico.

Find him at www.caseymoores.net.

#####

Duck Me by Melissa Olthoff

Karma Station

Bartertown

I should've known better when *Rebel* of all people wanted to go out drinking.

"Who names their bar 'The Sand Trap?'" I complained as my best friend dragged me through the door.

Charlee "Rebel" Holliday grinned over her shoulder. "Retired mercs who don't give a fuck what newbs who just earned their wings think."

I rolled my eyes and let her tug me through the rowdy bar. Normally, I'd be the one dragging her out for some fun, but I hadn't felt like partying tonight. She hadn't taken no for an answer. Again, that should've been a giant fucking cluebird.

The Sand Trap catered to Human mercs, but there were other races mingling with the predominantly Human crowd. At one end of the bar, a small pack of Zuul played flip cup with a trio of SalSha and a couple of Humans. As I slipped past an Equiri, shouts and good-natured heckling drew my attention to the left side of the bar, where a pair of Lumar were absolutely killing it in the cornhole competition.

Rebel made a beeline for an elSha standing on a high-top table near the bar and slipped him a credit chit. He gave her a toothy grin and hopped down, leaving the empty table to us.

"Okay, this place is pretty cool." I slid onto my barstool and pinned Rebel with a firm stare. "But just one drink. I've got to be up early."

"Come on, Bree, lighten up a little." The elSha trotted back with a beer in each hand and set them on the table with a wink. Rebel tipped him with another credit chit and slid a beer over to me with a grin. "Who knows when we'll get the chance to drink together again."

I shot her a pointed look and rapped on the table, despite the fact that it wasn't real wood. "Don't jinx us like that."

"Superstitious bullshit." Rebel snorted dismissively but knocked on the table too. "You could've been in the Silverhawks with me, you know. Better contracts, better pay… but no, you had to go for the Phoenix Initiative start up."

I tapped my fingers on the cool bottle. "I didn't want charity. I can stand on my own, thanks."

"It wouldn't have been charity, dumbass." Rebel scowled and rested her forearms on the table. "Your VOWS were great—you would've gotten in on your own merits with no *charity* from me. Now you've got to suffer the growing pains of a new unit. Like a dumbass."

I just shrugged. "The Phoenix Initiative is a good idea. I'm right where I want to be."

If anything, Rebel's scowl deepened. "What the hell is a Combat Wombat, anyway?"

"As of last week, *me*," I replied cheerfully. "Wallace's Combat Wombats might be new, but the commander's experienced, and he's got a lot of veteran mercs mixed in with newbs like me. Something about stiffening the buckwheat with buckshot."

Rebel shook her head, the beginnings of a smile breaking through. "Okay, buckwheat, it's your life. Just no dying on your first contract. You come back in one piece."

"Only if you come back too."

Rebel picked up her beer and held it up. "No promises."

I lifted my own beer with a grin. "No promises."

It's what she said to me every time she went out on a contract. It was the first time we'd said it to each other. We clinked our bottles together and drank.

A smirk pulled at my lips, and I tilted my head to the side. "That hottie over at the bar is checking you out."

Rebel glanced over and immediately turned her nose up. "I wouldn't touch anyone from *that* company for all the credits in the galaxy." The only thing I could make out on his patch was an orange and black cat of some sort. "Besides, girl, tonight's about *you*."

There was something evil in her grin that set off the alarm bells. "No."

"Yes," she said triumphantly as a frosty bottle of Jeremiah Weed was slammed onto the table by my new dropship commander, Captain Samuel "Mace" Wendel.

I glared at my former best friend. "Traitor."

Rebel smacked Mace's shoulder. "Just helping out an old friend."

A group of pilots from the Wombats crowded close, herding two other newbies, Francis Burns and Toshiro Inoue, with them. Rebel produced three shot glasses from who knew where and set them on the table in front of us.

"Okay, you nameless fucks. You know the rules." She poured the first round of shots. "Toast before you drink. If you don't like your name, you can drink to get another one." Her smirk said there'd be many stupid names before they got to the real ones they'd already picked. "Let the naming commence."

Burns picked up his shot glass and took a tentative sniff. "Oh hell."

"Don't smell it, man." Inoue grabbed his with a grimace. "Just swallow."

"That's what she said." I raised my shot glass and called the first toast. "Here's to honor..."

"*...Get honor, stay honor, and if you can't come in her, come honor!*" We all roared and knocked the shots back. It tasted like jet fuel and regret.

I squinted at Rebel through watering eyes. "Why the hell do we drink this shit again?"

She grinned. "Because it tastes like fuck."

* * *

The next morning, I woke up to the hangover from hell, the taste of misery in my mouth, and my best friend standing over my bed with a shit-eating grin on her face. I winced at the bright light and groaned.

"Why is there a rubber duck on my chest?" I eyed it suspiciously when it started to vibrate. "Please tell me this thing is new."

Rebel snickered. "You called yourself an awkward duck last night after you accidentally punched Burns in the balls. Twice. You meant 'drunk' but then we made you sing the Rubber Duckie song." Her grin widened. "Which you did, at full volume, while standing on top of the bar."

I tried to bury my face in my hands, but she wasn't having it. She grabbed my arms and yanked me upright. The whole damn room spun, and my guts tried to crawl into my throat.

"I hate you."

"Yeah, sweetie, I know you do." Smug didn't begin to adequately describe her expression. "But you need to get your ass in gear or you're going to be late."

I stared at her, my brain still swimming in the fumes of too much crap alcohol to comprehend what she meant. Then my eyes bulged, and I lurched out of bed.

"Shit!"

She grabbed my shoulder when my knees threatened to dump my ass straight to the floor. "Easy there, killer. You got this?"

"Fuck yeah, I got this," I muttered as I swept my chin-length hair out of my face.

She slapped my shoulder when I managed to stand unsupported, though puking was still a very real possibility. I'd been smart enough to pack before I let Rebel drag me out, so I just needed to get dressed—and find my lucky coin. *Where is it…*

I dug through last night's dirty clothes and relief shot through me as my fingers closed around the cool metal. It was my luck talisman and insurance all rolled into one, and there was no way in hell I was going out on my first contract without it.

Rebel watched in amusement as I zipped it into my inner pocket and jammed my feet into my boots. She tapped her wrist. "Five minutes."

"Fuck your five minutes," I growled and grabbed my gear. "I'm ready."

"Atta girl," she said with a wide grin that did nothing to hide the pride in her gaze. "Have fun on your first contract. Ducky."

I blinked down at the nametape she'd crookedly velcroed to my shoulder. "…fuck me."

"That's what the duck is for."

She ran out of my room with a cackle, just barely avoiding the stupid duck I threw at her face. It hit the doorframe, bounced on the floor a few times, and started vibrating again. Despite my pounding head, I cracked up. I really did have the best friend.

* * *

Solstice

Mategir System

The trip through hyperspace was uneventful. Possibly because I'd spent most of the time hiding in my bunk recovering. I knew I needed sleep when I saw a trio of Flatar dressed in red, blue, and green run through the chow hall on the first day. Nobody else seemed to notice them, so I went back to bed.

Rather than use our own ship, we were berthed on the *Solstice*, the armed transport ship utilized by the Badass Blades, another new merc company formed from the remnants of the Bushido Bandits and the Bladestorm. While it wasn't odd for two merc units to come together—so to speak—they were definitely unique. Not only was it rumored the two companies had nearly destroyed each other shortly before they'd merged, one company was comprised of *Goka*.

The Blades had accepted an assault contract on an old Science Guild facility located on an otherwise uninhabited planet. Guarded by MinSha and staffed by XenSha, the anticipated force was too big for them to handle alone, so they'd subcontracted us to assist.

A few hours ago, we'd emerged into the Mategir system and were getting our final briefing by our commander.

"The Combat Wombats will conduct a low altitude drop via the Phoenix dropships, while the Badass Blades will HALD in." Colonel Dave Wallace paced across the front of the briefing room as he spoke.

"The timing will be a one-two punch, otherwise we'll be all asses and elbows with our penguins eaten by the hippos."

The man was incredibly intelligent, and a seasoned commander. He also occasionally talked in jumbled up metaphors that made zero sense. None of the seasoned vets seemed bothered by his... unique method of communication.

One of the other pilots, Quirk, raised a hand. "Sir, how are the Goka getting to the facility?"

The veteran pilot sounded wary, and I honestly couldn't blame her. I didn't want them on my ship either with their creepy eyes and stabby blades.

Wallace grinned. "As I've already briefed, the Blades will HALD in. All of them."

"With the *CASPers*, sir?"

"Apparently, it's now a thing they do." He shrugged. "Our job is to engage the MinSha so they land in one piece. Once on the ground, they'll act as the shock troops and smash through the line. We'll exploit the openings and push deeper into the facility in a coordinated assault. Our dropships will gather here." He pointed at a location on the map well away from the facility. "And will extract everyone once the mission is complete..."

He kept talking, but I zoned out again.

Blah blah blah, get stupid CASPers to drop point, fly away, pick everyone up when it's over, big damn heroes.

I swore I felt my eyes glaze over as the commander went off on some tangent about shady employers and a chipmunk, of all things.

"Not sure why the chipmunk thinks he's in charge, but Colonel Adams of the Blades seems to humor him for some reason." He shook his head. "The shady employer part is slightly more concerning, but I have every confidence the Blades can hold up their part of the plan…"

I slumped low in my seat as he droned on about details outside my realm of give a shit.

Mace elbowed my side. "Pay attention, Ducky."

I grimaced and sat up straighter with some effort. It had been nearly a week since my naming, and I swore I was still hungover.

Wallace frowned at a question from someone in the front and shook his head. "No, there's too many penguins on the iceberg for that to work. We'll have alligators circling the canoes before you know it."

Um, what?

I shot Mace a confused glance, half convinced I'd misheard thanks to my lingering headache. "Translation?"

He snorted a quiet laugh. "Don't worry about it. Just stick to the plan and we'll be fine." As the briefing wrapped up, he arched a brow. "Remind me what the plan is again."

I sighed. "We reenter atmo in a low-threat area, fly in low and fast along our predesignated route, drop off our CASPers and rendezvous with the rest of the Phoenix dropships until it's time to pick them back up. I got it."

"Great. You've also got preflight. Don't fuck it up."

Down in the dropship bay, I ran into the other newbs from our naming buffoonery.

Burns, who'd been saddled with the unfortunate callsign Fancy, grinned. "And how is everyone this fine day?"

Toshiro "Tex" Inoue stared at him with a blank expression. "Fuck off, Fancy."

"Oh, come on, Tex, it's our first contract. You should try smiling." When that didn't happen, the wiry man waggled his eyebrows at me. "How 'bout you, Ducky? How you doing?"

"Living the dream." I pulled up the preflight checklists on my slate. "So, burning question. Why was Colonel Wallace talking about a chipmunk, and does the chipmunk really think he's in charge of this op?"

"That's two questions," Tex said without an ounce of humor. "He was talking about one because he's part of the command staff. I think."

Fancy chuckled. "There's actually three of them on board. He must've meant Alvin. Aren't they Flatar though?"

"I dunno man, I'm still hungover."

Tex glanced up from his slate. "It's been almost a week. That's not possible."

"Tell that to my headache," I shot back before I paused. "Wait, there really are three of them? Holy fuck, I thought I was hallucinating. So there's a trio of Flatar pretending to be chipmunks? Why the hell would they do that?"

Tex shrugged. "Who gives a shit so long as they don't get in the way? All we need to do is keep our heads down, do our jobs, and get paid. We don't even have to kill aliens, we just ferry the fuckers who do. You copy?"

I grinned. "Hell yeah, I copy."

I returned to preflighting with a bounce in my step, more energized than I'd felt in days. As I rounded the rear of my dropship, I was greeted by the sight of a walking, wobbling trench coat. A legit trench coat with a hood and… eyes? I blinked, rubbed my own eyes, and blinked again. There was nothing there. Cautiously, I walked up the open ramp and stuck my head in the cargo compartment.

"Uh... hello?"

Still a whole lot of nothing.

Clearly, the aftereffects of too much Jeremiah Weed hadn't worn off yet. I made a mental note to hydrate when I was done with the preflight and stuck my nose back in my checklist.

As long as my head was clear when we made our drop, everything would be fine.

* * *

Phoenix Dropship, Whiskey Two
Rubired

Our reentry through Rubired's atmosphere was uncontested. Mace was old and crusty, so we had the honor of flying on the formation commander's wing. All eight drop ships routed through a post re-entry rally point, then we split up along our individual flight paths to get our complement of CASPer drivers to their low altitude drop point.

We had a dozen in the back under the command of Sergeant Keiser. Listening in on their comms proved entertaining, and also made me exceedingly grateful I wasn't ground infantry.

We flew through the scrub lands, barely clearing the scraggly trees that struggled to grow in the arid environment. This was my favorite kind of flying—hugging the ground, balls to the wall, with little room for error. My grin stretched ear to ear, because Mace had let me fly my cherry drop. He must've figured it was a low-threat insertion, and I wasn't about to complain.

Everything went exactly according to plan. Right up until it didn't.

A missile lock tone blared through the cockpit, a deafening screech that sent my heart rate into overdrive.

"Break left!"

Mace's scream jolted my frozen brain into action. Everything felt like it was moving in slow motion. Honestly, I was shocked he didn't take the controls, but I didn't have time to question his command decision.

As I wrenched the dropship into a steep left bank and fought to keep it level, Mace dumped countermeasures. The missile tone went silent for a single second before blaring again.

"Second missile locked!"

This time I didn't need his instructions. Fear sharpened my reflexes, and I broke right as Mace released another round of countermeasures. My hands tightened on the controls when the missile tone didn't stop. *Come on… come on!*

I'd never been more aware of the cargo we carried.

Mace snarled and dumped a third round. The blaring tone finally fell silent as the missile bit off on the chaff, but it detonated too close, and our engines were fragged by the resultant shrapnel. The blast knocked us into a spin, and I gritted my teeth as I fought to recover and get the wings level again. We were *not* losing any of our troops before we'd even made it to the battle.

Dropships had less than zero glide capability, though, and we were pretty much a brick without thrust. Somehow, I managed to get the belly flat and the nose up before we slammed into the ground.

It wasn't my prettiest landing ever, but we were in one piece. I exchanged a shaky grin with Mace and activated the comm for the cargo compartment. "Everyone okay back there?"

"For now. You're not going to try to kill us again, are you?" Sergeant Keiser grumbled.

Alive. They were alive. I slumped back in my seat and patted the pocket with my lucky coin, as if the damn thing had anything to do with us not dying.

"No appreciation."

Mace took over on the comm. "Get the hell off my bird, Sergeant. She ain't flying again today. Keep your eyes up, whatever shot us down might not have been an automated defense." He switched to the command freq. "Whiskey Two is down, zero fatalities. We'll head in overland, ETA unknown."

"Wombat Actual, acknowledged. All other ships made their drops and reached the rendezvous point."

Because of *course* they did.

"Ditch the canoe, watch out for gators, and get those penguins to the iceberg!"

"Understood. Whiskey Two out." Mace blew out a breath and thumped my shoulder. "Not bad, Ducky. Just… maybe don't mention I let you fly."

I raised my brows. "Why did you?"

"As a lesson." Something grim touched his expression. "Just because something starts out as a cakewalk doesn't mean things can't go sideways *fast*."

As the CASPers dropped the ramp and evac'd, we shut everything down. I checked the charge on my laser pistol and followed Mace off the ship. Despite the dry heat, I shivered and tried not to feel naked with just a helmet and body armor over my flight suit.

The surrounding scrub looked as uninhabited as every other bit of land we'd flown over, with no sign of whoever had shot us down. Sergeant Keiser had most of his CASPers deployed in a defensive formation around the rear of the dropship while two others worked to unload supply crates. It was mostly extra ammo that was supposed to drop with them. While other ships would've dropped supplies of their own, our troops would need to ruck in as much as possible. Or at least, that's what I gathered from the sergeant's barked orders.

The two CASPers strode past me carrying one of the bigger crates between them. So, at the light patter of footsteps on the ramp, I spun around with my gun up. There shouldn't be anything on the ship right now, but I was ready for anything—anything but a trio of Flatar in red, blue, and green battle armor. One darted up to me with a hypervelocity pistol in hand. I was so dumbfounded it didn't even occur to me he might be a threat.

Fortunately, he just smacked my leg and said, "Nice flying, Ace!"

My jaw dropped. "Screw you, buddy."

At a loud bang, I whipped my head around, but it was just the CASPers dropping the heavy crate with the rest of the supplies. When I looked back down, all three had vanished.

"Did anybody else see that?"

Mace glanced over from where he conferred with Sergeant Keiser. "See what?"

"Chipmunks… fuck, I mean Flatar in battle armor. I swear to God I just saw three of them run off."

"Did you hit your skull, Ducky?" He scrutinized me with a concerned frown. "There aren't any Flatar on this op. Get your noggin in the game."

I stared at him flatly. "You can say 'head' you know."

The older man grinned. "No. No, I can't."

Over the wireless comms built into my helmet, somebody bellowed, "*Contact!*"

The call was accompanied by the roar of MAC rounds unleashed on the enemy. I tried to run up the ramp, but Mace grabbed my arm and hauled me behind the haphazard pile of crates.

"Wouldn't it be safer back on the dropship?" I flinched as a round pinged off the top of a crate. "At least it's not a literal pile of *ammo*!"

Mace stared at me. "Yes, because sitting inside a fat, stationary target is so much better."

Over the comm the sergeant barked orders. It was all a jumble of infantry terminology I didn't even try to understand. All that mattered to me was the last bit.

"*Simmons, Bash, guard our squishables.*"

The two CASPers who'd been unloading stationed themselves near our highly explosive cover before firing MAC rounds of their own. When Mace leaned out to one side and fired his laser pistol, I put on my big girl panties and did the same. At the sight of the towering, mantis-like MinSha, two emotions battled for dominance—entirely reasonable fear, and annoyance. As my second and third shots reflected off carapace, annoyance won.

I ducked back behind the crate and glared at my laser pistol. *Fuck me, I need a bigger gun.*

"Gotta aim for the joints or the eyes," Mace shouted.

I barely heard him over the overwhelming sound of the battle. It was so much louder than I'd thought it'd be. The roar of the MACs, the lighter rattle of machine guns, the pops and snaps of lasers, all punctuated by the occasional blast of a K-bomb, had my ears ringing. The noise was like a living thing, invading my brain and making it so damn hard to think. So I stopped trying.

I leaned around the crate when I could, squeezed off shots when I could, and actually remembered to swap out my mag when the first tapped out on me. The CASPer on my left ran out of ammo for his MAC and snapped out his arm blade, while the one on my right fired at a slower rate and tossed a K-bomb like it was a party favor.

A MinSha leaped to the top of the pile of crates and looked down at us. Maybe she thought the CASPers were guarding something more important than two squishable dropship pilots. Maybe she was just looking for an easy target. It didn't matter. The CASPer driver slammed his blade through her side and flung her into the thick of the fight, where another CASPer dropped her permanently with a few well-placed MAC rounds.

While he was distracted, a second MinSha jumped onto his back. Before she could fire her rifle at close range, the CASPer on my right leaned over, snatched her with one hand and slammed her into the side of my dropship.

"Damn it, isn't my poor ship busted up enough?" I shrieked. If he heard me, he didn't give a fuck. He kept bashing her until she stopped struggling. Then he did it a few more times for good measure.

Oh, holy fuck that's gross.

Even a grizzled vet like Mace looked a little grossed out at the broad smear of blue blood and bug guts all over the side of our ship. "Nasty."

"Nice one, Bash."

The CASPer chucked what remained of the alien into the brush. *"Thanks."*

In the next instant, everything stopped. No more rounds fired, no more stomping CASPers or charging MinSha, no more explosions. My ears ached in the silence. Cautiously, I leaned around the crates and stared at the carnage. When Mace holstered his pistol, I followed suit. It took me three tries.

Simmons flicked his combat blade, sending a spray of blue blood flying, then retracted it with a snap. I swallowed hard as nausea rose and focused on the CASPer stalking over to us instead.

Mace gave him a calm nod. "Status, Sergeant?"

"No casualties on our side, but we're banged up for sure. Just our dumb luck to fly right over a gods damned MinSha patrol," Sergeant Keiser said. *"And where there was one, there might be others. You two should come with us. It's not safe for you to stay here."*

Mace shook his head. "Thanks, Sergeant, but we can head to the drop ship rendezvous point. Ducky, go grab our gear and prep the ECEV."

I blinked at him. "Huh?"

Mace slapped me on the shoulder. Hard. "Mental breakdown later, Ducky, gear and ECEV now."

"Right… right." I nodded my head jerkily and trotted up the still open ramp without looking around too much. There were some things I didn't really want to see. My steps slowed when I got near the Emergency Crew Equipment compartment. The door was ajar, as if somebody had already rifled through it. I brushed it aside as unimportant for now and jerked the handle for the Emergency Crew Evacuation Vehicle.

"Stupid name," I muttered as the handle stuck. I threw my weight into it and the panel slammed to the deck. "Should have just called it a hover…"

The compartment was empty.

I checked the compartment's external hatch to see if it'd been damaged in the crash and maybe the bike had fallen out, but it was secure. I glowered at the empty space for a long moment before I swore viciously and nutted up. A sharp breath, and I marched out of the ship to give Mace the good news.

"How can it just be gone?"

Nothing. I had nothing.

"Damn it, Ducky." Mace grumbled. "I told you not to fuck up the preflight."

My jaw clenched. "I swear it was there when I preflighted the ship!"

"You also swear you saw a trio of chipmunks in battle armor," he said with a strange glint in his eyes before he turned to the sergeant. "Fucking copilots, I tell ya. Looks like we're going with you after all. Can we get a lift?"

"*Not a problem, sir.*" The sergeant paused. "*Once we reach the facility, we can't guarantee your safety.*"

Mace strode over to one of the dead MinSha, picked up her rifle, and checked the charge. "I'm aware."

"*Simmons, Bash! Finish reloading and get your asses over here. You're on squishable duty for the rest of the op.*"

"Great, if one of them dies it'll be our fault," Simmons muttered as he stomped over.

"*Shut your cakehole, Simmons.*" Bash crouched down. "*Hop on, honey.*"

I rolled my eyes. "How long have you been waiting to use that line?"

I could hear the grin in his voice. "*All my life.*"

"*That's obvious,*" Simmons muttered as he crouched so Mace could swarm up the back. I tried to copy his handholds and prayed I wouldn't do something embarrassing—like fall on my ass.

Mace looked over with a smirk. "If you weren't already named Ducky, we could call you Piggyback."

"Respectfully—fuck you, sir."

* * *

Suspicious Science Guild Facility
Rubired

The march to the Science Guild facility sucked. If there was any way I could've kept up with the CASPers on foot, I would've dropped off Bash's back in a heartbeat. We hadn't crashed too far from the drop point, and they were hustling to make up for lost time. By the end of the day, I'd probably be one giant bruise... assuming I survived. I hadn't signed up for ground combat for *reasons*, damn it. *Stupid MinSha patrol.*

After a short eternity of misery, a shining citadel appeared on the horizon. It was the only marker of civilization we'd seen on this god-forsaken rock, and it shone like a beacon in the hot sun. I wiped the sweat off my face and blinked my eyes clear. *Yep, that's really a no-shit pyramid in the middle of nowhere. Because that's not suspicious at all.*

By the time we were in range, the rest of the Combat Wombats had already engaged the MinSha defenders. I flinched as a CASPer staggered backward and fell.

I knew casualties were expected on an assault contract, but I hadn't expected to see them up close. Silently, I urged him to get up again... but he didn't.

Ten CASPers bounded forward, while Simmons and Bash hung back so we could dismount. Mace dropped to the ground like he rode CASPers into battle every day. I jumped down with a wince and quietly hated life for a long moment.

"Look up," Mace said.

I craned my neck back and gaped. We'd arrived just in time to see the Blades HALD in. The battle had subtly shifted in our favor when our CASPers had joined the fight. The arrival of the Blades decisively turned the tide.

"*Damn, that's badass. I want shoulder-mounted Goka for my CASPer,*" Bash said.

Simmons turned toward him. "*Do you? Do you really?*"

We all watched as a pair of Goka swarmed a MinSha and kept right on moving, leaving a bloody corpse in their wake.

"*Uh, maybe not.*"

I drew my laser pistol and watched wide-eyed as the defenders fell back toward the pyramid gates. "Hey, Mace… are we the bad guys?"

He gave me a distracted frown. "Just because we're assaulting the facility doesn't make us the bad guys."

"Yeah, but we have Goka." I shuddered as another pair of Goka scuttled past, stabby blades in their hands. Claws? "Lots of Goka."

"Just be glad they're on our side." He cast a pointed glance at the Blades' CASPers. "All of them."

There was a difference in the way the two groups of CASPers fought. Our green and gray-painted Wombats relied on their MACs, and all the things that went boom, and only used their arm blades as a last resort. In stark contrast, the black and red-painted Blades whirled through the battlefield, double-edged long blades whipping around in a graceful dance of death and flying body parts. It was hypnotic and highly preferable to watching the Goka slaughter every MinSha in their path.

My trance was broken when our CASPer guardians strode toward the fight. Mace stayed close to one of the CASPers, rifle at the ready and a grim expression on his face.

"Wait!" I ran after them. "I thought we were going to hang back here!"

"*They need us in the fight,*" Bash replied without slowing. "*Stick with us. We'll keep you safe best we can.*"

"I'm a dropship pilot, not infantry," I said in protest and ducked low as a K-bomb exploded nearby and pieces of MinSha went flying. I was pretty sure a head skipped right past my feet but decided not to examine it too closely.

"*You are today.*" Simmons stopped, ripped a laser rifle out of a dead MinSha's claws, and thrust it in my face. "*You know how to use one of these, right? Point the bang-bang end at the bad guys and pull the trigger.*"

His condescending attitude ruffled my feathers, and I holstered my pistol and took the heavy-ass rifle from him with a scowl. "I think I can handle that."

I might not have been able to see his face, but his skepticism came through loud and clear. "*Just don't shoot one of us in the back. And if you see us firing in a certain direction, feel free to join in.*"

A MinSha burst out of concealment from beneath a pile of bodies and aimed her rifle at Simmons. He cursed and lit her up with his MAC. She dropped, and he put an extra round through her chest to make sure she stayed down. It happened so fast I didn't even have time to raise my rifle.

"*You can always stay here if you want,*" he added before he hustled off to where the MinSha tenaciously defended the pyramid entrance.

I suspiciously eyed the fallen CASPers and MinSha, all more than capable of hiding who knew how many bad guys.

"Hard pass," I muttered as I grabbed an extra mag from the MinSha, stuffed it in a pocket, and hustled my ass after him. Incredibly aware that, outside of Mace, I was the most squishable thing on that battlefield, I quickly caught up to Simmons and did my best to become his personal shadow.

"*If you're going to be that far up my ass, at least keep an eye on my six,*" he grumbled as he took aim at a pair of MinSha attempting to sneak around the side of the fortifications they'd thrown up in front of the entrance. Before he could shoot, a pack of Goka swarmed them, blades stabbing and blue blood flying. The MinSha fought back, but their lasers reflected right off their shiny carapaces. One of the Goka was brutally kicked, recovered almost instantly, and charged back in. At that point, both MinSha tried to retreat behind the fortifications.

They didn't make it.

I swallowed hard. "Okay, really fucking happy they're on our side."

As brutal as the Goka were, the MinSha weren't exactly slouches. It looked like we were about to stagnate at that barricade until one of the Combat Wombats stepped forward and lobbed a double-handful of K-bombs at the center. The instant the bombs flew from his hands, he snapped out the laser shields on his arms and hunkered down behind them. Without a CASPer, I couldn't see the lasers fired at him, but I could guess from the way his shook under the invisible barrage that he took considerable fire for his heroics.

The K-bombs hit the barricade and exploded.

"Damn, *the sarge is badass,*" Bash said.

Two CASPers darted forward into the breach, long blades stabbing and slashing as they danced through the line. A veritable flood of Goka followed in their wake and widened the gap. The remainder of the Blades CASPers added their swords to the mix, and the Combat Wombats surged forward to hold the barricade.

As much as I wanted the battle to be over, the MinSha defense wasn't broken. They executed an orderly retreat into the facility as the

Badass Blades pressed them hard. Periodically, I darted a nervous glance behind me, trying to do what Simmons had probably only meant sarcastically and watch his six. I wasn't sure what I'd be able to do even with a rifle, but I'd try to guard his back.

"*Hurry up, squishable. We're going to miss all the fun.*"

I cast one more lingering stare over my shoulder and sighed when a MinSha didn't magically appear to shoot him in the ass. *Such a shame.*

The inside of the pyramid was just as tacky as the outside, with shiny walls and way too much chrome, though the blue blood splattered everywhere somewhat detracted from the shine. I winced when I caught sight of a dead Goka and remembered that their blood was blue as well. Just inside the entrance, there was a CASPer crumpled to the floor, red slowly seeping out from beneath the twisted metal.

Bash didn't even pause as he strode past and neither did Simmons, so I assumed there was nothing to be done for the driver and kept going. I'd lost track of Mace before we'd even breached the barricade, so I stuck with Simmons and hoped my crazy-ass pilot was still alive somewhere in this mess.

The long halls echoed with the sounds of combat. If I'd thought it was loud outside, it had nothing on the sheer cacophony currently assaulting my ears. It was difficult to tell with all the echoing, but it sounded like the main fight had quickly moved deeper into the facility.

Simmons cursed and staggered forward half a step before he caught himself. Both CASPer drivers spun as one and opened fire on a MinSha leaning out from a side corridor. She vanished down the corridor before either CASPer driver could kill her.

"*You good, brother?*" Bash asked with poorly concealed concern.

Simmons flexed his leg and took a few experimental steps. There was a noticeable hitch in his previously smooth stride and a brand-new laser hole, but it must have hit below his actual leg, because there was no sign of blood on his CASPer or pain in his voice.

"*Good to go. Looks like we're on clean up as well as guard duty*," Simmons said with an aggravated sigh. "*Stick close, squishy.*"

"Cute." First I was squishable, now squishy. I clutched my stolen rifle tighter and trotted down the side hall after them. "I have a name you know."

"*Don't care.*"

Bash snorted. "*Could you not be an ass for once?*"

Simmons actually laughed. "*Don't ask for miracles.*"

In the lead, Bash slowed as we reached an intersection. He swung around the corner, the MAC on his arm sweeping the arc from one side to the other. "*Clear.*"

Simmons followed, and I trotted at his heels like a damn dog. *Stupid fucking MinSha patrol shooting down my beautiful ship. I should be sitting in my cockpit right now, not going into combat with dickhead and—*

At a faint scrape behind me, I jerked my head around. Ruby eyes glowered at me from behind a laser rifle. "Check six!"

Simmons spun around with a roar echoed by his MAC. I executed a poor excuse for a combat roll and did my best to get out of his way, banging my elbow and nearly dropping my rifle in the process. *Shit, maybe I am an awkward duck.*

The first MinSha dropped in an explosion of chiton and blue nastiness, and I exhaled in relief. Just because Simmons was a dick didn't mean I *really* wanted him to get shot in the ass. Or anywhere else.

Before I could get back up, a second MinSha popped out of nowhere behind Bash. Her first shot reflected off his laser shield, and I flattened myself to the floor with a squawk as both CASPers returned fire.

Cautiously, I lifted my head when Simmons and Bash abruptly stopped firing.

"*Where the fuck did she go?*"

"*I have no idea.*" Apparently fearless, Simmons stalked over to where we'd seen the MinSha last, but she was well and truly gone.

Unease shivered down my spine as I scrambled to my feet. "Anyone notice we didn't pass a single door along the corridor?"

Simmons growled in frustration. "*Let's keep moving. If we can't track this bitch down in the next few minutes we'll rejoin the main battle.*"

The corridor ended in a suspiciously familiar atrium.

"*How the hell did we end up back here?*" Bash asked.

"*We didn't,*" Simmons said impatiently. "*No blood, no CASPer. This is a different entrance.*"

"*Yeah, but there was supposed to be only one and it's back that way,*" Bash countered even as he stalked toward the double doors. He wrenched them open while Simmons covered him with his MAC. We all stared at the solid wall behind the doors.

"*I hate this fucking place,*" Simmons muttered.

"*It's a real mindfuck,*" Bash said in agreement. He marched over to the only other exit from the atrium and took a long look down the corridor. "*Clear. What's the play, man?*"

Before Simmons made a decision, the seemingly solid wall opposite the fake doors slid aside and a dozen MinSha rushed out and opened fire. Bash ducked into the corridor, but Simmons and I were in the middle of the damn atrium. He snarled a curse, shoved me behind one of the doors, and planted himself in front of me.

"*Stay down.*" He deployed the laser shield on one arm and held it in front of his chest as he fired his MAC. I crouched low and peered around the edge of the door. The rapid fire abruptly slowed, and he snarled again. "*Almost out.*"

He ripped the other door off its hinges and launched it at the MinSha like an oversized frisbee. One wasn't fast enough to get out of the way and was smashed to the floor like a bug. Bash leaned out of the corridor and tore into them with his MAC, but he had to be running low on ammo too—and there were too many for him to engage alone. Simmons' CASPer shuddered and more than one smoking hole appeared where the shield didn't cover.

"*I got you, brother.*" Bash tossed a K-bomb into their midst. One of the MinSha tried to smack it away and her arm vanished in a spray of blood and chiton as it exploded. Several others were wounded, but the rest propped up the door as a makeshift barricade and continued to fire at Simmons.

A MinSha, quite possibly the same wily bitch who'd been popping in and out like a damn weasel, crept down the corridor behind Bash. Before I could scream a warning, she shot him in the back. The CASPer dropped to its knees, and Bash let out a strangled groan.

"*Bash!*"

Pinned down behind his shield and doing his best to protect me, there was no way Simmons could get to his battle buddy… but I could. I braced the heavy rifle against my shoulder and squeezed off a shot, remembering to aim for the bitch's eyes. I missed, but she ducked when I kept firing, trying to buy Bash time. Her mandibles clacked with rage, and she spun toward me.

My wide gaze locked onto the end of her rifle. It honestly hadn't occurred to my dumb ass that if I had a clear shot on her, she had one on me. I had no cover, and nowhere to go.

Simmons lunged sideways and dropped his laser shield in front of me, leaving himself unprotected. Meanwhile, Bash flipped out his arm blade and spun around with a wild slash, forcing the MinSha to focus on him again. She leaped back just far enough to avoid the clumsy strike and aimed her rifle pointblank at his cockpit.

Simmons let out an anguished shout—and a Goka dropped out of a vent in the ceiling and landed on the MinSha's head. Two blades flashed and stabbed, and blue blood went flying with wild abandon. She screeched and shook herself violently. The Goka went flying as a second appeared in the open vent over her head. She snapped her rifle up—and Bash lunged forward and stabbed her through the chest.

He snapped his arm sideways, and she flew off the blade and hit the wall. Her rifle fell from her claws as the first Goka darted back in and drove his blades into her thorax. The second dropped from the vent and stabbed her in the throat. Seemed a touch overkill to me, but I wasn't about to tell a pair of Goka they should stop stabby stabbing the enemy. Even if she was already dead.

With a guttural snarl, Simmons pivoted back and unloaded everything he had left on the MinSha behind the barricade. When his MAC fell silent, he snapped out his arm blade and charged. The Goka ran right at his heels, and Bash lurched out of the corridor to stand in front of me.

Beneath the thunder of the CASPer's footsteps, I caught the distinct crack of hypervelocity pistols. Before Simmons crossed even half the distance, several MinSha dropped. One fell outside the protection of the barricade with a neat hole through her head, and I caught a glimpse of red, blue, and green. For a fraction of a second, my eyes locked with the Flatar in blue. I shook my head in disbelief as the trio disappeared as quickly as they'd appeared, like little fluffballs of chaos incarnate.

Between an enraged Simmons and the stab-happy Goka twins, the rest of the MinSha fell quickly. Without stopping to chat, the Goka tossed Simmons a casual salute and scuttled off into another vent.

"*I've changed my mind,*" Bash said with a strained laugh. "*I want shoulder-mounted Goka.*"

Simmons strode across the atrium, the hitch in his stride even more noticeable than before and blue blood splattered all over his CASPer. "*Status?*"

"*Nothing a round of nanites and a band-aid couldn't handle,*" Bash replied with a strained laugh. "*Besides, chicks dig scars. Right Ducky?*"

"Totally." Fear belatedly slammed into me, and I slumped against the wall. "Fuck me, that was close."

"*Little idiot.*" Simmons stalked over to me with a growl. "*Make sure you have better cover before you attract the enemies' attention with stupid heroics.*" He towered over me, and I had to crane my neck back to glare in the general vicinity of where his face would be. His gruff tone didn't change in the slightest when he added, "*Are you okay?*"

My glare faltered. "I'm fine."

Bash snickered. "*Never trust when a woman says she's 'fine' in that tone of voice.*"

I flipped them both off, but my heart wasn't really in it. My adrenaline was crashing, and I couldn't stop shaking. "I really didn't sign up for this," I said hoarsely.

"*We don't have time for you to have a little pity party, so suck it up and get your ass in gear,*" Simmons barked. "*We need to get back in the fight, and we can't do that if you're huddled against the wall.*"

"*Dude.*" Bash sighed. "*He could've said it better, but he's not wrong. Chin up, little duck. We gotta move.*"

"Right… right." I drew in a deep breath and marched over to the dead MinSha. Nausea rose at the scattered blood and viscera, but it didn't stop me from scavenging a fresh mag from the closest body. I dropped my spent mag, swapped it out, and added a second mag to the one I already had in my pocket.

"*So, you do have some training in there somewhere.*"

I shot Simmons a glare over my shoulder. "We're trained in the basics, same as any merc. And you just let me know whenever you want to try flying a dropship, you smug bastard."

Bash snorted a laugh and kicked at the MinSha with a perfect little hole in her head. "*What the hell took this one out?*"

I thought about mentioning the Flatar, but the thought of Simmons' derision was enough to keep my mouth shut. It wasn't worth the ridicule.

"*Who cares. Let's move.*"

Bash pointed at the wall the MinSha had appeared from. "*Do we explore that way, or go back the way we came?*"

"Back," Simmons and I said in unison.

The trek back to the actual entrance took a little longer with Simmons limping. From his occasional pained grunt, I was fairly certain it wasn't just his CASPer that was damaged, while my arms ached from carrying the heavy rifle without a sling. It was still better than the laser pistol on my hip, and I knew better than to complain about the weight.

Bash, on the other hand, complained enough for all of us, but at least it was cheerful. Despite his incessant chattering, neither merc let their guard down. As we neared the atrium, Bash finally shut up, and they swept the area.

"*Clear.*"

Bash paused at the far end of the atrium where a vaulted corridor led deeper into the pyramid. "*Is it me, or is the fight moving this way?*"

I took a nervous step back as the roar of battle swelled. "Uh… it's definitely getting closer."

An ear-splitting alarm blared through the facility, and all of the lights flashed red.

"*Oh, that can't be good,*" Simmons muttered.

Over the blaring alarm, a pleasant, computerized voice announced, "*Facility destruction sequence activated. Total nuclear meltdown will occur in three hundred seconds. All personnel evacuate.*"

Pounding footsteps echoed down the corridor, and a group of XenSha bounded past a startled Bash like a tentacled horde of evil space bunnies. They ran outside without slowing.

"*Definitely not good,*" Bash said as he backed up toward Simmons.

A MinSha darted out of the corridor next. Simmons took a swipe at her with his combat blade, but she just ducked the blow and kept running.

Over the command freq, Colonel Wallace shouted, "*Retreat to fallback point Charlie. I repeat, retreat to fallback point Charlie. The damn iceberg is melting. No penguins left behind!*"

I didn't need a translation for that order. Unfortunately, neither did anyone else. A stampede of MinSha, XenSha, and CASPers ran down the corridor, their fight temporarily buried under the urge to escape—and I was the only squishable person in the atrium. I darted a glance over my shoulder, but no way in hell was I getting to the door first. Instead, I threw myself into the side corridor, barely avoiding getting flattened by a half-running, half-staggering CASPer.

"*Ducky!*"

It was impossible to tell which of my reluctant guardians roared my name, but both were trying to cut across the fleeing mercs to get to me.

"*Total nuclear meltdown will occur in two hundred forty seconds.*"

A vent popped open and a veritable flood of Goka poured out and joined the mad dash for the door. Several slammed right into Simmons' bad leg, and Bash had to spin back around to brace him.

"Just go! I'll catch up!" Both CASPers hesitated, immobile rocks caught in the flow of an unstoppable tide. "*Go!*"

One of the CASPers grabbed the other by the arm and dragged it toward the entrance. After a staggered step, they both ran. I caught sight of a few dismounted CASPer drivers in the crowd, but every last one was carried by a CASPer. If Mace was among them, I didn't see him.

"*Total nuclear meltdown will occur in one hundred eighty seconds.*"

Fuck, fuck, fuck. Come on!

The last CASPer thundered past my little side corridor. A gap opened up, a fleeting break in the pandemonium. Further down the main corridor, a solid mass of MinSha sprinted hard for the atrium, several XenSha bounding along just ahead of them. This was my chance.

I ran.

A XenSha caught up and tried to shove me out of the way. I bared my teeth and slammed my rifle into its face. Another XenSha clawed at my heels—I dropped the heavy-ass rifle and ran faster.

I burst through the door and into the searing light of a dying day. Behind me, that pleasant voice called out, "*Total nuclear meltdown will occur in one hundred twenty seconds.*"

There was no way I could run fast enough to get clear in time.

A CASPer darted over from my right, paused just long enough to sling me over its shoulder, and took off at a dead sprint.

A second CASPer limped along next to mine. "*You didn't think we'd actually leave you behind, did you?*"

A grin stretched across my face despite the discomfort in my midsection. I looked back at the pyramid just in time to catch a glimpse of a trio of Flatar running down the slanted side like their little tails were on fire. They disappeared into the brush before I could demand we go back for them.

I hoped they made it.

If riding a CASPer piggyback was uncomfortable, being slung over a shoulder was an order of magnitude worse. But since it was highly preferable to blowing up or glowing in the dark for the rest of my life, I kept my mouth shut. Behind us, the pyramid didn't so much explode as collapse in slow motion with a dull roar.

We caught up to the rest of the CASPers and Goka at fallback point Charlie, one of the farthest areas identified as a pickup location, just as the seven remaining dropships landed.

Bash set me down a hell of a lot more carefully than he'd picked me up. "*Sorry for the rough treatment.*"

I grinned up at his CASPer. "I'll take a few bruises over dying any day. Thanks for the save."

"Hey, Ducky!" Mace strolled over with his rifle propped on one shoulder and his helmet dangling from his hand. He had a black eye, a bloody bandage wrapped around one bicep, and was grinning like a lunatic. "Have fun on your first contract?"

My pilot was clearly insane… but he was alive. I'd take it.

"Oh, tons. I love it when our dropship gets shot out from under us and we get to go into combat with the ground troops. Let's do this every time."

"*Let's not.*" Bash laughed, tossed me a casual salute, and strode up the ramp of the nearest dropship. "*See you around.*"

"*Glad you made it, squishy,*" Simmons said as he stopped next to me and waited for his turn to load.

I glared up at the cockpit. "For the last time, my name's *Ducky*, not..."

My voice trailed off when he popped the canopy. Green eyes, sweaty brown hair sticking up in short spikes, devilish grin. Holy *fuck*. Simmons might be a dick, but he was a *hot* dick.

Mace leaned over and gently pushed my mouth closed.

"You okay there, squishy?" Simmons' grin turned smug before it fell away. "Thanks for what you did back there. Bash might not have made it without your help—even if you were stupid about it."

My lips twitched into a smile. "I'm not sure if I should say you're welcome or fuck you."

He winked. "Both is always an option."

My jaw dropped again as my brain short-circuited. All the things I wanted to say got lost somewhere between rage and amusement, and I ended up spluttering incoherent nonsense. Simmons roared a laugh and closed the canopy again before he stomped up the ramp after his friend.

I was saved from further embarrassment when a trio of Flatar pulled up on a hover bike. *Our* hover bike. I grabbed Mace's arm and pointed like an idiot. "I told you! I told you it was there when I did the preflight! I told you I saw three chipmunks... Flatar, *whatever!*"

The chipmunk in red hopped off the bike and ran onto the dropship. The one in green scuttled up the ramp right after him, but the one in blue paused long enough to shrug with an apologetic expression.

Mace grinned. "Oh, I knew they stole it. I was just fucking with you."

I stared. "You know what, *sir*? Zero respect; all the 'fuck you.'"

As I stomped up the ramp, Mace called back, "Aw, come on. *Ducking* with a new copilot is tradition!"

I flipped him off over my shoulder to the sound of his laughter.

* * *

Karma Station
Bartertown

I held up my shot glass. "No promises."

I barely tasted the burn. Numb. I was so damn numb and it wasn't even because of the shit alcohol. The cheerful roar of the crowd packing The Sand Trap didn't touch me. I sat at the end of the bar, a bottle of Jeremiah Weed in front of me. Alone.

I'd been so damn excited to tell Rebel about my first contract. A successful one, because our shady employer hadn't minded that we'd somehow blown the place up rather than secure it. We'd even gotten a bonus. The moment we'd returned to Karma system, I'd sent her a message. When she didn't respond fast enough, I'd looked up the status of the Silverhawk's contract.

Lost.

Bile that had nothing to do with the crap alcohol rose in the back of my throat. It was supposed to be a cakewalk.

This time, I didn't bother with the shot glass. I took a swig straight from the bottle and hoped the burn would make me feel… something. *Anything.*

My eyes watered. It was just the stupid whiskey though, not actual tears. I hadn't cried yet. All my grief was trapped behind that awful wall of numb. I hated the numb.

When I blinked my eyes clear, a trio of chipmunks stood on the bar in front of me. I looked from them to the bottle of Jeremiah Weed and back.

"Duck me," I slurred. "Not this again. Go away. I'm not in the mood for hallucinations right now."

The one in the red shirt stepped forward. His eyes narrowed to slits. "Our boss has a message for you."

My own eyes narrowed at his menacing tone, but the one in blue elbowed him sharply.

"Be nice, Alvin." He looked at me with too much sympathy in his eyes. "Your friend is alive."

I froze.

"We don't know much, but we think the Science Guild captured—"

Alvin shoved him aside and gave me a regal nod. "We'll see what we can do to help her."

I just stared as the first two hopped off the bar and disappeared into the crowd. The slightly chubby one in green awkwardly patted my arm before he scampered after his friends.

For a long time, I just sat on my barstool and let the noise wash over me. The desperate hope that the chipmunks weren't a drunken hallucination warred with the numb certainty that Rebel was dead, along with every other Silverhawk who'd gone out on that damn contract.

But if they weren't a hallucination…

Almost of its own volition, my hand dipped into my pocket and pulled out my lucky coin. Its cool weight in the palm of my hand normally soothed me, but not tonight. I flipped it over and over, until I finally set it on the bartop with careful precision.

If Rebel was still alive out there somewhere, she needed help… more help than I could give her. I slammed back one more shot for courage, picked up my comm, and made the call.

"It's Bree Alcuin." I looked down at the token, the silver standing out like a beacon against the dull wood. "I'm calling in my favor."

* * * * *

Melissa Olthoff Bio

Melissa Olthoff is a military science fiction and urban fantasy author who delights in sneaking in romance wherever she can. She is a lifelong geek of all things scifi and fantasy, as well as a veteran of the United States Air Force, both of which are incredibly useful when writing. Her degrees in meteorology and accounting are slightly less applicable to writing, but absolutely useful when it comes to supporting her family. She is published by Chris Kennedy Publishing, and is best known for her Salvage Title Universe novels, Hit World Valkyries, and numerous short stories. She can be found at her website melissaolthoff.net, Facebook, Twitter, and on her Amazon Author Page.

# # # # #

Safari by Dan Bridgwater

Vesril Station

Coro region, Tolo Galactic Arm

"OK, Marauders! Saddle up! We've officially signed our first contract!" Captain Tran's voice echoed through the ship's common area, and a chorus of cheers greeted him. He continued, "Grab your go bags, we're loading up to knock out a nice monster hunt!"

Sergeant Rik Mariso, Moose to his friends, jerked up in his chair. He was one of the few veterans in the newly formed Channo Colony mercenary unit. He regarded Tran with a questioning look on his face. "A monster hunt? What the hell kinda contract is that?"

Tran looked smug. "This is a sweet deal, boys. Better than we could have hoped for, really. We've been hired to provide security for a gem and precious metals mine on Frotith III, which I can't imagine anyone has ever heard of. Native species are called the Hrot. Non-mercs, burrow dwellers, mostly peaceful, built like gorillas but about half the mass. Anyway, they've been getting the crap kicked out of them by a local beastie they can't handle. It's a predator species that has recently developed a taste for Hrots. We are tasked to help set up a perimeter and hunt the bastards. Easy peasy."

Rik liked to think he wasn't a cynical man, but he'd been doing this work for over a decade. Big piles of crap came along a lot more often than rose gardens. "So, we're being hired to hunt a non-sentient species that can't shoot back. And they're going to pay us to do it. I gotta admit, sounds good. What's the catch, and how can they afford us?"

Tran smiled. "That's the beauty of it. The Hrot are working a small red diamond operation. Huge to them but insignificant by Galactic standards. They were headed to Vesril Merc Pit to post the contract when their rep ran into our agent. Once he understood what they wanted, he talked fast at 'em and basically grabbed it no-bid."

Captain Tran walked toward the Tri-V as he activated the screen. "Now for our beastie." He turned to face the group, and a scaley, grey-green creature, resembling a long-necked cross between a leopard and a crocodile, popped onto the viewer. "As near as we can tell, this is called a grekel. Since the Hrot are kinda new, and very minor as galactic races go, they're still working on the translation matrix. Now these grekel critters are fast—capable of short distance sprints of up to ninety kph and sustained speeds around sixty. They like the surface, but they can burrow, which is the real problem. They've been breaking into the Hrot warrens and grabbing up Hrot snacks. Oh, and for scale…" In the image, Rik's modified Mk 6 CASPer appeared. The three-meter mech, slightly larger and wider than the standard Mk 6 and with heavier armor plates, was taller than the shoulder of the grekel, but not by much. "Now before you all get excited remember, it's just an animal. Not sentient, no weapons. This is literally a safari. So pack up; we're going hunting."

As the mercs stood and headed to their quarters, Rik looked back at his CASPer on the display. Despite all the talk of loans and credits for new startups, the used Mk 6s, the same model he'd driven until he retired twelve years ago, had been the best a dirt-poor colony like Channo had been able to afford. No one wanted to throw good money after bad. He hoped they were enough.

* * *

Frotith III, Day 1

The dropship touched down in a clearing on the border between a scrubby forest and a minor mountain range. The ramp dropped, and Rik saw a few ramshackle buildings scattered around a clearing. Little more than small pavilions and lean-tos, they served as limited over-ground storage for mining equipment for the subterranean Hrot. The perimeter wall itself was almost wide enough to seem squat, despite its near six-meter height. Dry, dusty air blew into the open bay of the dropship and disturbed the stack of notes at the comm station where Chief Klein sat, engrossed in her work. Rik put a hand on the papers, stopping their slide. The chief jerked and blinked as she lifted her head and looked out the hatch. "Thanks, Moose," she said. "I didn't know we'd landed. There's a lot of radio traffic out there and some of it is giving the computer fits." She refocused on her station and made some adjustments.

Rik quirked an eyebrow, surprised that there was anything in this backwater that could stop the Marauder's comm hacking software. "What do you mean fits? Why? What kind of encryption are we dealing with?"

Klein glanced up. "Encryption? Oh, no. Dialect," she clarified. "It's the translation matrix. It doesn't match what we uploaded from

Vesril at all. The Hrot we spoke to back at the station apparently weren't speaking Hrot standard. Not sure if there is a Hrot standard." She pointed to a readout. "Since we dropped out of hyper, we've picked up three separate languages, and half a dozen local dialects. It's just going to take a bit to work it all out. When I briefed the Mage, he told me to get a solid translation code out first thing." Like some of the older Marauders, she referred to Major Cross as "the Mage," both a callsign and a play on the major's rank.

Rik used his 'plants to query the net and frowned. She was right. Even as he examined the summary, the net added a seventh dialect. He nodded to the chief and headed to the area of the hanger bay set aside for Third Squad. Corporal Jannsen, one of his more solid NCOs, was waiting for him. "OK, First Squad has overwatch while we disembark," Rik said, pointing over toward the ramp where four CASPers and a host of support personnel were prepped to step out into the clearing. "Round up Third and make sure everyone has their gear squared away. The boss is tasking us with supporting the Communication section, so that's first priority. Then we'll get the rest of the company gear and set a perimeter. By the time we have that knocked out, we should have an idea of where the hell the barracks are. This might not be a combat drop, but it ain't a vacation. Don't get sloppy. If Third looks like an ass in front of the boss, I will figure out a way to get remedial training in."

Jannsen smiled and turned toward a knot of mercs. "Moore, Lee," he called out. "Grab your fireteam and go see Chief Klein. She's gonna have a ton of comm gear. You're hers until she's done with you. Lalande, grab your people and start getting our gear out of lockdown. I expect a function check on the combat gear in one hour."

Rik watched Jannsen head off and nodded. Third would take care of business. His 'plant pinged. The major was calling a staff meeting. Based on the slug of data he received, this would be the final deployment order and watch schedule. He headed off and let his corporal take care of the immediate taskings. Good NCOs were worth their weight in gold.

* * *

Day 4 - Morning

"See what I mean, Kyle?" Rik asked the armorer from the open hatch of the Mk 6. He and Corporal Kyle were working in the barn-like garage the Marauders had thrown up to serve as an armory. "Definitely a lag in the MAC tracking movement."

"I see it, Moose," Kyle replied. "Just not sure what's causing it. Did you take any damage in training on Channo?"

Rik thought about the thick-barreled chert tree he'd bounced off of in their last night training evolution and shook his head in the negative. "Nothing comes to mind, or at least nothing that should have been able to damage these systems."

"This is what we get for buying used," Kyle muttered.

A klaxon ripped through the armory. "Perimeter breach. Perimeter breach," a voice blared over the speaker system. Rik recognized Chief Klein's voice. "Third Squad to Bravo immediately. Breach expected in eight minutes."

Rik started to button up the canopy of the CASPer. "OK, Kyle, get clear." He had been working with the armorer on the MAC targeting systems. Since the mech was mostly booted up, Rik was about fifteen seconds from being ready to stomp out of the bay and head for the tunnels. His squad was currently the quick-reaction team, and his battle systems already showed the other CASPers moving out.

Kyle staggered back. "What? No! This CASPer is not cleared for action, the MACs are still in test mode!" he protested.

"Doesn't matter," Rik shot back. "Can't use MACs anyway. We'd bring the tunnels down. No, we'll be doing this old school. Very old school." The CASPer's right arm dipped low behind his back and came out gripping the handle of a well-used, meter-and-a-half mace with a flanged head a bit smaller than a pony keg. "Either get the MACs off or lock 'em down so they don't get in the way. You have sixty seconds before I'm out the door."

Kyle looked back at his slate and considered for a few seconds, then started jabbing the screen. "They're going to have to stay. Can't get 'em off in less than ten minutes." The barrels started to rotate toward the rear. "Best option is to lock them backward; it'll give you better arm movement. I just hope the Hussars don't see any pictures. You're going to look like their logo." Yellow indicators started going green as the various panels Kyle had opened were secured. "Clear! CASPer locked. Get out of here, Moose."

Rik headed for the exit. "No school like the old school," he muttered and jogged toward the Bravo tunnel entrance. At the Marauders' request, the Hrot had dug an oval tunnel around the camp, large enough for three CASPers to walk side by side or two CASPers to fight. The Humans had reacted with some amazement at the speed at which the Hrot could work. Between their heavy equipment and natural ability, the ape-like aliens had proven their skill, having dug and shorn up the two-kilometer loop in the thirty-six hours it had taken the Marauders to make the trip in system from the gate. He activated his comm. "Chief Klein, what have we got?"

"We're picking up what sounds like tunneling," she replied. *"Based on the sensors, I'd estimate they are about 50 meters out, but moving fast—like abnormally fast. I'm guessing you have less than three minutes before it comes through the wall looking for snacks."*

Rik stopped beside the three CASPers standing at the top of the ramp leading into the tunnel and addressed the senior trooper, "You guys are the reserve. You need to be on top of any additional threats that come in." The tunnels were too tight to bring the whole squad down. He switched to a private channel. "Tell me again, Chief, why we aren't just using shaped charges to kill them in their tunnels?" Still in the bright sunlight, Rik paused in front of the shadowed mouth of the tunnel and thought about just how much he disliked fighting underground. He flipped through his monitor's display spectrums until the opening was revealed in all its grainy green glory.

"The Hrot tried. It didn't work. In fact, it pissed the grekel off. They popped up out of the crater and trashed everything above ground. That's when the miners decided they needed help."

"I had to ask," Rik muttered. *Never ask your troops to do anything you wouldn't do*, he thought to himself and started down the tunnel. Thirty meters later, he was standing next to Jannsen. He switched to the squad channel. "OK, there're six of us down here, but only room for four to engage. We'll split up into a two-one formation, two blocking and one back up on each side of the breach. Chief says they're going to come through right about there." He pointed a laser designator to highlight a spot on the dirt wall. "Jannsen, you take Lalande and Benett ten meters down and block that side. Mason, you and Lee are with me here. No lasers unless you know, and I mean *know*, you aren't going to make a friendly fire incident, and no MACs at all. If you bring the tunnel down on us, that would be a Very Bad Thing." A few chuckles came over the radio, and he saw arm blades deploying. "All right, gents, let's get ready to greet our guest."

Jannsen and his crew walked down the corridor and turned about with Lalande and Benett squaring off up front. Mason and Lee settled in front of Rik and faced the outer wall. Lee's voice came over the channel, *"You're in back, boss. Can't be having you scuff your suit."* More chuckles, and Rik smiled. If he was honest with himself, he knew he preferred getting right into the mix. With his heavier armor, his CASPer could absorb a shocking amount of punishment. Further, while some armor systems out there might turn or stop a CASPer's arm blade, he had yet to run into the alien mercenary, or small vehicle for that matter, that easily shrugged off the damage inflicted by his mace.

Chief Klein's voice came over the squad channel. *"Standby. I'm starting to get vibration off the wall. They're…"*

Her voice was drowned out by the noise of the collapsing wall just behind Mason's left shoulder. A great head and arm burst into the corridor. Mason turned. With lightning swiftness, the beast locked eyes on the CASPer and backhanded Mason into Rik, knocking them both off their feet and into a heap on the floor. He saw the grekel break the rest of the way into the corridor and leap onto Lee's chest and shoulders, bearing the mech down and into the floor and wall behind him. As the huge beast savaged Lee's arm and shoulder joints, the claws on its back legs raked down the CASPer's stomach plate leaving great gouges in the armor. As Rik struggled to get out from under Mason, he saw Lee's damage indicators dropping from green into yellow on his HUD. He could see Lee on his back ineffectively striking the body of the creature, his arm blade turned by the heavy scales along the ribs. From his position beneath it, Lee simply couldn't seem to get the proper angle to do anything else.

Rik heaved himself to his feet and scrambled to recover his mace. He gripped it in both hands and swung it back over his head but stopped. Any overhead strike put Lee in the impact zone. He shifted his grip, stepped forward with his left leg and, using the full strength of his heavy CASPer, drove the head of the mace forward like a battering ram. It slammed into the crouched body of the grekel behind the right shoulder, knocked it off the stricken Lee and drove it down the corridor toward the other group of CASPers. He reached down to Lee and, clasping the other mech's hand, pulled him to his feet. "You good?" he asked, seeing what he hoped was hydraulic fluid running down the left arm and the lower body of Lee's CASPer.

Even over the comm, Rik could hear the shock and panic. "*Christ! What the hell just happened?*"

"Snap out of it, Lee! Are you good?"

"*Hell, no! It looks like a Christmas tree in here. There's damage to systems I didn't know I had! Right leg and left arm are at 60%, and the left leg is thrashed. I can stand, but it's gonna be flaky as hell.*" Lee took a glacial step forward, dragging the left leg. "*Shit. It works, but no dancing.*"

Glancing toward Janssen and his team, Rik saw that they had fared much better. Braced and ready, Lalande and Benett chopped at the beast. He could see black blood stream from gashes in its side, but even injured, the beast moved like a snake, agile and lightning fast. It dodged under a wild swing by Benett and drove forward to strike the off-balance mech. As it did, Lalande was able to deliver a glancing blow, not damaging, but enough to cause it to miss Benett.

Rik noted Mason had made it back to his feet. "All right, Lee. You stay back. Mason—" Before he could finish, a second grekel flew out of the blackness and slammed into him, knocking his mace loose again. He managed to stay on his feet, and a small voice in his mind expressed its concern about a weapon he spent too much time trying to retrieve. The beast struck him again mid-body and drove him backward until he was braced against the far wall. Its tail thrashed and Mason was once again knocked back, spinning to fall on his hands and knees. *Looks like I'm on my own*, Rik thought.

With his right hand, Rik grabbed the beast's neck directly under the jaw and pushed its head and gnashing maw back. He could hear the suit's servos humming under the strain. With his left hand, he gripped the grekel's right front paw and pushed it back, stopping it from tearing into the suit's shoulder joint. His cockpit shook as the creature hammered the abdomen of the suit with one of its back legs, but with his heavier armor he wasn't worried yet. For the moment, CASPer and beast were at an impasse.

It didn't last. The grekel, no longer able to bite at the shoulder and MAC mounts, dropped its left paw onto Rik's right arm and tried to turn its head to bite at Rik's forearm and elbow. The metal plate on the CASPer's arm was much lighter than the rest of the suit and Rik had a sudden vision of it biting through and tearing his arm off.

A desperate thought came to him. A CASPer wasn't built for judo, but in the tight confines of the tunnel and disarmed, he really didn't have a lot of options. He shifted his weight, turned himself away from the wall, and stepped forward into the body of the grekel. Squeezing hard, he collapsed backwards, tucking his legs as he rolled. He jammed one foot up into the creature's ribs and the other into its neck and pushed away, simultaneously dropping his right hand next to his left to grab the captured paw and twist. The beast began to shriek. Still flat on his back, he twisted the animal's arm and felt something pop in the grekel's shoulder. It began to flail violently but the CASPer's hands locked down. He wasn't going to let go now.

Suddenly, a blade pierced the twisted hide at the monster's shoulder and sliced into the already damaged joint. The skin ripped, and as it thrashed, the grekel's arm tore from its body. The beast screamed its agony and fled back into the tunnel breach, leaving a trail of gore behind it. Rik looked up and saw Lee, gory blade extended. "*Sorry, boss,*" Lee said. "*I got here as quick as I could.*"

Rik collapsed back into his harness and blew out an explosive breath. According to his 'plants, less than 2 minutes had passed since the first breach in the wall. His heart was thudding heavily, and he realized he was soaked in sweat. "Crap, Lee. You are forgiven." He rolled forward to get a better view down the hall toward Jannsen and his team. Three CASPers stood over the body of the first grekel. As he watched, Benett extended his blade and jabbed it. There was no reaction. Rik leaned back down. "Damn, that was something," he breathed.

"*No kidding,*" Lee sighed. "*Those things are as fast as anything I've ever seen. Thank God there were only two.*"

Rik agreed. He rolled to his knees and got up, the arm of the grekel that had escaped still firmly in his grasp. He pulled up the status board in his HUD and saw a couple of yellow indicators. Some plates had been damaged, but those were easy enough to replace. He switched to squad view. Mason was all green, having spent most of the fight getting back to his feet. Jannsen and his crew were green across the board. Lee, on the other hand, showed a lot of red with some sprinkles of yellow. His CASPer was going to be spending some quality time with the armorer.

* * *

Day 4 - Late Evening

Twelve hours had passed since his personal nightmare in the tunnel. The corpse of the dead grekel had been dragged out, and Rik found himself at the entryway of the underground room the Hrot had dug to provide Major Cross a command bunker. Nodding to the officers, he moved to an available chair.

"First things first, gents," the major began. "Chief Klein won't be joining us in person for this. She indicated there are some critical fails in our translation matrix with the Hrot. Since this is a combat debrief, her time is better spent where she is. All right Mariso, I've read your after-action report, and I've seen the armorer's statement on Lee's CASPer. Damn, son," he paused, looking down at the slate. "That is a lot of damage. What happened?"

"Well, sir, you've read my report," Rik started.

"Yes, but that's not the same as being there. I want your impressions of the combat," the major interrupted.

"Yes, sir." Rik paused. His mind flew back to the fight in the tunnel. Already it was starting to feel detached, like it had happened to someone else. The speed and strength of the creatures had been staggering. The first grekel had only been partially in the tunnel when it backhanded Mason off his feet. A CASPer was a solid piece of gear, and the onboard gyros worked extremely hard to keep it upright. Knocking one over in that situation, using nothing but muscle power, was terrifying. The biggest shock had been the claws. Much like the Besquith, these grekel were capable of penetrating and tearing through the mech's armor plate using only what nature had given them. "Well, first I think we're going to need to re-think our strategy if we are going to be dealing with any more of them. In the tunnels, everything is too tight. We can't maneuver. Those things move like lightning, so we're reduced to hand-to-hand," Rik explained. "As you saw from the damage report, these things can tear into a CASPer. I took minimal damage because of the heavier plates, but you can see the gouges in the metal. Lee's suit was trashed and will be in the shop for a couple of days at least. The hides are tough. If you can get a good swing on one, the arm blade will cut it, but not badly. Again, we were hindered by the tightness of the tunnel. Lalande and Benett were having better luck using their blades to stab rather than trying to chop. Even then, the grekel are tough SOBs. Hell, I tore the arm off one and it got away. I mean, I assume it ran off to die. Hell, I hope it's dead." He shrugged. "No, the tunnels are bad. We need to get them up on the surface where we can engage them with the lasers, or the MACs."

Sergeant Tucker, his face grim, shifted in his seat. "You know, Moose, I was going to give you a ration of crap for coming out of that hole with a fricking arm, but I went to medical and saw it. These beasties are something else. The upper section of the arm is almost a meter thick, and the hide is tough. The scales overlap and spread the impact energy. I'm confident a MAC would drop 'em, but I wouldn't want to take a shot with any kind of normal infantry slug thrower. I just don't think you'd get any penetration. As for the claws, they're like some sort of super hardened crystal. They'll slice through rock. We might be able to slow them down by fusing the walls solid down in the tunnels, but that ain't gonna stop them. Heck, if our plate can't, I'm not sure what we have that would." He shook his head.

The major sat back with a thoughtful expression. "I agree. Engaging them in the tunnels is not our best option. You handled it well, Moose. We lose our advantages down there, and I have absolutely no interest in fair fights. We need to get them on the surface. The question is how. We don't have the water to flood the tunnels, and we don't have enough information about their physiology to know if we can gas them. Davis, I want you to get with the medical team and assist with the examination of the body. Find out everything you can. I know we aren't done. I spoke to the Hrot headman and he was not happy. He insists that there is at least one more grekel out there, and he was pretty emphatic about it."

Chief Klein's voice came over the intercom. "I think I can help with that, Mage," she said. "I have been listening in while testing the new translation matrix. We just went from 68% to 94% certainty. I'm pushing an update slug to everybody's pinplants, but here's the problem. Our contract clearly indicates that the Hrot hired us to address the entire family unit of these grekel."

The major looked up at the speakers. "We knew that, Chief. How have things changed?"

"Simple, boss. Based on the requirements and definitions in the contract, this particular family unit consists of three creatures. The two encountered by Third Squad were the cubs."

"Cubs?!" Major Cross exclaimed. "You're telling me that those two creatures, weighing in around 4000 kilos, were cubs?"

"Yes, sir," the chief replied. "And based on the data I'm getting from the Hrots now, properly translated, young cubs. The good news is there's no daddy. The bad news is momma is at least twice as big, probably more."

Rik felt his stomach drop. He scanned the faces around the table and heard the major voice what was on everyone else's lips. "Well, shit."

* * *

Day 5 - Morning

Twenty-four hours had passed since the tunnel attack, and the last twelve had been very busy for the Marauders. After the meeting the night before, Major Cross had reached out to the Hrot headman for a face to face. Now that the language matrix had been updated, new information was coming both from the retranslated contract and directly from the Hrot themselves. The major had been behind closed doors for most of two hours and when he had come out, the orders had started fast and furious.

The first order of business had been to push the regular drone patrol out from five to ten kilometers. Next, all three squads started clearing trees, followed by expanding and reinforcing the perimeter. Previously, the perimeter had been light with an emphasis on cameras and seismic sensors. Now they knew what else was out there. The adult grekel was estimated to weigh in at 7000 to 9000 kilos. The Marauders, expecting to face simple rhino-sized nonsentients, had packed fairly light for this safari. Exhausted, Rik sat on an empty ammo crate, mulling over the most recent information. He wasn't sure they had anything in the inventory that would actually stop the monster.

"*Hey, Moose, ya got your ears on?*" a soft voice came over his radio. Rik smiled. Chief Kara Klein was another of the specialist veterans hired for a staff position in the new company. During the initial creation and training of the Marauders, he'd never really had any call to interact with her beyond the requirements of the tasks at hand. Now that they were actually out on contract, he found he was talking to her pretty much every day.

"Hey, Kara. For you, I got time. What's up?" He adjusted his seat on the ammo crate so he could lean back against another.

"*Checking on you, Rik. I happen to know you've been going for about twenty-eight hours straight, and you've been using stims to stay on top of it.*" Her voice sounded a bit tart, and he raised an eyebrow. "*You've rotated your teams, but you haven't taken a break yourself. What is your plan for rack time?*"

"Why Kara, your interest in my rack time is touching. Is this an offer of some sort?"

"*Ha ha. Seriously, it's time for you to recover,*" she chided. "*If you don't, you're going to be worthless to your men when they need you. Now, as a staff officer, I technically am not in your direct chain of command, but I do rank you. If that's not enough, I was just about to give the Mage his morning status brief.*" Her voice took on a whimsical tone. "*He might accidentally find out that you've not taken a break yet. It would be unfortunate, but I just have that feeling.*"

Rik knew when to retreat. He even smiled a bit at the way she was manipulating him. "Fine. I surrender," he said, getting up from the crate and twisting his spine. "I know when I'm beat. So… you tucking me in?" he asked, trying to put a bit of a leer into his voice.

"*You wish. But I tell you what, I'm always looking out for you. Tucker just came out of the chow hall. I can send him over to tell you a bedtime story if you need it. I'm sure he'll even hold your hand if you ask nice.*" Rik now knew it was possible to hear an evil grin.

"You win. I'm sure if I wasn't so sleepy, I could come up with something witty."

"*Whatever you need to tell yourself, cowboy.*"

"Goodnight, good morning or whatever. I'll talk to you later." He headed toward his bunk.

* * *

Day 6 – Late Morning

Rik stood on the perimeter wall, a blocky half circle extending out from the rocky face of the mountain. In front of the wall, where a forest once stood, was now a large dusty field cluttered by stumps, craters and fortifications.

He wasn't sure there was anything left for the Third Herd to do at this point. They had built up and fortified their own section of the wall and set explosive charges across the front. In this, they were actually doing fairly well. The major had leaned heavily on the Hrot headman and, as a result, the Hrot had provided a seemingly endless supply of mining charges. The armory had been using them to build out massive shaped-charge land mines in the kill zone. With any luck, they might be able to detonate a few into the hopefully softer belly of the mother grekel.

There was movement across the wall and Rik spotted Sergeant Tucker's CASPer moving among the men of Second Squad. Tucker was another of the veterans in the unit, having served several years with a Canadian unit out of Edmonton. They had bonded in the onboard training and, honestly, he felt closer to Tucker than his actual brother. Over the last six months, they had become family by choice. He faced his own CASPer toward Second and pinged Tuck. "Well," he said, "this is another fine mess you've gotten me into, Stanley." On the way to the Frotith system, he and Tucker had been watching holos of some of the earliest talking movies on record. The humor was often low and slapstick, but that tended to appeal to mercs.

Tuck stopped and turned back toward Rik. There was a chuckle over the comms. "*Hell, Moose, you should be thanking me. Another combat command under your belt, and with a new company to boot! Think how good this is going to look on your record when we,*" his voice took on a deep, serious tone, "*valiantly defend this backwater from the depredations of the monster.*" In a more gleeful tone he said, "*It's gonna be great!*"

Rik shook his head. "Yeah, no," he shot back. "I was in the tunnels. I think I've had enough greatness for one trip. When we get back to Channo and write the after-action report, my recommendation is that we never deploy without the heavy antiarmor systems ever again. In fact," Rik went on, "I think I'm going to recommend we invest in a drone that can carry the damn things to the target. If we could engage that thing from the air, we'd be done and packing back into the damn shuttle."

"*Quit whining! Hell, we already have a rocket launch system that uses a laser designator you can mount on one of the drones.*"

"Yes we do," Rik gritted out. "But we didn't bring it with us, did we? We decided it was too expensive to pay what the Buma wanted to charge to freight it and it's currently sitting in a storage unit on Vesril

Station collecting dust, isn't it? Please keep reminding me about weapon systems we own, but don't have here. It's making me feel so much better."

Tuck laughed again. *"Easy, DangerMoose,"* he shot back, using the nickname that only close friends could get away with. *"We got this! That thing is gonna come around the corner and get lit up by nine light MACs, nine medium lasers, and your medium MACs. It's a damn huge target. Even you should be able to hit it."*

Earlier in the day, the chief had shared video of the beast that had been located several kilometers away in the pre-dawn twilight. Their estimates had been wrong. The cub they'd killed weighed in at 4500 kilos, about the size of large Asian elephant. The mother was easily four times the mass, probably closer to five. There simply wasn't a living Earth land animal to which you could compare it.

Rik and Tuck continued their banter. An outsider might worry, but Rik knew this was just how he and Tuck blew off pre-combat jitters. They'd stay on their private channel and take turns bitching until the shooting started.

"OK, Moose, I gotta go. Time to give my boys another pep talk. Beer after on you, ya old woman."

"No problem, Tuck. I'll buy the beer as long as you're buying the food." Rik laughed. After a fight, Tuck could put away a few beers, but Rik could close down a buffet.

"Sheesh! You trying to break me? Later, brother."

"Later, brother," Rik replied.

The link went silent. Using his pinplants, Rik began reviewing health and status of the squad CASPers. He had completed Jannsen, DuBois, and Mason when Chief Klein's voice came over the command channel. *"Command Staff. Command Staff. Please report to the bunker in ten minutes."*

* * *

Major Cross looked across the table at the assembled staff. "OK, mercs," he said. "We have some new information about our prey. Lieutenant Davis, if you'd like to start?"

"Thank you, sir." Lieutenant Davis looked out at his audience. "During the debrief, I was surprised by how poorly the arm blades performed. Stabbing worked well, but the scales pretty much turned the slashing blade with minimal damage to the beast. Now I know why."

The lieutenant pulled up a magnified and enhanced picture of the beast's hide on the screen. "As you can see, there is significant overlap of the scale pattern that will deflect a slashing attack, but it's actually more complicated than that. The scales, the hide, and even the bone structure of these animals seem to be based on a crystal-silica matrix, making them very resilient. The scales themselves are structurally similar to some of the ablative armor we've experimented with in the past. Based on the thickness of the cub's hide, depending on how it goes as they mature, we might not get the penetration we need from the light MACs. I'm sure the MACs will sting it, and we might be able to use that to slow it down or herd it into the minefield, but I'm not sure the MACs are going to seal the deal on their own."

The major looked out across the table. "There you have it," he said. "We need options, people."

Lieutenant Guillard, the first squad commander, spoke up. "What about the mines?" he asked. "Are they going to work?"

"We up-sized the mines considerably over what the Hrot initially tried, so I actually think we're good there," Davis replied. "After looking at the dead one, I'm convinced a contact or close proximity shot would damage it badly."

"That's good news," the major said. "What else?"

"Actually, I might have an idea, sir," said Chief Klein. "It's something I saw in my previous unit before I came to the Marauders. The armorer crafted a specialized penetrator round for the MAC. It had a shaped head with a sabot jacket so the round had a smaller cross section. In the case of an armor strike, the penetration and velocity usually blow right through the target, pretty much igniting it on its way by, but in the case of hitting something like the grekel, something organic…" She shrugged. "I'm not sure what it would do."

"Crap, I like it," Rik exclaimed. "I'll take a case."

"No good, Moose," the chief replied.

"What do you mean?" he asked.

"They won't feed properly. The length required and the shape of the sabot means that it can't auto feed into the MAC. They tried a bunch of variants, but by the time you got one sized down to where it would feed, it was no more effective than a normal MAC round, less even. No, you have to load the individual round by hand, and then you only get the one shot."

"I like it less."

"I thought you might," she said.

"I hate to say it," the major said, "but it has possibilities."

"Sir?"

"The plan is to light the grekel up when it gets close to the wall. We have twenty-nine effective suits, sixteen lasers, and fourteen MACs. Between that and the mines, I think we win. But it's like Davis said. We may not be given the time for the lasers to really do damage, and the light MACs might not hurt it at all. Frankly, if they can't, your medium MAC, as it stands, really isn't all that much bigger." The major paused to think and nodded. "If the armory can craft it, I think we have a better chance with you loaded with the penetrator. You'll only get one shot… well, two, since you actually have two MACs, but if all else fails, those will be the shots that have the best chance of killing it. What do you think, Sergeant?"

Rik thought his stomach might hit the floor. He tried to come up with alternatives but couldn't. "I think if it goes pear-shaped, we're putting a whole lot on two experimental rounds, sir, but I haven't got any better ideas."

* * *

Day 6 - Afternoon

The armorer had listened to their proposal, nodded, and had immediately gone about improving the idea. "The problem you have with your design, sirs, isn't penetration, it's over-penetration," he had said. "It'd do an absolute number on maybe a medium-armored vehicle, but on an animal? More than likely, it'll blow right out the other side of mama and she'll just be pissed. You may kill her, depending on what you hit, but it probably won't be a fast kill, and I think we all agree we want to drop her in a hurry. We gotta build something better; something that'll mushroom after penetration, maybe." At that point, he had turned to his fabricating equipment and started sketching on a pad. "Gimme an hour or so, boss, I'll have something special."

It had been closer to three hours, but true to his word, Kyle had turned out an impressive weapon. The sabot-jacketed penetrator was capped by a sharp, crystalline point designed to penetrate the hide and shatter. The softer head would push back into the round, causing it to mushroom and expand the wound channel, greatly increasing the damage. "Remember, Moose, you need a minimum of thirty meters to allow the round to discard the jacket," Kyle said. "Closer than that, it just isn't going to work."

Now armed with the sabot shot, Rik was back on the wall. He looked left to check the positioning of his men. The remaining seven CASPers of third squad stood about three or four meters apart, restlessly waiting for the monstrous grekel to appear. They knew it was close. Chief Klein had the scout drones out in force, but it wasn't in sight of the perimeter yet. Occasionally, they could hear a great roar. Down the wall to his right, Rik saw Tuck and his nine CASPers spread out in a similar manner to Third, facing out from the wall and ready for combat. Rik's and Tuck's squads formed the front line, with Major Cross and Lieutenant Guillard's First Squad forming the reserve. Depending on how this went, First would be ready to deploy to either side of the defense to support, should either Second or Third falter.

The first indicator of contact was the rhythmic thudding. Rik's suit microphones picked it up before the grekel came into sight. Soon after, he could feel the vibrations coming up through his feet. An acquisition icon came up on his display. He knew the comm shop, using the microphones from several mechs, had triangulated the source to provide targeting data. On his HUD, Rik saw Jones and Benett, the two CASPers on his immediate left, shift. He watched as Jones readied a medium laser rifle and the shoulder mounted light MAC attached to Benett tracked left, right, up, and down before settling toward the gap in the trees where he expected the creature to appear.

Major Cross's crisp baritone came across the comms. *"OK, Marauders. Second and Third, you will fire on my command. Standby."*

The trees shook and parted as the grekel moved into the edge of the clearing. At first, it was difficult to make out, partially obscured by the terrain. It moved in a half crouch, its head sweeping back and forth low over the ground. The massive creature paused, raised its head, and focused its gaze across the cleared ground. The weaving head froze and seemed to look directly at the base. Rik felt his jaw drop. Momma was huge. Even crouched, she was nearly four meters at the shoulder and massively built. One third of her fourteen-meter length was lashing tail. Despite everything he knew about the grekel, despite the encounter in the tunnel, part of Rik's brain still expected the sluggishness he associated with the large lizards of Earth. That was not what he saw now. The movements of the creature were quick and smooth, more like that of a mountain lion or the bobcats he had occasionally seen growing up in the Canadian Rockies.

The major's voice, still calm, continued. *"OK, that's a big sonofabitch. Doesn't matter though. We've had time to prepare the ground and it's not ready for what we are about to give it."* Warning indicators came up on Rik's combat display as the major activated the minefield. *"Ladies and gents, we are live. This grekel has 40 meters of very ugly minefield to cross before it gets to Point Alpha. If it gets that far, we'll start lighting it up with the MACs and then the lasers at Bravo."*

As if on cue, the creature started moving slowly forward, head low and sweeping over its path. Abruptly it stopped, backed up a little and then started moving to one side. It started forward but after a few yards, paused again, and moved to the side. Rik felt a cold sweat break out on his spine. Something was wrong. He was trying to see what it was doing when Tuck broke in on the command net. *"Major, we got a problem."*

Major Cross came back immediately. *"What do you see, Tucker?"*

"Sir, it knows about the mines."

"What? What do you mean?"

"Just that, sir. It knows. I don't know how, but it's moving through the field and actively avoiding the mines. Me and my boys laid out that section; I know where all the mines are and it's moving around them. I think… I think it can smell the explosives, sir."

"OK. We adapt." The major paused a moment. *"Well, if it isn't going to be courteous enough to step on the mines, then we'll just have to remote detonate them. Klein, you get a bonus duty. I want you and your team to trigger mines as the grekel moves near them."*

"Aye aye, sir."

"All right." Rik heard the click as the major shifted to the all-hands channel. *"Okay troops, we're twenty seconds in, so it's time for the plan to change."* There were some chuckles across the net.

* * *

Out in the cleared zone, the enormous grekel had moved out from the tree line. It crept slowly, cautiously, worming its way forward. Its head turned toward the movement of one of the drones. It regarded the device but then turned away. Before it could resume its course, the first mine detonated three meters off its right flank, sending dirt and debris skyward and staggering the beast. It stumbled to its left and a second mine, now only a meter and a half from its left front leg, exploded. A raging scream rang out from the creature. It quickly scuttled back into the tree line, hissing, and was gone from sight.

Rik leaned back into his harness, a look of concentration on his face, as he studied the display. He didn't think the mine did enough damage to drive it off. As he thought about it, he noticed two drones move out of the station and start following the creature.

Chief Klein's voice addressed the staff. *"The grekel is retreating. I've tasked two drones to track it. It's moved back into the trees about fifty meters and is now moving right, parallel to the tree line."*

Lieutenant Davis came on next. *"Sir, I was reviewing the video. We hurt it, but not bad. I don't have a great angle, but it doesn't look like there is much damage to it; the hide is just too thick. When we were building the charges, we were expecting the thing to step directly on the mines, or at least be standing over them when they went off. It was limping a little, so that second shot did... something, I guess... but it was still moving pretty well."*

"Agreed," Chief Klein responded. *"I'm tracking it now and it's moving slow, but not because it's hurt. The movement is more stalking. It may be looking for another way in."*

"Yes, I see," the major replied. *"Okay, it's moving south. That's still minefield, but it's shown that the minefield is only going to slow it down. All right, plan B. Everybody up on the wall. We let it get in close, too deep to get out. It gets near the wall, and we tear into it with everything we've got. Just light it up. We should be able to hit it with the command detonated mines at that point. It'll be too busy taking fire to avoid them."*

Rik dedicated one corner of his display to the drone feed following the grekel. It had circled around and now approached the southern end of the perimeter, the area manned by Second Squad. He checked his men's deployment again. Now that First had joined them on the wall, taking position on his left flank, he wanted to make sure Third hadn't moved so close to Tuck and his crew that they'd get in each other's way. He nodded to himself, satisfied, and opened a channel. "Hey, Tuck. Looks like you guys get to start the ball."

"*Yeah, I see it.*" Tucker's voice came back. "*We have a few minutes before it's in sight. Coming in on the flank like it is, it almost seems smart.*" A green dot appeared on Rik's HUD map. "*If it comes in here, or further south, I estimate only about half the suits will have a direct line of sight to it. We'll see how it moves, but as it stands, we aren't going to be able to put all the guns on it.*"

"Yeah, I see what you mean. First isn't going to be able to play with the rest of us." Rik looked out at the approach. "This works for me. I'll take what I can get, but the best bet for this penetrator is a flank shot and that looks like what I'm going to get." It was a good plan. He had given it a lot of thought and knew it was dangerous, but given the task and the tools, it was the best plan they had.

The grekel emerged from the wood line. Once again, its head was low over the ground. It began to slowly advance through the minefield, weaving its way between the mines. "Big sonofabitch, ain't it?" Rik said to Tuck.

"*Just a bitch more like. 'The female of the species is more deadly than the male,'*" Tuck said, quoting the ancient poet. "*To be honest,*" he went on, "*I'm a little disappointed in the major. He didn't use my idea.*"

"And what was your idea?"

"*Well, I figured since you had the super guns,*" Tuck said, "*we could just put you out there about fifty meters or so and dangle you like bait until it charges. Then you could just pot it. As a concession to your safety, I told him we could tie a rope to you and pull you back in if we needed to.*"

Rik grinned. "Well, you know, Tuck, it is a rare plan that is perfect at birth, and yours is so close. Don't you think it would be better if, instead of me, we put you out there? When it stopped to eat you, it would present the perfect shot for me, and there would be no risk to anyone actually important in the company."

"*Oh, that's a good one,*" Tuck laughed. "*Okay, time to get serious. It's about halfway to the kill box.*"

Rik watched the grekel, still stalking through the field. It split its attention, looking down at the ground and then up at the Marauders lining the wall. Each time it looked at the CASPers, it let out a low, malevolent hiss. It occurred to Rik that the grekel might have connected the death of its offspring to the Marauders.

The major's voice came over the speaker. "*Okay Marauders, it's time.*" Rik adjusted the rifle into firing position.

"*FIRE!*"

On both sides of Rik, the staccato thuds of MACs cut loose, accompanied by discharging lasers. He joined them, firing his rifle at the head of the beast. Like lightning, it was already jerking away, screaming its outrage. Rik could see the beast's hide dimpling as MAC rounds hit and failed to penetrate. He cursed and pulled up the squad channel.

"The MACs aren't penetrating. MACs hold fire until it gets closer and target the head. If we're going to hurt it anywhere, it'll be the head." As he closed the comm, a mine detonated beside the grekel and it twisted in pain and anger.

As if it recognized the danger, the grekel turned, bounded to the right past Rik's position and then dove forward. In a single motion, it sprang onto the six-meter wall and drove into two of Third Squad's CASPers, scattering them like bowling pins into the courtyard below. Rik watched as the damage indicators for Jones and DuBois dropped from green to yellow. The beast turned and roared its defiance. He could see its right eye was damaged, possibly gone. As he activated his MACs, red lights lit the cockpit. Cursing, he opened comms. "She's too damn close, Tuck, I can't target her!"

"*Dammit!*" Tucker bounded forward and activated his jumpjets. He shot upward and Rik saw his arm blade snap out. At the peak of his arc, the jets cut out and Tuck dropped like a stone to the grekel's back, blade leading. He crashed into it, the blade sinking into the monster, driving it onto its belly on the wide walkway topping the perimeter wall. The beast screamed, thrashing around and twisting to seek its tormentor. As it spun, its tail came around and struck Rik's CASPer, sweeping him from the wall and through a temporary building. At the same time, Tucker was thrown, landing further down the wall and flat on his back.

Stunned, Rik worked to get back on his feet. Red and yellow warning lights blazed across his HUD. Over his own wheezing, he could hear Tucker gasping over the open comm. Through his visor, Rik saw the grekel turn and spot Tucker's downed CASPer. It roared and began to move forward as other CASPers engaged it with laser and MAC rounds. Rik readied his weapons. As it advanced, the beast had presented itself broadside to him, and he could not ask for a better shot. He placed the crosshair right behind the beast's left shoulder and triggered the right MAC. Unlike the thunk sound made by the lighter MACs, there was a tremendous crack-BOOM as the sabot fired. It slammed into the wall below the grekel a full four meters from his point of aim and blasted a crater big enough for a CASPer to stand in. Rik didn't know if the miss was from the damage he took from the tail, or from being slammed through a building. He cursed and looked up. The grekel bounded forward, slamming through the remainder of Third Squad, heading for Second's section of the wall. Rik saw lasers flash ineffectively and the creature's body dimple as light MAC rounds impacted and failed to penetrate. The beast looked annoyed as she bit down on Laland, shook him twice and threw him out from the wall. On the HUD, Rik saw Lalande's systems drop to yellow and red. The life signs were still strong, though. The monster hissed and bounded again, falling among the lead CASPers of Second Squad.

"*Oh, no you don't, you big bastard!*" Tucker's voice thundered over Rik's suit's speakers as he staggered back to his feet. The beast screamed at the new challenge, and Tucker's MAC ripped off a string of rounds that impacted the wounded right side of the grekel's head and neck. The beast roared in pain and rage, and it pounced. Both front legs slammed into the chest of the CASPer, drove it into the stone walkway, and pinned it much like a cat would trap a mouse.

"Shitshitshit!" Rik gritted his teeth and scanned his displays. He knew he couldn't trust his targeting systems anymore. He scrambled to disable the traversing motor and locked the left MAC forward. Using his whole body, he then pointed the weapon toward the grekel.

The beast turned to swipe at another round of laser fire, shifting more of its weight to the clawed paw resting on Tuck's unmoving CASPer. Pointing at center mass, Rik fired.

The round exploded out of the barrel and crossed the open courtyard, the sabots peeled off by the tremendous velocity of its passage. The revealed fins bit into the air, and the core dart stabilized. Once again, the round impacted a notable distance from its point of aim, this time entering the upper neck of the beast slightly left of center. As it exited the lower skull, it took with it a significant portion of brain and bone. The grekel dropped like a marionette with its strings cut.

Rik staggered. He could barely think. He could hear someone yelling at him, but it seemed to be coming from far away. His head still rang from being bounced off a building.

"Third Squad, status!" He struggled to keep his voice steady as he lurched toward the wall. Electricity seemed to jolt through his body. He staggered again, but forward, picking up speed. Only half his attention was on the comm chatter, his mind on Tuck, who had not responded to anyone yet. He climbed the stairs to the top of the wall and picked his way through the suits that had gathered around his downed friend. Corporal Wills of first squad was dragging the grekel's arm off Tuck's CASPer. Rik helped push it the rest of the way. "Tucker! Answer me!" he demanded over the link as he reached down to the canopy release. He could still hear people yelling as he pulled the handle. The canopy popped, and he knocked it away.

Rik popped his own canopy, hitting the emergency releases on his harness and dropped down next to Tucker. "Buddy! Buddy, hang in there." He knew it was bad. Tucker's face was a mask of blood from a cut across the forehead, and he could see a massive amount of blood down his chest, where the grekel's claw had penetrated the armor.

Tuck coughed, frothy blood on his lips. One eye opened, focusing on Rik. "Are we done?" he whispered.

"Yes! Yes! It's dead!" Rik turned and spotted Sergeant Tams of first squad. "Where are the medics?" Tams pointed at a knot of people coming up the stairs. Rik could see them, but they seemed so slow.

"Hey," Tuck coughed again. "We got it." He took a labored breath. "Yay, us. Next time… you're bait."

* * *

Hyperspace, Day Two

With the death of the grekel matriarch, the major had been able to wrap the contract and claim a tidy bonus for doing it in less than the originally projected month. Contract completed, they had packed up and headed toward the gate.

Tucker was still confined to medical and griping the whole time. It had been a near thing, and he'd be stuck there for a while longer as the nanites repaired his lung. Rik had been stuck there himself for the first day. The doc had diagnosed him with a mild concussion and had hit him with medical nanites. Once the concussion was cleared, he'd been thrown out and told to limit visitation to one meal a day. He and Tucker together had driven the medical staff up the wall.

"This sucks," Tucker said as he looked down at what the medics called lunch.

"It does indeed, my friend," Rik replied. "It's your own fault, though. You got stabbed through the lung, stomach, and a little bit of intestine. You're lucky the grekel missed the liver or you would have been dead before we popped the canopy. So you get… what is that, anyway? Some sort of gruel? Nasty."

"They say it's protein paste. They say it tastes like chicken," Tuck said bitterly. "Bullshit. Hey, why aren't you eating?"

"This crap?" Rik asked, gesturing. "Thank you, no. Besides, I have a date."

"Bullshit."

"Sorry, buddy. Kara, oh, I mean Chief Klein," Rik said, smiling, "says she'd like me to come watch some movies with her. Since you're all laid up, I didn't think you'd mind. So, enjoy the gruel, we're having burgers." Rik patted Tucker on the shoulder, grinned, and left medical.

* * * * *

Dan Bridgwater Bio

Some of Dan's earliest memories include watching Godzilla movies and Star Trek (The Original!). This love of monster movies and TV Sci-Fi led to his reading every bit of science fiction and fantasy he could get his hands on. Eventually, all those stories in his head reached some sort of critical mass, and now he's creating his own. An Army brat and a Marine veteran, Dan has lived on both coasts, the Midwest, Korea, and Kuwait. He now lives with his wife and daughters in Colorado, where he supports training for the US Military.

# # # # #

Something Beautiful by Chris Kennedy

Now

"That's just fucking great," Major James "Foster" Grant muttered as he looked through the binoculars. "I haven't seen that many ants since my last fucking camping trip." He lowered the binoculars, blinked a couple of times, and then brought them back up again. The flashes of black moving between the rocks on the other side of the valley resolved into giant armed aliens, darting from cover to cover. "We've definitely found the Altar."

"The altar?" Private Sebring asked. "You mean, like from a church?"

"No," Sergeant Jistala said. His ears flicked forward, and he jerked his muzzle toward the other side of the valley. "The missing mercenaries, you moron."

The private sniffed. "I knew that. I was just kidding."

Corporal Jernigan chuckled. "Maybe if we lay out some sugar or honey, we can get them all to follow it into a nice little kill zone."

"I meant to ask Sergeant Tragonic but never got the chance," Sebring said. "If they look like ants, do you suppose he's going to be afraid of them?"

Jernigan cuffed the private in the back of the head. "Elephants are afraid of *mice*, not ants. The sergeant's right; you *are* a moron." He looked across the valley. "Although… maybe if they were Veetanho, we'd have to worry about the sergeant."

"Neither of you should laugh," Jistala said. "In fact, you'd better hope they keep coming the way they are."

"Why's that?"

"Altar really aren't seen that much as mercenaries," the Zuul said. "And they really don't take very many above-ground contracts. Like the ants of your world, they're diggers, and you don't want to meet them underground. That's where they're at their best." He turned back to Grant, who had his binoculars back to his eyes. "Can you tell what they're doing?"

"Not sure," Grant said, "but I can tell you what they're *not*. They stopped advancing. Looks like they're setting up observation posts."

Jistala winced. "And they've got three hundred of them on the other side of that hill."

"If they have hundreds," Jernigan said, his voice full of disbelief, "why don't they just attack? They've got us like six to one. If they did it right, they could overrun us."

Sebring turned to the sergeant. "They've seen our CASPers, right, sir? They're probably afraid of us."

"That's not the way they fight." The Zuul shook his head. "Right now, they're digging. Don't worry; they'll be coming. But it'll be underground."

Grant nodded. "Come on. Let's go get our CASPers. We have to let the CO know."

* * *

Three Months Earlier
The Mangy Merc

Just Outside Miami Startown, Earth

Grant set his drink down and chewed his lower lip. "So, you're serious about doing this?"

"The time is right," Dave Arnett replied. "With what Shirazi and the government are doing, it's now or never. I've got the credits from the last few contracts, and I'm going to give it a go. I'm starting a merc company. It'll be a small, combined arms organization, company sized, built around two platoons of Mk 8 CASPers."

"And you think you can be successful?"

"I think so, yeah." Arnett stared across the booth at Grant for a moment. "That's more likely if you take the XO spot."

"Me? XO? I've never been more than a lieutenant. Jumping to XO… I don't know if I could, and more importantly, I don't know if the troopers will respect me."

Arnett scoffed. "You've completed almost as many contracts as me. You've seen and done plenty. The only reason you've moved around and not up is you just got into bad situations. This time, the situation is made for you. Literally. When I decided to start a merc company, I knew you needed to be part of it."

Say no, Grant's subconscious said. *You're retired.* Grant sighed and pushed aside the thought. He'd been retired for four months, and they'd been the longest and *most absolutely boring* months of his life.

"Who else do you have?" Grant asked, stalling.

"Mostly a lot of junior guys. The ones coming over from the old unit only have a contract or two under their belts, and neither were particularly difficult. We'll need to find some good NCOs."

"Where the hell are you going to do that? Anyone you try to steal them from—"

Arnett held up a hand. "I'm not stealing from anyone." He smiled. "There's a reason we're meeting here." He waved a hand toward the main room. The bar was packed, with all its tables full and plenty of people standing in between them listening to the loud, awful music. Although most were Humans, there were also a few aliens at a couple of the tables. "What do you see?"

Grant surveyed the room and shook his head. "A bunch of has-beens and never-weres. People who couldn't cut it as mercs. Even the aliens look iffy. If a fight broke out, you and I could probably take the whole lot of them. If you're going to start a new company, you need *hard* men for NCOs. These ain't them."

"True." Arnett acknowledged the comment with a small nod. "Anything else?"

"Cheap booze sold for exorbitant prices?"

"Speaking of which." Arnett chuckled and tapped his empty glass. He caught the attention of the Zuul waiter—an alien that looked like a large, bipedal German Shepherd—and signaled for another round.

Grant frowned and sighed. The only problem with Arnett was that sometimes, he liked his own jokes just a bit too much. "Are you going to tell me?"

"Nope."

"Then what the hell are you talking about?"

"I'm not going to *tell* you." Arnett smiled. "I'm going to *show* you." He nodded toward the Zuul now weaving his way through the crowd toward them.

A man got up from a table suddenly, and his chair slammed into the waiter. All the drinks ended up on the table and several of the patrons behind him. The men—Humans all—came up swinging. The first one took the edge of the waiter's tray in the side of the forehead and went down, along with the one to the left with him.

The server ducked a swing from a guy that yelled, "Fucking mutt!" as he charged in, stomped on the merc's foot, then stood up suddenly, using the back of his head to slam into the man's jaw.

Several teeth flew as the man collapsed.

The fourth man started to draw a laser pistol, but the server threw the tray like a discus and caught the man in the throat. He went down gasping.

The server turned back to find the second man now on his feet. The man picked up one of the wooden stools and slammed it into the floor, breaking off one of the legs. He then advanced, holding the chair leg like a baseball bat. The Zuul dodged the man's swing, then was on him like a flash. He grabbed the man's arm in a nerve pinch, and the chair leg fell from his grasp. The Zuul caught it midair, flipped it to catch the small end, then brought the large end down on the man's head. He fell.

The Zuul looked around the circle that had formed around the combatants. "Anyone else?"

When no one stepped forward, he dropped the chair leg and nodded to the bouncers that were just arriving on the scene and motioned toward the downed Humans. "Toss them out, but make sure they pay for all the busted stuff."

The Zuul turned toward Arnett. "Give me a minute on the drinks; I'll go get a new round."

"Not necessary." Arnett smiled and waved him over.

"You guys done?" the alien asked. "Want your check?"

Arnett chuckled and jerked his chin toward where the bouncers were dragging out the mercs. "Nice moves."

The Zuul shrugged. "Beating up on drunks isn't anything to be proud of. No honor in it."

"How'd you like to fight with honor?"

"I look forward to it. Another year or two of this and I'll have enough credits to get back to my clan."

"Stranded here after the war?"

The Zuul scoffed. "Is it that obvious?"

Arnett nodded. "I'm starting a new merc company and need people with experience. You interested?"

"I might be. Depending on the situation."

"I need NCOs to help run it. You look like you can show the new folks hand-to-hand combat. Any good with machinery?"

"What kind of machinery?"

Arnett smiled broadly. "Ever wanted to drive a CASPer?"

"Every time I had to face them on the battlefield."

"What's your name?"

"Jistala."

"I'm Colonel Arnett." He held out his hand. "Welcome to the Knights, *Sergeant* Jistala."

"A CASPer and a promotion?" His lips pulled back showing a lot of sharp teeth. "I think I'm going to like the Knights."

"You know of any other stranded aliens that might be available?" Arnett asked.

"I might." Jistala stroked his muzzle. "Are they all CASPer positions?"

"Yeah. Mk 8s. Top of the line."

"Oh." Jistala's shoulders fell.

"What's wrong?"

"There's a Sumatozou on days here. Tragonic. Too crowded for him to work nights, so he gets stuck with the day shift and shitty tips. I know he'd be interested. Too big for one of the mech suits, though."

"A Sumatozou?" Grant asked. "We'll take him."

"Are you sure?" Arnett asked. "They aren't particularly mobile on the battlefield."

"No, but they're heavy weapons teams, all on their own. Trust me."

"Fine." Arnett turned back to Jistala. "Bring Tragonic and anyone else you know to the starport tomorrow and ask for the Knights' hangar."

The Zuul nodded. "I will."

"Hey, Dog Breath!" the bartender yelled. "Get back to work!"

"Fuck you, Stevens!" Jistala yelled back. "I quit!"

* * *

The Next Day
Arnett's Knights' Hangar

"Come on," Arnett said. "Let's go see what Jistala brought."

Grant looked up from the CASPer he was preflighting. The suit was so new it still had some of the oil and shipping material on it. He'd climbed into it and closed the canopy just to experience the "new car smell" of it, as he'd never been in one that didn't already smell like someone's ass—or worse, their blood and entrails. The aroma had rendered him momentarily speechless, and it had taken him a few moments to convince himself to open the canopy and continue the preflight.

"Sure," Grant said, standing. "I take it they're here?"

"Yes."

"That's all I get? A 'yes?'"

"I'm not sure you'd believe it if I told you."

Grant chuckled. "Well, lead on then."

They walked quickly, and as soon as they stepped out of the relative cool of the hangar and into the tough Florida sun—after Grant's eyes adjusted, anyway—he could already see some of the aliens at the gate. The massive, elephantine Sumatozou was hard to miss, as was the large, black shape—

"A Tortantula?" Grant asked, incredulous, as he looked at the enormous, three-meter-long spider.

Arnett laughed. "Looks like it."

"We can't take him."

"It's a her."

"How do you know?"

"They're all female, or so I've been told."

Grant shook his head, unable to believe the collection of aliens. In addition to the Sumatozou and Tortantula, there was a Flatar seated on the spider, as well as an Oogar, a Lumar, and a MinSha standing behind Jistala and another Zuul.

"That's quite a collection," Arnett said. "Although you're missing a few of the merc races."

Jistala shrugged. "You wanted experience; I brought the most experienced folks I could find. I already told you about Tragonic," he said, nodding to the Sumatozou.

"This is Elpka." Jistala nodded to the other Zuul.

"Gron." The Oogar—a large purple bear—nodded and yelled, "Good to meet you!"

Grant winced at the volume level. It had been a while since he'd been near an Oogar, and he'd been partially deafened by an exploding shell. *They really* are *as loud as everyone says.*

"Truda." The hulking, four-armed humanoid waved both left hands.

"Shatayl." The enormous praying mantis bowed.

"And finally, Zzelator and Treetar." The Tortantula and the oversized chipmunk riding it both waved.

Arnett nodded. "Thanks for coming. Yes, the Knights are recruiting. I know most of you got stuck here at the end of the war. If you sign on with us, I promise I'll drop you at Karma at the completion of our first contract."

"We will have that in writing?" the MinSha asked. She waved a hand at her surroundings. "Because we were all promised that before, and yet, here we are."

"Absolutely." Arnett chuckled. "I think you'll find that my promises are far more solid than the Mercenary Guild's or anything that comes from the mouth of a Veetanho." He turned back to Jistala. "Where did you find them all, and what experience do they have?"

"They have all completed at least five contracts. I know most of them personally, and the others were vouched for by Elpka." The other Zuul nodded. "As we will potentially be going into combat with them, it's safe to say that neither of us would recommend someone who'd get us killed."

Arnett nodded. "Makes sense." He turned to the Tortantula. "What do you do?"

"Sssort garbage," the spider replied with a lisp. "Yummy, yummy garbage."

"No, I meant your combat skills."

"If the enemy has things," the Flatar said, "we take them. We lead the assault."

"Dessstruction." The Tortantula nodded. "Ssslaughter."

"Treetar?" Arnett asked. "That was your name?" The Flatar nodded. "Can you keep her under control? Destruction and slaughter are fine, up until the enemy surrenders. The Knights will honor any enemy's surrender, and we will not eat their dead."

"I can eat their living?" Zzelator asked.

"No. Unless otherwise instructed, we're not eating any of the enemy. If you can't promise that, I don't have a place for you."

"We're not going back to the dump," Treetar said. His nose twitched. Whatever Zzelator liked, he obviously did *not*. "I will keep her under control."

Arnett nodded. "You're all provisionally hired. Be here tomorrow at 0800 for your first day." He handed Jistala a piece of paper. "Send me all of their resumes."

Jistala nodded as the rest of the group turned and walked off. "I'll get them to you shortly." He hurried off to join the group.

"You can't be serious," Grant said as they walked back to the hangar. "Most of them can't operate a CASPer."

"No, they can't. The two Zuul can, though, and maybe the Lumar."

"You'd put a Lumar in a CASPer?"

"Not if I can help it."

"So, what are you going to do with them?"

"Honestly, I'm not entirely sure."

"So why hire them?"

"Because the government is going to pay us 100,000 credits a piece to take them off planet."

Grant shook his head. "The money's no good if we're dead because they either can't or won't integrate into the company."

Arnett stopped, turned toward Grant, and winked. "True. Happily for me, I have someone that's worked with alien races before who can figure out how to integrate them."

"Me?"

Arnett nodded. "That is about as diverse a group as I've ever seen. Don't look at them as square pieces that you're trying to put into round holes. Look at their individual characteristics and find square holes to fit them into. This is our company, and we can structure it any way we want to."

"We'll never get that collection past the Merc Guild, though."

Arnett smiled. "Yes, we will."

"How do you know?"

"Because I just got the approval to start Arnett's Knights." He pulled out his slate and turned it to where Grant could see. On it was their certification to operate and accept contracts. "I sent this in several months ago, and it was approved. The only manning issue is that Humans have to make up at least fifty-one percent of our roster. That won't be a problem. The only problem we have—"

"Is figuring out how to use them." Grant nodded. "Got it."

"I'll forward you their resumes once I get them. I look forward to seeing what you put together."

Yeah," Grant muttered. "So do I."

* * *

"What have you got?" Arnett asked when Grant walked into his office in the morning.

Grant lifted an eyebrow. "Besides a headache from lack of sleep?"

"Don't worry, there's plenty of time to sleep when you're dead. I just accepted our first contract, so we—"

"You what?" Grant thundered. "You can't—"

"I can." Arnett smiled. "I'm the CO, remember?"

"But we're—"

"Not ready." Arnett nodded. "I know. Which is why I took one that doesn't start for a couple of months. We'll have time to train and get ready."

Grant winced. "Where is it? Do I want to know?"

"A couple of jumps past Karma."

"So, we're only going to have about a month to train?"

"Something like that. I hope your plan is good, because we don't have a lot of time."

"Isn't that what I just said?"

Arnett chuckled. "No, I meant before they get here. It's 0715, and they'll be here in forty-five minutes." He smiled. "What's your plan to integrate the aliens into a Human CASPer unit?"

Grant stood, looking at his CO, unable to close his mouth or speak coherently.

"Oh, come on," Arnett said. "It's not that bad. We've both had worse."

"Sure, but we didn't have aliens; we just had knuckleheads we had to train."

Arnett winked. "Just think of the aliens as exceptionally large knuckleheads. Or, in the case of the Oogar, exceptionally loud ones." He waved his XO toward a chair. "Now, what have you got?"

"Fine," Grant said, sitting. "Let's start with Gron, then, since you brought him up. First Sergeant Gron is your new senior enlisted advisor."

"What?"

Grant smiled as Arnett's mouth fell open. "He's got about twenty-five years of service, making him the most experienced, other than you and me. Besides. With his voice, the troopers won't have any problem hearing him on the battlefield."

"Neither will the enemy."

Grant shrugged. "You asked me to assign them where they fit. Gron is qualified—and then some—to be the senior NCO."

"And always be yelling in my ear." Arnett rolled his eyes, then he put his hands up in surrender. "Fine. That's my payback. What else?"

"The two Zuul and the MinSha are your new platoon sergeants. The Zuul have the added benefits of being able to fit inside a CASPer, so they'll have all the communications capabilities we do. All three have the experience and the leadership to handle the position. And, in case you forgot the barfight the other night, Jistala can take anyone behind the woodshed if necessary and realign their attitude. Shatayl and Elpka actually have more experience with such things. All will have the rank of Sergeant First Class."

"We only have two platoons, though, remember? The standard company size in the Merc Guild is two platoons with two squads of ten men each."

"Each of our three platoons will have two squads of seven, plus we'll have a separate weapons squad. That's forty-two. You'll need to buy two more suits, but that's the best way to do it."

Arnett sighed. "Fine."

"Cheer up. I'm using all eight of the aliens. You'll get almost a million credits from the government."

"True, but there are other expenses—"

Grant raised an eyebrow.

"Okay." Arnett's shoulder slumped. "What are we doing with the other ones?"

"They'll be our heavy weapons and assault squad."

"The heavy weapons squad is support. They don't lead the charge."

"Ours does." Grant smiled. "And if you saw a Tortantula and a Sumatozou charging at you, supported by an Oogar and a Lumar with chain guns, and a whole pile of CASPers, you'd have second thoughts about the life you were leading."

Arnett chuckled. "That much is true." His slate buzzed, and he picked it up. "Yes?" Grant couldn't hear the response, but then Arnett added, "Be right there."

"This I have to see," Arnett said as he stood.

"What?"

"Come on. I'll need you for this."

The two men hurried out to the gate. The group of aliens was back, along with what looked like a large wasp.

"Never seen one of those before," Arnett said. "Any idea what it is?"

"SleSha," Grant said with an involuntary shudder.

"What's wrong with them?"

"Nothing," Grant replied. "I just hate bugs. Especially stinging ones."

"What do they do?"

"The SleSha? They're a failed merc race, and most are pirates or worse. Some of them are excellent pilots."

Arnett's eyebrows rose. "Some of them?"

Grant shrugged. "Some are just drones, with almost no independent thought. They take their orders via a hive mind thing from a queen. Their front-line warriors and pilots are intelligent, as is their leadership caste."

"Which do you suppose that one is?"

"It's talking to the others, so I'm guessing it's intelligent."

Arnett nodded, and they walked the rest of the way in silence.

"I brought you one more recruit," Jistala said as they approached.

"Really?" Arnett asked. "What's he do?"

"I'm a pilot," the SleSha said. "Best you've ever seen. I'm not a 'him' though. I'm female."

"Sorry," Arnett said with a nod. "We don't need a pilot, though. We don't have a shuttle."

"Oh, I fly those, too, but my specialty is battlefield intelligence. I also fly drones."

"And you're good at that?"

"The best. I can get into and out of almost anywhere unseen."

"Prove it."

The SleSha nodded. "You have forty-eight CASPers in your hangar. Two of those are Mk 7s, the rest are Mk 8s."

"I didn't think we had enough CASPers," Grant said. "If that's true, we have plenty."

"I wanted to have some spares," Arnett replied. He turned back to the alien. "What's your name?"

"Shishtik."

"It's an accurate count, Shishtik. You're hired."

* * *

One Month Ago
Common Room
Maki Transport *Blade of Grass*, Hyperspace

Arnett and First Sergeant Gron entered the room. The ship was coasting, so there was no gravity, and they used magboots to walk. Grant chuckled softly in the back of the room. Arnett, for all his prowess in battle and management, had never figured out how to walk well in them, and the massive purple Oogar seemed far more comfortable—and walked more normally—as they took their places at the front of the space. The last two months had flown by in a blur. Grant had taken a lot of notes—what had worked and what hadn't—and he intended to write a book on it, assuming he survived this mission.

But that was a story for another time, and he focused on what the CO was saying.

"So, here we are," Arnett began. "I won't sugar coat it; the last couple of months haven't been easy. Integrating new ways of doing business for... well, for everyone, myself included, hasn't been easy, and it's meant that we've all needed to get out of our comfort zones from time to time."

"Yes." Sergeant Truda nodded. "Florida hot."

Treetar shook his head at the Lumar. "That's not what he meant, moron," the Flatar said.

Truda tilted his head. "What he mean?"

"Focus," Grant whispered, motioning to the front of the room. Two of the things that had become apparent were just how sarcastic the Flatar could be, and how much the Tort rider loved to screw with the Lumar. To his benefit, though—or maybe he really *didn't* get it— the Lumar always smiled and went along with the teasing without ever getting annoyed. Which only made the Flatar madder, so he tried harder. Which went on in a vicious circle that always left the taunter—Treetar—far angrier than his intended target. "We don't have time for that shit now."

"Tomorrow, we emerge in the Nunki system. It will take a couple of days to get to the planet from there, and then we'll have one day to turn over with the company that's currently got the contract."

"Who's that?" Sergeant First Class Jistala asked from the front row.

"The Queen's Own," Arnett replied. "It's an Altar company, I believe."

Jistala shook his head slowly.

"What's wrong with that, Sergeant?" Grant asked when the CO didn't see the reaction and started to move on.

"A packmate of mine was on a contract where his company followed the Queen's Own on a contract one time. That company is either the luckiest or the unluckiest one I know."

"What does that mean?" Arnett asked.

"I come from the same region they usually operate in. The Queen's Own has a reputation for finishing contracts. However, I know of three occasions where the company that followed them was wiped out."

"What happened to your packmate?"

"We don't know." Jistala shrugged. "His company was never heard from again. The next people in the system found everyone dead and the thing they were guarding—a mine—looted."

"Were the Altar to blame?" Tragonic asked.

"Nothing could ever be proven. The Altar had left the system, and no one else had been there. It was an unsolved mystery."

"I see," Arnett said. "Well, we'll make sure we're ready for anything before we take over from them. Here's what we're going to do."

* * *

"What do you think about what Jistala had to say?" Grant asked later in Arnett's office. "The setup seems awfully similar."

"It does," Arnett agreed, "but I can't do anything about it. If we back out now, we'll lose the deposit I put down on this contract, and I used the last bit of our funds to contract with the Maki to get this transport. If we don't finish this contract—successfully finish it, that is—then we're broke and out of business. Worse, our return trip is contingent on having the funds from completing the contract to pay for it."

Grant's jaw dropped. "So, if we don't complete it?"

"We're stuck there, just like the aliens in our company were left stuck on Earth."

"What happened to all the money you had? The good deals on CASPers and the credits for hiring aliens?"

"A merc company is gear intensive. Even with a discount, CASPers aren't cheap. And weapons and ammunition aren't, either. Add in food, transportation, and salaries, and we need to complete this contract. When we do, we'll have funds to float us going forward."

"Let me guess—this contract paid well. Perhaps a little more than it ought to. And it was on the boards a while, even though it was fairly lucrative."

Arnett couldn't meet his eyes. "Yes. To both."

"The other companies probably got wind that it was following the Queen's Own." Grant shook his head. "Dammit."

Arnett squared his shoulders and met Grant's gaze. "I knew about the reputation of the Queen's Own."

Grant's eyes widened. "You did? And you took it anyway?"

"I did." He smiled. "But that's because I really believe in this group and what we've put together here. Most companies are fairly one dimensional; we're not. This company can solve problems that most others can't. When you're a hammer, you see every problem as a nail. The Knights are a whole tool belt, though. We're going to get through this, and we're going to get paid well." He chuckled. "The advertised fee would have paid us well. Based on the Queen's Own thing, I got them to double it."

"So we'll be well off if we complete it?"

"*Very* well off."

Grant shrugged. "Then I guess there's no other option than to go in with our eyes open, figure out what's going on, and kick some ass. When we get home, though; this time I'm done."

"I like that."

"What? Me quitting?"

"No. The fact that you believe we're going to get through this." Arnett winked. "I'll let you in on a secret."

"What's that?"

"I believe it, too, or I wouldn't have signed us up for it."

* * *

One Week Ago
Mining Site, Auriga-5

"I've got good news and bad news," Staff Sergeant Shishtik said. The SleSha had become the company's reconnaissance "guy" and had been tasked with keeping tabs on the Altar.

Arnett sighed. "Good news first."

"The Altar transport finally gated out."

"That's good," Arnett said with a nod.

Grant scoffed. "Yeah, I was starting to wonder if they were all going to leave or just turn around and attack us." The giant ants had stayed in close proximity to the mine and the nearby industrial complex that served it for a couple of weeks after the Knights had taken over, and it had been fairly obvious that they were "casing the joint" in the old-time parlance.

It had seemed like no matter where Grant went—the bar in the small community to the east, the refinery, or *especially* the defensive emplacements—there were always Altar nearby. They didn't ever seem to be doing anything either; they just stood around, watching.

When Arnett had finally said something to their commander, he'd been told they were "just trying to learn from the Humans," but they'd pulled back, using their shuttle to redeploy to a camp about thirty kilometers away. *Probably because they already had all the info they needed.*

"I didn't say the Altar had left," Shishtik noted. "I said their *transport* had gated out."

Arnett chewed his lower lip. "But the Altar weren't on it?"

"I don't think so. I watched the ship burn its engines, and the vessel's mass wasn't what it should have been. It was a lot lighter… about as much as if three hundred Altar—along with all their combat gear—had been left behind."

Arnett sighed. "So, where are they?"

"I can tell you where they're not. They're not at the camp they established. That's gone."

"Telling me where they aren't doesn't help. I need to know where they *are*. Having three hundred soldiers show up unexpectedly will not make my day."

"Sorry, sir, but I have to sleep sometimes, and it looked like they were leaving. I just don't think that they did, in fact, leave. Even though they are trying to give that impression to anyone who might be watching."

"And you think an attack is imminent?"

The SleSha nodded. "I do."

"So do I." Arnett nodded. "Get your drones in the air and find them."

"I'm on it."

* * *

"Bad news," Shishtik said two hours later.

Arnett shook his head. "I'm sorry, Sergeant, but you've already used up your bad news quota for the day."

"Well, this can go for tomorrow's. I went back and looked at the tapes. In all the running back and forth the Altar's shuttles did between their ship and their encampment, they pulled one over on us. They left a shuttle behind. I analyzed all the goings and comings… and there was one fewer trip to space than trip to the planet."

"So they still have a shuttle here and could be—"

"Nearly anywhere," the SleSha said.

"Well, the one good thing is they can't put all of their troops on a single shuttle," Grant said. "They'll need time to mass, because they're going to have to hit us with most of their troops if they hope to beat us. One on one, we kick their ass."

"True." Arnett looked at the SleSha. "Thanks for the info. Even though it isn't what I wanted to hear, it will help us beat them in the end." He turned to Grant. "XO, I need you to push out the observation posts as far as you can. We'll have a limited window to prepare when they come back, and we'll need as much lead time as possible."

Grant nodded. "Yes, sir." He motioned to Shishtik. "C'mon, Staff Sergeant. I have a feeling you and your drones are going to be busy."

* * *

Now

Knights' Command Center, Auriga-5

"Got them!" Shishtik said. "Entropy!"

"What's going on?" Grant asked, looking up from his slate.

"The good news is I found the Altar. The bad news—"

Grant held up a hand. "Does there always have to be bad news with you, Sergeant? Just once, can you give me good news without anything bad?"

"Yes, sir, I'd love to. That time isn't now, though. I found the Altar where we'd least expect them, just like you said."

Grant nodded. "We have fewer defenses to the north, and it's mountainous, making it harder for them to get around as easily, so that's where they are."

"Yes, sir, and they're in about the last spot I would have looked for them if you hadn't said anything. A small valley with no easy way in or out—"

"Unless you have a shuttle, and then the terrain masks anyone looking for it."

"Yeah, that." The SleSha nodded.

"So what's the bad news?"

"I thought you didn't want it."

Grant frowned.

"The bad news is they know we know where they are."

"And why is that?"

"Because they saw my drone and shot it down. The worse news is I can't watch them anymore; that was my last drone. I can go build another, but it will take a couple hours."

"You're not impressing me, today, Sergeant."

"Sorry, sir, I didn't honestly think—"

"No, you didn't." Grant stood and turned to Sergeant First Class Jistala. "Grab a couple of your folks and your CASPers. We're going to go scout the old-fashioned way."

* * *

"So, you found them?" Arnett asked when they got back.

"Yes, sir," Grant replied. "They're about five kilometers to the north, or about three ridgelines up. Sergeant Jistala thinks they're going to tunnel from there and break into the mines. They'll probably distract us with an aboveground assault and use that to distract us from the main effort, which will be below ground, through the mines."

"Any idea how much time we have to prepare?"

Grant shrugged. "I looked at the GalNet. It ought to take three or four weeks for them to tunnel the five kilometers, based on what's known about Altar tunneling methods."

Arnett's jaw dropped. "That fast?"

"The only thing they do better than fight in tunnels is dig them out. They can excavate about a kilometer and a half a week. There's no telling how long they've been at it, either."

Arnett rubbed his chin. "Well, we can't let them hit us from two directions at once. They outnumber us too greatly; we'll be chewed up. We need to come up with a plan. Get with the Caroon miners and see what they think. Maybe we can dig a tunnel past them and hit them from behind."

* * *

"Okay," Grant said a few hours later. "I talked to the Caroons. They say that tunneling past the Altar tunnel and breaking through into it really isn't an option without knowing where it's coming from. Even if they knew the exact direction, they might miss it high or low."

"Damn," Arnett said. "I thought I'd come up with something clever."

"Well, my talk with them wasn't completely without benefit."

Arnett leaned forward. "What have you got?"

"The current tunnel system has bent off to the west, following the ridgeline. Apparently, there's an ore seam they're following. They said they have no issue with us rigging the northern section with explosives so that we can drop them when the Altar show up." Grant chuckled. "They even agreed to help our demolitions folks set them up."

Arnett nodded. "So, when the Altar get here, they break into the tunnel, we let them advance a bit, and then drop it on them?"

"Yes, sir. That frees up the company to focus on the aboveground attack."

"It would, anyway."

Grant's eyebrows knitted. "What does that mean?"

"The strength of this unit isn't in its defense. I mean, sure, we can park Tragonic somewhere, and he takes up a lot of space, but the company's lifeblood is its mobility—its ability to attack."

"If that's the case, why did you take a defensive garrison contract?"

Arnett smiled. "Just because we're defending something doesn't mean we have to be static, though. Didn't someone once say that the best defense was a good offense?"

"They did… but I think they were talking about it as it related to something in sports."

"It's just as relevant on the battlefield. Here's what we're going to do."

* * *

A Week Later

Knights' Command Center, Auriga-5

The Caroon scampered into the command center on all fours, then stood to survey the room. Mammalian, with a long nose and ears, it could have passed for an anteater in a dim alley. It raised a long, sharp claw and asked, "Where is Major Grant?"

"He's on assignment," the CO said, standing. "What's going on?"

"The foreman says the Altar are coming! He can hear their digger approaching our tunnels. They will likely break through today!"

Arnett nodded. "Please thank the foreman for me and ask him to take the rest of the day and night off."

The Caroon nodded once and ran back out of the room. "Twitchy little thing," Sergeant First Class Elpka said. "Are all of them like that?"

"Pretty much," Arnett replied. "Put out the word. It's time to move."

* * *

10 Kilometers North

"If we ever get out of this," Grant muttered, "I'm changing my name to Hannibal." He braced his CASPer's legs and pushed with all his mechanically enhanced strength.

"What does that mean?" Treetar asked. He slid backward out of his seat so Zzelator could duck her head and use her shoulders to help push Tragonic up the hill.

"Nothing," Grant replied. With a final grunt and some assistance from Gron and Truda, who were pulling from the front, they finally got the Sumatozou to the ledge just below the ridgeline. He took a moment to wipe the sweat from his forehead. "We'll rest here until it's time to go."

The star had already gone behind the mountains, and the light was fading fast. Grant had worried they wouldn't make it in time. They had, but just barely, and the entire team dropped down to relax.

If someone had ever told me I'd be commanding a team consisting of an Oogar, a Sumatozou, a MinSha, a Lumar, a Tortantula, and a Flatar, I would have laughed at them. The three Caspers, sure, but the rest? Grant shook his head.

"Movement on the far ridge," Shatayl said softly.

Grant eased his way forward and zoomed in on the ridge across the small valley. The Altar there were up and moving. All of them seemed focused in the other direction, but he didn't move quickly in case any of them were looking back. Tunnel dwellers, the Altar had better vision in the dark than most other races. They couldn't see as far as most, of course, but there was no sense in moving quickly and potentially highlighting himself.

The call had obviously gone out, as the Altar boiled out from the camp and from a number of tunnels in the area. Within minutes, a dark stain formed as the troopers formed up.

"We go now?" Truda asked. He held two rifles in his hands and looked excited to get to use them.

"Not yet," Grant said. "Wait."

With a roar, their dropship screamed up and over the ridgeline from the west. Before the Altar could do anything, its nose had rolled back down toward them, and a barrage of missiles roared off from under its wings.

The troopers were all armed, though, and lasers streaked up to meet the dropship as it thundered past them, dropping a string of bombs. The shells opened up, and a number of smaller bomblets dispersed from the cluster bombs to cover a large portion of the Altar.

The dropship climbed to avoid the next ridgeline, and Grant could see the lasers had been effective—one of the engines was smoking heavily.

"Go now?" Truda asked.

"Just another few moments…" Grant replied. He watched the opposite ridge and could see the Altar there dropping as First and Second Squad continued their advance. The Altar in the valley—now much fewer in number—began to organize and move in their direction.

"Now!" Grant said. "Charge!"

Weapons Squad started down the hillside. While the Sumatozou had struggled to get up the steep incline, it now had gravity in its favor, and it slid quickly down the slope, its legs churning as fast as they could to stay under him.

This probably wasn't the brightest idea, after all, Grant decided as he jumped off the ledge to follow the massive alien and the rest of the squad now racing down the mountain. *Just because Hannibal did it, doesn't mean that we should have, too.*

The CASPers had one thing the aliens didn't though—jumpjets—and Grant saw a flare as one of the troopers tried to catch himself. The rockets were bright in the night, and Grant winced, hoping none of the Altar had seen it.

But of course, they had—it was too bright for all of them to totally have missed it. Grant's low-light camera showed a handful spinning to come in their direction. He chuckled—the Altar hadn't sent anywhere near enough to deal with what was coming.

Zzelator reached the valley floor first, and with a scream of "Slaughter!" used her speed to race forward. Grant and the MinSha were next, then the rest of the team, with Gron rolling to a stop. He got up with a growl and launched himself after Zzelator, with the rest of the team close behind.

A number of flashes illuminated Treetar as he fired the MAC mounted to his saddle, and the Altar headed toward him returned fire with their weapons. Grant arrived as Zzelator killed the last of the Altar by biting its head off in a spray of dark blood. She looked around as if trying to decide whether to eat any of the others.

"Zzelator, no!" Treetar yelled as he slapped the massive spider. She spit the head back out.

"It tasted awful anyway," she muttered. "More slaughter!" she yelled and raced off again.

Grant looked up and saw more Altar headed in their direction, and the team began firing. Gron cut loose with his chain gun that had—miraculously—survived the Oogar's tumble down the hill, and the rest poured a combination of MAC and laser fire into the approaching aliens.

Then Tragonic cut loose with the multiple rocket launchers strapped to his sides.

Woosh! Woosh! Woosh!

Missile after missile streaked across the valley into the incoming Altar. Although each was small, he had a *lot* of them stacked up on their launchers, and he ripple-launched all of them while on all fours, then stood and threw off the launchers and grabbed his chain gun.

Grant glanced to the ridgeline as he deployed his laser shield. First and Second Squads were coming over it, but they'd be too late to the party and the heavy weapons team was still outnumbered four to one as the groups crashed into each other.

A warning light illuminated on his right leg; an Altar had gotten close and fired a laser into it. His sword blade snapped out as he spun, and the blade decapitated the trooper. Another warning light illuminated on his left arm and all the fires of hell blossomed on his left bicep. Another Altar on the left had snuck under his shield and was trying to use its laser rifle like a scalpel to cut off his arm. He spun back the other way, ending the threat.

As he turned back, he realized there were more—a lot more—Altar around him. Perhaps he seemed like an easier target than the Tortantula, the Oogar, or the Sumatozou, but a large number clustered around him, and he knew there were more than he could deal with.

Then, with a roar of jumpjets, Third Squad arrived, having jumped out of the dropship as it passed back over the battlefield. His suit identified Colonel Arnett as the CO landed on one of the Altar in a pillar of flames, roasting it, then he fired his MAC into another one at his side.

With the entrance of Third Squad into the fray, the resistance collapsed, and the few remaining Altar surrendered.

* * *

The Next Day
Knights' Medical Tent, Auriga-5

"How are you doing?" Arnett asked as he came to stand next to Grant's bed. "You look like a mess."

Grant looked at the swath of bandages around his arm. "What? This?" He chuckled. "You should see the other guy."

"I did. There weren't many left when we got there. You guys did a hell of a job."

Grant nodded. "That group puts out a lot of punch."

"They do."

"Did you get any info out of the surviving Altar?"

Arnett shook his head. "They're all junior troopers; they don't know anything." He scoffed. "Something interesting happened this morning, though."

"Oh, yeah? What's that?"

"A ship jumped into orbit."

"A ship jumped in? You don't mean in orbit, though, do you? You mean it came out in the emergence area."

"No, I meant exactly what I said. A ship jumped into orbit, on the other side of the planet from where the stargate is."

"That's impossible." Grant shook his head. "You *always* come out of hyperspace in the emergence area."

"Not this time. It appeared and made a couple of transmissions, then it jumped back out again." He shrugged. "We got some video of it."

"I understand how you jump out of a system without using the stargate—internal shunts—but how the hell do you just jump into orbit?"

"I don't know, but I intend to find out."

"And then what are you going to do?"

Arnett shrugged. "We're the Knights. I'm going to do something chivalrous and go kill the evil doers."

"They've pulled this stunt several times that we know of. They're going to be well financed."

"Probably. But they're sitting on a lot of credits. It will be a pretty good payday, I think."

Grant nodded. "I'm looking forward to it."

"I thought you were retiring?"

"I hate claim jumpers and people who stab you in the back." Grant shrugged and winced as it pulled his arm.

"Careful with that," Arnett cautioned.

"I know. The doc's had nanites working on it all night, though; I should be out of here later today."

"Hating claim jumpers isn't any reason to come back."

"I know." Grant smiled. "But the call to do battle better is. I look forward to getting back to it. Charging into battle with a bunch of different aliens was really cool, but it could have gone horribly wrong, too. I have some ideas that will integrate this company into something that's never been seen before."

"So you're back?"

Grant nodded. "Yeah. I think this is just the start of something beautiful."

* * * * *

Chris Kennedy Bio

A Webster Award winner and three-time Dragon Award finalist, Chris Kennedy is a Science Fiction/Fantasy author, speaker, and small-press publisher who has written over 55 books and published more than 500 others. Get his free book, "Shattered Crucible," at his website, https://chriskennedypublishing.com.

Called "fantastic" and "a great speaker," he has coached hundreds of beginning authors and budding novelists on how to self-publish their stories at a variety of conferences, conventions, and writing guild presentations. He is the author of the award-winning #1 bestseller, "Self-Publishing for Profit: How to Get Your Book Out of Your Head and Into the Stores."

Chris lives in Coinjock, North Carolina, with his wife, Sheellah, and is the holder of a doctorate in educational leadership and master's degrees in both business and public administration. Follow Chris on Facebook at https://www.facebook.com/ckpublishing/.

# # # # #

Sub Rosa Infiltration Company by John M. Olsen

The rough side of startown on Imago had a life of its own under a cloak of darkness and misdirection. It harbored an ebb and flow of shady characters doing things off the books. A sour miasma scared off those who didn't have any business in the seedy bars and tech shops. In the background, an occasional roar announced the departure or arrival of a ship on the backwater settler world.

Jonathan Smith, as everyone called him, swam through the undercurrents of dark deals like he was born to it. He knew the benefits of using both carrots and sticks to deal with shady characters, but he had built his reputation on giving people what they wanted. Then his best contacts moved on, leaving him with zero deals and climbing bills. The area was becoming more civilized every day.

Getting a mercenary team registered through the Phoenix Initiative was a lucky fluke, and he wasn't about to pass up the chance to take out a big loan and get some fancy equipment to bootstrap a new opportunity. It was a grand step up.

He still had a few networking contacts in a world where who you knew made all the difference, and he had called in all his favors to make the best of the new deal.

It wasn't like he was going to take on any high-profile mercenary gigs. He did his best work under a cover of darkness and misinformation. One more pickup, and he'd have his team.

Inviting alleys stretched to either side as he walked along the damp sidewalk, but his goal was a door farther down the street. Despite the darkness, he knew the way by heart, not having to rely on directions from his pinplant. Local service techs had given up here and moved to safer territory after having dozens of streetlights shot out over and over.

He stopped at a nondescript door and rapped twice, waited, then rapped two more times. A thin window slid open to show a yellow eye for only a moment. A Zuul opened the door to let him in.

As far as aliens went, his contact was as scary as most, if not more so. Jonathan was never sure if his expression was a snarl or a smile. Canine features were hard to read even after working several deals with one.

"Jotala. Good to see you."

The Zuul snarled a sequence of noises, and Jonathan's pinplant translated. "If you're here to complain about the hardware I sold you, it wasn't designed to be used underwater."

Jonathan spread his hands despite the rebuke. "You were quite clear, and I take full blame. I'm not here to complain."

"More equipment, then?"

"Not quite," Jonathan said as he eased into the room and leaned against a workbench covered with half-assembled actuators and transmitters. "I have a mercenary company registered with the Phoenix Initiative. I'm looking for a technical specialist, and I have a non-human slot to fill. Are you ready to get off this mudball and back into space?"

"Blunt as ever, and just as ambitious. Why would I leave what I have here? I build things for people, I trade in electronics and tools, and I sell to the highest bidder."

Jonathan eyed the shabby workshop and smiled. Jotala had been hit by the same downturn in clients. "I have a budget, and my team is negotiating for our first job from a local merc pit. I can't do this one without you."

"Ever since the war, everyone wants me to work for them. I work on only what I want to work on. I value independence."

With a flick of the wrist, Jonathan set a 100,000 credit chit spinning on the workbench, its red diamond catching the light as it came to a stop. It was a significant percentage of the upcoming contract payment. "Here's your budget for specialized equipment. Or parts to roll your own. I trust your judgment, but I need to know if you're on board."

Jotala showed even more teeth as he picked up the chit. "Independence is overrated. How much room can you spare for cargo, and where is your base of operations?"

"Two pallets of gear. The rest can go to a small warehouse. First, I'll introduce you to the team. If the contract negotiations work, we leave tomorrow."

Jotala looked around the shop and shook his head. "Two pitiful pallets? I'll pack after meeting your team."

"Not my team. Our team."

Bystanders of dubious repute found sudden interest in neighboring streets at the sight of an armed Human and Zuul walking purposefully through the dim streets.

The merc pit crouched on the border of the underbelly, which was convenient for merc companies who needed unusual gear. This wasn't like things back on Earth. There, you had to put actual work into finding black-market dealers.

Toward the back of the room, three mercenaries sat, not looking much like mercenaries at all. Gibbi, his CozSha accountant, sat with a short glass of some unknown liquid. His dark gray fur showed black splotches, which helped him to blend into the shadows, especially given his three-foot stature and stubby, goatlike horns.

Beside Gibbi sat Assam Alami, his weapons specialist. An empty plate sat nearby, and several parts of a weapon sat in a neat line in front of him as he examined one component with a magnifier.

The last occupant, a XenSha named Peek, scanned the room in a constant sweep as his long ears twitched nervously. Peek spotted Jonathan at the door and waved him over.

Jonathan stepped up beside Peek. "Where's Bevin?" He'd expected to have the full team here. His single fireteam barely met the minimum requirements for the Initiative.

Assam waved toward the door. "He left on an errand some time ago. It might have involved picking up a stock of alcohol."

"Great," Jonathan said. "Just what we need. And you let him go?" Bevin was the only one trained to use their old surplus Mk 6 CASPer.

Assam shrugged. "You're the boss, and you weren't here."

"We're a team. We have to act like one." Counting Blevin, the team consisted of three Humans and three not. Barely enough to meet the fifty percent Phoenix Initiative requirement. The team would grow as soon as they finished their first contract.

Four combatants and two support crew sounded insane on the surface, but Jonathan had a method to his madness. Running in stealth mode suited his team and his personal style perfectly. He could track down small undercover contracts the big mercs wouldn't look twice at.

Gibbi rolled his eyes and tapped his slate as he spoke. Jonathan's translator kicked in again. "We have a few hours to track him down. The client accepted the contract modifications."

Jonathan sat at the table and looked at Gibbi's slate from the side. "What did you fix?"

"Terrible loopholes. It had no combat pay bonus and no allowances for equipment damage. Cargo space was too small to house our CASPer, and the food was all made for SleSha. They also wanted three fireteams on rotating shifts."

"On a babysitting mission? It's a high-pay cakewalk. That's why I picked it."

Gibbi showed his square teeth in an approximation of a smile. "That is why it was so easy to get the proper clauses added. Insurance for us, no actual cost for them. The contract was sloppy. Written in a hurry with nobody like me to clean it up. We now qualify to bid on it with our limited numbers."

"That's great, Gibbi. Let me introduce our final team member for this assignment. This is Jotala. He does electronics and hardware and will bulk up our stealth and offensive potential."

Jotala nodded and glanced over the weapon parts on the table. "You should replace that spring if you want to shoot that thing more than once."

"Why do you think I have it field stripped, furball?" Assam leaned back in his chair and flicked the spring toward Jotala's head.

Jotala snagged it from the air and pocketed it in one smooth motion as his eyes narrowed and a growl rumbled deep inside his chest.

"Smooth it out. We're a team, remember?" Jonathan hoped it wouldn't feel like riding herd on a preschool to keep his team aimed in the same direction.

Jotala ran a hand along his scruff, but he sat. He still glared at Assam.

"Better lock in the contract before someone snipes it from us, Gibbi."

"Done. Team of six to board with our gear tomorrow morning. Sign this, sir." Gibbi slid the slate in front of Jonathan, and he confirmed the contract before copying it into his pinplant's storage.

* * *

The next morning was a disaster. Jotala's pallets were late, so he paced nervously with only his backpack of tools. Assam found new warning lights on the CASPer. Bevin didn't show.

To top it off, a pair of Human guards frog-marched a guy out of a neighboring berth and shoved him to the ground. Someone had worked over his face. The security team laughed as they boarded their ship and shut the hatch. Jonathan didn't need more drama.

He looked over his crew and shook his head. "Let's get on board."

"We can't," said Gibbi. "We have five. Contract says six."

A distant look came over Jonathan as he diverted his attention to his processing pinplant and searched the startown network for news of his wayward mech pilot. It didn't take long. Jail would have been one thing. He could have bailed him out. But the search showed Bevin at the hospital with severe injuries, along with a local news article about a bar brawl.

He couldn't afford to go nuclear and make a scene in front of his team. He clenched his jaw and looked at his options. Terminating or withdrawing his first contract before starting would be a black mark, but without his full team, he couldn't board at all. "Bevin's not coming.

I've got his medical bill covered, so we can take him on our next contract. Options? We need one more Human. Assam, go buy us a little more loading time with the captain. Jotala, you have a few minutes to search for your gear."

The two team members scrambled, Assam toward the ship and Jotala away from it.

Peek pointed at the figure slumped at the neighboring berth. "There's a Human."

"We need more than just a warm body, Peek."

Gibbi ticked a hoof on the pavement impatiently and said, "One more warm body would get us on board. Shall I prepare a contract for him?"

"No! We don't know anything about him."

Peek came to Gibbi's defense. "He's a CASPer driver. Look at the callous patterns on his hands, and observe his haircut. Looks like he's got a pinplant. Horde?"

How Peek could see all that from such a distance was mystifying, but it was worth checking out. XenSha like Peek were great spotters. "Not Horde. They never quit to work for another company. I'll go talk to him."

Jonathan strolled over and stood in front of the man who sagged against the wall with his eyes closed.

"You already took everything but my clothes. You want me to strip?"

"Wrong target. I'm boarding another ship."

He glanced up with a bruised eye, the other still squinted closed. "I'll leave as soon as I can stand up. No need to call security." He leaned forward and grunted in pain. "Just give me a minute."

Jonathan sat beside him. "Got somewhere to go?"

"Know anywhere free within easy walking distance?"

"I'm Jonathan Smith. And you are?" Jonathan held out a hand.

The pilot took his hand and winced as he moved. "Gary Trolleyman. Pleasure to meet someone not kicking me."

Jonathan plugged the name into a search along with the slim information he already knew. In a few moments, he filtered the results down to what looked like a match. Ex-merc turned ship pilot. The merc company had shut down.

From the loading dock, Gibbi pointed at his slate and gestured. Jonathan nodded.

Gary leaned against the wall and took a ragged breath. "Am I about to lose my kidneys in a medical chop shop?"

"Nah. I'm the owner of the Sub Rosa Infiltration Company. We've got a Phoenix Initiative charter, and we could use a mech driver, but this isn't a great spot for an interview." Jonathan stood and offered his hand, helping Gary to stand.

"Wait. How did you know I'm a mech driver?"

"My team is good at what they do."

"Sounds better than rotting here, but you'd better watch out for that sketchy group hanging out in front of the next ship over." Gary grunted and bit his lip as he stood, but Jonathan kept him vertical as they walked.

"That's my team."

"Oh."

"Do we have a problem?"

"I've been working with aliens since my merc company got blown out from under me. We're good as long as you haven't hired a Tortantula. That's what shredded us."

Jonathan stopped and eased Gary down to sit on a box beside the CASPer.

"Wow. Is that a Mk 6 CASPer? Don't see them much these days." His hand traced a maintenance panel on the machine's leg.

Gibbi brought over his slate. "Sign now?"

Gary held up a hand and tapped his head. "Slow down. I don't see any record of your company on the net."

It was a good sign that Gary had done his own search of the local network. "We do stealth operations, so I've set up a couple of shell companies to hide behind. I prefer to find customers instead of having them find us." Jonathan teased him along with the idea of stealth over combat, given how his last merc employer had fared. "We're down a team member. Interested in joining us provisionally for a simple watchdog mission?"

Down the concourse, the same pair came out of the neighboring ship and scanned the area as Jonathan eased to the side to block their view of Gary.

Gibbi held the slate out to Gary as the thugs marched toward them.

"Sounds better than another kick to the gut." Gary signed the contract.

Gibbi nodded. "Permissions verified. We may board."

One of the thugs approached and rested a hand on a sidearm. "Hold up, there."

It wouldn't do at all to get into a shootout with another ship's security team, especially right outside his customer's ship. Gibbi and Peek wouldn't fight, and he had his two best combatants on errands. That left him alone against the two. One brain against two meat lumps might still work.

"What can I do for you, gentlemen?"

"That man's unemployed, and a menace. We ordered him to leave."

Ah, bullies. Jonathan knew the type. It would be best to keep them off balance. "The thing is, I just hired him, so he's employed."

Behind him, Gary shifted closer to the CASPer and leaned against its leg.

The front thug drew his weapon. "More tricks, Gary? You're a slow learner."

Behind Jonathan, the CASPer raised an arm to point a humming chain gun at the thug with the drawn sidearm. Things were spiraling out of control. He might lose the contract if he had to stop and explain two deaths to the authorities before boarding.

He gave their uniforms and equipment a quick scan. New enough that a small bribe would only make them angry. He flashed a pair of hundred-credit chits. Bribes were going to get expensive if he had to keep this up.

"I'm sure there's been a simple misunderstanding. You should probably go the other way to find whoever it is you're looking for. I'm sure your employer will appreciate how thorough you are looking over there. Nothing to see here."

Jonathan gestured past the other ship and held his hand out with the coins in his palm.

The thug eased his gun back into its holster and shook Jonathan's hand, taking the chits.

The thug nodded. "I think we'll look over there for, say, ten minutes."

They backed away, turned, and hurried past the entry to their ship.

Assam returned from the ship. "The captain has a tight schedule to keep. No delays."

Ten minutes would be plenty of time if Gary didn't go nuts and kill them all with the CASPer. "Gary? We cool now?"

Gary reached up and unplugged a maintenance pinlink cable from his pinplants and tucked the cable back into the CASPer's open leg panel. "Hope you didn't mind me stepping in, being a new employee and all. I haven't even been through new employee training."

Jonathan wiped a bead of sweat from his forehead. "Chain guns are frowned upon at the ship berths. But since you can drive that thing remotely, how about you walk it into the open loading bay? Assam, keep him standing while he moves it. He's with us now."

As the team loaded the CASPer and other gear, Jotala came back with an oversized duffel hanging from each shoulder and a scowl even Jonathan could read. "This is all I could grab. This isn't what I signed up for."

"I'm sure you can work wonders with what you brought. Let's board."

Jonathan entered the ship's cargo bay and found the cargo master, a SleSha. The wasp-like race had a dodgy reputation. Jonathan understood dodgy. "Jonathan Smith and company checking in."

"Ah, yes. The hired security team. Once your gear is all in the transfer hold, we will shift it to a hold reserved for you. The ship XO will send you a crew work schedule. A drone will show you to your quarters."

"What about training space?"

"There will be sufficient open space in your assigned cargo hold for limited training exercises. Gather your team and stand along the wall near that door, please." He pointed to the back of the cargo staging area.

Shortly, a SleSha drone arrived to lead them through crisscrossing corridors in the ship. It stopped at a hatch and opened it, then stood aside. Three pairs of stacked bunks lined the left wall, with footlockers attached to the floor for each. The drone spun and returned the way it came.

"Bunk assignments, sir?" asked Assam.

"You take Gary to the back and monitor his recovery. Apply some healing nanites from the emergency kit if necessary. Jotala, you're up front where you can tie into ship's data interfaces near the door. Peek, take the other bunk up front to keep an eye on things. I'll take the middle above Gibbi. Consider this our forward base. We are a team, and we are now deployed."

* * *

Captain Snistet sent a message soon after liftoff with the full trip itinerary and enough patrol and maintenance tasks to bury them. "All crew are required to work during transit. We are not a pleasure cruise ship. We requested three strike teams, and you have only one, so you will work more."

Assam sat back on his bunk. "They can't be serious. Don't they know we're here to guard and defend them?"

A chuckle came from beside him as Gary laboriously sat up. "The captain's put you on his schedule to cover drone jobs. Jobs are all about where to be and what to do when you're there. No initiative, all grunt work."

Jotala snarled as he pulled a gadget from a duffel and plugged it into a panel beside the door. "But we're not drones."

Jonathan smiled. "No. We're not. But we can make this work, all from the shadows. He won't check where we are. He'll only check that things get done. We're going to improvise and optimize. Consider every job as an intelligence mission. Anything we can do to cut hours without cutting quality, tell me. I want to know this ship better than the captain does. How we doing on that data interface, Jotala?"

"Basic data is there. Ship internal and external cameras, atmospheric sensors, automated janitorial equipment, non-secure data. Secured bridge data will take a few hours."

Jonathan held up a hand. "Don't annoy the customer. If you see a way into their data, save it for later without going active. Peek, you're up. We need plans to respond to a variety of ship breaches. This may be an undercover babysitting mission, but I intend to do it right despite Captain Snistet's ideas. Gibbi, you're on shift scheduling. And see if you can get the heat turned down in here."

The team members knew their jobs, but they didn't have experience working together. While Jonathan was used to weaseling people into thinking things were their idea, he didn't have time for that. He had to trust his team and let them step up.

The plan from the captain showed the ship piggybacking on a *Behemoth* for transit in three days. They'd spend a hundred and seventy hours in transit, then pop out three days from their destination for an in-system delivery at an orbital station. From there, they'd repeat the process and come home. The contract was for the trip out, and the free ride home was a bonus.

While the plan was simple and small-scale on the surface, a lot of details had to be handled. His team had the specializations to cover those details. What he lacked was warm bodies to cover everything on the captain's schedule and still do his defensive planning.

"Jotala, I need those ship labor optimizations as soon as you can get them to me."

* * *

Their third-day rendezvous with a *Behemoth*-class ship arrived without incident, and their position on the outside of the spinning *Behemoth* gave them more than half a gravity. The giant ship could take on Captain Snistet's ship with barely a bump in its total capacity. The thing was nearly a mile across.

Outside of the rendezvous, nothing had gone according to plan.

"Jotala, any word on the climate control? This heat is killing me. And the smell? Everyone has to shower. Daily." The odd mixture of body odors from four different physiologies caused a problem that would likely plague every company that created a team with diverse life forms.

"Priorities, captain. Some of the internal cameras were not on the ship network, so I set up some feed taps of my own. The cameras work, but the wiring was faulty. Peek was rather insistent on observing the entire ship to keep us from being surprised."

Peek sat at a makeshift desk with multiple slates showing surveillance views. "I'm thinking of shaving my fur to cool off, but at least I can see the ship now." He ran a damp cloth over his head, soaking the fur. No wonder their cabin smelled funny.

Jonathan looked over Peek's shoulder at the views of hallways and cargo holds. "Careful on any updates that could be considered damage to the ship, Jotala."

Gibbi let out a braying, goatlike laugh. "Not a problem, sir. You know the contract modifications I made? The one for ship damage does not require combat. Jotala could repurpose a great deal of equipment before exceeding the limits."

Jotala's ears perked up. "I could do what, now? Why didn't you tell me this before? I need to check the ship's inventory. This ship is riddled with narrow access passages where they've stored old gear I can repurpose."

Jonathan fanned himself. Was it getting hotter? "Don't go wild, Jotala. If you plan to use something, let me know first. And don't mess with their cargo."

The ship inventory flashed onto one of Peek's screens, then he twitched his nose. "That's weird. One hold where Jotala fixed the cameras has zero cargo, according to Gibbi's list. But the hold isn't empty. I hadn't noticed since our work details avoid the area."

Before his Zuul tech wizard could comment, Jonathan interjected, "Don't touch that stuff, either."

"There's good news on that one. After my mods, the contract says it must be on the cargo manifest for us to be responsible for guarding it."

Now that was a conundrum. A captain with probable smuggling ties hired his team to guard their cargo, but his team wasn't obligated to guard unregistered cargo, the stuff the captain most likely wanted to protect. "Gibbi, make sure we're running by the contract on everything, and keep me advised. We need to complete this job with flying colors, and I don't want any surprises."

* * *

Transition to hyperspace was an unpleasant moment of discontinuity. Jonathan wasn't a fan, but it also wasn't his first time. From the front of the room, Jotala made gagging sounds. "You never told me you don't tolerate transition. Anyone else forget to mention that?"

A furtive glance between Peek and Gibbi was his only clue. If they held their breakfast, it couldn't be that bad. Jonathan made a mental note in the personnel records of each team member.

Now they had a hundred and seventy hours filled with double shifts of mindless ship duties. On the bright side, the contract included basic crew pay to keep up appearances. "Jotala, once you're done emptying your stomach, get me a list of optimizations to tasks. Double shifts will wear us down too fast. Gibbi, revise our schedule based on that. The past three days have spread us thin and run us ragged."

Gary sat up. "Put me on the able-bodied list. I can get around now."

"Done," said Gibbi.

Jotala wiped an arm across his snout and bared his fangs in a vain attempt at a Human smile. "I've automated two of the ship's duct cleaners, and they can cover several assignments with only a few minutes of programming per task. I sent the data to Gibbi right before transit."

"The new schedule will be done in a few minutes," said Gibbi. "That gets us down to a single shift each per day."

Finally, some good news. "Any word on the heat yet?"

"You said to leave that unregistered cargo alone. The heat in our quarters is because that hold is being held at cryogenic temperatures. The extracted heat has to go somewhere on its way out of the ship." He pointed to ducts running along the ceiling.

"Fine. Gary, let's head over to practice with that CASPer. It's cooler over there."

As soon as they arrived and got Gary into the machine, Gibbi's voice came over his pinplant. "*I don't know if this is important, but the external cameras on the ship show a merc company riding along beside us for the transition.*"

While hyperspace was a uniform white to Humans during transition, there were dozens, if not hundreds, of ships on the shell of the *Behemoth*.

"It's probably nothing but keep an eye out. It's nice to have each other's back if something goes wrong out in the black, but we're riding undercover. Don't contact them."

"Got it."

Once Gary was set up inside the CASPer, they discovered why Jonathan got such a good deal on the old equipment. Something had gone wrong with the adjustments to make it fit various body types.

Gary grunted from inside the ill-fitting mech suit. "I can use it, but it rides up funny. Maybe Jotala can get me set up with a data relay so I can run it remotely instead."

With their exhausting schedule of drone work on the ship over the past three days, Jonathan hadn't had time for a solo conversation with Gary as he recovered. "Good idea. I'll get him on that. While we're talking about driving stuff, how about you tell me what happened on your last job to get you ejected from the ship?"

Gary paused before answering. "The captain had his daughter on board."

Jonathan envisioned a host of directions the story could go, all bad. "You didn't."

"Of course not. How stupid do I look? But when I turned her down, she made accusations. End of story, he booted me from the ship without pay and threatened to kill me if I ever talked about it. The way I see it, you deserve to know about it as my new employer."

The situation became clear. "I see. It looks like a con job."

"A what?"

"Let's say the captain wanted your driving services and didn't want to pay you. Let's say he has a daughter that's in on the scheme. Once she professes her love and/or lust, you're stuck unless you've got recorded evidence on your side. If you go along with her, he has video evidence, and he boots you for cause while she sheds crocodile tears. If you don't go along, then she lies, and the captain *still* boots you for cause. I'm not saying that's how it went down, but the odds are good."

Gary popped the front of the mech open and rubbed his chin. "If you have a daughter, I quit."

"If I did, I wouldn't drag her along on mercenary contracts. We're good."

It took practice to get into and out of a mech as smoothly as Gary did. He'd clearly spent time in one back with his last merc company. Later, he could dig up what happened without putting Gary through a detailed retelling. It was a fine art to know when to dig in person and when to dig online. Jonathan preferred the buffers of digging online.

As they returned from their training session, Peek waved Jonathan over. "Our mercenary friends have at least one Mk 8 CASPer."

He replayed a video segment showing a mech marching between ships on the outside of the *Behemoth*. The first segment showed it carrying a box of some sort, and the second showed it returning empty-handed.

"Where did he go?"

Peek shrugged. "Either to our ship or past it. The tail end of our ship is a blind spot."

"Gibbi, I need to know what job they took. That's your top priority."

"You could still walk over or ask. Maybe even just call on the radio."

And that would work out great if their target had something to do with this ship. "Let's see what gets found first. I'll ask Captain Snistet about getting Gary out in the CASPer to look for that box."

One call later, he had a flat rejection from the captain until they had transitioned to normal space and had detached from the *Behemoth*. "Gary, suit up and stand by at the rear airlock. The captain says we'll be in freefall for a few minutes to get clear of the *Behemoth* with no engines. That's enough for a quick look outside."

Gibbi let out an uncomfortable cough. "I've narrowed down the possible contracts for the other mercenary company. One is tied to remote political unrest on the planet we're going to. The other is a hostage rescue."

"Thanks, Gibbi. I want to see the outside of our ship before we burn toward the planet; something's not right. Everyone put on your armor." All but Gary would be in standard non-powered armor, but that was typical for ship-bound work.

Assam reappeared with armor that covered him head to toe. It wouldn't stand up to heavy weapons, but he could hold his own for a while against anything smaller than a crew-served gun. "Follow Gary and run the airlock for him. I don't want anyone alone."

Peek and Gibbi rushed to their lockers and were armored and back at their desks in under two minutes. Neither would fight other than as a last resort. Jotala pulled on a vest and picked up a small remote with exposed wires and non-standard switches.

"What, no weapons, Jotala?"

"Show me fighting and you'll see weapons. The ship had more cleaning bots than it needed. I rebuilt them and added some enhancements since you left most of my gear behind."

Jotala was never going to let him live down their fast exit, and the pallets that got left behind. "What's the remote for?"

"This one? Psychological warfare."

Jonathan clapped him on the shoulder. "And here I thought of you as more of a blunt trauma specialist."

"Would you rather I blow a hole through the hull with a missile? That would end badly."

The transition to normal space went as it always did, with a momentary falling sensation before the normal spin-based gravity returned. The Behemoth ejected its cargo of smaller ships several at a time, sending them out in a fan.

Gary called out on the radio from inside the CASPer. "*Good to go as soon as they kick us off.*"

The drill worked well to get everyone into armor, but it had taken twice as long as it should have. His team needed more practice.

An alarm sounded through the ship, "Ten seconds to zero gravity."

The clamps holding them opened, and they drifted away from the massive ship.

One slate in front of Peek floated free. He grabbed it and fastened it down as Jonathan glared at the oversight. Nobody ever wanted to be the reason for a new safety briefing.

Whether his team was in stealth mode or not, the basic organizational problem was the same. He had to make use of his team's specializations and prepare for the million things that could go wrong.

Jonathan had just begun to reorganize his list of training exercises when Gary called across the comm. *"Warn the captain immediately. Do not fire the primary engine. We found something."*

A series of images and video arrived from the mech as it jetted around the primary engine of the ship. The box from the other merc company sat inside the main engine exhaust nozzle.

Once the captain had been warned, Jonathan floated over to Gibbi. "Looks like the other mercs are not on a political unrest mission. I need you on the hostage rescue angle to confirm or eliminate it right now. I don't want to tangle with another Human-based merc company. We're supposed to look out for each other just like everyone in a merc company looks out for each other."

Jotala snarled. "What? We're mercenaries, and we need to not kill Human mercenary opponents? Where is that in my contract?"

"Paragraph forty-three," said Gibbi. "But it's more like avoid killing them when possible. The contract takes priority."

"Some sanity at last. I'm getting the rest of my equipment." Jotala pulled himself through the door and into the hall beyond.

Gary's mech suit sounded a pressure alarm over the communications link as he made his way back toward the airlock. Jonathan called across the radio, "Status, Gary?"

"I'll make it back to the airlock, but I'm done going outside. This piece of garbage suit blew a seal. I've got the mystery box. If I had to bet, I'd say it's a heat-activated, low-yield explosive designed to disable the ship. Maybe an EMP. Hard to tell."

The babysitting mission had taken a whole new and dangerous turn.

Gibbi let out an exasperated sigh. "No crew or passengers match as a potential hostage. There's nothing on the cargo manifest."

"The off-limits hold?" said Peek. He pointed at the camera signal that had originally been out of order. "The hold contains cryo equipment. It could be someone in deep freeze."

If Jonathan brought it up with the captain, he'd have to admit to rewiring the cameras and snooping through the ship. Surrender to the well-armed mech company would be a mission failure, and that would set a terrible precedent. There had to be a path through the maze, but the situation was too foggy.

"*I'm inside,*" said Gary. "*Airlocks sealed. I'm leaving the CASPer holding the box in the airlock. It's not much use until I can pilot it remotely.*"

Jonathan got on the intercom to the bridge. "Captain Snistet, we are clear to fire the engines. My team believes an attack is imminent based on what we found, so I advise that you get everyone to their stations and lock down access to your crew."

"*That sounds prudent. I will take the ship to a two-gravity burn to see who follows. You will protect the ship,*" said the captain. "*Keep me advised.*"

A general-quarters alarm sounded throughout the ship as the engines came online. Jonathan called out across his fireteam radio frequency. "Roll call."

Each team member sounded off, verifying the connection through their linked helmets.

Peek tapped one of his screens. "The merc ship has begun to follow. It can overtake us easily, but it's keeping pace for now."

It was time to plan. "Gibbi, if you were to attack this ship, how would you do it?"

"Attack? Why would I attack?"

"Okay, if you were sending a team to attack, where would you send them?"

"Ah, I understand. There are several scenarios. If Captain Snistet stops to allow them to board, they fight in the halls to reach their objective. If he continues to run, they will send boarding craft to either connect to a shipping hold, or to burn a new entrance through the hull. Then, they fight in the halls to reach their objective."

Assam stood in the doorway. "It sounds like fighting in the halls either way. We don't have the manpower to go toe-to-toe with the firepower they can throw at us."

Jonathan wasn't naïve enough to think there was a solution to every problem, but this one had potential if he played it right. All he had to do was survive long enough to figure out how to give everyone what they wanted. "Jotala, now would be a good time to tap into the bridge. Radio traffic, an open microphone, chatter between the bridge and engineering, whatever you can weasel your way into. I don't trust our client to keep us in the loop."

"*I'll be right there to activate the links.*" A metallic clomping noise sounded from the hall as an eight-legged monstrosity of metal appeared outside the door with Jotala riding behind a welded barrier on top.

The smell of machine oil and ozone wafted into the room as Jonathan stared. "You've been busy. What is it?"

"Extra firepower. It's three cleaning bots, two heavy laser rifles, and some plating scavenged from access panels in our cargo and training hold. I can drive it remotely."

Anything to even the odds was welcome, but the remote control brought up another issue. "Can you set up remote access on the CASPer for Gary, too? It's no good for a trip outside the ship right now."

"I only have one remote module. If I put it on the CASPer, we don't have the Claws of Doom. Now, if I'd received both my pallets of equipment…"

Jonathan ignored the implied insult and gave the metal contraption a closer look. "Does this thing have loudspeakers?"

"The cleaning bots had a warning claxon, so yes."

It took a few moments to locate the appropriate saved video clip with his pinplant, then Jonathan pushed a sound file to a slate. "We're going to use the Claws of Doom to keep the attention of our boarders."

Gary arrived, stepping gingerly around the thing in the hall and into their quarters. "What's that?"

Peek played the audio file, and the screech of a charging Tortantula horde filled the room.

With a scream, Gary turned to run, but fell to the floor in the high gravity. He scooted toward the back of the room before noticing he was the center of attention.

Peek cut the audio. "It seems to work on Humans."

Jotala rubbed his hands together. "I'll have that copied to the Claws of Doom as soon as I have the bridge communication tap activated."

The tap was in place and routed to Peek's slates so quickly that Jonathan had to assume it had already been put in place. Jotala was good at what he did, and he'd warned Jonathan he worked on what he wanted. There was a fine balance between encouraging initiative and losing control of the team. In this case, it had worked in the team's favor.

Peek's slate shared a radio message as it arrived on the bridge, *"This is your last warning. Submit to boarding, or we will disable your ship and board, anyway."*

An external camera showed a detonation in the distance. A warning shot. Acceleration dropped from two gravities to a half as the captain activated an intercom message to Jonathan. *"Jonathan Smith, we have no choice but to submit to boarding. It is now your job to defend us."*

Defending the crew was more of a derived requirement from the contract. He needed someone to pay him after completion. "Captain, we will protect you with everything we've got according to our contract. I recommend you stay in lockdown and grant me access to all hatch locks so I can steer them to where we will have the greatest measure of control and least damage."

The intercom went mute, but Jotala's data tap carried a conversation to the team. Another voice on the bridge said, *"All doors? We can't do that. The cargo is too important to risk them bumbling their way into it."*

The captain said, *"I will give them access to all locks except to the bridge, engineering, and the special hold. Anything less would hamper their ability to defend us."*

The intercom came back to life. *"Granted. What is your plan?"*

That was the rub. It wasn't much of a plan yet. "See if you can get them to connect to airlock 4C. We're going to lead them away from you and work to get them off the ship."

Jonathan cut the connection. "Jotala, park the Claws of Doom in the hall up near the bridge. If they go for the offered airlock toward the middle of the ship, we push them from there aft."

Too much of the plan forming in his head depended on last-minute choices in response to the boarders.

Peek sent a message across the team radio despite having nearly everyone within easy voice distance. "Boarders incoming. I give them three minutes. I see a hull breach device."

Jonathan was the first to reply to the worst-case scenario. "If we lose pressure, we'll be stuck in here. Everyone into pressure suits."

The cheap pressure suits barely had room for full body armor, but at least they would still be mobile and armored.

Gary shook his head. "I can't wear the pressure suit inside the mech."

"Then stay close to airlocks in case pressure drops. Assam, can you get through the access tunnels with that pressure suit on?"

His combat expert stopped long enough to roll his eyes. "Not a chance. Even if I *could* fit, I'd probably tear the suit."

"That puts you in the side halls near the skin of the ship as we steer them from wherever they breach. Take a heavy laser rifle and whatever magazines you can carry."

Jotala was the first to be suited and out the door. "I'll grab the other heavy laser rifle and get the Claws of Doom set up near the bridge."

Jonathan hated to split and scatter his team, but it was the only choice he had. *Get between the enemy and the employer, then push them aft past all the cargo holds as quickly as possible to keep them from investigating every hold and ruining things.*

The end game still depended on too many variables. He had to get the boarders off the ship, he had to protect the cargo, and his employer had to survive. He'd assumed the cryo chamber was their target. If he was wrong, he'd already failed. His team was outgunned by a good margin, leaving his only hope of success to psychological advantage, and knowing his enemy enough to predict his actions. That had gone poorly so far.

For the moment, Jonathan's best option was to watch the incoming data streams with his pinplant. It gave him the same screens that sat in front of Peek, but with zooming and targeting capabilities at the speed of thought. The ship came in from the side and impacted with a thud felt through the ship. After several sharp impacts, a section of hull crashed into the hallway.

Air pressure held steady, but that would change in a hurry when the enemy ship detached from the hole they made. That had to be part of their escape plan. They would force bulkhead hatches to seal with the pressure drop, cutting off any pursuit as they left.

Six CASPers and six figures in advanced body armor entered the hallway. Two of those in body armor bore large backpacks. "Jotala, get ready to crank up your audio to full. Get the Claws of Doom to stomp and scrape as loud as you can. I want the crew and the boarders to all hear you. It's your job to keep those CASPers near the entry guarding their retreat. You're a go in five seconds."

Twelve boarders to his four combatants, plus more on the shuttle, and more back on their main ship doing overwatch. This would be tricky. Any direct conflict could destroy his team.

Tortantula screeches and metal scraping against metal echoed through the ship, and the boarders flew into action. CASPers took position to watch all the nearby tunnels as the six armored figures sprinted aft through the central corridor, away from the noise. Maybe they knew where they were going, but he couldn't leave that to chance.

"Assam, you have targets inbound. Let five go past, then target number six. Fire to disable. Then move to your second crossing and repeat if possible."

Assam's chemical laser fired. "*I got in a leg shot. Moving now before they see me. You notice they're not prepared for vacuum? We're safe from decompression until they leave.*"

Thank heaven for small favors. So long as his team could ghost from spot to spot in parallel, they could leapfrog the slowed enemy. "Peek, shut down lights in everything but the main corridor. Let's encourage them to stay there as they move back. Jotala, keep up the noise. Stay away from the breach, or those CASPers will turn the Claws of Doom back into spare parts. If you get a shot to slow down the CASPers, take it. We need to stay in the shadows and snipe for this to work."

Gibbi's voice came across everyones' radios. "We're scattered all through the ship and we still don't know your plan. We can help more if you fill us in."

Things had been going so fast with the boarding that he hadn't had time to explain. "We give them what they want, but we can't make it look easy. If they're after the cryo equipment, that's not cargo. They can have it."

"But how do we keep Captain Snistet from claiming we're colluding?"

"That's where it gets fun. We have to make both the captain and the boarders think we gave it our all. If you see a chance for a disabling shot, take it. That puts one of them out of the fight and another to haul him to safety. I put the Claws of Doom near the bridge on purpose so the captain would hear it, too. Jotala, be sure to leave a lot of scratches on the floor and walls."

Jotala's tone conveyed his annoyance. "*So, we're back to not hurting Humans? We're just putting on a show?*"

"We're mirroring what they've done. Their CASPers are still near the entrance covering a retreat path. If they'd taken the mechs through the halls, we would have had no choice but to stay out of their way. We're outmatched."

A camera near the breach point showed a bright flash, and a boom reverberated through the halls of the ship. Jotala said, "*One CASPer has lost the ability to hold air. It may have lost a MAC, but I can't tell for sure from here. They're holding position but finding better cover.*"

Another bright flash appeared on a main hall camera closer to the aft. Assam said, "*Sorry, I missed. We've got a new hole into an interior bulkhead.*"

More flashes illuminated the hall from the scout team's weapons as they poured fire down the hall he'd fired from. Assam grunted over the radio. "*Armor is holding, but my vac suit has a new hole. Moving to the next crossfire location.*"

The scouting team had passed right by several cargo hold hatches. Jonathan kept his team up to date. "It looks like they know where they're going. They must have either been tipped off, or they have equipment to scan for an energy signature."

Jotala barked a laugh. "*They sat next to us for a hundred and seventy hours inside the* Behemoth. *If they don't have detailed scans and know exactly where they're going, I'll eat the Claws of Doom.*"

"*They beat me to the intersection,*" said Assam. "*That was the last crossfire spot. Gary's up next.*"

If it came down to it, Jonathan would sacrifice the boarding party to save his team, whether or not the enemy was Human. One CASPer against six mercenaries in body armor wasn't exactly a fair fight. But if he took out the scouting party, things could devolve into a bloodbath as the six mechs set out for rescue. Or vengeance.

A hall camera showed the scouts stopping at a door. A momentary check of the ship plans confirmed it was the cryo hold. Jonathan wasn't sure whether to be relieved at being right, or terrified at what would be worth so much effort to guard or retrieve. The injured team member and two others set up to guard side passages while the other three worked on the door. One of those side passages led directly to where Jonathan sat with Gibbi and Peek.

Jonathan had spent most of the fight deep in his pinplants, watching monitors and issuing orders. He felt like he was cheating, leaving his team to all the danger, but he was the best one to coordinate everything because of his speed with data.

He pulled out to pay attention to the world around him. "Gary, keep an eye out. They're down near you. Move forward to the next cross-tunnel access."

Jonathan left the suite before closing and latching the hatch. His laser pistol only had twenty shots, but it might be enough to steer them away from his team if plans fell apart.

If the boarding party got away with what they came after, he still had to deal with Captain Snistet. "Gibbi, we're going to need to make a mess of that special cargo hold before the captain sees it."

"*I'm on it.*"

The ship rumbled, with the noise coming from aft. Peek broke into the radio channel. "*They've cut the hinges off the hatch into the hold.*"

Jonathan dropped back into his data feed to watch the signals from the various cameras as the team in the hold staged some complex equipment from their packs and set to work moving wires and tubes from wall ports to their personal gear.

The hall cameras closer to the center of the ship picked up more screeching of metal and the hideous noise of Tortantulas as it poured from Jotala's remote control monstrosity. The mech suits had spread out to block all travel between ends of the ship. "Jotala, don't leave the fore sections. They've blocked everything off."

Jotala had his creation in one tunnel and had gone over to an adjacent one. He and the fake Tortantula opened up with laser fire, causing the CASPers to pull back around the corners they guarded.

A mech reached an arm around the corner and fired blindly, spraying machine gun fire down the hall. Jotala had been too slow to retreat behind a corner of his own and took several hits that knocked him to the ground. He scrambled around the corner, dragging one leg behind him as the Claws of Doom continued to pour laser fire down another corridor. Its magazines couldn't last much longer.

Peek said, *"They've put wheels under the cryo module and they're rolling it into the hall. Hold on. They've turned around and are headed to the aft airlock. Maybe they got a report that it's too hot the way they came in. Gary, you're up."*

Jonathan rushed forward, approaching a corner where he could get a direct view of the door they'd removed to get into the hold. One of them remained in the room as the ductwork on the ceiling came apart in a shower of sparks. Gibbi dropped into the room.

Jonathan called out a warning. "Gibbi! There's one in there with you still."

Next, Gary broke into the conversation. *"How sure are you that these guys get to live? I've got them right in front of me, stopped in their tracks."*

"Do NOT fire."

"I can't fire without shooting through this stupid box we pulled from our engine. I'm still carrying it around."

"Keep carrying it."

The hall guards had joined the team carrying the cryo chamber, allowing Jonathan to peek around the corner with a lower risk of getting his face shot off.

Within the room, Gibbi let loose with a laser pistol firing at random, and the lone mercenary in the room tumbled out and ran to rejoin his team in front of the Mk 6 CASPer. The new guy raised a pistol, and two other mercs batted it out of his hand and gestured to the mech.

Jonathan smiled. "Whatever that box is, they really don't want to shoot it. Step forward slowly. Push them back to the way they came in. I'm ducking into the hold to see what Gibbi's doing here."

"Just what you told me to do. It was supposed to be empty. I'm here to break things and make a mess. Now you've made me shoot at people, and they might shoot back. I'm supposed to pull *data*, not triggers!"

Smoke filled the room from Gibbi's random laser fire, but Jonathan could still monitor the hallway cameras. "Just hold still. Let them pass by. Gary, keep moving toward them one slow step at a time."

With the smoke and haze of the hold to obscure him from the team outside the room, Jonathan tapped back into the cameras. A member of the team with the cryo unit gesticulated wildly as he looked between the mech and the path they'd taken to get to the hold.

"Jotala, back off. They think things are too hot up there for their mobile team to come back."

Jotala gasped, then said, *"Backing off. They winged me again."*

The screeching sounds and scraping of metal faded.

After a few seconds of what had to be an interesting conversation, the cryo recovery team pulled their load after them as fast as they could move, hauling their wounded team member with them.

Assam's voice came across the radio. "*I'm lined up to take a shot as they cross my path.*"

"Let them pass. If they're not firing close to that box, then we don't fire, either."

The cryo team made it back, and exited through their makeshift entrance, followed by the Mk 8 CASPers.

Magnetic clamps released their boarding craft, and the ship pulled away, leaving air venting into space. Jonathan yelled, "Everyone out of the venting section. The bulkhead hatches will seal it off."

Within seconds, hatches slammed, and the air stilled.

"Everyone check in."

Each team member responded except for Jotala.

Jonathan scanned his hall cameras. The first thing he saw was the Claws of Doom. Then, nearby, lay Jotala. Jonathan let out a sigh of relief as he realized Jotala was in a pressurized section, and not exposed to vacuum.

"Gary, leave that box in the rear airlock, then get Jotala back to our suite. Assam, take his remote and put the Claws of Doom in the cryo hold. Then tear it apart along with everything in the room. Gibbi's there to help."

As two of his team trashed the cryo room, Jonathan helped Assam to get Jotala out of his armor. Gary extracted himself from the mech and joined them. The Zuul was breathing.

After a quick examination, Assam said, "His fur's been burned off in multiple places. Typical laser injuries. Two bullets damaged his left leg. I see exit wounds for both."

After moving Jotala back to their suite and a spray of Zuul-specified healing nanites, Jotala twitched and groaned, blinking his eyes.

Assam held him to his cot with a hand. "Easy. You gave us a bit of a scare, furball. Hold still and I'll dress those injuries."

With his team taken care of, Jonathan called the captain. "The boarders have been repelled, and all the cargo holds you gave us access to have been protected. Your crew can come out and begin repairs. We're tending to our injured. I'd like to get to the delivery location at best speed."

"Very good. I will send out my teams. Our status shows one small section breached. Power systems are... One moment. Smith, report to my quarters immediately."

There was no way the captain would admit even having the cryo chamber, but Jonathan was about to have some serious negotiations. He pulled up the contract and highlighted the sections defining cargo and responsibilities, proving they did exactly what the contract required. Jonathan didn't even feel bad about losing the non-cargo since the captain had never brought him into the loop.

He preferred to offer carrots when he could, but every once in a while, the stick had to come out. A few messages back and forth between the captain and the Mercenary Guild representative in system confirmed that the contract had been filled, much to the annoyance of Captain Snistet.

It was a very tense day and a half as the captain returned to a two-gravity burn to be rid of Jonathan's team as soon as possible. The free trip home was no longer an option.

* * *

Jonathan entered a small merc pit on an orbital station, looking to blow off a little steam. Jotala had improved to where he could limp his way along with the rest of them. They stumbled their way through the combination bar and restaurant within the merc pit and found a table against a side wall where they sat and ordered food fit for a menagerie.

Two tables over, a merc waved his arms as he told a story. "It had to be a Tortantula, and it was on a trade ship. Not sure how they hired one. You saw the sharpshooters. We're lucky nobody took a laser shot through the head. Then there was the CASPer driver playing chicken with a neutron bomb. If that had gone off inside the restricted hallway, we would have all been blown down the hallway and out the nose of the ship like a giant shotgun. That's one for the record books. This was supposed to be a simple hostage retrieval from a poorly armed ship. I can't wait to get back to Imago."

Jonathan strolled over to their table and joined the conversation with a wide smile. "Sounds like a rough one. We ended up getting shot up on what should have been an easy babysitting contract. Things are never what you expect, are they? I'm Jonathan Smith. If you're headed to Imago, could six of us bum a ride home with you?"

*****

John M. Olsen Bio

John M. Olsen is an award-winning author who edits and writes speculative fiction across multiple genres. He loves stories about ordinary people stepping up to do extraordinary things. His short stories have appeared in dozens of anthologies.

He loves to create and fix things through editing and writing both short stories and novels, and also when working in his secret lair equipped with dangerous power tools. In all cases, he applies engineering principles and processes to the task at hand, often in unpredictable ways.

He lives in Utah with his lovely wife and a variable number of mostly grown children and a constantly changing subset of extended family and pets.

# # # # #

Hogan's Zeros by Nick Steverson

My jaw ached as I clenched it to keep my teeth from rattling in my head. It was obvious the pilot hadn't done many combat drops, if any at all. My Mk 7 CAS-Per vibrated hard as the shuttle ran through what seemed like every bit of turbulence the pilot could find. I could barely read the information on my screens without getting dizzy. I guess I shouldn't have been surprised.

Warden Drieger's voice came over the combat channel. *"Two minutes to drop! When you hit the dirt, find your designated officer and await instructions."*

I clicked my comm twice in acknowledgement. No sense in all fifty of us crowding up the channel. Then I grinned as more than one officer told the other morons on the channel to shut the hell up and double tap their mics instead. Rookies. Not entirely their fault though. They were inmates, not mercs. My story was a little more complicated. I was a merc *and* a convict.

"Hey, Troy," Jose Nunez said over a direct laser link, *"who's my officer again?"*

I shook my head and sighed. The man could smuggle drugs into any system and keep track of every ounce, but ask him to keep track of who his commanding officer was? Newp.

"Lieutenant Anderson. The NCO is Sergeant Cliff. They oversee all of D-Block. Christ, man. Pay attention during the briefings."

"*I can't, bro. Captain Jenson is always in there. You know what that woman does to me.*"

"Didn't she mace you two months ago and toss your ass in the hole for making a pass at her?"

"*Eh, she's just playing hard to get. If she didn't care, she wouldn't have told me not to get myself killed before we left.*"

"She said that to the whole company during the briefing, you fuckin' moron."

"*Yeah, but she looked right at me when she did. I can read between the lines.*"

Another laser link comm came through. It was Hondu Rorke, a third member of mine and Nunez's D-Block group. None of us were affiliated with any gangs and had formed a friendship of sorts. We watched out for each other. There was no such thing as a lone wolf in prison. You made friends, or you became a target. It was a brutal world to live in.

I created a private channel and looped them both into it. "This has to be quick, Rorke. The commander doesn't want us bullshitting on private channels and he can see we're in one. Nunez is already taking up too much time with his ridiculous guard fantasy."

"*You talking 'bout Jenson again?*" Rorke asked. "*She's gonna do more than mace you next time. Keep it up, and you'll catch a whole new charge. Then you'll be stuck in here even longer.*"

"*Not if I bust out three successful missions,*" Nunez countered. "*Then I can ask her out as a free man.*"

"Yeah, yeah, you're a regular fuckin' Don Juan, Nunez. Rorke, you know who to report to?"

"*Anderson and Cliff,*" Rorke replied.

"See, Nunez? That's what happens when you pay attention at the briefing instead of creeping on the lady guards."

"*Whatever. That's what I got you two for. You guys got my back.*"

"*Only if your stupid ass makes it to the right group,*" Rorke quipped.

"You two fucktards shut up and listen," I snapped. "This isn't a training drop on the compound and it's not a goddamned sim. When that door opens, shit gets real. Stay close on the fall and make damned sure you don't hit your thrusters too late or too early."

"*Geez, mom, chill out,*" Nunez groaned. "*We got this.*"

"*I hear you, Troy,*" Rorke said.

"When we hit the ground, we group together before we find the LT and Sarge. You both know good and damned well we'll be fighting a two-sided battle down there."

"*Are we having a wonderful fucking party over here in the local chat and chew?*" Warden Drieger's voice screamed over the channel. "*Do you ladies think you're too good to share with the rest of us lowly mercs?*"

"No, sir," I said. "Just making sure they understand what we're supposed to be doing, sir. There was some confusion. It's cleared up now."

"*It damned well better be! Drop in twenty seconds. Time to shut up and sack up!*"

The shuttle floor split apart as the drop bay opened. Far below, the forest canopy rolled by. The internal buzzer sounded, and the light turned green. Two seconds later, the clamps released and I was falling toward the ground of a planet I didn't even know the name of. I splayed my arms and legs to level out and control my descent. Using my external cameras, I located both Nunez and Rorke. Both looked good. Nunez even managed to shoot me a CASPer-sized thumbs up.

My brow furrowed when I caught sight of Lieutenant Anderson. His CASPer was limp, and his fall looked uncontrolled.

"Lieutenant Anderson!" I shouted over the comm. "Lieutenant! LT! Can you hear me?" He was close to critical velocity.

"*I think he passed out!*" Warden Drieger shouted. "*I've been calling him, but he's not responding!*"

Damn it! I thought. Of course, it would be *my* lieutenant who passed out on the jump. *Fucking rookies.* I oriented myself and dove to catch up with his limp form.

"*What the fuck are you doing?*" Rorke shouted. I ignored him and concentrated on Anderson's CASPer.

As I neared, I splayed my arms and legs back out again and slowed just enough to match his fall, reached out, and ripped away the emergency parachute handle on the upper rear of his Mk 8. The dual chutes deployed at the same time my altitude alarm began to scream. I aimed my feet at the ground and fired my thrusters with everything they had. I gritted my teeth and fought to stay conscious as the g-forces hit me. Twenty-five feet from the forest floor, I cut the thrust and dropped, bending my knees to absorb the impact.

There were thuds all around me as the other CASPers touched down. I looked to the sky and saw Anderson's chute disappear into the trees about a hundred meters further in. His landing was off target, but not so far he would land amongst enemy troops. Without waiting for orders, I hustled off in his direction. Technically, I was supposed to report to him anyway. So, I was actually following the previously issued orders.

"*On your six,*" Sergeant Cliff said. "*His vitals look fine, but I can't get him on the comm. Any thoughts?*"

"He's out cold. He should've regained consciousness by now, though."

"*You ever have this happen before?*"

"Once, but it was because we jumped from over 10,000 feet and the driver didn't have his oxygen on. If you say his vitals look good, then it's something else."

Ahead, a pair of shredded parachutes clung to the branches above and the Mk 8 swayed two feet above the ground. The cockpit appeared undamaged other than some scrapes and scratches from busting through the canopy. Without hesitation, Cliff reached out and pulled the emergency handle on the CASPer's cockpit. The clam shell rose to reveal Anderson slumped over in his harness.

Without waiting for further instruction, I popped my own canopy and got as close as possible. I unhooked my harness and stepped up and leaned into Anderson's machine and felt his neck for a pulse. There was nothing. I checked for breath but came up short there too.

"No pulse and he's not breathing." I opened his mouth to make sure he hadn't bitten his tongue off. It was then the smell of burnt ozone hit me. I looked down and saw smoke rising from a panel. The one containing the circuits for his life support. "Shit! His life support shorted out. Froze all the other systems. That's why you didn't see the change in his vitals. He made the fall without oxygen. I'm gonna give him an epi-shot and nanites."

"*What's the status on Anderson?*" Warden Drieger asked.

"*Not good, sir. He made the jump without life support. No pulse, not breathing. Doing what we can. Stand by.*"

I ripped open the emergency med kit, pulled out the nanite injector, and gave him a full dose in the neck. Next, I grabbed the epinephrine.

"Sorry, LT. This is gonna suck—a lot."

The movies always show some dramatic scene where the hero crams a long-ass needle into someone's heart to get it going. It's all Hollywood horseshit. To get a needle around the sternum and all the ribs and body's natural protection and straight into the heart under crazy stress in a combat situation would require all the skill and luck in the world. The more muscular parts of the body are the best places to inject.

I jammed it into the meaty part of his shoulder. A thigh would have been preferable, but I couldn't exactly get to one while he was hanging two feet higher than my own CASPer and me having to lean up and over his consoles. The auto injector engaged. After a minute, his eyes shot open, and his entire body went rigid as he fought to suck in a breath. His back arched against the restraints and his hands stiffened into claws. After what felt like an eternity, Anderson let out a ragged scream of both agony and relief. Sweat beaded on his forehead as he clutched at his shoulder straps and sucked in air.

"*Got him back,*" Cliff called over the radio. "*He's alive.*"

"*Good,*" Drieger replied. "*You three hightail it back to the LZ. We're moving out in ten. We lost four in the drop. Puts us down to forty-six and we need every walking dick we have if this mission is going to be successful.*"

"*Understood, sir,*" Cliff answered.

"How do you feel, Lieutenant?" I asked. The last thing I wanted was for him to go into shock. "You need to take slow, controlled breaths."

"Couldn't... fucking... breathe," he choked out. "Goddamn fuse... blew. Couldn't reach it."

"I gave you an epi-shot and nanites. You'll feel like you can outrun a cheetah for a while."

Anderson rubbed his chest. "It feels like my heart is about to beat out of my chest."

"Better than never feeling it beat again," I said. "The effects should wear off in about thirty minutes. Get ready to have the worst headache of your life though."

Anderson nodded. "Good thing our roles weren't reversed. I wouldn't have known what to do."

"*Same*," Cliff said. "*I was useless as shit.*" He pointed at me. "*Monterey didn't just save you down here. He's the reason you didn't hit the ground Wiley Coyote style. He risked crashing himself to pull your emergency chutes.*"

My eyes dropped to the ground and my face got hot.

"That true, Monterey?"

I looked back up to the lieutenant and gave him a nod. "Yeah, LT. Couldn't let you go splat. We're in this shit together." I waved vaguely around us. "Out here, inmate, guard, warden—it doesn't matter. If I let you die, you won't be there later to save *my* ass when I need it."

Anderson nodded, then grinned. "Teamwork makes the dream work."

I snorted. "Something like that."

The smile faded and Anderson's brow furrowed. "Thanks, Monterey. You're probably the only non-guard who would've done that. I won't forget it."

It was my turn to smile. "Hopefully you remember it when you guys are deciding who gets new equipment."

Anderson rolled his eyes. "There's the inmate. Let me get this damned circuit swapped out and we'll get back to the rest of the company before Drieger throws us all in the hole."

* * *

"*Damn fine work, Monterey!*" Warden Drieger said as we approached. "*Never seen anything like that. Glad we have someone here with your experience, convict or not.*"

"I keep tellin' you guys I'm innocent," I replied. "Crazy ex, her dirty cop side-dude, and an unfortunate rich old guy. You all know that age-old story."

"*Yeaaah, right. You're all a bunch of damned saints.*"

"*I'm Catholic, Warden,*" Nunez said. "*I could totally be a saint.*"

"*Eternal Patron Saint of the Misery Hole if you don't shut the hell up, Nunez,*" Drieger snapped.

"*Shutting up.*"

The warden's voice became even more stern. "*If you pukes are done running your traps, we've got a job to do. You all have your designated officers and positions. We lost some on the way down, so four of the squads are down to nine CASPers. We'll have to make do with what we have.*"

A map of the surrounding area appeared on my HUD. "*As you can see, the facility is enclosed by a concrete wall. Autocannons are positioned every ten meters along the top. Outside the main gate are two crew-served lasers. Teams Two and Three, the lasers are yours. Take them out as fast as possible. Teams One and Five, concentrate on the autocannons and roving guards. Data is unclear how many there should be. Approximate number is fifty on the grounds. Could be more, could be less.*"

"*Any indication what race we're up against?*" Anderson asked.

"*Jivool,*" Drieger answered.

I ran a hand over the right side of my head. Three thick lines of scar tissue rubbed against my calluses. Black claws and snapping jaws flashed through my mind. *Fucking Jivool. Of course, that's what it is.*

"*Look on the bright side!*" Dreiger shouted. "*At least it's not Oogar or Goka.*"

A shiver ran down my spine at the thought of the giant cockroaches. I'd take all the Jivool and Oogar in the universe over those nasty bastards. Never mind how deadly they were with their blades.

"What's the actual mission?" I asked. "Are we capturing the facility? Is there a hostage?" Us cons had been left in the dark about the mission for the most part. It was all in the name of "security." That way we wouldn't know where we were, preventing anyone from calling in outside contacts for a possible escape. It was in the name of bullshit if you ask me. How the hell were we supposed to properly do our jobs if we didn't even know what the fucking job was? All we knew was blow up the big guns and kill the Jivool. While that sounds like all kinds of fun, it doesn't really help with tactics.

"*Facility recovery,*" Dreiger said. "*These assholes came in, killed everyone, and took over. The owners hired us to return the favor. The mission, Monterey, is to kill every fucking teddy bear you see with extreme prejudice. Think you can handle that?*"

"Yes, sir." I did my best not to sound condescending. I mostly succeeded… I think. "We really should get moving, sir. There's no way the Jivool didn't spot our shuttles and watch us jump. They're likely headed right at us. Furthermore, it's a bad idea for us to be huddled together like this for too long. We need to spread out. The heat signatures from our CASPers are probably presenting one hell of an easy target while we stand here talking. None of this would be necessary if we'd been given all the mission intel prior to the jump."

Dreiger turned his CASPer to fully face mine and pointed a very drill sergeant-worthy knife hand at me with the machine. It was actually pretty impressive.

"*Who the fuck's in charge here shitferbrains?*"

"You, Warden."

"*Goddamn right I am! We'll move how and when I fuckin' say so. If you've got a problem with that, then you can—*"

BOOM!

The warden's CASPer disappeared in a spray of blood, steel, and dirt. The surrounding war machines were all thrown back by the concussion from the Jivool mortar rounds.

BOOM! BOOM! BOOM!

My screens blacked out, and I had the sensation of falling as I was launched into the air. The sensation was replaced by skull-splitting pain as my CASPer slammed into something hard. I dropped to the ground. My head spinning, I began rebooting my systems. No less than three fuses had blown, and it took me way too long to replace them, fumbling around in the dark. Finally, my screens and comms came back to life. The remains of a shattered tree filled my HUD. Lying next to it was half a CASPer, intestines trailing from it. All around me the sound of artillery thundered. It did nothing to drown out the screams of dying men over the open comm channel.

In quick order, I was back on my feet and scanning the area. The carnage before me nearly turned my stomach and visions of past battles came rushing back. Bits and pieces of CASPers littered the ground around a dozen impact craters.

"Nunez! Rorke!" I shouted over the comm. "Anderson! Cliff!" I didn't bother calling for Drieger. He was paste in the bottom of the first crater.

"*Troy?*" Nunez answered. "*Is that you? Fuck, man. What the hell happened?*"

"Mortars!" I shouted. I checked my HUD, searching for his indicator. There were only twelve CASPers still operational, most of them in the yellow. The rest were black. "I'm going to make my way over to you!"

I brought my left arm up, armed the mounted minigun, and brought my MAC online. On my left shoulder was a rack of rockets, but at such a close range, they were as much of a danger to me as an enemy. The artillery had stopped, which could only mean one thing. The Jivool were coming in to clean up. Scanning for enemies, I rushed as fast as I could to Nunez's location.

He was backed up to a tree cluster, his rear toward where the enemy fire had come from. At least that's where I assumed it came from. It was the direction of the compound. As I approached, three more CASPers joined us. I was pleased to see Cliff, Anderson, and Rorke.

"Looks like it's your lucky day, LT."

"*The fuck it is. I should've stayed my ass on D-Block patrol.*"

"*At least we're outside,*" Rorke said.

"You all good?" I asked.

"*I've got a hitch in the left leg and one of my cameras is out,*" Cliff said.

"*I'm green except this,*" Nunez said and held up the stump where his CASPer's right hand had been. "*Minigun still fires though.*"

"*My shit's green all around,*" Rorke said.

"*Same,*" Anderson added. "*Besides the stuff from the jump.*"

A roaring war cry came from the trees toward the facility. A second later, dozens of armed and armored Jivool erupted into the area. One took aim at a CASPer headed in our direction and released a spray of tungsten rounds on full auto. The bullets tore through the CASPer and shredded the driver within. At such a close range, the armor did next to nothing to protect the con.

"Fire!" I screamed over the comm and fired a MAC round right into the bear-like alien's chest. There was an explosion of blood as the round made its gruesome exit through its back. The alien behind him also fell as the through and through impacted his face.

As if by magic, another Jivool was at my side and dug its claws into the front of my canopy. The screech of steel rang through my machine as I fought to shove him away. The blade on my right arm snapped out, and I drove it deep into his side and twisted before ripping it back out. The ravaged teddy bear dropped to the dirt. I raised my minigun and stitched another charging Jivool from crotch to face.

Charging into the fray, I saw two more Jivool had Nunez cornered at his tree cluster. I fired my MAC into the legs of one while he fired his minigun into the other. I stopped dead in my tracks when I saw something I couldn't believe.

Twenty yards ahead, two CASPers marked as cons on my HUD had Anderson's CASPer gripped by the arms and one of them was waving a Jivool over. The motherfuckers were trying to make a deal with the bastard and offering the lieutenant up as some sort of payment.

"LT!" I shouted over the comm and charged in.

"*Monterey!*" Anderson replied. "*I can't get free, and they ripped my MAC off!*"

"*Stay the fuck back, Troy!*" the CASPer designated Torento warned. "*If we give them the officers, they'll let us go! Fuck this bullshit! Are you a con, or a little snitch?*"

I ignored his taunt and hit my jumpjets. Both cons opened fire on me with their miniguns. Rounds impacted the armor of my Mk 7. I aimed my MAC at Torento and pulled the trigger while simultaneously firing the minigun at the Jivool. I cut the thrust and landed on the

Jivool with a wet crunch. Toronto's CASPer spun from the impact, and I put three more rounds into his back. He hit the dirt face-first and didn't move again.

Anderson slammed his CASPer's free fist into the shoulder joint of the machine still holding him. The con lost his grip on the lieutenant and stumbled back. Before he could regain his balance, Anderson fired his minigun point blank into the cockpit. The CASPer fell flat on its back and didn't move again.

"*That's three times you've saved my ass with some heroic shit.*"

"Eh, who keeps count of that sort of thing?"

Someone screamed over the comm. We both turned to see only six CASPers still standing and more than a dozen Jivool still attacking. Two toppled another machine while a third fired a laser rifle through it. I fired my MAC three times. Three Teddy Ruxpins lost their heads. I watched as Nunez and Rorke worked together to herd two more into a tree cluster and shred them with their miniguns. A CASPer designated Jenko backhanded another while the alien tried to reload, then stomped its head into the dirt. Jenko rotated his MAC and blasted a hole through the next closest Jivool and ran after a third. The alien merc didn't last long under the con's fury.

I noticed two more trying to make a quiet escape back to the facility by creeping behind the trees. They were a good seventy-five yards from my position.

"Fuck it," I said as I locked onto them with one of my rockets and let it fly.

A stream of smoke trailed the projectile as it screamed through the air. The two Jivool turned with looks of horror on their furred faces. Their fear was short lived as the warhead blew them into chunks of meat and gore.

"Goldy Locks sends her regards, assholes."

"*Really?*" Sergeant Cliff asked as he stepped up next to me. "*Puns?*" His CASPer was covered in blood and dented in numerous places.

I shrugged, even though he couldn't see it. "I thought it was punny."

"*Dear god…*"

"*Yooo, Troy, that was some stone-cold killer shit, my boy!*" Nunez shouted. He came strutting up in his one-handed machine. "*Like, you obliterated those fools.*"

I looked around as Anderson, Rorke, and Jenko joined us. The previous carnage, courtesy of the artillery, was now more like something from Jeffery Dahmer's worst nightmare. And that's saying something.

"*Are we all that's left?*" Anderson asked.

I looked around and sighed. "Looks that way." I checked my HUD. Forty-four of the previous fifty CASPers were black.

"*Fuck!*" Cliff shouted. "*What the hell are we supposed to do now?*"

"I don't know about you guys," I said, "but I intend to finish this mission. Successfully." I turned to Anderson. "What do you say, LT? You wanna go back to Hogan with a loss, or do you wanna bring him a victory?"

"*The hell you asking me for? You're the only actual merc here. I'm just a prison guard who made the stupidest decision of his life by signing up for this stupid shit.*"

"You're in charge now. Warden's dead. Hell—" I waved my hand at the massacre "—they're *all* dead. Cliff is a sergeant and you're a lieutenant. You're up. Make the call."

"*I say we go for it,*" Rorke said.

"*Agreed,*" Jenko said. He motioned to me, Rorke, and Nunez. "*If we can pull this off, it puts us one successful mission closer to gaining our freedom back. You guards got nothing to lose by going back with a loss. I mean, Hogan might chew your asses, but that's about it. We gotta go back to that hell hole and back into our cells. At least if we do this, we can do so knowing we're one step closer to getting the hell out of there.*"

"*Three successful missions and you go free,*" Anderson said, understanding in his tone.

"Exactly," I said. "We didn't sign up for this because it sounded like a fun work detail. We did it so we could earn our lives back." I gave a snort of derision. "Hell, some of us aren't even *supposed* to be in prison. But here we all are."

I could feel Anderson staring at me through his CASPer. Since my arrival at Hogan Penitentiary, I hadn't been shy about proclaiming my innocence.

"*As much as I hate to say it, LT,*" Cliff said, "*he's got a point. We can at least give it a shot. Scout the facility out and see how many Jivool are left.*"

Anderson sighed and turned his CASPer to survey the carnage. "*There's at least fifty of them dead out here. Maybe more.*" He turned back to me. "*Intelligence indicated only about seventy-five of them could occupy the facility. It's not a large building. The outer wall covers more square footage than it does.*"

"No wonder Drieger wasn't taking this seriously. He thought it would be a cakewalk. I bet Hogan sold it to him like that too. What's in the building?"

"*Unknown. The Cochkala said that information wasn't our business. Whatever it is, they want it back.*"

I chuckled. "Fits the company motto perfectly, doesn't it? Hogan's Zeros, we re-steal what you lost! Kind of the exact opposite of the Golden Horde."

"*Rumor has it they all started off as criminals too,*" Rorke said. "*So, we're sort of the same.*"

"*Did you really just compare us to one of the fuckin' Four Horsemen?*" Nunez asked.

"*Okay, Monterey,*" Anderson said. "*We'll follow your lead. Let's go kill all the gummy bears and take their damned gummiberry juice.*"

* * *

I watched through my HUD as Jivool mercenaries rushed around the facility. The six of us were twenty meters deep into the tree line and keeping to the shadows. There were four stationed at each crew-served laser. One in the gunner position and three hunkered down behind the barricade. There was an additional dozen crouched behind the two barricades in front of the gate. They were all armed with rifles and armored. I had no doubt they also had RPGs hidden behind their cover too. There were corner barricades attached to the wall where two more guards were positioned in all four stations.

The rear of the facility butted up to a river backed by an open plateau. On the east side of the facility, two armed shuttles sat ready. I could see from my HUD's IR that the engines were running and ready to go. That meant there were an additional two more Jivool in each shuttle. Pilot and copilot. It also left the possibility that there were more waiting in the shuttle.

"I count twenty-eight around the wall and four in the shuttles," I said. "There could be more waiting inside the craft and inside the wall. My IR isn't picking up bodies, but that doesn't mean shit. Either way, looks like your intelligence was off."

"*Shhhit,*" Anderson hissed. "*What do you think?*"

"I've got twelve rockets and Jenko has the same."

Before trekking down to spy on the facility, we'd cannibalized the downed CASPers for ammunition and to replace damaged weapons. All but Nunez's hand. It would've taken too long. Ammo and weaponry were snap and go for speed under duress.

"*So, we take out the shuttles with the rockets?*" Cliff asked.

I nodded, then remembered he couldn't see me. "That's what I'm thinking. Nunez, you and the LT aim for the trigger men on the crew-served lasers. If we can neutralize them and the shuttles, we stand a chance. Rorke, go for as many autocannons as you can. The rest of us will switch over as soon as the other targets are dealt with. Everyone needs to keep their eyes open for anyone raising an RPG. Get hit with one of those and you're likely not going back to prison."

"*Never thought that would sound like a* bad *thing,*" Jenko said.

I grinned. "Yeah, no shit. Everyone ready?"

"*Fuck no I ain't ready for this shit!*" Nunez shouted.

"*Suck it up, buttercup,*" Anderson ordered. "*On your word, Monterey.*"

"Everyone have their targets locked?"

"*Locked on the closest shuttle,*" Jenko replied.

"*Locked on the first crew served,*" Nunez said.

"*Locked on the second crew served,*" Anderson added.

"*Watching for RGP fire and locked onto the closest autocannon,*" Rorke said.

I took a deep breath and locked onto the shuttle further away. "Locked on shuttle two. *Go!*"

As one, we all rushed from cover and out into the open. Jenko and I halted side-by-side and fired all twenty-four of our rockets at the waiting shuttles. We didn't have time to watch and see if we hit our targets as we immediately began taking heavy fire.

I activated my jumpjets, as did Jenko, and leapt for the closest barricade of Jivool, firing my MAC and minigun. Rounds ripped into the concrete and tore into the aliens. With our combined fire, half the Jivool hit the ground, dead. When I landed, I grabbed the closest alien and smashed his head into the barricade, crushing his skull and helmet. My blade snapped out, and I stabbed another in the throat.

Two massive eruptions shook the ground. I turned to see both shuttles ablaze, black smoke rising into the air. More than a few Jivool ran around the ruined craft, rocket-fueled flames cooking them alive as they screamed. The ping of rounds impacting my CASPer redirected my attention back to the Jivool at the wall. I aimed my MAC and dispatched the two Jivool at the front left corner of the building as Jenko literally ripped the head off the last merc at our barricade.

To the side, I heard another explosion and turned to see the furthest crew-served laser in pieces. Anderson had done his job well. He was racing toward the mercs at the two corner stations on the other side of the wall.

I raised my minigun to fire at the remaining Jivool working the closest crew-served laser. Nunez was running to catch up to Anderson but had left a cowering Jivool alive. Before I could fire, half my arm disappeared.

Thank fuck that wasn't my real *arm.*

Instinctively, I fired my jumpjets to retreat. The autocannon above thundered as it fired again and again. Frantic, my heart beating in my chest, I aimed my MAC at the cannon… and missed. I fired twice more and finally hit the damned thing.

"Stupid!" I chastised myself. I'd completely forgotten about them in all the madness.

"*Look out!*" Rorke shouted. "*RPG!*" He was steadily firing at swiveling autocannons.

As it turned out, the cowering Jivool hadn't been cowering at all. He'd been arming his fucking rocket launcher and now had it aimed directly at *my* ass. I fired my jumpjets again and was met with an alarm letting me know I was out of jump juice. A flash of fire erupted behind the merc and smoke streamed through the air as the grenade rocketed toward me in what seemed like slow motion.

So, it's a fucking Jivool that takes me out after all. Ain't that a bitch?

A huge weight slammed into me, there was an explosion, and then a scream. I hit the ground with a grunt. Immediately I shoved the weight off and rolled to my knees. Cliff's CASPer lay next to me, missing half an arm and both legs. His screams from inside his Mk 8 rang over the comm.

"*Cliff!*" I shouted. "*Cliff!*"

Rage overtook my mind and body. I stood and charged the Jivool. He was desperately trying to reload the RPG. He wasn't fast enough. My CASPer's fist slammed into his fat gut. I used the stump of my shattered arm to pin him against the laser's housing. With my remaining hand, I ripped a K-bomb from my belt. I crushed his foot under the steel boot of my war machine, and he screamed. When his mouth opened, I armed it and shoved it as far down his throat as I could. There was a sickening pop as his jaw bones snapped. With a roar I grabbed him by his armored collar and threw him at the gate doors. He bounced off the steel and fell to his knees. The K-bomb detonated, showering me in a red mist of severely fucked up gummy bear.

Anderson, Rorke, Nunez, and Jenko ran up to me.

"Check on Cliff!" I shouted and pointed to Anderson. I looked around the area. There didn't seem to be any remaining enemies. "Status?"

"*All hostiles eliminated,*" Rorke answered. "*Out here anyway. I knocked out all the damned autocannons too. Not a clue what's inside the walls.*"

"Hand me your K-bombs," I ordered. "Let's find out if anyone's home on the other side."

I took all five remaining K-bombs and stuck them along the seam of the two-door gate. I synced the timers and stepped back to cover. They exploded, destroying huge chunks of each side of the gate.

"On me!" I yelled and rushed forward, my MAC ready to cut down any son of a bitch that showed their ugly face.

I kicked one side of the gate open and turned right, Nunez at my side. Rorke and Jenko cleared the left. There was no one in sight. The courtyard of the building was empty, save for some shrubbery. A scan of the facility revealed no further weapon emplacements, nor did IR pick up any warm bodies inside.

"Courtyard is clear," I radioed to Anderson.

"*Good. Stand down. Our orders were to remain outside the building and not enter. Whatever is inside, they don't want us to see it.*"

"How's Cliff?"

"*Bad. His legs are gone at the knees and his arm is shredded. He needs a MEDEVAC. I hit him with a double dose of nanites. His haptic suit's tourniquets stopped the blood loss, but he needs a doctor.*"

"Call it in," I said. "Tell the ship to move their ass. We'll continue to patrol the area until they get here."

A few minutes later Anderson said, "*Shuttle is inbound. ETA twenty minutes.*"

"I hope he can make it that long. He saved my life. I can't repay the favor if he doesn't make it. Hell of a thing for a guard to die saving a con's life."

"His vitals are holding steady. I think he'll survive. And I thought you said you weren't a real con, Troy…"

I didn't respond. It had taken me years to come to terms with my bullshit situation. Dwelling on it at a time like this certainly wouldn't help. I also tried to ignore Andersons' informal way of speaking to me. No guard had ever called me by my first name. Not unless it was for some sort of roll call or something like that. I did my best to ignore it. Best not to read too much into things, especially at a time like this. Once we got back to the pen, things would go back to the way they always were. Cons on our side of the yellow line, the guards on theirs. One mission wouldn't change that status quo.

It didn't take long to figure out we'd, by some miracle, managed to take out all the Jivool mercs. As it turned out, using our rockets on the shuttles had been the smartest thing we'd done. There were no less than twenty crispy bears in each one, no doubt waiting to ambush what remained of our forces. We'd have bit the dust in no time if they'd been allowed to charge. Hell, we'd barely managed to survive as it was.

The whining of engines filled the air as the shuttle sat down. My eyes immediately went to the company emblem painted on the fuselage. Three inmates dressed in stereotypical black and white stripes all chained together at the ankles in a crude depiction of an old-school chain gang. Each man had tattoos on their forearms, held sledgehammers, and broken rocks were scattered about their feet. "HOGAN'S ZEROS" was written in curved block script above and below the cartoon prisoners.

Once you see all those zeros in your bank account, you'll be calling us heroes.

* * *

Cell block D was quiet. Nunez and Rorke were on kitchen detail, so their constant chatter from cell to cell wasn't there to keep me distracted. Jenko was from A-Block. Anderson said there was a possibility he might be moved over with us. I didn't know the guy all that well other than he was a survivor, and I wanted him with me on the next mission. If there *was* a next mission.

With nothing else to do, I grabbed my combat boots from the locker and a tin of polish. I was nearly done with the first one when I heard someone clear their throat. My head snapped to the cell door, and I saw Anderson standing there with an amused look on his face. Two baby-faced rookie guards stood behind him.

"Old habits die hard, don't they?"

I gave him a half smile and nodded. "Scuffed boots earn you extra PT, Warden."

After the battle, Lieutenant Kyle Anderson was the senior officer still alive. He'd been promoted to Warden upon our return. I wasn't unhappy about it. Drieger had been a real bastard. Though, I suppose his retirement could've been a little less messy. Then I remembered all the times he tossed me in the hole. *Nah, fuck that guy. Bombs away, bitch.*

"You sound more like a merc than an inmate."

"If only."

"You don't still consider yourself a merc?"

I snorted. "I consider myself expendable. I'm just a body for Hogan to throw at his contracts until I eat it. Then he'll put some other poor sap in my place until they meet their own sticky end."

Anderson nodded and bit his bottom lip. "Funny you should mention Hogan."

"Yeah? Why's that?"

"Because he wants to see you."

That was a surprise. No inmate ever saw Hogan. The guy made sure no con could ever get near him. Rumor was that Hogan was actually an ex-con himself, and that made a lot of guys mad. It was the whole "turn on your own kind" mentality. I wasn't sure if he actually was an ex-con or not. It wasn't like I had access to the GalNet to research the guy and verify the rumor. I also didn't really give a shit.

"That's—unexpected."

One of the new guards unlocked my cell door and swung it open. I stepped to the yellow line, turned around, placed my feet shoulder width apart, and placed my hands on the back of my head. It was standard procedure so the guards could safely cuff an inmate before moving them.

"Not really," Anderson said. "I'm surprised he didn't ask for you sooner considering what happened on the mission."

There was a rattle of chains, and I braced for the pain of overly tight steel shackles being slapped around my wrists and ankles before being marched through the corridors.

"Those won't be necessary," Anderson said.

Instead of cold steel, I felt a hand on my forearm, pulling mine down from my head. I lowered my arms and turned to see the new guards outside my cell and the new warden on my side of the yellow line, looking me dead in the eyes. His gaze wasn't stern though, it was… friendly.

"He won't be a problem, gentlemen." One side of his mouth rose in a half smile. "Right, Troy?"

There it was again. My *name*.

"Uhh… n-no, Warden."

Anderson gave me a single nod, then did the last thing I ever expected. He turned his back on an uncuffed con while his backup was outside the cell, leaving himself open and vulnerable to attack. The man showed *trust*, real trust, to a *convict*. More than one guard had lost their lives to makeshift shanks by doing this exact thing.

He stepped to the cell's threshold. When my stunned ass didn't follow, he turned his head and asked, "You coming?"

It took a second, but I finally remembered how to walk and talk. "Yes, sir."

He motioned for the guards to lead the way and followed. Still shocked at his behavior, I followed. It was the first time I'd ever walked the halls of Hogan's Penitentiary unshackled.

"How's Sergeant Cliff?" I asked. I hadn't gotten any updates about the guard who'd sacrificed half his body to save my life.

"Recovering fast," Anderson answered. "The docs had to further amputate up above his knees to accommodate for prosthetics. He got lucky with his arm. It's below the elbow."

I lowered my head. "He should have just let me eat the grenade."

"He said to tell you to shut the fuck up when you said that." Anderson grinned at me as we passed through the gen pop rec-room. "Said he only did what you'd already done for me. Plus, now he gets some badass upgrades and will be better equipped for the next mission."

"Still, he's a guard, I'm a con."

Anderson came to a dead stop and spun on me, a hard expression on his face. "We're all mercs out there. That's what you said, right? That's why you saved me... *three times*. There's no guards, no cons, just mercs, right? How are you supposed to save Cliff on the next mission if you aren't here, Troy? How are you going to pull my ass out of the fire *again* if you're six feet under?"

"I guess I can't." I didn't really have a better response than that.

The truth was I didn't expect anyone else to feel that way out there besides me. I was the only real merc on the roster. The rest were gang members, drug dealers, rapists, murderers, and prison guards. Sure, we trained and ran sims, but they weren't the real deal. They'd never stepped foot on a battlefield before, never brushed their lips against those of Lady Death. They didn't know what it was to fight for one another. How could I expect them to think like a merc? Like a warrior? They just weren't. Or, at least, that's what I'd thought before. Nunez, Rorke, Jenko, Anderson, and Cliff… they were all blooded now, bonded in battle.

"Then stow that shit and practice what you preach." He turned and led us up a flight of stairs.

We came to a door I'd never been through before. He swiped an access card and the locks clicked. It opened into a well-lit hallway. On both sides were doors with glass pane windows. Through each one, I saw men and women doing clerical work. A few of them looked up as we passed. The confused looks on their faces told me I was the first inmate they'd ever seen on their level.

At the end of the hall, an intricate, hand-carved set of wooden double doors screamed, *"I'm important!"* Rich people always felt the need to show off how much better they were than everyone else. In this case, it might have been more of a power move. Guards tended to run on a high protein and testosterone diet and regularly needed to be knocked down a notch by their superiors. Walking up to a set of doors like that before getting an ass-chewing from the big boss was sure to do the trick.

The two new guards took up posts on either side of the doors. Anderson stopped and knocked twice.

"Come in!" a gruff voice called.

Anderson shoved the right door open and waved me through. I stepped in and instantly felt completely out of place in my prison scrubs. I didn't need to examine the walls to know they were made of cedar. The smell was plenty. A haze of cigar smoke floated in the air, illuminated by the sunlight shining in from the expanse of bay windows behind Hogan's huge, mahogany desk.

Marcus Hogan, dressed in a white business suit, sat in a large, leather wingback chair, a thick cigar tucked in one side of his mouth. A white hat sat on his desk, alongside a pile of paperwork, several slates, two ashtrays, and no less than five bottles of high-end whiskeys and bourbons.

Fuckin' Colonel Sanders lookin' motherfucker. Are you shitting me with all this cliche shit?

"Mr. Monterey, I presume," Hogan said around the cigar. He pointed to one of the two empty leather chairs in front of his desk. "Have a seat. Warden, you too."

Anderson sat in the other chair, then gave me an expectant look. Fully aware that Hogan would have to have the leather scrubbed after I left, I sat down.

Hogan tossed his cigar in the ashtray, folded his hands, and leaned forward on his desk. "First, I want to say thank you for saving my men and commend you on a job well done. Warden Anderson here tells me you're the only reason anyone survived at all."

My eyes darted to Anderson, then to the floor. As a con, you didn't dare make a guard look bad. As far as you were concerned, each one was the best guard in the whole damned facility and never made a single mistake. They were perfect. Each and every one. If I told Hogan, the owner of the whole god-damned prison and Anderson's employer that he and every other guard who'd gone on the contract didn't know their ass from a hole in the ground as far as mercenary contracts went, I'd find myself beat to hell and in the hole before the end of the day.

"Warden Anderson and Sergeant Cliff performed their duties admirably, Mr. Hogan."

"Bullshit, Troy," Anderson snorted. "You know damned well I didn't have a clue what to do. Neither did Cliff, or any of the rest of us. Don't blow smoke up Mr. Hogan's ass. Tell him the truth." A smile crept across his face. "Wait, are you doing that thing where the prisoners make sure the guards look good so they don't get tossed in the hole?"

My cheeks burned, and I cleared my throat. "I don't know what you're talking about, Warden."

"More smoke." He backhanded me on the shoulder. "Tell the truth, Troy. Come on. You've got my word, nothing's gonna happen to you. This is important."

"Listen to the warden, son," Hogan said. He picked the cigar back up and crammed it in his mouth. "I didn't call you up here so you could kiss my ass and tell me what I want to hear. Out with it. You're an ex-merc, right? Well, I'm the commanding officer, and I want a full after-action report. Now, out with it."

I glanced at Anderson again, then the floor, then locked eyes with Hogan. *Fuck it.*

"To be honest, Mr. Hogan, you could have sent me in there with a team of high school JROTC rejects, and I'd have probably fared better."

Hogan's eyebrows rose. "That bad, huh?"

"Worse."

I proceeded to give him the entire story from my perspective from drop to pick up. He didn't interrupt other than to ask a few questions here and there but seemed to be actually listening. When I was done, he leaned back, twisting the stub of his cigar.

"What would you have done differently?"

"Everything. For starters, if you're going to send guards in as officers, you should probably think about hiring guards with experience as mercs. Or, hell, just hire some damned mercs. I get why you use us prisoners. We're a free, never-ending source of expendable forces. You don't even have to pay out death benefits on us. But your officers need to know what the hell they're doing. Drieger didn't have a fucking clue."

I paused, expecting him to ask who the fuck I thought I was talking to him like that. Instead, he picked up a pen and wrote a note down on a pad of paper. "Go on."

Might as well keep going. If he's going to actually listen, it could save lives on the next campaign—including mine.

"Well, not letting us in on the planning was stupid as fuck too. How the hell are we supposed to complete a mission if we're essentially blind? We need all the details. If you don't want to give out exact coordinates and planetary names, fine, but we need to know what we're walking into. Also, the training has to be better. You can't run us through eight weeks of CASPer sims and expect us to perform up to par on the battlefield. If you're going to do that, just pull new recruits from the cells as soon as we leave. 'Cuz you're going to need them.

"Also, if we're going to do a drop, don't drop us two klicks from the fuckin' enemy's base of operations in the middle of the day. They knew exactly where we were and how many of us there were. Then

Drieger had us form a little party and took his sweet time getting us moving. We should've never been close enough to form one group like that. We had fifty CASPers. There should've been ten shuttles dropping us in ten different locations *at least* five klicks out. Then we could've surrounded the facility and shredded those fuckers. Likely with minimal casualties, if any. I got the feeling from Drieger that you sold this mission as a cakewalk."

Hogan grunted and dropped his pen. "That's because it should've been. I gave Drieger control of the operation, and he assured me he could handle it. He led the SWAT team at his old police precinct before coming here, so I figured he had some sense about him. I wasn't involved with the strategy."

"He was wrong. You both were."

"I see that now." Hogan stood and walked to the window. "I assume you've heard the rumors that I'm an ex-con."

My seat was suddenly very uncomfortable, and I really wanted to leave. "Uh, I may have heard something along those lines."

"Still with the bullshit," Hogan said, still staring out the window. "It's true. Did my time in Soga's Palace."

"Never heard of it."

"Count your blessings. But, yeah, I have my own demons, same as everyone else here. Anyway, my own mercenary days are long behind me. You ever heard of Dan Walker?"

My eyes widened. Who *hadn't* heard of Dan Walker of the Golden Horde? "Yes, sir. He took down a MinSha with a pair of kukris in hand-to-hand combat. That's a bad man. Never knew he was a con though."

Hogan nodded. "Not under that name, no. That was after he got out. And you're wrong, he was a *good* man. Should have never been in prison, if you ask me. Well, maybe he should have, but I get why he did what he did. Many a man has lost his mind over an unfaithful wife. I was happy to hear he got a fresh start. When my own freedom was earned, I came to Tabula Rasa in hopes of starting over with my own mining company. Once I got here though, plans changed. The colony was new, and crime was out of control. This far out on the edge of the galaxy, people tend to think morality doesn't matter anymore."

"Not to mention even aliens start hearing banjos out here," I said.

Hogan chuckled and nodded. "You're not wrong. Anyway, there wasn't a proper holding facility, and it cost too much to transport the riffraff out, so the local law just kept setting them free. They simply couldn't accommodate. I saw an opportunity and jumped. I sold all my mining equipment, scrounged up all the credit I could, and sweet-talked some investors into backing me." He waved his cigar in a circle over his head. "This fine establishment is the end result. You can imagine the irony I felt for years. But, at the end of the day, I make more doing this than I ever would have as a miner. Not only do we hold the criminals from this planet, but also from several others. Prisons overflow everywhere. I have plans to expand to other worlds, even thought about building an entire station, but that's a discussion for later."

He walked back to the desk, opened a drawer, pulled out a thick file, and tossed it on the desk in front of me. "I tell you all this, only so you'll know I understand your situation—intimately."

I felt my eyes widen. "Is that... *my case?*"

"It is. Anderson brought it to my attention that you maintain you're an innocent man. I took it upon myself to take a look." He sat back down in his chair and pointed at the stack. "Sure did have a lot of evidence against you. Prints, DNA, hair, murder weapon, complete and total lack of an alibi, everything needed to put you away."

I shook my head and clenched my jaw. "Talk about bullshit. Every bit of that was planted."

"I'm inclined to believe you. A trained merc, such as yourself, would have enough sense in his head not to leave all that behind. Besides that, you made more on one contract than was taken from the old man. Why the hell would you do something so stupid?"

"I used that argument too. Didn't do me any good."

"I know. It's all there in the file." Hogan rubbed his snow-white beard. "Fact is, I think you're telling the truth. I did some more digging and found your ex and her boyfriend bought themselves a swanky new house, new cars, a boat, and blew tons on jewelry and other stupid shit. They'll be out of money in another two years, tops. My question is where did they get it all? The old man's property was never found, and your last payout mainly went to lawyers and court costs. What was left wouldn't have bought her all this."

All the anger I'd spent years caging up was desperately fighting to escape. "Yeah, well, too bad you weren't the judge."

"True enough. And I can't change the verdict now." He held up a finger. "But I can do plenty to help you in other ways."

I snorted. "What? Extra yard time? A Tri-V in my cell? Wait, let me guess, you're gonna give me a new set of clean scrubs."

Hogan grinned. "Your attitude is understandable. I was the same way. No. I'm talking about really helping you. As you're aware, I need to train a whole new company of CASPer drivers and the remaining troops I have need to be re-trained."

"That's an understatement."

"And it's exactly why I need you."

"*Need me?*"

"Warden Anderson here needs a second in command." Hogan reached in the desk drawer, then dropped two silver bars in front of him. "I need a lieutenant who knows what the fuck they're doing. I'm old and have been out of the game too long. You want the next two missions to be successful so you can punch your ticket and get the fuck out of here? Help get this company on its feet. Shirazi's Phoenix Initiative presented me with a unique opportunity, and I don't want to waste it. I'll take your suggestions and do what it takes, but I need you to step up as more than a con. I need a merc. I need a fucking *leader*."

"And you think they'll follow *me*?"

"The other inmates will," Anderson said. "Once I have a word with the new guards, they will too. I'll explain your situation. It won't be perfect, but it's doable. You'd be like a trustee officer. You can pick some second lieutenants to help you out."

I already knew who my seconds would be. Rorke, Nunez, and Jenko. "Would I get to have a say in which inmates get in?"

"You'll have a hand in everything," Hogan said. "And, when your third mission is a success, not only will I cut you loose, but I'll pay you, then offer you a job."

The deal to serving in Hogan's Zeros was if you participated in three successful missions, your sentence was commuted. Death row inmates dropped to life, provided they weren't executed first. Lifers dropped to a thirty-year sentence, and if you had anything less than life, you went free. You dropped a tier every three missions. The risk was high, but worth it if you could survive.

I narrowed my eyes. "Define *job*."

"I'll officially employ you as an officer in Hogan's Zeros at the rank of Lieutenant Colonel, second only to Colonel Anderson."

I raised an eyebrow at the Warden. "Colonel, huh?"

He just shrugged.

"What about Cliff?"

"Sergeant Cliff will return to work in six months," Hogan answered. "We'll decide what to do with him when he's healthy and ready to go. Until then, you and Anderson are what I have to work with."

I reached out and picked up the silver bars. Before being framed for murder, I'd been on the cusp of making second lieutenant with my old company. There was no denying that part of me wanted to pin them on and get to work.

"Well?" Hogan asked. "What do you say?"

I looked at Anderson, who gave me a reassuring nod, then turned back to Hogan. In the end, it was an easy decision.

"One down, two to go."

* * * * *

Nick Steverson Bio

Nick Steverson is your everyday, blue-collar liquor vendor. Using his Class-A CDL, he delivers wine and liquor from Pensacola to Tallahassee. When not on the road, he takes as many opportunities as possible to write down the chaotic musings of the deranged voices in his head. Since he was young, he has always wanted to write a book, but never took the time to actually sit down and do it. His wife and children were, and remain, his first priority, leaving little time for much else. Inspiration to make the time came from his father one night after sending a text about an idea for a race of characters in his father's books. The last answer he expected to get was, "*You* write it," but that's exactly what he got. So, he did. Sometimes, all it takes is a little nudge in the right direction, and the story writes itself. He now has multiple publications in the Salvage Title Universe including a wide variety of novels and several short stories. Additionally, he has short stories in the Four Horsemen Universe, Starflight Universe, and This Fallen World. He's not done yet, though. There are many more stories to come.

# # # # #

Sugar Foot by David Alan Jones

Chapter 1

When Steven Yardley came home to the ranch for the double funeral six months ago, the Colorado winter had been hard and bitter. Spring and then summer had come. The land thawed and Yard had stuck around. He rode six to ten hours a day, depending on the day, pushing the herd from one grazed-over pasture to another while the border collies yipped and nipped at the cattles' hooves.

Yard had sworn he would never come back. Not to work. Maybe to visit his folks and his brother, catch up with some of the ranch hands who refused to leave, but his life lay in the stars. Death before default and all that. And yet, here he was.

He guided his roan gelding across a knee-high stream that joined the Arkansas River a few kilometers south and gave it some boot to climb the eastern bank. Yard would have lost his seat doing that a few months ago. Now it was trivial. Funny how things came back to a man. He hadn't ridden a horse in twelve years. Yes, he had fallen a couple of times in those early days, and cultivated a crop of saddle sores, but the rhythm had come back to him, that clop-clop-clop beat of the hooves.

The old ranch hands had called him Sugar Foot at the beginning—back when he planned to help out for a week or two tops. Cowboys were no respecters of credits or surnames. Only skill could buy their regard. And Yard had earned it, eventually.

The cows lowed in the misty morning fog. Yard sent the border collies—Dusty, Ace, Peepo, and Ranger—running ahead to keep the herd packed close. He didn't know how he felt about his dad naming one of the herd dogs after the mastermind who had all but enslaved the Earth. Peepo was a hell of a good dog. She didn't deserve that name. And his dad had died not long after giving it to her.

Gusskal-Fa guided his Clydesdale to plod next to Yard. The Besquith looked at home in the saddle, ordered special to match his 2.2-meter frame. "Charlie's gone ahead to open the next gate."

"Good. I figure we'll trailer the horses to Glen Rock next. Pasture's nearly cleared up there. That herd needs driven down to Pipe's Bend."

Gus nodded his wolf-like head. "You remember the vet's coming to look at that calf and his mama this morning?"

Yard cursed. He had promised he would be there for that. The heifer had an infection of some type, urinary maybe, and her calf's eye was all runny. One thing hadn't changed about cattle ranching in the last three hundred plus years: vet bills sucked the marrow right out of profits. But you couldn't do without them.

"It's fine, Yard." Gus reached down to slap him on the shoulder with a paw the size of a steppingstone. "You go. The rest of us will drive the Glen Rock herd."

Yardley pushed his Stetson back on his sweaty brow to nod at his partner. He and Gus had met while serving together in Leonard's Legion, a small but respected mercenary company. Yard hadn't possessed a big enough imagination to picture himself befriending a Besquith before that. Humans and the werewolf-like creatures usually didn't get along. Not so with Gus. He had signed on with Leonard's within a week of Yard and the two had formed a solid bond clearing their six-month probationary period together. That bond had tightened as they mutually saved each other's hides a dozen times over on one godforsaken planet after another over the months that followed. Somehow, during all that, Gus had met and wed Motswen, his life mate. And she had given him a couple of pups. Yard figured Gus's family, more than anything, had prompted him to come along when Yard's mother had sent word she needed him back on Earth at the Tumbling Y Ranch. It didn't hurt there was a large community of refugee Besquith living in and around the startown of Denver now either.

"All right then." Yard whistled for the dogs and they came loping back, tongues lolling in that happy way dogs do when the morning is fine, the herd is in hand, and all is right in their master's world. "I'll take Peepo and meet you back at the house when you're done. Steaks tonight!"

"That's the best part of this job, Yard. No one's shooting at me, and there's steak every night!"

* * *

Chapter 2

The ailing heifer mooed from the other side of the fence. It was a plaintive sound. Her calf, flanked and trussed, heard it and bleated in answer.

"You'd think with the price of beef lifting for the moon, somebody'd do the research to produce nanite sprays for cattle." Yard stood with his well-muscled arms folded atop the barn stall's top rail, Peepo panting at his knee.

"You gonna do that, Sugar Foot?" Tracy Cantori, one of only three livestock veterinarians in the territory, didn't look up from her work on the ill calf. She and Yard had gone steady, as Yard's mother called it, the summer before high school. Yard had always meant to ask her out again later, but he had never made the time. In the end, he had gone off to pursue the merc life at a fake university while she had become an animal doctor. Of the two, she had made the better choice.

Yard ignored the Sugar Foot quip. She knew he had improved since his first days back on the ranch. "Hell no. Vetting is your thing. Maybe you should do it. Make yourself rich."

Tracy squeezed a tube of goop into the calf's runny eye and applied a sticky patch over it. "Rich is rich. I got all I need. There now, that patch'll drop off in a week or two. Keep an eye on him though. If the infection persists, I'll re-apply."

With a no nonsense grace, Tracy loosened the knot holding three of the calf's hooves. He sprang to his feet and ran to the fence separating him from his mother.

"How long should I keep them isolated?" Yard opened the gate for Tracy.

"Three days." She came out shouldering her vet kit and turned to look at the animals. "I know you've got branding and vax days coming up. He might as well be with his buddies when that happens."

"You'll be here for that?" Yard wasn't looking forward to the branding days. It meant combining two or three herds and driving them to the homestead so the hands could rope out the calves. Branding and vaccinating them would take all day. Maybe even two. But it was worth it to keep down the respiratory and other diseases that might otherwise cull the herd and cut the ranch's profits. All the hands looked forward to it. Not Yard.

Tracy pushed a damp strand of auburn hair from her eyes and grinned. He could tell she wanted to say something saucy but refrained. "Wouldn't miss it."

Not for the first time since coming home, Yard considered asking Tracy out. They were twenty-four now. Middle school was long gone. He recalled they had broken up after a fight but couldn't remember the reason. Whatever it had been was probably his fault. Perhaps he could make amends for it now?

Yard had drawn breath to ask when his comm beeped an alert message. He frowned. Amelia Broady, the Tumbling Y's foreman, had sent a priority call. A tingle of concern zigzagged up his spine. Broady wasn't the sort to contact the boss unless something dire had happened.

"What's up, Broady?"

"Yard, God..." Her voice broke, making Yard's hackles rise.

"What's happened?"

"Yard, it's Gus. He's dead."

* * *

Chapter 3

Whoever had shot Gus had done it pointblank with polymer-jacketed lead slugs. Three in the chest. Besquith were tough customers, but the large caliber bullets had made a mess of Gus's furry upper back. The entrance holes looked like little more than tears in his western-style blue shirt. Same couldn't be said for the exit wounds.

He lay in the sage grass on a rolling prairie half a mile from Pipe's Bend. His blood had colored the grass crimson. Most of the ranch's hands stood around the body in a semi-circle, hats off, faces long.

"Sheriff Leiter's on his way." Broady patted Yard's back. She didn't seem to know what to do with her hands.

"Who could have done this?" asked Paul Whitchurch.

Yard shook his head. "Damned if I know. But damned if I'm not going to find out."

"Has anybody told Motswen-Fa?" asked Franklin Huey.

"I didn't have the heart to call her yet," Broady said.

"You don't do that. I will." Yard dreaded making that call, but he wouldn't leave it up to Broady or, God forbid, his mother. She didn't need that sort of thing so soon after losing Dad and Patrick. Neither did Yard. But he was a merc at heart. Losing people came with the armor.

Gus's mate, Motswen-Fa, was no mercenary. She was an alien living on a planet that didn't much like her kind, and that went double for her babies. The world government was offering all sorts of incentives to get refugees off Earth since Peepo's failed seizure had left so many non-humans stranded here. They called it the Phoenix Initiative. Nothing said welcome like mercenary start-up bonuses aimed at encouraging human company owners to take on alien employees just to get them off planet. Yard turned his head and spit in the dust.

A small flyer, its turbo fans humming, circled the gathering and landed five meters away on a grassy rise. Painted glossy silver, it bore the words "Oak Creek County Sheriff" in bold black letters on its side. Sheriff Casey Leiter climbed out, a laser pistol at his hip, his gold badge glinting on his fat chest. Yard hadn't seen Leiter since the summer of his junior year in high school when he had buzzed the office for a lark and accidentally crashed through the eastern wall. Leiter had threatened to send him away to juvie for five years. It had all been bluff and bluster meant to scare Yard. And it had worked. Thankfully, the judge had sentenced him to six months community service, part of which had involved helping to repair the school. In the end, Yard had grown from that experience, no thanks to one Sheriff Casey Leiter.

Leiter surveyed the body through dusty shades. "Who did this?"

"We don't know." Yard refrained from telling the sheriff that was his job. Instead, he asked, "Is the coroner on the way?"

Leiter shot him a cool look. "That's none of your business, Steven. Now move your people back. This is a crime scene."

The ranch hands moved back without Yard saying a word, though they wore sullen expressions. The scent of Gus's blood hung in the air. Flies had begun to accumulate on the body, crawling through the stiffening fur.

"Can I cover him with a blanket from my saddle bags?" Yard figured he knew Leiter's answer before he asked.

"No. We need the body pristine."

Yard doubted a synthetic blanket would make any difference, but he kept his thumbs hooked in his belt while Leiter made a show of walking around Gus's body with a slate, shooting 3D images, taking chemical samples, and marking where spent casings had fallen. Did he notice the imprints of three horses and a dirt bike leading down off the eastern rise? If so, he made no mention of them, nor did he pay them any special attention.

Yard did. He gazed at the ridge for a long while, wishing he could get away to investigate. He dared not with Leiter there. But later he would for sure send a drone or two that way.

It took another twenty minutes for the coroner to show. She and her team took more samples and more images before carting Gus's remains to their flyer on a stretcher. Soon, all that was left of Yard's friend was a stain on the prairie. Peepo showed some interest, like she wanted to lick it up, but Yard called her off.

"I don't guess you had any drones out this way at the time of the shooting?" Leiter asked as the coroner's air van lifted off, fans roaring to gain initial altitude.

"No."

"And your family still insists on no crime prevention flights from the county over your land?"

"That's right."

"Well, you're reaping what you sow there, kid."

Yard said nothing though his heart sped in his chest. Could he lay the sheriff out flat with one punch? He thought so. But doing it would be stupid.

"You get any leads, any hint who might have done this, you call me first thing, got it?"

Yard nodded.

Leiter pushed his sunglasses back onto his bloated face. "You've got a look in your eye that I don't like, Yardley. It's the same sort of look your dad used to get whenever the county council talked about ordering an easement across his land for the light rail track. Don't do anything you'll regret, son."

Yard fixed Leiter with steel-blue eyes. "I won't, Sheriff."

Leiter nodded and squeezed into his patrol unit. He was well into the air, the flyer's shadow dancing across the low hills, before Yard spoke again.

"I won't regret it at all."

* * *

Chapter 4

Firearms, as a rule, were illegal for regular civilians on Earth. Licenses could be had, of course. Though urban sprawl was fast eating away the planet's untamed wilderness, and had been for millennia, there were still places where a citizen could legally obtain and use a pistol or rifle for defense against wild animals. That might have been true of the ranch if Yardley's great-grandfather and his neighbors hadn't put up such a stink when the Earth Federation had first been formed. Back then, the General Assembly had ordered a worldwide gun buyback program. Everyone had known such an ambitious idea wouldn't go over well in what had been the United States of America. But the world government had been adamant. Unifying was their only means of joining the Galactic Union, thus affording Earth Union-member protection. Yard's great-grandfather and many others formed militias and fought several small skirmishes to keep their weapons, but it had come down to a matter of scale. They had no army, while the General Assembly had all the military forces of the planet, including the former United States, at their disposal. In the end, the ranchers disarmed. And because of their short-lived resistance, the Assembly decreed they could not obtain firearms of any kind in perpetuity.

The sins of the fathers had fallen squarely upon the heads of their children.

Yard was weaponless for the first time since leaving home at age seventeen. And yet never had he so wanted a gun. Almost as much as he wanted to follow those tracks leading down to where Gus had been shot, but he waited on that while the ranch hands broke off to drive the herd to a new pasture.

Once they were gone, he called Peepo to his side. She wanted to run off with her brothers to work the herd, but Yard needed her more right now. He scratched her head and she leaned into him for a hug. She smelled of dog and cow and the prairie where she made her living. He patted her flanks, thinking what he should do. In a few minutes, he would send a couple of stealth drones to follow the tracks up and across the ridge. Yard was fairly certain what they would show. Part of him wanted to see the people who had killed Gus. Part of him would rather they remain faceless monsters. It might be better that way.

He stared for some time at the blood on the sage brush and decided he would make a call before sending the drones. No matter what they found, he had already chosen his path. He had done that years ago. He fished his comm from his jeans pocket and tapped a familiar name. He didn't have to wait long for an answer. The person he needed was in California.

Colt Maier's 3D image appeared looking hale, his caramel-colored cheeks bronzed from time in the sun. He grinned, but that expression died almost immediately. Colt wasn't always the best at reading people's faces. Yard must have looked pretty damned grim.

"What's happened?" Colt asked.

"I'll tell you, but first I want to know something."

"Okay."

"You still interested in forming a new merc company?"

Colt turned his head to peer at Yard's image with his right eye. "We went round and round about this when I was there for the funeral. We need a down payment to finance new CASPers and we need a job to get the credits for a down payment. No job, no payment. No payment, no job."

"That's not what I asked." Yard kept his voice even. "Do you want to form a company or not?"

"Of course, I do."

Yard nodded. "In that case, come out to the ranch. We need to talk. I've got a client lined up. You still in contact with Levin and Petrov?"

"Yes."

"Send them the message. Offer them each twenty-five percent. Might be after our first job before they can get here, but I want them in on it from the ground floor. That good with you?"

"You're serious about bringing back Fulcrum Mercenary Tactics?" Colt stared hard at Yard's image as if he half expected his old friend was playing a trick on him.

"No." Yard shook his head. "We had fun in FMT; don't get me wrong. But I'm not looking to rehash the past. I want us to build something new. Something without the stink of a con on it."

Yardley and Colt had met ten years earlier when they joined Fulcrum Mercenary Training, a supposedly prestigious merc university. Unfortunately, the school had been a sham. Same went for the cadre running it. And when it had inevitably fallen apart, Colt and Yard had managed to galvanize their former school into a legitimate mercenary company. Though it had been short-lived and fraught with hardship, Yard wouldn't trade his time in FMT for a billion credits. And he wouldn't go back there for double that.

Colt was nodding. "All right, we start fresh."

"Exactly."

"So, what are we calling this new company of ours?"

"Animals are the going thing. Have been since the beginning."

"But all the good ones have been taken." Colt shrugged as if this were a known thing.

"True. Let's think about it a bit—see if we can come up with something good by the time you get here tonight."

"Okay. But wait, Yard, who's this mystery client willing to hire us before we even have a name for our company?"

"Oh, that's easy. Me."

* * *

Chapter 5

"Mama, I've got Colt coming over tonight," Yard said as he entered the big house which had stood on the Tumbling Y Ranch since 1874.

"That's good, honey," she said from her spot where she lay on the living room couch. "I like that Colt. He's a good boy."

Yardley's mother, whom all the ranch hands affectionately called Mama Yard, hadn't been herself since dad and Patrick had died. Perhaps it was the fact of their deaths that had changed her. The devil knew, no happily married woman ever celebrated the loss of her husband after thirty years of marriage. And no mother with a conscience ever felt like herself again after losing a child. But Yard thought the circumstances of dad and Patrick's passing weighed on her as heavily as the loss. It did on him.

Worse, it all came down to the family business.

The Galactic Union's first contact with Earth hadn't been the sort that heralded celebrations across the local spiral arm. Humans ended up contributing another merc race to the Union, and some considered that good. Others not so much. But Earth itself provided little by way of trade commodities alien races couldn't obtain from more convenient and better-developed planets. That was until the Union's meat eaters discovered beef.

Steak was a hit from day one. Yard's grandfather, and his father after him, had traveled extensively bringing this alien delicacy to the uninitiated. Sales had skyrocketed, revitalizing the cattle industry on Earth, making it possible for many struggling families to not only hang onto their ranches, but to actually earn respectable profits. Even after things had improved, Yard's dad continued making ambassadorial trips meant to expand the market. It was immediately after one of these excursions that he and Patrick had died.

They had been home three days. Winter was on and the combined herds were over the pass at Camstock Valley to wait out the cold months. Rather than trailer their horses out, or perhaps take a flyer, the two had elected to ride across the mountains to visit their stock. They hadn't been in the saddle for a while. They must have missed it.

No one could say for sure which of them took the first tumble. Sheriff Leiter thought it was Yard's dad. His horse, an otherwise sure-footed stallion, must have taken a wrong step on the heights with the snow driving into his face, and the cold making his muscles tremble. Why Patrick hadn't immediately called for help remained a mystery to Yard. Then again, he knew what fear could do to a man's common sense. Patrick must have seen dad's horse stumble off that cliff and panicked. Maybe he thought he could save dad. He had grown up on the ranch same as Yard. He knew the hills and the mountains like his own face in a mirror. Still, for whatever reason, Patrick had fallen too, leaving his horse alone. The painted gelding had walked home still saddled.

"When is Colt coming?" Mama asked. "I don't want to be out here napping."

"Soon." Yard didn't add that his mother had been out there napping on the couch for nearly six months. He had tried to speak to her about it—tried to make her see someone about her depression—but it was like trying to squeeze smoke in his fist. She was pliant as hell. Admitted she had a problem. Promised to see someone about it. Never did.

She rose, her face pale in the gloom. Mama kept the living room shades closed at all times, casting the place in perpetual darkness. The only light came from a lamp on the ancient roll top desk in one corner.

"Mama, you need—"

"I know, Steven." She drew a comforter about her shoulders like an oversized shawl, or perhaps a cape, and Yard glimpsed her arms. They were too thin and had acquired a saggy band of loose flesh under her triceps that had never been there before.

"I can call for you. Doc Rybeck will be happy to make a referral, I'm sure."

"I'll do it tomorrow, honey. I promise." She had already retreated down the hall, the blanket trailing after her like a puffy train.

That promise was so much air. Not that Yard could concern himself with it just now. One problem at a time, as Colt always said. Mama could keep for a day or three. He needed to call Motswen-Fa now.

* * *

"You think he was murdered?" Motswen-Fa's voice, much higher than Gus's, nevertheless grated low like a band saw. Unlike a human, she couldn't produce tears, but her canine-like nose glistened, and her ears drooped in anguish.

"I do."

"And the sheriff—"

"Probably isn't going to do anything about it, Mots. I have to be honest with you."

"You said you sent drones to follow the horse tracks, the ones leading down to where Guskal was shot?"

Yard thought a human female might choke up asking that question. Besquith were made of stern stuff. "I did. The tracks led to a ranch about fifteen kilometers away. It's not one of the old farmsteads. It's new."

"By that you mean it's non-humans who are running it?" She didn't pull any punches.

Yard wouldn't either. "The land's newly registered to a MinSha named Remtep. And when I say new, I mean new as in a little over a year. This Remtep took out a lease and hired every free hand she could throw credits at. My ranch hands haven't had any problems with her, but I called around a bit. Seems other ranches have had run-ins with what they call Rem-riders. These guys have been accused of rustling several times over, but the Sheriff's never caught them at it."

"You said the sheriff won't do anything anyway."

"That's right. Knowing Leiter, he probably hasn't even looked into it. Not more than the surface anyway."

"Too scared?"

"Probably."

"I'm afraid I don't have much clout with my alpha. Otherwise, I'd call my clan for justice."

Yard shook his head. "Mots, there's already too much bad blood between humans and the refugees stuck on Earth. Declaring a blood feud would be like setting off a fusion bomb right now."

Motswen stared into the 3D viewer, her dark eyes narrowed. "Isn't that exactly what you're proposing, Steven?"

"Maybe. But let it be human blood spilled on human land. Keep your pups out of it."

"And what are we supposed to do now? As you say, this isn't our home world."

Yard chewed the inside of his cheek for a moment. He hadn't discussed this with Colt, but once the idea struck him, it refused to fade. "How about if you hire on with me? I don't know how you feel about fighting—hell, I don't know how I feel about putting you in a fight with two little ones relying on you—but there's always work in a mercenary company that doesn't involve pulling a trigger. We could get you and your kids off Earth at least."

The whiskers above Motswen-Fa's eyes folded down as her brow wrinkled. "I am no warrior, but I'd be grateful if I might contribute to the company that brings my mate justice."

Yard nodded solemnly. "I'll send you a contract soon as we're official. I think Gus would have approved."

The barest twinge curled Motswen-Fa's lips upward to reveal her fangs and she growled, a sound that somehow combined heartbroken sorrow, chagrin, and mirth. "Don't think this makes you my alpha, Steven Yardley."

"Of course not, Mots. This is a human thing. It makes me your paladin."

* * *

Chapter 6

Colt arrived late in the evening around 2200 hours. Mama Yard was already fast asleep in her own room, and the hands had put in for the night at the bunkhouse. Peepo lifted her head and whined at the sound of a flyer touching down outside when the old homestead's front windows lit up. Yard stood in the doorway waiting while Colt shouldered his overnight bag. They shook hands and shared a hearty hug on the threshold. Then Yard ushered his truest friend inside.

"You hungry?"

Colt dropped his bag by the couch and fished a slate from it. "No, I'm curious. Last time we talked about starting a company—"

"I said it was too soon. I said we couldn't get the funding." Yard sat on the plush chair across from Colt, scratching Peepo's head. She licked his hand and pushed into his knee.

"All that, and you talked me out of it. So why am I sitting here with a letter of incorporation to form a new mercenary company? You said there was some trouble out here, but you didn't give me details. What's going on, Yard?"

Yard outlined what had happened with Gus and what the drones had found. It took less than five minutes. Sad how something so horrendous came down to just a few whispered words spoken in the night.

Colt shook his head. "I'm sorry, Yard. I know you two were close. The police aren't doing anything?"

"Let's just say I don't expect much. These rustlers have been skimming off my neighbors' herds for a while—changing brands and tags, and taking steers for their own. They'd never hit us until now."

"And never killed anyone before Gus?"

"Not that I know of."

"Did they steal any of your cattle?"

"I was so shocked, I didn't ask. I guess that's why they call me Sugar Foot out here. But Broady told me this evening we're down seven out of that herd Gus was driving."

"No one saw him get shot?"

"He had ridden out for some stragglers over a ridge. We had drones, but they were with the main herd. He was out of view. I guess the cows he was hunting for had been rustled, but he didn't know that of course."

"So he happened upon these rustlers, and they shot him." Colt keyed his slate on and placed it between them on a low coffee table that had probably been in Yard's family for two-hundred years.

"They shot him and left his mate and their two pups alone in the world. I don't know what it's like in California right now, but around here eighty percent of the day workers looking to pick up whatever ranch jobs they can get are from off planet. And that's pissing the humans off. All our hands are permanent, but I've heard from my neighbors there've been fights—mostly our kind hating on the local refugees for stealing jobs."

"It's about the same at home. Less rustic, more industrial, but yeah, same dynamic."

Not for the first time, Yard had to kick himself for the gratitude he felt over Colt's misfortune. The two of them, along with Colt's onagain-off-again girlfriend, Nichol Levin and their stalwart friend Feliks Petrov, had graduated from Burne's Academy, an intensive two-year mercenary training school. With the bright-eyed enthusiasm of youth, the four had assumed they would immediately start their own company and go to work. They had, after all, done it once before under worse circumstances. Unfortunately, launching a mercenary concern required far more capital investment than any of them could muster. And it wasn't like scads of venture capitalists were falling over themselves to back a handful of twenty somethings on what would have been a risky endeavor no matter their ages or experience. They had held onto their dream for about five months before the money ran out and they had each been forced to go their separate ways, joining various companies as lowly recruits.

While his own family tragedy had brought Yard back to Earth, Colt too had suffered a less severe version of the same. His mother, a professor at Stanford, had suffered a freak stroke last month. Colt might not agree with his parents' liberal political views, but that didn't mean he wasn't a dutiful son. He had given up a probationary commission with Bjorn's Berserkers, a monumental loss to his career by any mercenary's reckoning, and returned home to be with her and his father. Bjorn's might take him back if another spot opened up, but competition for a big-league commission like that was fierce.

That was unfortunate. But it left Colt a free agent, and for that Yard was grateful.

"So the job is protect your herds from any more thieves?" Colt asked.

"No. That's not the job. I'm not looking to stop more theft. I want whoever did this shut down permanently."

Colt blinked that way he did whenever his mind was working overtime. "You're skating too close to the justice system with that attitude. This isn't merc territory, Yard, and you know it."

Yard cracked his knuckles, and Peepo looked up at him in surprise. "That's why I'm telling you this up front before either of us puts a thumb on that contract. This first job ain't about justice. It's about what's right. One of my friends—one of my best friends—was murdered in cold blood on my family's ranch. I'm not bringing the bastards who did this to the law. I'm putting them in the ground where they belong."

Yard pulled the incorporation contract close and pressed his thumb to the slate, signifying his one quarter ownership in their company which would rise as part of the Phoenix Initiative. That done, he pushed it Colt's way. "Are you with me?"

Less than a second passed before Colt pressed his thumb to the slate.

* * *

Chapter 7

"You had RATs hidden down here this entire time?" Colt stood next to Yard with his hands on his hips as the cellar's automated doors whirled open, casting a broad beam of light into the darkness. Connected to the Tumbling Y Ranch's main barn, the original underground structure had been a storm cellar built by one of Yard's ancestors back in the twentieth century. Subsequent Yardleys had expanded it first into a fallout shelter during the early twenty-first century and later, as new building techniques arrived from the stars, a sprawling, multi-floored complex of storage facilities for farm equipment, emergency food supplies, and ever since Yard had returned home, battle armor of dubious legality.

"Short answer, yes." Yard led the way down a ramp into the cellar's steel corridors. The first set of rooms on the top floor contained old tractors, fifteen hauler drones equipped with motors powerful enough to lift some serious farm equipment, and pallets filled with sacks of fertilizer. The seventh room contained a dozen armored battle suits known as Reaction Armor Tech. Yard flipped on the overheads and the RATs gleamed a dull red where they stood on mounting brackets in two rows of six.

"How'd you get them down here? And for that matter, how'd you get them in the first place? I thought all of our equipment went back to the Mormons after they repossessed the *Uncanny Valley*." Though Colt had grown since Yard had first met him—he was twenty-one now and stood almost two meters tall—he looked like a kid in Santa's toy shop as he inspected the RATs.

"I still say the *Uncanny* should have been our ship after we saved those Mormons' planet for them."

"Are you still on about that? They financed our entire company for a year. We'd be slaves if it wasn't for them."

Yard shrugged one shoulder, unwilling to rehash an old debate between them. "Well, Petrov and I felt like they owed us a little more than what we got paid. So, we marked twelve RATs off the inventory and shipped them out with our effects when we left the Zion system. It wasn't hard considering the losses we had taken defending Brigham. And before you get all high and mighty, it sure as hell didn't hurt anybody's bottom line. These suits would have ended up in dry storage somewhere collecting dust. Petrov and I figured we would need them more than the Mormons once we got around to forming our own company. And here we are."

Colt turned away from inspecting a suit's outstretched arm and lifted an eyebrow. "Why didn't you tell me about this?"

"Colt, seriously?"

"What?"

"You know I love you like a brother, but you and secrets go together like soap on Teflon."

"I can keep a secret!"

Yard tilted his head to one side.

"Fine, sometimes I let things slip." Colt narrowed his eyes. "Does Nichol know about these?"

Yard shrugged. "Of course. She was our Top. Nobody keeps a secret like a Top."

Colt sucked his teeth and turned back to continue his inspection. He and Nichol Levin, the former FMT First Sergeant, had broken up for probably the fourth time a couple of months ago. It was a sore subject. Colt looked as though he might say something about her knowing before him but changed tack instead. "How'd you get these past the Earth Fed Inspectors?"

"Mixed them in with tractor and flyer parts. Ranchers need a lot of heavy equipment, and these days we order loads of it from off planet. Besides, strength-enhancing suits aren't illegal down here. And it's not like I have any weapons attached to them."

"Yeah but these strength-enhancing suits happen to be bullet, laser, and mostly concussion proof."

"That's just a bonus."

Colt laughed and threw an arm around one of the RATs like it was his best pal. "So, our nameless company might be incorporated, but we haven't got any sort of guns. Not even laser pistols. Unless you've got some old GenTok W80s buried down here, how are you expecting us to go after Gus's killers?"

Yard squared his shoulders and met Colt's gaze. This wasn't going to be an easy sell. But like taking any medicine, better to swallow it and get the tough part done quick. "We're gonna have to take out loans."

"Go to hell."

"Colt, I'm not talking about borrowing from loan sharks this time. I think we all learned our lesson doing that. These are Earth Fed loans. Hell, they've got Nigel Shirazi's endorsement backing them. You said it yourself; we've got no weapons. Besides, I'm not talking about buying CASPers—not yet anyway. Just a few thousand credits to purchase our initial loadout. The ranch can pay the mission expenses, all of them, in two months."

"You can't have spoken with Levin or Petrov about this," Colt said. "They're both out system. What will our co-owners say when they find out we're a day old and already in debt?"

"They'll think we're a regular mercenary outfit."

"So, it's going to be like old times, us running from one job to the next, scratching to pay last month's expenses with this month's contract?"

"A healthy company is a working company, right?" Yard knew echoing their mutual mentor, the late Captain Enrique Torres, was a low blow of sorts. Yard had come to respect Torres before his untimely death. Colt had loved him like a second father. Torres's words were bound to have an effect.

Colt twisted one of the RAT gauntlets free and fitted his hand inside. Servos whined as he opened and closed his fist a couple of times. He considered it for a minute, like a man choosing an engagement ring. "Even if I'm willing to take out loans, we can't get weapons delivered here. There's a ban."

"There's a ban for regular citizens. That doesn't hold for merc companies. In fact, the government's pushing to get units outfitted as fast as technologically possible."

"You're talking overnight?"

Yard shook his head. "I'm talking a matter of hours. We've got FedEx and we're not that far from Denver. It's a startown, Colt. They've got everything. You want merc weapons, they've got you covered."

Colt heaved a sigh. "Fine. Pull up the loan docs before I change my mind."

* * *

Chapter 8

Yard rode out on his roan at dawn without a weapon. In his younger days, and he had to admit that would have been as little as two years ago, he might have marched into Remtep's camp armored and ready for battle. But, as Colt had pointed out, they had no proof the Rem-riders had shot Gus. Assuming otherwise put him in the category of those who judged aliens before getting to know them. MinSha like Remtep came in every sort, just like any Human. You got good ones, and you got scoundrels. Yard figured he'd let time tell which category Remtep belonged under.

Of course, that didn't mean he was going in unprepared.

"You with me, Colt?" Yard asked as he cleared the ridge above where Gus had died.

"I'm here." Colt's voice sounded perfect over the near-invisible plug in Yard's right ear. "The suit's running at one-hundred percent optimal. Stealth systems are activated, and I've got you on drone cam."

"Any sign of a welcoming party?" Yard scanned the horizon where the Rocky Mountains stood like frost-covered teeth chewing the sky.

"Nope. Nothing moving ahead of you but some rabbits."

"Didn't figure there would be. We've got another three or four kilometers till we reach the border."

"These guys were ballsy coming this far onto your family's land."

"That's rustling for ya. Guess they could have done it with flyers or drones, but they must like stealing up close and personal."

"I wish we could have waited for Levin and Petrov to get here," Colt said. "I know why we can't. I'd just feel better with more back up."

"Hey, No Name's an all-new company, right? We all start out small. What's smaller than two guys and a RAT?"

"One idiot on a horse?"

"Ouch." Yard feigned outrage but couldn't stifle a chuckle. "Don't worry. You just stay hidden and close by. We'll make this work."

"So is that what we're calling this outfit? No Name?" Colt sounded like he was on the move. Piloting a RAT, he could run up to seventy kilometers an hour. Unlikely in this terrain, but he could nonetheless far outpace Yard's gelding.

Yard adjusted his riding position as his mount trotted down a small hillock. "I bet it'd be one of a kind if we went with that. We'd be Company No Name, topping the contracts completed lists in every pit this side of Karma-IV."

"What about a name related to the ranch? We're getting our start right here in Colorado on the Tumbling Y. I'm not opposed to calling it that: Tumbling Y."

"Nah." Yard shook his head. "That's my family's thing. Our company belongs to us. You wouldn't want to call it Stanford Inc or something, right?"

"Definitely not." Colt was silent for several seconds. Then he asked, "How about Taurus? Like the bull constellation?"

"It's better than Tumbling Y, but I don't know. Taurus Inc? Taurus Corp?"

"Taurus Templar. Alliterations are a big thing with the famous merc companies."

Yard twisted his lips to one side, considering. "Templar is like a knight?"

"Yep."

"Funny, I told Motswen-Fa yesterday that I'd be her paladin. I know it sounds cheesy, but it's how I feel."

"No, it sounds right. We don't let people get away with executing our friends," Colt said. "That mean you like the name?"

"Yeah. It's got potential."

They had reached the Tumbling Y Ranch's border. Yard crossed it and followed the mixed horse and dirt bike tracks a few more kilometers until they meandered onto a soft-packed trail. In the distance stood several buildings. The largest looked something like a wasp nest turned on its side, or perhaps a seashell. Tan and yellow in the morning sun, the structure appeared more cultivated than constructed. It was all rounded curves with no hard angles. Roughly the size of a small office building, it looked completely out of place on the prairie. Next to it stood a wooden barn of human design large enough to shelter two dozen horses. Four battery-powered dirt bikes rested on kick stands in front of it.

"Looks like you've been made," Colt said. "I count five bodies coming out of the… hive or whatever that is up ahead. One of them's a MinSha."

"I see them. You stay in stealth mode." Yard squeezed the gelding into a lazy trot, kicking up puffs of sand along the trail.

The MinSha, a being who resembled a two-meter-tall praying mantis, regarded Yard with red, compound eyes that put him in mind of enormous golf balls. Tilted upon one of her shoulders she carried a silver rifle as long as his horse. It looked like it belonged mounted on an assault shuttle. Three Besquith and a human flanked the MinSha. Each of them carried weapons of their own: rifles for the werewolves and twin laser pistols for the human, belted at his waist. The Besquith wore what Yard thought of as work clothes—denim pants, rugged work boots, and heavy-duty shirts of blue and black. The man wore light armor. Nothing so sophisticated as a RAT, but definitely not the sort of thing any sane person would wear for ranch duty.

Yard brought his mount to a halt about ten strides from the welcoming party. The gelding snorted and pawed the ground. He did not like the smell of these people. Neither did Yard for that matter.

The MinSha spoke in a discordant buzzing drone that made Yard think of pissed off bees. Yard's pinplants dutifully translated the irritating sound into words he could comprehend.

"I wondered how long it would be before we got a visit from you, Steven Yardley."

"You know my name, Remtep?"

"Any fool can use the GalNet." Remtep tossed her head side to side in a MinSha gesture that conveyed derision. "I make it a point to know my neighbors."

"Yard, I'm reading three more people near the hive entrance. All armed. My sensors can't penetrate too far into the structure, but I think we should figure there's more than that deeper inside."

Yard made no answer to avoid tipping off Colt's presence. Instead, he said, "And how often do you kill your neighbors, Remtep?"

One of the Besquith snarled and leveled his rifle on Yard. The other two growled as well but made no threatening moves. The human, his greasy red hair flapping in the light breeze, placed his hands on his holstered pistols.

Remtep made a calming gesture with her free hand, and the Besquith settled, though they remained tensed.

"Shall I speak frankly with you, Human?" Remtep chopped her chitin-armored hand at Yard as if breaking a block of ice between them.

"Yes, and I'll do the same."

"I ordered your father and brother killed because they were infringing on my livelihood. They insisted on selling their beef at prices I could not match. And they would not listen to reason on the matter."

A sizzle of pure feeling snaked up from Yard's toes all the way to his heart. He wouldn't call it anger, fear, or even hatred. It appeared too quickly for such labels. Shock might encompass it. Or perhaps realization. Either of those terms fit, and yet neither was quite right. His mind worked over what Remtep had said while waves of this unnamed sensation washed over him.

"I came about Gus," he said stupidly. He hadn't even realized he had spoken until the sound reached his ears.

Remtep looked at one of her Besquith and chirruped an inquiry.

"Gusskal-Fa. He was the Yardley's dog. I put him down yesterday when he tried to stop me from claiming seven of their cattle."

"And you didn't tell me this?" Remtep sounded offended, though not particularly surprised.

"I was going to tell you, Rem. Today for sure. It's been a busy week."

The other Besquith chortled, their furry hides shaking with their mirth.

"Yard," Colt said, his voice calm but rising. "Your pulse is up. I need you to remain calm right now. I know what you just heard wasn't part of our plan, but we've got to roll with it if we want this thing to work out in our favor. We can't go off half cocked."

"Roll with it? I'm supposed to roll with the idea that these animals killed my dad and my brother and poor Gus? How the hell can a body roll with something like that?"

"Who's he talking to?" asked the human on Remtep's side.

"It's obvious he has accomplices." Remtep turned her chitinous head this way and that, surveying the bleak landscape with her ruby red eyes. "They must have impressive stealth systems if the house lidar didn't pick them up."

"Won't matter once they're dead." The human drew both pistols. "Say the word, boss, and this cowboy's going off that horse with two smoking holes where his eyes used to be."

A small part of Yard's mind knew he should be afraid. He was, after all, outnumbered, unarmored, and essentially weaponless. Humans might be one of the galaxy's thirty-seven mercenary races, but unlike the MinSha, Besquith, and so many others, humanity was essentially soft and vulnerable. Yard lacked the natural defenses much hardier bodies could provide. Thus, seated on a horse in denim, cotton, and leather boots, he presented a defenseless target for his enemies.

Yes, he should be scared shitless right now.

But the larger part of Yard's mind was busy issuing commands through his pinplants to the seven industrial-sized drones hovering almost forty-six hundred meters above him. As one, they shut off their motors, and fell like an extinction level event toward Remtep's position.

"Yard!" Colt sounded frantic. "What are you doing? That's not part of the plan."

Yard leaned forward in his saddle to peer at Remtep. "Plans come in two types."

"What?" She returned her gaze to him, taken aback by his non sequitur.

"Two types." He held up two fingers. "Flexible and brittle. I don't like brittle plans. They break. Just like I don't like murderers and rustlers. I break them."

All seven drones' motors spun to life, arresting their plunge five meters above the ground while, in the same instant, they opened their articulated lifting claws to drop eleven RATs directly onto Remtep's crew.

The drones' buzzing was worse than the MinSha's voice, and an order of magnitude louder. Wind from their high-powered fans kicked up dirt, grass, and small pebbles in a glass bottle hurricane that momentarily obscured Yard's vision. Fortunately, the flying debris did not prevent him from witnessing the moment when the armored suits reached earth.

The human died instantly. One of the RATs crushed his skull like a hammer coming down on an eggshell. Two of the Besquith suffered injuries in the hail of falling armor, while Remtep and the remaining Besquith moved fast enough to avoid the danger, though they had another surprise coming.

The gelding reared and screamed, but Yard had already slid out of the saddle the instant the mayhem began. He slapped the horse's rump and sent it galloping away, thankful it didn't kick him for his efforts.

Crouching, and hurriedly pulling off his boots, he sent a command to ten of the RATs: ASSUME AUTONOMOUS BATTLE MODE.

Those ten, relying on rudimentary AI and a target set designated by Yard, attacked Remtep and the remaining Besquith. One RAT turned on its heels and ran toward Yard, spinning to place its back toward him once it was within arm's reach. A series of whirling sounds and the unit's rear armor spread apart like a deadly metal flower. Yard stepped into the suit and it closed around him. The RAT's sensor array linked to his pinplants, and he ceased being a guy in armor to become its pilot.

Seven more Besquith boiled out of the main nest and four humans came running from the barn. Everyone was armed and they all looked pissed. Yard drew a Mag-9 laser pistol from the holster strapped at his hip and fired on the humans coming from the barn because they presented a clearer target. Dressed in simple work clothes that afforded them no real protection, Yard was able to pick two of them off almost instantly. Clearly not complete fools, the remaining two ducked behind the parked dirt bikes where they took up firing positions with their rifles.

"Stay on the guys behind the bikes," Colt said over their comm channel. "I'm coming in to surprise Remtep and—oh, shit. No!"

"What?" Side-stepping to evade incoming fire, Yard couldn't turn to see what was happening with Colt. He prayed his partner hadn't just bought it, but there was nothing he could do if he had.

"It's Peepo!"

Yard fired three beams, tagging only the bikes but forcing the two sharpshooters behind them to keep their heads down. "Peepo? Where?"

And then he saw her. His brave, stupid, and apparently angry border collie raced down the nearest ridge like a black and white blur toward one of the Besquith. She growled and barked and latched onto the werewolf's calf muscle like a bulldog. Flummoxed, the Besquith howled in pain, his own growl not that much different than hers. He danced around in a half circle, babbling in his native tongue, seemingly forgetting the gas-powered, chemical sub-gun in his hands.

Unfortunately, one of the new arrivals suffered no such bout of forgetfulness. Taking quick aim, he shot Peepo through the flank with a laser that burned through fur and flesh with ease. Peepo screamed and opened her jaws. She hobbled a couple of meters, and fell in the grass, yowling in pain as smoke rose from both sides of her body.

* * *

Chapter 9

Yard screamed so hard he busted several capillaries in his right eye. He had heard people describe a red rage before, but he had never experienced it. Not until this very moment. He had always assumed such a state of mind would rob him of coherent thought. Not so. In fact, though he was literally seeing red, he nonetheless experienced a cold flush of analytic thought that was almost frightening.

The two riflemen behind the dirt bikes were a distraction. Not the main target and yet capable of crippling his mission, they were more than simply expendable: they were marked for death.

Bereft of explosives, Yard ordered one of his industrial drones to flip over directly above the two humans and then keyed its fans to full power. It slammed into them going better than forty kilometers per hour. Not fast really, but since the thing weighed more than a thousand kilograms, it didn't take much speed to inflict damage. It pinwheeled off its targets, motors screaming in protest as its uncovered blades ate up the ground, ruining the machinery inside. Yard didn't care. In fact, he wasn't even interested in what damage the drone inflicted on the men. He wanted a specific reaction.

And he got it.

Straggling to their feet, both clearly injured, the sharpshooters ran for the barn. They had gone perhaps two meters before a second drone, this one flying upright, simultaneously decapitated both of them in a spray of blood, bone, and brain. That done, Yard turned his attention to his remaining opponents, viewing them through a haze of red, and he grinned without realizing it.

The RATs, though powerful in their own right, and semi-smart running in autonomous mode, simply couldn't hold their own against the remaining three Besquith and Remtep. For hired muscle, and that's all these Besquith could be since they were working for a MinSha, the werewolf-like warriors fought well. They had already taken down three of Yard's RATs and a fourth was barely walking upright, its helmet and torso smoking from many holes blasted through the armor. Yard hadn't armed the autonomous suits. Doing so would have prompted too many questions from the authorities. Instead, he had set them to fight with armored fists, feet, and helms. They did so valiantly, but they were no match against laser and gunfire. Remtep's rifle alone was taking them down with one to two shots per kill.

Colt, who had joined the fray, did far better, firing his own pistol, but with so many suits in the way, most of his shots went wide of their enemies.

Time to even the odds.

Yard flung a dirt bike at the nearest Besquith. It clobbered him just as one of the RATs punched the beast in his ribs. The giant creature staggered, and Colt shot him through one massive eye. The Besquith fell, and his two remaining fellows turned their rifles on Colt. While the near point-blank fire didn't immediately penetrate Colt's RAT, it did inflict major damage. Sparks flew and a series of warning lights turned red for Colt on Yard's 3D status display. He would have tossed another bike, but Remtep took a pot shot at him. Thankfully, she missed, but the laser blast superheated the air around him and set the barn ablaze.

Yard dive-rolled to one side and came up firing. His G-9 wasn't the most powerful laser in the Union. Though he scored three direct hits on Remtep's chitin-covered thorax, the coherent beams did little more than scuff her armor.

She fired back, and Yard attempted a second dive. This time, part of the beam struck his left boot. Pain flared up his leg. He worried she might have blown off a portion of his heel, but he didn't have time to look. He rolled to his good foot and fired again. This time, instead of aiming for her body, Yard shot Remtep's rifle. He didn't know much about MinSha weapons, but taking a laser blast that could slice through steel probably wasn't good for the thing. He tagged it four times, three across the main stock, and one lucky shot right down the fist-sized barrel before she could scuttle out of the way and level the weapon on him a third time. She pulled the trigger and he tried to drop though he knew he had reacted an instant too late. Through his red haze, he realized he was about to die. His only regret would be leaving Colt to fight alone.

A series of static pops resounded across the hills. Remtep had enough time to look at her rifle and give it a shake before it exploded in her hands. The titanic boom caused Yard's defensive systems to lock out his hearing for a moment as a concussive wave sent him crown over ass crack into the dirt bikes. RATs, Besquith, and one surprised Colt Maier, went sailing over Yard's head. Well, bits of the Besquith did anyway. Colt's armor protected him from the worst of the explosion, though the status display showed he had suffered some gross internal injuries from the shock wave which the suit couldn't fully baffle.

Yard rose to his good foot to survey the damage. A blackened crater and a couple of azure legs was all that remained of Remtep. No more warriors came from either the giant nest or the barn. Those who had were dead.

"Colt, you conscious?"

"Barely," he croaked. He lay near where the sharpshooters had lost their heads.

"We won."

"Really? Yeah, makes sense. I remember this is what winning usually feels like. Is Peepo…"

Yard hobbled over to the dog where she lay several meters from the main battle. He placed an armored hand gently on her side. To his everlasting surprise and joy, her chest rose and fell. Relieved, he lay next to her and keyed his comm to send a distress signal.

* * *

Yard awoke on his back. Someone had opened his helmet, but he still wore the bulk of his armor. Tracy sat on her knees next to Peepo. She had shaved away much of the fur around the dog's wound and applied a bandage to it. She also had a drip running into Peepo's leg and she was petting her face.

Though he hadn't moved, Yard must have made a sound.

"Ambulance is on the way," Tracy said. "Sheriff too. I hope you have a good excuse for what happened here, Sugar Foot."

He nodded and swallowed. "Merc business."

"I see."

"Tracy."

"Yeah?"

"Would you like to go out sometime?"

She stared at him, her lips quivering on a smile before she outright laughed. "I thought you'd never ask."

* * * * *

David Alan Jones Bio

David Alan Jones is a veteran of the United States Air Force, where he served as an Arabic linguist. A 2016 Writers of the Future silver honorable mention recipient, David's writing spans the science fiction, military sci-fi, fantasy, and urban fantasy genres. He is a martial artist, a husband, and a father of three. David's day job involves programming computers for Uncle Sam.

You can find out more about David's writing, including his current projects, at his website: https://www.davidalanjones.net/.

# # # # #

The Battle of Bronzer Hill
by Benjamin Tyler Smith

"Is this seriously all we've got left?" Captain Paulie Bucco waved a suntanned hand at the mostly empty storehouse. "We brought weeks' worth of ammo with us! I saw you order it all, Melfi." *And damn near broke my back hauling all of it in, too.*

"Don't look at me, Paulie." Melfi crossed her arms tight against her body and glared up at him. "I bought as much as the government advisor said to buy for a company our size. It's not my fault he didn't account for how wild you boys are with all the plinking you do."

"It's called target practice, woman, and it's necessary." *Especially for rookies like us*, he thought, his cheeks hot with embarrassment. "How's our jump juice stash?"

"Worse than this. Like I said, you boys are too wild."

Paulie cursed. He and his Jersey Bronzers were only a month into their very first contract to defend a mining operation on Ceiras 3, and it was already turning sideways. The desert world wasn't exactly brimming with tourist hot spots, but it was rife with conflict. Part of the reason he'd wanted his boys practicing their shooting and jumping every day was to dissuade the locals from seeing them as easy targets. "What about Deego? That damned Zuul is a week late."

"And likely to be later still, if his last transmission means anything." Melfi pulled a tablet from her overalls and skimmed its contents. "He's in system, but contending with a few 'emergency' deliveries, as he calls them."

"Emergency deliveries. Yeah, right. They're paying him more than we are, most likely."

An alarm sounded from the watchtower the Caroon manned near the entrance to their mine. A second later, a chirp sounded in Paulie's head courtesy of his pinplants. *"Boss, we got trouble!"*

Of course we do. Trouble never came in small packages, not on Earth and not here, either. And it always loved company. "What is it, Tony?" he asked aloud.

"Dust clouds on the horizon, from the west."

"A sandstorm?" Melfi asked.

"Oh, it's a storm all right. A storm of Besquith."

Paulie cursed for what seemed like the hundredth time that morning. "Everyone, suit up! We've got some wolf hunting to do."

"And you." He leveled a finger at Melfi. "Get Deego on the horn. Those fancy Mk 8's we got on loan aren't gonna be worth much without ammo and jump juice."

Melfi ran past him and back toward the command bunker. "I'll see what I can do!" she called over her shoulder.

Paulie turned the other way and headed for the hangar where his CASPer was stored. He thought about Deego and cursed yet again. Maybe he'd show up now that the Bronzers were in an "emergency."

* * *

Jacquelyn Candace Warren, founder and CEO of the Justin Warren Munitions Conveyance Company, tightened the strap that held her to her jump seat. She reached up and grabbed the electric guitar floating in front of her, then strummed a simple C chord. Musical notes echoed through the cargo hold of the dropship *Bunker Hill*, her home for the last two hundred hours, a hundred and seventy of which had been spent in hyperspace.

She would've preferred her quarters on the transport ship *Wardens' Justice*, but it was thirty hours behind her, still in hyperspace after an extended stay in orbit of Julvin 2. She and her bodyguards had taken the *Bunker Hill* with a load of weapons that needed to be delivered to her warehouse on Ceiras 4. A lot of green merc companies had sprung up in the last several months, and many of them had found their way out here, leading to a bit of a boom for her company.

Not only that, she'd had increased demand for concert appearances at Fenn's Den of Dren, the main merc pit on Ceiras 4. She had one scheduled for this week, and nothing new to present to the crowd.

Running a hand through her long, black hair, Jackie adjusted the pair of bunny ears on her head. She strummed a clean G chord, then sighed. The music wasn't with her.

Riku sat across from her in another jump seat. The Japanese-American man was the youngest of her bodyguards to have been hired by her late father, back when the company was a mercenary outfit named Warren's Wardens. He looked up from the classic sci-fi book he was reading, something by a guy named Steverson. "Depik got your muse, JC? Any way I can help?"

"Not unless you can travel through time." Jackie opened the case magnetically locked to the floor and placed her guitar inside. "I hate when people don't want to uphold their end of a bargain."

"Ah." Riku nodded and turned his attention back to his book. "Yeah, it's pretty infuriating."

"I know the Havlens don't leave their homeworld often due to their unique physiology, but they can't be that socially inept."

"Well, I know they'll think twice before trying to double-cross you or anyone else again."

"Oh, aye!" a voice boomed from above. A giant of a man lay in a sleeping bag strapped to the cargo hold's ceiling. His bushy red beard split in a grin. "Lassie, you did a number on them, an' no mistake!"

Jackie smiled. Another of her bodyguards, Big Al had been around since she was six, nearly fourteen years ago. Despite his height, the broad-shouldered Scotsman had reminded her of the bearded dwarves of Tolkien, Feist, and other authors she had devoured during her earliest days as a reader. "I merely presented them with an alternative."

"An' that's a fact!" Big Al pinched his mouth together and spoke in a stuck-up tone. "'Excuse me, Miss Warren. Would you kindly return our space elevator to us? We'll die without it!'" Then he smiled and continued, this time in a high-pitched, exaggerated southern drawl. "'Why, certainly, Mister Alien! So long as you pay me and my boys, we'll be happy to return it to you, and only partially damaged, too!'"

Jackie laughed. "I don't sound like that!"

"It's an accurate summary of events, though." Riku smirked. "Maybe you could do a song about it."

"Och, I can see it now! The Ballad of the Runaway Elevator!"

Jackie waved a hand. "You both know my policy. I don't write songs that show clients in a negative light, even if it's warranted."

A tall man with short, graying brown hair floated from the rear of the cargo bay, past metal containers full of MAC rounds, chemical laser magazines, and more. Marcus was the leader of her bodyguards and her late father's best friend. He wiped sweat from his handsome face with a towel. "That's it for the first three-hour workout of the day. Al, the machine's yours."

"Roger, boss!" Al reached into a pouch on the front of his sleeping bag and removed a set of gym clothes. He unzipped his bag and pushed off toward the *Bunker Hill's* stern, where the exercise equipment had been set up. "It'll be worth it to see Sayra and Roxie in their tight gym outfits!"

"I heard that, *garotinho*!" Sayra called from beyond the cargo containers.

"Aw, isn't that cute, Sayra?" Roxie added. "The big boy thinks he can keep up with us. Too bad for him we're already finished."

Jackie smiled when both ladies came into view. Sayra was the oldest member of her team of "Justin Timers," only a year or two past Marcus's forty-three. The petite Brazilian woman's long hair was held back in a ponytail, the coal-black locks without a hint of gray.

Roxie did triple-duty for Jackie. The tall blonde served as a driver when they were on the ground, a gunner aboard the *Bunker Hill*, and as the drummer in her company mascot's band, Gun Bunny and the Bandoliers. In all capacities, she acted as a bodyguard whose job was to get Jackie out of harm's way, no matter what. Jackie still wasn't sure where she hid her weapons when she was in her Foxie Roxie stage getup, and she wasn't sure she wanted to know.

"Mornin', Bunny!" Roxie waved. "How's things?"

Sayra smiled at Jackie. "Good morning, *garota*."

Marcus pointed. "You make a habit of wearing that off-camera now, Little Miss?"

Jackie reached up and touched the bunny ears. "It's for inspiration. I've got a new song to compose."

"No one ever said the company mascot had to sing and dance." Marcus strapped into the jump seat next to Riku. "Candy the Gun Bunny just needs to look pretty."

A wave of heat swept through her. "If it helps the bottom line, why not?" Jackie had come up with the idea back in the company's early days, shortly after taking what was left of the devastated Wardens and turning it into an arms conveyance organization, specializing in emergency deliveries. "Ready to hop when you need a drop!" had been an early slogan, and a popular one if merchandise sales on the company's GalNet page were any indicator.

"Is it helping?" Marcus asked. "The bunny ears, I mean."

"Not really." She smiled. "Maybe I need to put on the full getup. Would that work for you, Marcus?"

"It would work for me!" Riku said.

Marcus sighed but said nothing.

Jackie felt a flash of annoyance, but she tamped it down. Marcus had known her since she was a child, and still treated her as such, despite how much she had grown and… developed in the intervening years. She couldn't blame him. It was one of the qualities she found so endearing, even if it frustrated her to no end.

And no one said I couldn't tease the hell out of him.

She released her seat restraint and pushed off toward the partitioned area she shared with Sayra and Roxie. "I'll let you boys judge the outfit I've worked up for the next performance. Think Playboy Bunny, but with more bandoliers."

Before she could reach the canvas partition, her pinlink chirped. "*JC, it's Double-T,*" a deep voice said inside her mind. "*Intercepted some chatter from the planet we're about to slingshot around. You may want to listen to it.*"

Jackie grabbed a handrail to arrest her forward movement. She briefly considered tuning in to the *Bunker Hill's* comm system through her pinlink, then pulled herself toward the cockpit. When she opened the door, a pair of heads turned her way. Terrence Tremain—otherwise known as Double-T—was a big black man with a shaved head and a set of aviators almost permanently adhered to his face, day or night. He nodded and turned back to the instrument panel without a word, a clear sign he was troubled.

"Hey, JC." Ed saluted with a half-eaten protein bar. The *Bunker Hill's* main gunner tapped a sensor screen, which showed a dropship in high orbit of Ceiras 3, a yellow planet known for its mining ventures and not much else. "Got something juicy for you."

Double-T grunted and flipped a switch.

Gunfire, explosions, and the crack-whine of laser weapons echoed through the cockpit. Jackie grimaced until her pinplants dialed back the noise level to protect her ears. *"Bronzer Prime to all units,"* a man with a thick northeast accent called, *"Bronzer Prime to all units. Prepare LZ for hot drop, over!"*

A chorus of whoops and *"Right on!"* and *"About freakin' time!"* rang out, followed by a woman saying, *"Not a moment too soon! We're about to run dry over here."*

Double-T turned the audio off. "That was from a few minutes ago." He punched in a command. "This is live."

"—you're not here in the next ten minutes, Deego, we're all dead! Fuckin' dead, ya hear me?"

A new voice spoke, his alien tongue overlaid by an English translation. *"Captain Bucco, you must secure the LZ. I can't put my ship down with those Besquith missile batteries active."*

"Don't you have countermeasures? Chaff? Flares? ECM?"

"Countermeasures can and do fail. I can't risk my crew—"

"Listen here, you oversized mutt. We paid extra for hot drops! Get your fuckin' ass down here now, *or I'll drag you to the nearest vet clinic and—"*

A series of explosions drowned out the rest of the threat. "How are we hearing this?" Jackie asked. She used her pinplants to run a GalNet search for the name "Bronzer" and learned the company's full name was the Jersey Bronzers, a newly minted outfit based out of Atlantic City. Their maiden contract was an all-hands-on-deck defense of a valuable ore mine that a Caroon corporation owned. They had recently struck a new vein and attracted the notice of a few companies that wanted control of the mine, and these rivals didn't care who they killed to get it.

Captain Bucco had called the arms dealer Deego. If the term "oversized mutt" was any indicator, Deego was likely a Zuul. She ran a search for both name and race, and came back with Deego Arms, a single ship outfit that worked this cluster of star systems. The company promised fast, scheduled deliveries of munitions for militaries, private security firms, and merc companies of most races. There was even the option for combat drops, if a nonrefundable fee were paid in advance.

Deego's company offerings sounded an awful lot like Jackie's, with one glaring exception: she and her Justin Timers *never* ran from a fight. She balled her hands into fists. Her Papa and most of the Warren's Wardens merc outfit had died when their arms dealer had left them high and dry. She would never let that happen to another group of mercs, not if she could help it.

"*Bucco, I simply cannot risk my crew until you eliminate those anti-aircraft batteries!*"

"*You yellow-bellied, chickenshit—*"

"*Watch your mouth, Human!*"

"*You watch* your *mouth, or I'll deep fry your hot dog ass and make the biggest ripper my boys have ever seen!*"

Jackie leaned over and activated the mic. "Boys, what seems to be the problem here?"

"*Who the hell are you?*" Bucco demanded. "*This is supposed to be a secure channel!*"

Double-T tapped the comm screen, his dark finger touching Deego's name. "You'd have to ask your former arms dealer that," Jackie said. "It seems he's the one broadcasting this conversation for the entire system to hear."

Deego let out a choked gasp. "*Of all the nerve—*"

"*What do you mean 'former'? Who are you?*"

"I doubt you want to continue using Deego's services now that he's wimped out. Besides, why use him when you can use us? Name's Jackie Warren, and my Justin Timers are ready to assist."

"*Justin Timers? Why does that sound familiar…?*" Bucco muttered.

A second voice cut in. "*Hey, are you the ones with the sexy bunny girl mascot?*"

"*Candy the Gun Bunny!*" another said. "*I've seen some of her music videos!*"

"*Tony, Richie, pipe down!*" Bucco shouted. "*Although I do remember a fine piece of heavily armed rabbit tail, now that you both mention it.*"

She mentally stuck her tongue out at Marcus. *Told you it was good advertising.* "That's us! And like our advertising says, we're just in time, or you won't pay a dime."

"*Yeah, 'cause we'll be dead!*" Tony said, and laughter flooded the comm line.

Jackie smiled. *God, I love mercs.* Papa had enjoyed that kind of morose sense of humor. "It's our plan to make sure that doesn't happen." She read over the Bronzers' advertised strength and compared it to the *Bunker Hill's* manifest. "We can assist in clearing the LZ, and rearm and refuel you in the next fifteen minutes. Base fee is twenty thousand, plus expenditures and the standard combat bonus."

"*You drive a hard bargain, Miss Warren.*"

"*Don't listen to her, Captain!*" Deego shouted. "*She's bluffing!*"

"Am I? Shall I transmit testimonials from some of my customers? Hatfield's Hooligans? Wings of Odin? Philips' Phalanx?" She accessed Bucco's bio on his company's public paperwork. "How about Quentin's Qualifieds?"

"*Ol' Colonel Moreau's group?*"

"The very same! He's old and salty as ever, but a joy to work with."

"*You're telling me. He's back on Earth, training us greenhorns to venture into the wild black yonder.*"

"Oh, then I have him to thank for all the recent business I've been receiving. Next time I'm on Earth—"

"*This is ridiculous!*" Deego growled. "*There's a battle going on, and you're both reminiscing?*"

"You're still here, little doggo?" Jackie asked. "I figured you'd have run off by now."

"*Listen to me, you little—*"

"*No, both of you listen to me,*" Bucco snapped, his command voice booming through the radio. Jackie winced and was glad she wasn't tapped into the comm with her pinplants. "*At the end of the day, I don't care who gets me the ammo. Miss Warren, you've got a deal. Twenty, plus all the rest. And Deego, if you get here, you'll get the same pay she does. Whoever is first gets paid!*"

"*This is ridiculous!*" Deego repeated, his rage evident through the comm.

"What's the matter, pupper?" Jackie strapped into the seat behind Double-T and Ed. "Not up for a real-life arms race?"

"*Should you really be taunting the Zuul, Little Miss?*" Marcus asked through the comms.

"*Oh, come on, boss,*" Big Al said. "*You know that's how our blue-eyed lass rolls!*"

"*You won't get away with this,*" Deego growled. "*This is robbery!*"

"No, this is business. You had an unsatisfied client, and we poached him from you." Jackie tapped Double-T on the shoulder and gave him the thumbs-up. "And if you want to catch this Gun Bunny, you'd best get to running because we're already way ahead of you!"

With that, Double-T punched the throttle. The increased acceleration pushed Jackie back into her jump seat. "Is Deego following us?"

Ed watched his sensor readouts. "Looks to be the case. Damn, that bird's fast too!"

He turned the monitor so she could see. Deego's ship had a Zuul name that roughly translated to "Duchess." She smirked at the pet name as she studied the information. The *Duchess* was a variant of the Shrieker, a dropship design where some armor was sacrificed for speed. "At this rate, he might catch up to us," she murmured.

"Hardly. I'm barely pushing my baby!"

"Well, push her hard and fast!" Jackie slapped Double-T on the back. "Just like the ladies like, right?"

Double-T coughed and spluttered, while Ed snorted with laughter. The others snickered and chuckled through the comms.

"*Please don't upset the pilot, Little Miss. He kind of has all our lives in his hands.*"

"Everyone strapped in?" Jackie asked. "Sound off!"

"*Marcus, mounted up and ready to drop.*"

"*Al the Dwarf, snug as a bug in my CASPer!*"

"*Riku, also ready to go.*"

"Roxie, manning the portside cannon, ready to rock someone's world!"

"Sayra, strapped into one of these awful jump seats. How in the world can a chair be so uncomfortable, even in low-G?"

Jackie rubbed at the phantom pain in her butt. Even after years of traveling to this port and that planet, she never had gotten used to the jump seats. "It's about to get worse, Sayra."

"*Don't remind me,* garota."

Double-T pushed the nose of the *Bunker Hill* down as they entered the atmosphere. "It's about to get worse than worse, ladies! Hold onto your asses!"

The *Bunker Hill* dropped at a steep angle. A heat shield warning flashed on the main monitor, and a siren shrieked. As the shield neared its protective limit, Double-T deployed the flaps, flared the speed brakes, and yanked hard on the stick. The *Bunker Hill* leveled out with a sudden jerk, its speed dropping rapidly. He pulled the nose high and rolled the ship a hundred and eighty degrees to the left, banking toward the target LZ. He slammed the throttle to full burn. "Here we go!"

"Be ready with countermeasures," Jackie warned through gritted teeth. "We'll drop the goods once we reach the LZ, but don't tangle with the Besquith unless we're fired upon." She skimmed the enemy's company profile. Rashar's Reavers had a reputation for brutal, if sloppy, execution. They would get the job done, and revel in it. "I'd like to avoid a straight-up fight if we can."

"*Aw, but they're like space kobolds!*" Big Al grumbled. "*A dwarf like me lives for this kind of fight!*"

"Nerd," Riku said. "Besides, whoever heard of a six-foot-four dwarf?"

"*I'm six-foot-two, I'll have you know. I may be tall for my kind, but a dwarf I am. I've got the war hammer and bushy red beard to prove it!*"

"*Well, I guess you have a point.*"

"*Hey, what's my fantasy race?*" Roxie asked.

"*Roxanne, don't encourage—*" Sayra began.

"Incoming!" Ed shouted, his voice cutting through the chatter. "Break right, T!"

"On it!"

The *Bunker Hill* lurched to the right. Jackie grimaced at the sudden change of direction. "We're already taking shots from the ground?"

"No, behind us!"

"*I'll be damned if I let some Human spawn get the best of me!*" Deego shouted over the radio. "*Turn back or prepare to be shot down!*"

"You've got a lot of nerve shooting at a fellow merchant, Deego!" Jackie snapped.

"*There's no honor among thieves, mercs, or arms dealers, Human girl! Time you learned that the hard way. If you want on the ground so bad, I'll put you there permanently!*"

"Big words from a Zuul too craven to resupply his client only a few minutes ago!"

"Popping flares!" Ed called.

Bright blooms of red light appeared in the stern cameras. The incoming missiles flew off course and exploded. The force of the blasts rattled the hull of the *Bunker Hill*, but no damage alerts appeared on the monitors.

"Returning fire!" Ed punched in a few commands, then mashed a big red button next to him. "Missiles away!"

The *Bunker Hill* shook as its one rearward-facing missile launchers fired once, twice, and again. One of the cockpit's monitors switched to the aft camera feed. The three missiles shot through the yellow sky toward the barely visible *Duchess* in the distance. Several flares burst into blinding light around Deego's dropship, the brightness reflected by thousands of pieces of chaff. The missiles sailed off course and exploded.

Jackie keyed the mic. "That was a warning shot, Deego. Our next salvo won't miss!"

A barrage of cannon fire answered her. "So much for bluffing," she said as the missile lock alarm wailed once more.

The two ships screamed their way through the ever-thickening wind, exchanging missile and cannon fire. After Ed fired the last of the rearward missiles, Double-T dove into a cloudbank. A few more cannon rounds pinged off the hull, but the maneuver bought them a short respite.

In her head, Jackie heard the chatter between her Justin Timers as they did last-minute equipment checks. She hoped they wouldn't be needed on the ground and mouthed a silent prayer for their safety. "Captain Bucco, what's the status of the LZ?"

"*Besquith, Besquith everywhere, but not a spare MAC round in sight!*" Bucco's gruff voice was nearly drowned out in the explosions and gunfire rattling its way down his mic. "*If the cavalry's waiting for the most dramatic time to appear, it doesn't get more dramatic than this!*"

"Hold on, Bronzers. We're almost there!"

The *Bunker Hill* broke through the thick clouds, the craggy terrain below drawing closer by the second. Deego's ship flew out of a cloudbank a moment later, and a fresh volley of missiles and cannon fire soared their way. "Brace yourselves!" Double-T shouted as he pushed the throttle to the max.

They sped toward the ground, Jackie's heart in her throat. With an effort, she forced the fear down. Double-T had gotten them out of worse scrapes than this. Papa had placed a lot of faith in him, and she'd never had reason to doubt that.

At the last second, Double-T yanked back on the stick and flared the speed brakes. The *Bunker Hill* leveled out and blasted up from the ground. Behind them, explosions erupted as the missiles chasing them couldn't alter course fast enough.

"Incoming cannon fire!" Ed shouted. "From above!"

The cameras facing upward caught sight of a terrific barrage of tracer rounds coming from the enemy transport ship. Double-T did his best to dodge but rounds still pinged off the hull. The *Bunker Hill* shuddered, and a whining sound filled the cockpit. "Number two engine's been hit! Power's down a bit, but she can still go!"

Another siren blared. "What now?" Jackie demanded.

"Missile lock!"

"From Deego? How many missiles does he have?"

"Not from there. From the ground!" Ed swore. "The Reavers have AA batteries! And they're only targeting us!"

"Not the *Duchess*?" Something clicked in her mind. "Oh, so that's why Deego had the open channel." She keyed the mic. "You double-crossing sack of dog shit. You sold the Bronzers out!"

Deego's response was more cannon fire.

* * *

"Paulie, you seein' this?" Tony asked, his dark orange CASPer's face turned to watch the aeronautical display.

Rounds cracked through the air, punching into the sandbags Paulie crouched behind. He let out a burst of gunfire from his dwindling supply and ducked even lower. "A bit busy dealing with what's on the ground, Tony. Keep your head down! Your CASPer's got cameras all over, remember?"

Paulie had been watching on his camera display. The rolling gunfight between the two ships had been impressive. More importantly than watching, he'd been listening. It sounded like Deego was working with the Besquith against him and his Bronzers. While it was possible that this Jackie chick was just slinging mud at a fellow merchant, Deego's recent actions cast a lot of doubt onto his loyalties. "Anyone got eyes on those Besquith missile launchers?"

"*Tower says they're about nine hundred yards out from our position,*" Richie replied. "*Behind a rise, so none of us here on the ground are gonna see 'em.*"

"Any volunteers want to jump out there and back?"

"*What'd I tell you earlier?*" Melfi snapped. "*We don't have any jump juice, remember?*"

Paulie checked his own reserves and cursed. They'd have to remember to go a little lighter on the CASPer calisthenics routines in the future.

Besquith missiles sailed into the air as more rounds impacted around him.

If we survive this, he added.

* * *

"Popping more flares!" Ed called as the missile lock warnings continued to blare.

"Hey, how many more flares do we have?" Jackie asked. "Enough for a bit of fireworks?"

Double-T glanced at her. "You thinking of the time on Meridua 7?"

"9, but let's not worry about the details." She grinned. "Think you can pull that off again, or was it a fluke?"

Double-T laughed. "Well, there's only one way to find out, right?"

Ed groaned. "All right, I'll get the special loads ready!"

The forward monitor showed a hilly, crater-pocked landscape. One hill loomed above them all, with a squat facility at its center and a line of sandbag and ferrocrete barriers surrounding it. Human infantry and dark orange CASPers crouched behind the defensive works and traded fire with squads of Besquith advancing up the hill on all sides.

A pair of armored vehicles sat on one of the opposing hilltops, each topped with a triple rack of missile tubes. Those racks turned to face the *Bunker Hill*. "That could do some damage," Jackie murmured. "Double-T, ready?"

"Born ready!"

"Do it!" she shouted as the missiles fired.

Double-T throttled down and applied the speed brakes. A collision warning siren screeched, and then the *Duchess* thundered past, barely missing the *Bunker Hill*. Double-T pushed the lever to full throttle and climbed until they were right above Deego's ship. "Dropping the stickies!" Ed said.

More than twenty flares thumped out of the launchers mounted to the *Bunker Hill's* underside. The flares clattered against the hull of the *Duchess* and stuck fast, their luminescence blinding even in the harsh sunlight. Jackie squinted. "Damn, I think you made these even brighter than the last batch, Ed!"

"Stickier, too!" Ed dimmed the monitor screen. "It'll take days for them to scrape all that adhesive off."

"Assuming they have days," Double-T added. "Throttling back down!"

Ed fired another salvo of sticky flares as the *Bunker Hill* dropped behind the *Duchess*. They glided for a short time with the jets powered down to idle and cooled off, leaving a smaller heat signature in comparison to the gigantic one Deego's ship now emitted.

The *Duchess* bobbed and weaved as it fired flares and chaff. Most of the incoming missiles strayed off course, but a few stayed true to their new mark and slammed into the ship's armored hull in bright explosions. The impact sheared off one of the *Duchess'* engines, and the other trailed black smoke. The ship wobbled before it fell from the sky.

* * *

Richie let out a whoop that went over the comms. "*Yeah! Take that, you double-crossing mutt!*"

"*That's what he gets!*" Tony called as more Bronzers took up the cheer.

"Pipe down!" Paulie roared. He couldn't deny feeling a bit of vindictive joy at the sight, but that did little to fix their present problems. The Besquith were still advancing, and he and his boys were still perilously low on ammo. He keyed his comms. "Jackie, doll, we need you now more than ever!"

* * *

The *Duchess* dug a deep trench into the ground, its path leading it straight into the Reaver's antiaircraft battery. The vehicles disappeared beneath her bulky fuselage, along with some of the Besquith crewing them. The missiles still in the vehicles' racks exploded and flipped the *Duchess* over onto its top. It slid to a halt, its belly exposed like an animal attacked by predators and left to rot in the sun.

Jackie felt a touch of remorse for Deego and his crew. Mostly his crew. "Think anyone survived?"

"Possible," Double-T said. "Those Shriekers are tough beasts."

"*I wouldn't worry about it, Bunny,*" Roxie said. "*They started it!*"

Jackie couldn't argue with that.

Rounds pinged off the hull. Ed checked the cameras. "Taking small arms fire! The Besquith ain't happy!"

"Are they ever?" Jackie pointed. "Get us over the LZ, Double-T!"

"Roger!"

"Man, Bucco wasn't kidding!" Ed said. "There really are Besquith everywhere!"

Below them, the craggy landscape teemed with the tall, wolf-like aliens. The Besquith mercs pushed forward under an ever-thinning barrage from the entrenched Bronzers at the hilltop mine. Jackie tuned into their radio frequency with her pinplants, and the sounds of battle spilled into her head.

"*Anyone got a spare mag?*"

"*Negative, Richie! Switch to your sidearm!*"

"*That was my sidearm!*"

"*Dante here! More Besquith pushing hard to the east!*"

Jackie placed a hand on Ed's shoulder. "Cut us a path."

"We could just drop the stuff and leave," Double-T offered. "No need to stick our necks out any more than this."

She shook her head. "No, we're already involved. Like it or not, their only other arms dealer's out of the picture now—"

"*I like it!*" Riku chimed in from his CASPer.

"*Same here. The bloody mutts had it coming!*" Big Al added.

Jackie smiled. "Regardless, we owe it to the Bronzers to see this through to the end. Besides, this way we can get our combat bonus!"

Double-T looked back and flashed a grin. "Haven't done a CAS run in a while. This sounds like fun."

"*We're ready to go back here, Little Miss. Drop the ramp and we'll jump.*"

"*Loaded up with as much spare ammo as we can carry, too!*" Riku added.

Jackie released her straps and opened the door. "I'll man the starboard Vulcan."

Three Mk 7 CASPers stood on the far end of the cargo hold, near the ramp. Each was heavily laden with magazine-filled bandoliers and ammo belts. In addition, each had a full weapons loadout: a magnetic accelerator cannon and laser rifle for Marcus, a hammer and pistol for Big Al, and a double set of chain guns for Riku. She wished she'd brought their shoulder-mounted missile launchers, but they were back on Ceiras 4 getting a much-needed upgrade.

"Bunny, here!" Roxie held up Jackie's carapace breastplate, then tossed it. "These Besquith are about to get their furry little balls rocked!"

Jackie caught the breastplate and snapped it into place. "Couldn't have said it better myself!"

Sayra waited at the starboard hatch, a tether connecting her lithe, tan form to a handrail at the opening. The Brazilian woman rested her M40A9 sniper rifle in the crook of an arm and smiled. "Ready to save some lives, *garota?*"

Jackie took a tether off the wall, hooked it to her belt, and secured its other end to the mounting frame of the hatch's M61 Vulcan rotary cannon. She grinned at Sayra. "To quote Double-T: born ready."

A red strobe light came to life, and an alarm sounded as the ramp lowered. The *Bunker Hill* slowed, and Jackie spread her legs to keep her balance.

"*We're over the LZ!*" Double-T barked. "*Get your fat asses off my baby's back!*"

"*Justin Timers, go!*" Marcus stepped off the edge and dropped from view.

Riku bounded down the ramp and leapt into the open sky.

"*Show-off,*" Big Al muttered. "*Ladies, watch this!*" He tried to run, but one of his CASPer's metal feet caught on the other. He tripped, fell forward, and slid down the ramp on his belly in a shower of sparks. "*Woaaaaaah!*"

Sayra, Jackie, and Roxie all shared a look. Roxie threw back her head and laughed. "Hey, Jackie, you want to incorporate pratfalls into the stage routine? The fans would love it if Gun Bunny and Foxie Roxie fell flat on their faces or asses every now and then."

"No, thanks. I like my face and tailbone in their present condition." Jackie pulled herself into the gunner's seat and lowered the Vulcan cannon so she could aim at ground targets. "Let's get to work, people!"

* * *

Marcus took in the battlefield as he dropped toward it. His HUD highlighted the enemy Reavers in red, and the allied Bronzers in green. And there was a lot more red than green. The cameras mounted on top of his CASPer showed the *Bunker Hill* hovering overhead, its hull growing smaller. Riku's CASPer jumped out a second later, his unit outlined in blue.

Big Al slid out and tumbled end over end. "*Woaaaaaah!*"

"*Try to get control, big guy!*" Riku called.

"*I'm a wee busy trying not to heave up last night's dinner!*"

"Well, get less busy," Marcus said. "Ceiras 3 has enough craters already."

"*Hey, if you want to cannonball it, aim for that knot of Besquith over there.*"

On Marcus's HUD, a squad of Besquith pushing up the Bronzers' hill was suddenly painted yellow.

Marcus checked his altimeter, then fired his jumpjets. His descent rate slowed considerably. With this kind of drop he would burn through most of his fuel before he hit the ground, but it would be worth it.

Riku pulled up alongside him. He burned his jumpjets intermittently to match speeds with Marcus. "*Looks like we'll land right in the middle of the Bronzers' position.*"

Big Al shot past them, his CASPer rolled up into a semblance of a cannonball. The Scotsman's comms broadcast a mixture of laughter and groans. "*If I can't have a good landing, I'll make sure the Besquith feel it, too!*"

"*Al, I was kidding!*" Riku said. "*Don't do it!*"

"He'll be fine." Marcus studied the landing points his computer estimated for all three of them. "Be ready to provide covering fire when we land."

* * *

Shanshen advanced up the hill at the head of his squad, his broad shoulders hunched to make him a smaller target for the Human defenders who still had ammunition. The Reaver bared his teeth in a menacing grin. He hadn't tasted Human in a while and couldn't wait to get his hands on one.

A dropship hovered high over the hilltop mine, its ramp lowered. Shanshen's grin turned into a scowl. Deego had fouled things up, but it was Commander Rashar's fault for getting the little Zuul involved in the first place. *He should've listened to me.*

Through his earpiece, he heard Rashar order the long-range squads to engage the dropship while the close-combat squads continued their advance. Shanshen returned his focus to the hilltop and its beleaguered defenders. His squad didn't have the range to deal with the Human dropship.

A shrill whistle filled the air, and Shanshen assumed it was the portable rocket launchers the long-range squads had. But the whistling grew louder, and louder. He raised a paw to halt his squad and scanned the sky above the hilltop. Two CASPers dropped through the air, their jumpjets burning at regular intervals to give them a controlled descent. He barked a laugh. Two CASPers wouldn't make any difference in this fight—

"Shanshen, look out!"

One of his subordinates tackled him, and the two Besquith rolled a short way down the hill. Shanshen threw his subordinate off him and opened his mouth to demand what he was doing.

The ground where he'd been standing exploded in a shower of hot dirt and rocks. Shanshen flattened himself to the ground as clumps of earth pelted him.

A CASPer strode out of the settling dust of a newly formed crater, a giant hammer in one hand and a pistol in the other. The machine's external speakers boomed with laughter as the CASPer shot one Besquith, then pounded another to the ground with powerful hammer blows. "Now, that's an entrance!"

Shanshen shouldered his rifle and fired three-round bursts as he advanced. Some of his bullets connected and dented the CASPer's armor, but the Human operator dodged most of them. It always amazed Shanshen how agile those machines could be if the operator was good. And this one was very good, and brave, to fall straight into a pack of angry, hungry Besquith.

Shanshen stepped on something soft, and he glanced down. One of his squadmates lay there, his body torn in half and burned horribly. Other bodies were scattered about, either in or near the crater the CASPer made when it landed. His eyes widened. He'd landed right on top of them, only seconds after he'd ordered his squad to a halt.

Rage boiled up in Shanshen at the cost of his mistake, and he switched his rifle to full auto and charged at the CASPer. He fired from the hip as he emptied the weapon's drum magazine in seconds.

Bullets whizzed past him, and one clipped his arm. Shanshen tumbled to the ground, his spent weapon falling from his hands. He rolled to his feet and drew a sidearm, but before he could fire, a laser bolt burned a hole in the ground next to his knee. Two CASPers stood on top of the hill, their sleek hulls laden with bandoliers of fresh magazines. One aimed a laser rifle his way, while the other's arm-mounted chain guns fired in slow, steady thumps.

Shame mixed with anger in Shanshen as he considered his options. They'd been ambushed, and there was only one survivable option left for him and his squad. "Fall back! Find cover and regroup!"

He fired a few rounds at the accursed hammer-wielding CASPer, then turned tail and ran down the hill, his left arm hanging limp.

* * *

"*Think it's a good idea to let them go?*" Riku asked.

Marcus kept his weapons trained on the retreating Besquith until he was sure they were gone. "No, but that's how the Little Miss operates."

"*'Today's enemy is tomorrow's client,' and all that!*" Big Al strutted up the hill, blood and dust covering his once-clean CASPer's body. He rested the gore-spattered hammer against his shoulder and laughed. "*Oh, but that was fun! Well, except for the vomit-inducing descent.*"

"*Wait, big guy, you didn't—*"

"*Let's just say the outside isn't the only thing that's filthy.*"

"*Nice work, everyone!*" Jackie's voice crackled over the comm "*We could see it all from here!*"

"*Did you see my cannonball, lassie?*" Big Al asked. "*I waited until the very last second to fire the jumpjets. Burned a few of the furry bastards with 'em, too!*"

"*Flawless execution, my giant dwarf! Except for the vomit part. Ew. Someone's showering as soon as he's aboard.*"

"What, no hug for the conquering hero?" Marcus asked.

"*Quiet, you.*"

The three of them crested the hill and approached the earthworks the Jersey Bronzers had erected. A few Human mercs in dark orange fatigues pointed and waved. "Hey, you crazy bastards!" one of them called. "Over here! Get behind cover!"

"Beginning resupply now," Marcus said. "Little Miss, keep their heads down for us."

"*Incoming!*" Double-T shouted.

Marcus looked up in time to see a salvo of missiles and tracer fire fly toward the *Bunker Hill*.

* * *

The *Bunker Hill* banked hard as flares thumped out of the launchers and bloomed to life. The gyros in Jackie's gunner seat kept her on point while she aimed at a line of advancing Besquith and smashed the trigger button. The Vulcan cannon spun up and spit out a slew of depleted uranium rounds with a loud *brrrrrt*. Down below, a line of dust appeared where the rounds chewed through the dry earth. Besquith dove in every direction, and a few disappeared in sprays of blood.

Roxie's husky laugh echoed through the cargo bay. "Nice one, Gun Bunny! Now it's my turn!"

If Jackie's Vulcan were a crossbow, Roxie's gun was a ballista. She manned a 120-millimeter howitzer, an artillery piece modified for close air support use. Similar to what the old AC-130 Spectre gunships used, it was capable of deploying a variety of rounds, from high explosive ordnance to white phosphorous shells to bunker buster rounds. They even had some airburst canisters stuffed with flechettes, and it was these she selected. "Target in sight... Firing!"

The ship shuddered as the gun fired, and the cargo bay filled with the scent of burnt powder. Down below, a shell burst over the heads of a squad of Besquith, and they fell, their bodies shredded.

A rocket exploded nearby, and Jackie's targeting screen went black. "*Shit, we've been hit with EMP!*" Ed said over a wash of static. "*Most of the cameras are out.*"

"*Engines and controls are fine for the moment,*" Double-T reported. "*Thank God for heavy shielding. JC, how about you?*"

Jackie tapped the dead screen. "My targeting system's fried."

"Mine, too!" Roxie pounded her armrest. "Dammit!"

"We'll have to depend on our eyes." Sayra leaned out of the hatch next to Jackie, her rifle tight against her shoulder. She stared through the scope for a long moment and squeezed the trigger. Before the report could finish echoing, she had cycled the bolt and taken aim again. A hint of a smile played at her lips. "Oh, wait. I do that all the time."

"Smartass." Jackie raised the opaque targeting HUD and peered at the ground through the clear ballistic shield mounted over the gun's six barrels. The Vulcan cannon didn't have any iron sights, but if she fired short bursts, she'd be able to walk her fire to the enemy. She opened her mouth to suggest the same thing to Roxie.

A barrage of bullets struck the ballistic shield and edges of the hatch. Sayra threw herself flat as bullets sailed overhead. Then she pulled herself into a crouch and took aim, a steady stream of Portuguese flowing from her mouth. Jackie didn't need to load her pinplant's translation circuit to know it wasn't flattering speech.

Jackie started to turn back to her gun, but something caught her eye. Sayra's security tether lay on the floor, its end nothing but frayed thread. A lucky shot had somehow severed it. A thrill of fear shot through Jackie. "Sayra, secure yourself!"

Sayra looked down and cursed. She reached in her pack for another carabiner.

The *Bunker Hill* suddenly banked hard to port. Sayra banged her head against the handrail at the hatch entrance. She collapsed and slid across the floor toward an open hatch.

No, no, no, no! Jackie unhooked herself and ran after Sayra. The dropship had banked so far to port that the view outside the hatch was more ground than horizon. Jackie started to fall, so she dropped onto her smooth carapace armor and slid, much as Big Al had but with a lot more control. She sped after Sayra, but she knew she wouldn't make it in time. "Roxie!"

The tall woman reached for Sayra, but her hand just barely missed the Brazilian's boot. Sayra went over the side.

Jackie held up her tether. "Secure me!" she screamed and pressed the carabiner into Roxie's waiting hand.

And then she was out the hatch, falling after Sayra. Jackie dove headfirst, her body and legs straight as an arrow for maximum acceleration. She reached out with both hands. *Please, let me reach!*

One hand grasped a boot, while the other took hold of a calf.

Her descent came to a jarring, painful halt an instant later when her tether went taut. The air flew from Jackie's lungs, and she struggled to draw breath in the rushing wind. The force of the jolt tore Sayra's boot from her foot, but she still had a grip on the unconscious woman's leg. She dropped the boot and grabbed Sayra's leg with both hands. The two dangled there for a long moment. One of Sayra's arms hung free, while the other was tangled up in her rifle sling.

Jackie's arms burned from the effort. "Thank God you're light, Sayra," she muttered.

"*That makes two of you.*" Roxie's voice sounded strained. "*Ed, get over here and help me haul them up!*"

"You're holding onto us?" Jackie's eyes widened. "I thought I told you to secure my tether!"

"*Well, you only gave me a split second to do that, Bunny,*" Roxie growled. "*I wrapped it around my arms and prayed neither my wrists nor my tether would snap.*"

"That's a drummer for you." Jackie chuckled. "Arms made of steel!"

"*No shit. How's Sayra?*"

"Unconscious, but fine." *I hope.* Head blows were always an iffy thing.

Movement down below caught Jackie's eye. A wave of Besquith swarmed the hilltop. "*Little Miss, where's our fire support?*" Marcus asked. "*We're resupplying the Bronzers, and the Besquith don't like it very much.*"

"*Everything all right up there, Miss Warren?*" Captain Bucco demanded. "*Why'd you stop shooting?*"

Because our targeting computers are fried, and half the crew's in mortal peril? Jackie bit back the frustrated retort and took a deep breath. Until they were hauled up, there was very little the *Bunker Hill* could do. The Bronzers and Justin Timers on the ground would have to hold their own.

She studied the battlefield. If anything could turn the tide, it was information. A weak part of the enemy advance, a defensive position about to get flanked, a leader giving orders—

Ah ha, right there. She focused her attention on a spot about five hundred yards out. A Besquith armored personnel carrier sat in a depression that she was sure wasn't visible from the Bronzer hilltop. It was painted to match the landscape's drab yellow. The only part of it that rose over the lip of the depression was a long communications antenna, also painted in desert colors. A group of Reavers stood in a line next to the APC, while a large Besquith paced about, powerful arms flailing as he yelled at the others. "Hello, Mr. Alpha Wolf," she muttered.

Sayra groaned.

"Stay still, Sayra," Jackie warned as the older woman's eyes fluttered open. "Stay still. We're going to haul you up in a moment."

Sayra looked around. Her body tensed, but she obeyed Jackie's warning. She clutched at her rifle as if it were a lifeline and closed her eyes. "Don't let go, *garota!*"

"I won't." Tears filled Jackie's vision until the wind blew them away. "I've let go of too much already. I can't lose any more of you, so stay with me!"

"*Dammit, Ed!*" Roxie shouted. "*Get your old ass out here and help!*"

Jackie took a steadying breath, and activated her comm. "Hey, Marcus—"

* * *

"*—I've got eyes on the Besquith commander!*"

Marcus fired a burst from his MAC, then ducked behind the ferrocrete barrier as a hail of bullets pelted their position. "Can you take him out?"

"*I'm a little tied up at the moment, and the ship's targeting computer's down.*"

That explained why the steady rain of covering fire had stopped. "Show me where he is."

After a second, an image taken directly from Jackie's pinplants appeared on his HUD. His computer compared the terrain in the picture to what his CASPer's cameras had picked up the moment he dropped.

Next to him, Captain Bucco dropped an expended chemical laser magazine and fished for a fresh one. The Bronzer commander cussed up a storm over the local comm network. "*We need to do something about these Besquith, and fast! How come your ship isn't doin' anything?*"

"EMP." Marcus stood and blasted at a trio of Besquith who crested the hill. He tagged one, but the other two dropped from sight. "Plus some other issues."

Bucco swore. "*Any good news?*"

"We may have a bead on the enemy commander. Problem is he's about five football fields that way." Marcus pointed, then ducked back down.

Bucco crouched next to him. His bronze-painted CASPer was an older Mk 6 variant, a dated but still formidable model. It had taken a beating over the last several days, and it was showing signs of the strain. "*A few of my boys have a little bit of jump juice left, but we really can't spare the manpower to go after him. We're hard-pressed as it is!*"

"Yes, you need to keep holding the hill." Marcus checked his reserves. As he had feared, his fuel was almost depleted from the near constant burn he'd made during his descent. Riku's suit reported a similar condition.

On the other hand, Big Al had nearly half his juice left. Marcus smiled. "Al, your recklessness may very well have saved the day."

"*Lord, I hope so.*" Big Al jumped on top of the ferrocrete barrier and swung his hammer down into a Besquith who got too close. The Besquith dropped into the dirt, his smashed head shoved down into his torso. "*It'd make this awful smell worth it!*"

Marcus sent the estimated coordinates over to Big Al. "Mind if I hitch a ride with you?"

"*Piggybacking a jump?*" Bucco whistled. "*Ballsy and stupid. I like it!*"

Big Al laughed. "*Me, too. Sure, hop on! It'll take a few jumps, so keep me covered.*"

"Can do." Marcus clambered onto the backside of Big Al's CASPer. "Riku, hold down the fort with the Bronzers."

"*Sure thing, boss!*"

"*Covering fire, boys!*" Bucco shouted. "*Give the Justin Timers the opening they need!*"

"*There's girls here too!*" Melfi complained.

With a roar, the Jersey Bronzers stood up and fired an impressive volley. The approaching Besquith ducked into cover or were torn to ribbons. Once their heads were down, Big Al fired his jumpjets. He and Marcus blasted high into the air, their trajectory carrying them off the hilltop and in the direction of the enemy APC. Marcus tried to look for it, but they weren't high enough.

The first landing was uneventful. The closest Besquith unit was entirely focused on engaging the *Bunker Hill* and was too far away to notice two CASPers. Marcus considered taking them out, but the enemy commander was more important. *Be safe, Little Miss*, he thought.

With their second landing, they surprised a small group of Besquith carrying ammunition and other supplies up to the front line. Marcus hopped off Big Al's back long enough to engage them with laser rifle and MAC rounds. The Besquith fell quickly.

"This next time should get us there," Big Al said. *"And a good thing, because I'm almost out of juice."*

"Carrying twice your weight will do that." Marcus topped off his ammo. "All right, let's go!"

This time Big Al burned the jets as hard as he could, and it carried them high over the battlefield. *"See anything?"*

Marcus scanned the ground and finally spotted the enemy APC. Reaver commander Rashar still paced back-and-forth in front of a line of underlings, just like Jackie's picture had shown. "Bingo."

"Rally-ho!" Big Al bellowed through his external speakers. It was a dwarf war cry from some old role-playing game. Marcus shook his head and tried not to laugh. Justin sure had known how to pick a strange crew, and his daughter Jackie had the same knack for keeping such people loyal.

The Reavers looked up at the last second. More than one pointed and raised a cry of alarm, while fewer still reached for holstered pistols or slung rifles. Commander Rashar glared up at them, teeth bared and ears flat against his skull. He drew a massive pistol from his chest rig and took aim.

Marcus had no idea what size caliber that pistol was, but he didn't like the idea of getting shot by it. He pulled himself up onto Big Al's armored shoulder and kicked off with a metal foot. Marcus shot into the air while Big Al plummeted at a different angle.

Rashar's first round went wide. He hesitated a moment, his eyes darting from Marcus to Big Al. By the time he adjusted his aim again, Big Al was already among the Besquith, his sidearm barking and his war hammer swinging.

Marcus landed thirty yards away from the melee and opened up with his MAC. He took time to place each shot, since Big Al was downrange, and the unpredictable Scotsman had a habit of getting in the line of fire during his wild, lethal dance.

Before they landed, Marcus had counted eleven Besquith, including Rashar. Now they were down to six. The remaining Besquith had dropped their rifles and switched to long combat knives. They surrounded Big Al but didn't approach, except for Rashar. Human and Besquith circled one another, trading blows with knife and hammer as each sought a weakness in the other.

A collision alarm sounded in Marcus's CASPer, and he spun in the indicated direction. The APC barreled down on him with a sudden burst of speed, its engine roaring. Marcus tried to roll out of the way, but the bulky vehicle clipped his left leg and sent him tumbling. Warning indicators flashed, and he found the leg couldn't fully support his weight. It hadn't broken through the armor to damage his actual leg, but the servos in the foot were toast.

He tensed when the APC's twin-barreled machine gun spun toward him, but its rounds went well over his head. In his comm, Big Al cried out and let loose with a string of curses. *"Bloody crazy bastards! Shooting at me when their own men are here!"*

"They're not men, but I see your point." He pulled a K-bomb from a belt pouch and thumbed the detonator button with the force only a CASPer's hand could manage. He cocked his arm and threw it high.

The turret gunner noticed the movement and adjusted his aim. The twin-barrels stared straight at Marcus, who prepared to roll out of the way. Then his grenade bounced against the hull and landed right on top of the turret.

It exploded in a blinding flash, tearing through the turret and ripping a hole in the APC's armor. Smoke poured through the vehicle as it rolled to a stop. Hatches flew open on all sides and Besquith stumbled out, clutching at shrapnel wounds or coughing from the smoke.

"Boss, behind you!" Big Al shouted.

Marcus rolled to his knees. Rashar charged at him, long knife clutched in both hands like a spear. The alien beast roared, and Marcus reached for his sidearm. The knife filled his vision, and he realized he wasn't going to be fast enough. If that knife punched through, he was dead.

A bullet punched through Rashar's knee, and the Besquith toppled. He tried to stand and crashed to the ground again. Screaming in rage, Rashar flipped the knife in his hand so he could throw it.

Marcus finished his draw and lined up the weapon's iron sights on Rashar's forehead. He squeezed the trigger.

Rashar's head snapped back from the shot just as a third hole blossomed in his chest. The Reaver commander let go of the knife, then slowly sank to the ground, his eyes glazed over in death.

Marcus let out a breath. Big Al stomped over to him, bloody hammer once again resting against his shoulder. He reached down with his free hand. *"Fine bit of shooting there, boss."*

"Only one was mine," Marcus admitted. He took the offered hand and looked up. The *Bunker Hill* hovered high overhead. "Sayra, that first shot was sloppy. Second one was a perfect heart shot, though."

"My apologies," Sayra said, her voice oddly high-pitched and shaky. *"The shooting conditions are... unfavorable."*

* * *

"JC, Sayra, please don't do that again," Ed called, voice strained.

"That was so cool!" Roxie grunted as she hauled on the tether. "But, yes, don't do that again."

"I agree," Jackie said, her arms ablaze with pain. The recoil from Sayra's M40A9 hadn't been pleasant for any of them. "Great pair of shots, though."

Below her, Sayra clutched the rifle to her chest and closed her eyes. "I was aiming for his head both times. That's a horrible grouping."

"Well, considering you were upside down and swaying in the wind..." Jackie's chuckle turned into a pained grunt. "We'll say it's a pass."

* * *

Bucco held out a tan, callused hand. "We owe you one, Miss Warren. Thanks for the save!"

"Oh, it was our pleasure, Captain Bucco." Jackie accepted the offered hand. "We're happy to help a customer in need."

"Please, call me Paulie." Bucco flashed a weary grin. "And the pleasure's mine. You doing anything after this? The boys and I can fix up a mean plate of sausage and peppers. We're out of wine, but the Caroon make something that's passable as beer, if you stand in the right light and pretend the movement in your glass is fizz."

Oh, yum. "That sounds appealing, Paulie, but my policy is business before pleasure."

Marcus took a long drag on a cigarette. "Haven't had good sausage and peppers in a while."

"You won't find better than my family recipe!" Bucco puffed up with pride. "Mama always knew how to keep her boys fed."

In front of them, elated members of the Jersey Bronzers removed ammo cans from the cargo containers Jackie's team had unloaded from the *Bunker Hill*. In the distance, the staccato sound of gunfire echoed as the merc unit's newly resupplied forward elements harried the retreating Reavers.

Another container slid down the ramp of the *Bunker Hill* and skidded to a halt in the dirt. *"That's the last of it, JC,"* Riku said from his CASPer. *"Ready to go when you are."*

Bucco jotted something down on a slate and jabbed the stylus against the screen. Jackie's pinplants pinged, and a transparent message overlaid the vision in her left eye. It was notification of a funds transfer request, to be carried out the next time she reached a trade hub.

"Is it all there?" he asked.

She smiled. "All there, and then some. Thank you for the bonus."

"It was well earned." Bucco looked around and ran a hand over his mud-spattered face. "You gonna be in the area for a while? Our contract is to hold this wonderful piece of real estate for another three months, and we could use a dependable arms dealer." He coughed. "Your appearance would also do wonders for morale. Not exactly a lot of eye candy here, if you know what I mean."

"Hey!" Melfi shouted. "I heard that!"

"Pipe down, woman!" Bucco yelled back.

Jackie's pinplants pinged again with a different chime. She glanced at the calendar reminder, and her eyes widened slightly. "I won't be around, but my company can certainly make regular runs out here. If it's all right with you, we can discuss the details over the radio. Normally I would stay and do this in person, but I really have somewhere I need to be."

"Ah, an important meeting?" Bucco grinned. "Or another high stakes run?"

"A little bit of both, actually." She spun on her heel and hurried away at a fast walk. She waved over her shoulder. "We'll be in touch momentarily. Justin Timers, let's go!"

"So much for sausage and peppers." Marcus dropped his cigarette and stomped it. "You heard the Little Miss. Our gun bunny is late to a very important date!"

"Quiet, you," Jackie snapped, her face flushing at the laughter from the rest of the team.

She strode toward the *Bunker Hill*, where Double-T, Ed, and Roxie were enjoying a much-needed smoke break. Roxie kept rubbing her arms, and no wonder. Jackie's arms didn't hurt now, but she knew they would in the morning.

As she walked, the beginning of a tune entered her mind. Jackie hummed, occasionally mouthing a word or lyric when one came to her. Her annoyance at Marcus vanished, replaced with the joy of composition. She nodded to the others, then bounded up the ramp.

Sayra sat in one of the jump seats and ran a bore brush through her M40A9. She smiled, and Jackie felt a flood of warmth in her chest and fresh tears stinging her eyes. She had come so close to losing one of her closest companions today, and it was so good to see her tending her weapon like usual. She returned the smile and settled into her jump seat.

The sound of running water emanated from the *Bunker Hill's* tiny bathroom as Big Al cleaned himself of vomit and grime. He sang some kind of folk ditty, his words muffled through the steel door. Jackie's humming blended with Al's singing and a new tune formed in her mind. She reached for her guitar case, a smile lighting up her face.

"The Battle of Bronzer Hill" would make a great ballad.

* * * * *

Benjamin Tyler Smith Bio

By day, Benjamin earns his bread as a necro-cartographer (which is a fancy way of saying he makes digital maps) for a cemetery software company, and by night, he writes about undead, aliens, and everything in between. *Blue Crucible* was his first novel. Other works include short stories set in Chris Kennedy Publishing's Four Horsemen military sci-fi universe. He had stories that were Baen contest finalists in 2018 and 2019.

# # # # #

Training Mission by Kim M. Schoeffel

Shenli was used to other races staring at him as he slithered along a corridor in an older section of Karma Station. It wasn't often they saw a two-meter-long eel with arms, in a worn environmental suit, moving on its tail. Shenli stopped at his intended address, then he checked his notes again. It was the location the hiring notice had indicated.

> I SPY CONSULTING SERVICES
> "WE FIND WHAT IS HIDDEN"
> SURVEILANCE RECONNAISANCE ESPIONAGE
> (A NEW MERCENARY COMPANY)

The last few months had been hard on Shenli. As the former Reyq representative at Karma, all he had heard were rumors of what was happening to his race. When his credits finally ran out, he survived as best he could. He tried relying on business associates, but then was forced to move on to petty crime, sleeping in alleyways, and scrounging food from the trash. Now his environmental suit was beginning to show signs of impending failure. Without the moisture and humidity provided by the suit, he would die from dehydration in days. There were no options other than employment if he hoped to live. He steeled himself before opening the office door.

The interior of the office was worn but clean and had an antiseptic smell.

"Welcome to I Spy Consulting Services, do you require our services?" a disembodied voice asked.

"Uh, no, I applied for a job." He paused. "Let me see, it said 'apply now and see if you have the skills we need.' The reply I received said my application had been accepted and told me I was hired."

"Did you completely fill out the application listing all your qualifications? Some applicants have been reluctant to list unpleasant experiences."

"Yes!"

"Please present your UAAC for scanning." A scanner bent out from the wall and confirmed he was a new hire.

"Please take a seat, someone will attend you shortly."

Shenli looked around the room, finding old but serviceable seating for many varied races. Just as he was getting settled, a hunchback bear in a camouflage uniform emerged from a hallway. The bear looked around, saw him, and gave a shrug before beckoning. "Follow me."

Shenli thought to himself, *That's a Jivool?*

They went around the corner to a set of double doors. "Go in and join the others. The colonel will be in next. Good luck," the Jivool said.

The doors opened inward, revealing a small conference room with varied seating. Shenli saw other races he recognized from his time on Karma Station. There was a skinny Veetch, a Blevin, a one-eyed Goka, a huge Jeha, and a nervous-looking Zuparti. Before Shenli got comfortable, the doors were thrown open.

"Attention in the room!"

Everyone who had been seated jumped up, and the Zuparti started twitching. Two small, yet muscular, Human women with short-cropped hair strode into the room. They wore combat fatigues, light body armor, and slug throwers. One stopped at the doors, closing them quietly; the other came to the end of the conference table and stood at attention.

In a booming voice, she said, "What a sorry lot of desperate applicants we have here, but beggars can't be choosers. I am Colonel Ryherd, and this is *my* company. I Spy was formed in response to the Phoenix Initiative. We're just starting and are searching for qualified candidates from any race. As you should have noted on our sign and in our application, we are not a combat unit but instead bill ourselves as an intel and recon outfit. We fight when we must, but that's not our primary mission. If we do the job right, violence is not expected. If any of you want to reconsider this job offer, now's the time. It's no skin off my nose whatever you choose."

The colonel paused, taking a moment to look directly at each of the trainees. If possible, the Zuparti's tail started twitching faster, but no one left.

"In that case, if you are successful with your on-the-job test and training mission, you will be offered a permanent spot here. If not, I won't see you again. The sergeant will give you the details of your training mission."

With that, the colonel turned sharply and left the room. The sergeant closed the doors and took the position where the colonel had stood. "At ease. Your training mission will consist of entering the Dream World Consortium's office here on Karma, copying any files you find, gathering any other potentially useful information, then returning, as a team, all within thirty-six hours from now!" She slammed her palm on the table, emphasizing the "now." Everyone jumped. "You are a very jumpy lot, especially you, weasel." She pointed at the Zuparti. "Here is the information given to us for this contract. You are to be discreet. You will use the least force necessary to complete this mission. You have fifteen minutes to figure out your team roles and another forty-five to determine your equipment needs, which I

Spy will provide. Use this slate to select your equipment. I will return in an hour. Get going." With that, she turned sharply and left the room, quietly closing the double doors behind her.

The dark-brown Blevin stood. "I'm Occar, and I'm taking command of our mission. Any objections?"

The room was silent.

Occar smiled. "This sounds like a snatch and grab operation I was part of back when I was in a small-time crime ring."

The Goka muttered quietly, "If it worked for your crime ring, you'd still be there."

"I know what needs to be done, and I'll assign all the roles. We'll go around, tell me your name and any pertinent information. I have the slate with all our applications along with the Dream World office details." Pointing at the Veetch he said, "You first."

"I go by Grey," she said as she spread her four arms wide to reveal clothing in various shades of grey. "I've been a pilot, not useful here and now. I frequently multitask when I pilot. I can focus my eyes on two different tasks and use my four arms to do both tasks."

Occar pointed again, this time at the Goka. "You next."

"Zoxur here. Barely survived a near hit from a Flatar hypervelocity pistol. Shrapnel partly destroyed my left eye. Kicked me out of the unit when we returned to Karma. The skill I know best is killing. I prefer close combat; I like using my knives," he said, pulling them out quicker than anyone could follow. "Don't know why they might want me if they don't want to fight, but this is a merc outfit. One other thing, a snatch and grab doesn't sound like how I Spy operates."

"Enough from you. I'm in charge. Be quiet now. You there, Zuparti. You're next."

"What, yes. Carque, yes, I'm Carque. I don't, don't think I have skills. I'm pretty good at hiding and watching, yes, hiding and watching," he stuttered.

The group stopped and stared at him. Carque continued to shake as he sat down in the corner.

"You, Jeha."

"I'm Tlt'Ch'tk, just call me Chak. I've worked as a ship's engineer and can deal with anything mechanical. Break it down, analyze, then repair. I've been involved in defensive shipboard combat too. That's about it."

"Lastly, you. And what is a Reyq?"

"I'm Shenli. The Reyq are a small merc race. Our home world was engulfed in a gamma-ray burst more than a century ago. We are an amphibious race with electrical abilities." He demonstrated by arcing sparks between his fingers. "My specialty was contracts, but Reyq have an inherent knack with any electrical or computer system."

Zoxur mumbled again, "Even with my busted eye, I see a whole lot of nothing around this table."

Occar set out his snatch and grab plan. The Veetch and Zuparti would scout the area around the Consortium's office. If no problems were found, they were to remain there and not report back, finding a place to watch the break-in, then provide backup if needed. The remainder of the team would leave in about an hour, after getting their gear, and would go directly to the Dream World office. It was to be in and out, quick and quiet, then return to I Spy.

Zoxur muttered, "I've seen better plans from a drunk Lumar." He sighed as only a Goka could.

*　*　*

MISSION TIME REMAINING: 35 HOURS 10 MINUTES

Carque talked rapidly as he and Grey left the office. He stuttered less, the faster he talked. "We'll split up now. You find a good place to watch the main corridor and the side corridor where the Dream World office is." Grey continued to walk on while Carque disappeared.

The section of Karma Station where the Dream World offices were located was not the high rent area. The walls were grimy. The floors were dirty and sticky with discarded food, litter, and other unidentifiable filth. The lighting was poor and intermittent. Legitimate businesses were closed at this time of the night. Automated kiosks populated many intersections. Some of them were working; others had been vandalized. All were old and needed maintenance or repair.

Grey found a pair of working kiosks near the corridor to the Dream World office. One dispensed food, and the other had drinks. She thought she could see both the main and side corridors from this location. Thinking about her cover, she went to the food kiosk and reviewed the limited menu while keeping one eye on the local traffic. She was surprised there was any food offered she could eat. Foot traffic was usually sparse this time of day, but the kiosks were busy. There were scattered benches and tables in use by various races. Nothing was clean, but that wasn't surprising here. She noticed two HecSha arguing over a dice game.

The grime-encrusted dispenser signaled and opened, revealing her order of obsingnata. The lavender-colored worms were covered in a lime green mrsa sauce, lying motionless in the steaming bowl. The enticing aroma would only be fully appreciated by a Veetch. Grey moved off to the side to eat her meal and watch the corridors.

The HecSha argument had gotten louder. Glancing over, she heard them arguing about who would buy the next round of drinks. Both suddenly stood up, their metal benches falling over with a clang. The HecSha staggered toward the drink kiosk, still arguing loudly.

"Admit it, Dit, you lost the bet. You need to pay for the next round of drinks, and someone needs to hire a better bunch of idiots."

"You are right, Juk; I buy the drinks," Dit said as they stumbled into Grey.

Rough hands grabbed Grey around her neck and trapped her pistol.

"You see, Veetch," Juk said and flashed his teeth, "eating with one eye on your food and one hand holding the bowl is stupid, even for a Veetch. You deserve what's gonna happen." The HecSha laughed, low and rumbling.

"But this is just a testing and training mission," Grey gasped when she could finally talk.

"Sure, a training mission. Who do you work for?"

* * *

MISSION TIME REMAINING: 34 HOURS 55 MINUTES

Carque separated from Grey shortly after leaving the office. He reached the side corridor where the Dream World office was located, nervously hiding, watching, his head on a swivel. There were both legitimate businesses and vacant offices along the corridor. The pristine sign at the Dream World Consortium's office indicated, "Business by appointment only." There were vacant offices on either side, their doorways coated with a crust of grime. He used the electronic lock-breaking set I Spy had provided to break into the office on the left, quickly closing the door behind him. Turning on a hand light, the room revealed nothing. There was a thin layer of undisturbed dust on the floor. There was no furniture, no trash, not even dead bugs. Carque checked the walls, the floor, and the ceiling. Nothing but grime, dust, and now his footprints. It appeared as if no one had been in this office for months, maybe longer. Carque exited and relocked the first office door before proceeding to the office on the right. Here also he found nothing. He took more time, sure he was missing something important. Maybe it was only the paranoia inherent to his race. Carque opened the door a crack to check the corridor before leaving. A scaled hand shot forward, grabbed him by the throat, and pulled him into the corridor before he had a chance to react. Two other hands grabbed his wrists.

"Now, who do we have here, Dit? Is this another careless trainee? Let's put this idiot in the pit with the other one and see who shows up next."

Carque shuddered and his bowels let loose as he passed out. Both the HecSha shrugged and shook their heads, laughing. "Typical Zuparti."

* * *

MISSION TIME REMAINING: 35 HOURS 30 MINUTES

The remaining trainees waited in the conference room after getting their gear. Occar found a comfortable seat and promptly fell asleep. Shenli went over to Chak, as Zoxur watched.

"Chak, will you help me? My environmental suit needs maintenance. It's not working well."

"If you can get out of the suit, I'll check it and see if I can do anything."

"That I can do. I can be out for a couple hours with no harm, but only if the conditions are not too hot or dry. It's not bad here."

Shenli slithered out of his environmental suit, like losing a second skin. Chak went to work, carefully inspecting the suit before deconstructing some sections and then rebuilding them. A few minutes later Chak indicated he was finished. "There were some worn seals, clogged filters, and a blocked recycling line. It should work better now."

Shenli reentered his suit, checking the seals and settings before turning it on. The misting jets sent an invigorating moisture over his body. "This feels like a brand-new suit. Thank you."

Chak nodded in reply.

"I have one other request. Not that important, it's something I've seen some Reyq mercs play with. It's a toy of sorts involving our electricity," he said, sending some sparks between his fingers.

Zoxur moved closer as Chak started working on Shenli's toy.

"It seems you two are getting along quite nicely. Tell me what you think of this team and this mission."

Chak was busy with the project, so Shenli answered. "I know contracting. In contracting, I get all the information I can before entering negotiations. Risks, costs, rewards, expenses. That's what 'I Spy' does but not what Occar is interested in. He thinks sending the Veetch and Zuparti out is getting information, but he won't wait for them to report. No news is good news in his world. No news is no information in my line of work. He split the team up before we could find out what we were facing. Not smart. Next, he's dictating, not asking for any input, not that he would listen. He cut you off earlier. I think you would have been a better choice to lead. And that point about the drunk Lumar was dead on."

"I would appreciate it if you didn't use the word 'dead' with this group. I've got a bad feeling about him leading us. Make sure you watch your backs," Zoxur offered quietly.

Chak interrupted the discussion. "Here you go, Shenli. I think this is what you asked me to make." Chak handed over two small ovoids connected by a length of fine, superconducting wire.

Before Shenli could reply, the conference room doors opened again, and the sergeant reappeared. "Time to leave. Return in less than thirty-five hours when you've completed the testing and training mission, or don't return at all."

* * *

MISSION TIME REMAINING: 34 HOURS 45 MINUTES

Occar led the team directly to the Dream World office door. He turned to the group and asked, "Did anyone see Grey or Carque?" No one answered. "That's good, it means no one is watching the office or us," he said as he rolled his shoulders to loosen up.

"Chak, Shenli, get the door open now," Occar said with an impatient tone. Shenli detected no electronic field. Chak found no obvious mechanism to open the door. There was a call button below the Dream World sign with instructions to press to schedule an appointment. Chak pressed the button.

A voice replied, "Dream World Consortium, do you wish to schedule an appointment?"

Chak glanced at Occar, who nodded. Chak answered, "Yes we do."

The reply was immediate, "When would you like to meet our representative?"

Chak again glanced at Occar, who shrugged this time. Chak continued, "As soon as possible. Time is valuable."

"The Dream World Consortium understands your need for urgency. Please enter the office and make yourselves comfortable. Our representative will be with you in less than thirty minutes." The door slid open onto a spacious, well-appointed office.

Occar beamed. "See, we've got an invite. Everyone in, now."

The team filed in; Zoxur was the last to enter. He was hesitant, uneasy. The door slid shut. There were Tri-Vs on the walls that came to life as they entered. They showed what Dream World had to offer their clients. There were seats scattered around the office, usable by multiple races. There was a platform at the back wall with a large desk and an expensive-looking executive chair that dominated the room. The floor was richly carpeted in the half nearest the door. The rear floor had ceramic tile in an intricate pattern. A lone slate rested in the middle of the desk.

"Shenli, check out the slate. Everyone else, search. Grab files, brochures, anything." Occar stepped up on the platform, went around the desk, and settled in the chair.

Chak noticed there was no way to open the now-closed door. He pointed this out, but Occar was unconcerned. "We can force our way out when the representative arrives," he said, brandishing his gun. "That won't be a problem."

The Tri-Vs covered the two side walls, floor to ceiling. Each highlighted a different planet, with different environments and climate types. The ceiling and back wall had a pattern of small inset dimples set in an eye-catching design.

Shenli was confused when he accessed the slate on the desk. It had power and an operating system but there were no files or other programs. Occar seemed unconcerned when told this, saying, "With the muscle I have with this team, I will intimidate them and get the files."

As the search continued, Chak found a hidden control on the floor, where the carpeting, tile, and Tri-Vs met on one side. Occar, watching, indicated Chak should try the switch.

A three-meter by three-meter section of the tile floor dropped a short distance then slid under a section of the carpeting. Lights came on illuminating a set of steps leading down. Chak peered in and called with a quivering voice, "Occar, you need to see this."

Before he had a chance to leave the chair, the message on the Tri-Vs changed. They now displayed a well-dressed Zuparti.

"Welcome to Dream World Consortium. If you truly were potential clients, I would be seeing you shortly, to find ways to accommodate your needs. Instead, you entered this office under false pretenses and as such will suffer the consequences. I will meet you shortly, but you will be expected to accommodate *my* needs at that time."

The Tri-Vs went dark, and a hissing sound was heard throughout the room. The small inset dimples opened, and the room's air was vented to space. Chak scurried to the door but there was no way to open it. As the air pressure decreased and oxygen levels dropped, their thoughts became fuzzier and their actions uncoordinated. The last thing they heard was Zoxur mumbling, "Damn it, Occar!"

* * *

MISSION TIME REMAINING: 34 HOURS

Shenli awoke in a clear cage. Chak was in the cage too, but still unconscious. The other trainees, including Carque, but not Grey, were bound by their arms and legs, but only Zoxur showed any sign of being awake. There were three large HecSha in the room, slug throwers in their hands. The well-dressed Zuparti reclined in the designer chair Occar had recently occupied. He surveyed the group as they slowly regained consciousness. The chair appeared to fit the Zuparti like it was made for him. There was a sheet of plastic polymer covering a large portion of the carpeted floor near the pit.

Once they all started to awaken, the Zuparti said, "I'm glad to see most of you still live. It's hard to get useful information from a corpse." He paused for a moment before he continued, "What do you think of my trap, venting the room to vacuum once the pit is found?"

He paused again, then directed his attention toward the largest of the HecSha. "Juk, please ensure their bonds are secure and vital signs are stable, considering their situation."

Shenli observed and assessed the predicament the team was in while the Zuparti continued talking. Every member that could be bound was bound by race-specific restraints, their arms fully extended. That seemed strange to him. How did they know what they needed? The teams' weapons and tools had been arranged at the base of the desk, on the platform. The HecSha must have thought the ovoids and wire were part of Shenli's environmental suit because he still had them. The cage they were imprisoned in appeared to be made of transparent aluminum with small ventilation holes and an electronic lock.

Juk holstered one of his automatic slug throwers, then went to each captive and confirmed their vital signs. "They're all alive boss, except the Veetch, but the Zuparti is, let's say, in a fragile condition. He should be able to answer questions in a few minutes."

"Put the Veetch's body back in the pit. She may have company soon."

The walls had reverted to advertisements of various Dream World locations, but the sound was silenced. Shenli thought it was a pity the Reyq didn't know about Dream Worlds before now. They might have helped the Reyq rebuild.

"Dit, get me my bottle of Cumuni, the good stuff. I feel a need to celebrate," the Zuparti said.

Dit went to one of the Tri-Vs they had checked, held his red diamond-encrusted bracelet to the seam, and a refrigeration unit slid out. Checking the labels carefully, he chose a large bottle with a fancy design, then brought it and a chilled goblet to the Zuparti. He poured a small amount of a thick, black liquid into the goblet then offered it up. The Zuparti swirled the liquid in the goblet then brought it to his nose, inhaling deeply before tasting.

"Yes, this is exquisite."

Dit filled the goblet more than halfway before he resealed the bottle of Cumuni. He placed the bottle on the desk near the Zuparti then returned to guard the prisoners.

By the time the Zuparti had finished enjoying his drink, the entire team had completely awakened, realizing their dire circumstances.

Refilling his own goblet this time, the Zuparti began interrogating them. "I'll ask you questions, and you will *only* answer my questions. Failure to follow this rule or give me useful information would be unfortunate. Juk, please demonstrate why."

Juk picked up a laser rifle that had been leaning against the wall. Going to the desk, he picked up the largest pistol, the one Occar had brought, and cut through the barrel like it was made of soft lead. Juk left the pistol pieces on the desk and returned to his previous position.

"I have most of the information I need here," the Zuparti said, pointing to his head. "Get the Blevin first. He was in charge. His name is Occar."

When the Zuparti said his name, Occar struggled against his bonds. He blurted out, "How did you know my name?"

The Zuparti shook his head. "Someone was not listening well. Juk please show him what happens when one doesn't listen."

Occar began to scream, as only a Blevin could, as two of the Hec-Sha laid him on the dirty plastic sheet. He obviously knew what the sheet was for.

Juk came over with the laser rifle and shot him in the knee. Occar passed out, and blood leaked from his leg.

"Put him in the pit with the dead, for now," the Zuparti said as he took another sip from the goblet, then he continued, "Did everyone else learn from Occar?" No one replied; they just stared in horror. "I'll answer his question though. I know, because I was the one who contracted this 'testing and training mission.' I did this through multiple dummy corporations. I Spy, and others before them, willingly gave me your information as negotiated in the contract." Waving a jewel encrusted hand, he said, "I need to ensure my guards and traps will protect me. Now, who should be next? Let me see." He looked over the remaining trainees. "I choose Carque."

At the mention of his name, Carque fainted. "Dit, just leave him there. I'll get back to him when he wakes. I'll make it more interesting for him, and me, at that time."

"Get Shenli; he intrigues me. I've never met a Reyq before. I have much to learn," he said, waving a hand at Juk.

Juk opened the electronic lock on the cage. The HecSha had no idea how to handle a Reyq, so he took the laser rifle and pointed it to the midpart of the environmental suit as Shenli moved in front of the desk. The Zuparti paused, looked down at him for a minute, and pondered his next question. He sipped his Cumuni. "Tell me about your race and why I've not heard of it?"

Shenli began, "Over a century ago our sun began to flare. The Science Guild said we had nothing to fear so no precautions or preparations were made. They lied to us. There was a gamma-ray burst that sterilized our home world. We were a minor race, a member of the Mercenary Guild. Those who survived were off planet on contracts or doing business when the flare struck. We've been a lost race since then. There are little more than 100,000 of us remaining. We've tried to rebuild, but we are few. We took those mercenary contracts that focused on swampy worlds; those that suited our bodies. When we're not in a humid or watery environment, we require these environmental suits to function. If we had known what Dream World could have offered us, we would have come to you as clients."

"Interesting," the Zuparti said, steepling his fingers. "Why do you think your team failed?"

Shenli picked up his head and continued, "We were never a team. We were six mismatched trainees. Most of us had no experience as team leaders or desire to lead. Occar took charge and no one argued. Well, Zoxur made comments, but Occar didn't listen. Just like he didn't listen to you here. He paid no attention to the missions of I Spy: surveillance, reconnaissance, and espionage. He thought like the small-time criminal he was. Then he panicked. Zoxur could have been a good leader if the team had a chance to bond. He watched and listened. After that, the next issue was the time limitation of thirty-six hours. The final unknown was that this mission was a trap."

The Zuparti continued, while still enjoying his Cumuni, "And if you had been in charge?"

"I would have done the reconnaissance by scheduling an appointment to hear about what Dream World could offer the Reyq. I would have seen the layout, recognized your guards, interacted with you. The result would have been unchanged since you had all the information on our mission."

"I may have more questions for you later." Waving his hand, he sent Shenli back to the cage. Shenli watched intently as Juk opened the lock, then the door. He placed a hand by the electronic lock as the cage door closed.

"Bring me Zoxur next," the Zuparti demanded. Zoxur was brought, arms bound, before the desk. The Zuparti snidely said, "Tell me your assessment, warrior!"

"Shenli made valid points. Occar being in charge was the first mistake, but none of us would have been better. I'm not a leader. I fight. The only reason I applied for the job was I needed work. If I could find a role at I Spy, I would stay. If you had a role for me, I would join you."

"Well done, Zoxur, well done," the Zuparti said with a smile. "You asked a question without asking a question. Intelligent. Resourceful.

All points to consider later. Return the Goka and bring the Jeha next. Lastly will be our reluctant Zuparti."

Shenli had been watching everyone and everything from the moment he was fully awake. The oxygen supplied in the humidity of his environmental suit had blunted a portion of the effects of the vacuum on him. The HecSha guards had become lax as the questioning progressed. They knew they had total control of their captives. He started to unspool the wire connecting the two small ovoids as soon as he returned to the cage. None of the HecSha were paying attention to the two caged captives, knowing they couldn't get out. Placing his hand on the door, Shenli quietly disengaged the electronic lock. He waited there, at the door, and placed one of the small ovoids in his mouth, coating it with sticky mucus.

One of the two HecSha returning Zoxur released his grip, and he knew that was his chance. Pushing the cage door open, he spit the ovoid, like a seed pit, and struck the HecSha on the side of his neck. It stuck, the attached thin wire trailing behind. Shenli held the other ovoid and sent a powerful electrical shock through the superconducting wire. He had seen Reyq mercs playing with this toy as they shocked each other for fun. The lax HecSha guard dropped to the floor, spasming. Shenli, weakened by the discharge, staggered at the open door.

Zoxur and Chak recognized the momentary confusion and struck. Chak's mandibles crushed the ankle of the guard that held Zoxur, then Zoxur used the small, sharp heel spurs on his feet to slash the now-crippled HecSha. Chak released Zoxur's arm bonds, and he moved to the platform and swept up his knives.

Juk saw this and panicked, and he fled to the outer door. The Zuparti spoke in a loud, measured voice as he touched his head, "I'm not going to open the door until they are restrained once more or dead. It's your job to protect me, so do so."

Juk knew a knife fight with a Goka was unwinnable. He drew his automatic slug throwers, and he fired, wounding the Goka, but it was not enough. The knives won.

Shenli slowly recovered his energy and balance. The three free trainees mounted the platform and surrounded the Zuparti, who was still seated behind the desk. "Very impressive, very impressive," he said, as he raised his goblet in a toast. "It's obvious I need a new set of guards. Are you interested?"

"No. Why would we be interested in working for you?" Zoxur asked.

"So, you've moved from non-question questions to actual questions. You think you have the gripping hand?"

"We do," Chak retorted. "We have weapons and are free. What do you have?"

"I have this room! Remember what I said about traps? This *room* is a trap. I'm both bait and a trap. I can offer you credits and a profitable job. More importantly, I can offer you your lives. That is, free and not enslaved by the HecSha, which you would have been if you survived my questioning."

Zoxur flashed his knives in an intimidating manner and continued, "Just give us the files and we'll leave. You can live. You know you'll get the files back since you arranged this contract."

The Zuparti stared at Zoxur for a moment. "I'm the only one who can let anyone leave this office. If I die, this room will vent to vacuum with nothing to stop it. My regrets, but your leaving is not an option." The Zuparti began to laugh.

The vents opened. Zoxur whipped his knives in a complex pattern, leaving the Zuparti dying, blood pouring from a dozen deep slashes.

Chak sped to the door but there was still no access panel; nothing to work with. Shenli paused for a second then rushed over to the Zuparti, his own thoughts becoming fuzzy with the decreasing oxygen.

Placing his hands on both sides of the Zuparti's head, he delved for any electrical signature. The Zuparti's brainwaves were slowing but there was a pinplant and it remained functional. He searched the pinplant for a command circuit and found it just as he began to lose consciousness. *Air!*

The vents snapped closed, and air returned to the room. Zoxur, as all Goka could, had the ability to withstand a short exposure to vacuum and was unaffected. As Chak and Shenli never lost consciousness, they recovered from their brief anoxia as Zoxur went to check Carque. He was dead. Zoxur found a medkit and raced to the pit. He treated Occar then helped him up and to the desk.

* * *

MISSION TIME REMAINING: 33 HOURS 10 MINUTES

"I'm still in charge," Occar stated.

"No," Chak replied. "Shenli was the one who made our freedom possible. We—" he indicated himself and Zoxur "—decided Shenli was in charge."

Zoxur leaned against the wall, sharpening his knives and muttered, "Or you could stay in the pit."

Occar shuddered.

"If I'm in charge," Shenli said, "then everyone needs to listen up and work together. I must keep a small charge on the pinplant, or the encrypted files there might get erased. This means my usefulness in searching is limited. If we're to be part of I Spy, information, any information, is important. Search all the bodies, including the corpses in the pit, for anything that might be useful. I'll be working on a plan while you're doing that. And see if you can find any case or bag that we can use to carry what we find back to I Spy."

Chak and Zoxur went down the steps into the pit while Occar hopped around, searching the HecSha. Shenli was able to search the Zuparti's body while keeping the charge on the pinplant. After twenty minutes, they regrouped to examine what had been found.

There were five slug throwers from the HecSha, the laser rifle, multiple UAACs, jewelry, and the blank slate.

Shenli got their attention. "Chak, check the UAACs from the pit first, then those of the HecSha. We may be able to have I Spy pass on information on how Dream World played their con on others."

Occar stopped, "What con? What did I miss when I was in the pit?"

Zoxur turned and stared. "Exactly why you weren't a leader." Zoxur continued, "Dream World, through dummy corporations, hired units to test their security. They issued false contracts and set their traps. They were told who was coming and when. Survivors were questioned, then sold into slavery by the HecSha. You need to get on board."

Chak chimed in next. "The UAAC interfaces still work. That's some information to work with. What should we do with the credits on the HecSha UAACs? They also list where their quarters are; we could check them out."

Shenli looked at Zoxur and Occar. "Leave the credits for I Spy to decide. Any objections? Those ideas sound solid to me."

Occar said indignantly, "So we have found credits and expensive jewelry. You're taking it all back to I Spy. Why? We're the only ones who know. We should divide it among ourselves."

Shenli shook his head. "No, that's up to the colonel to decide."

Occar spun the chair around and ended up facing the three of them with one of the HecSha automatic slug throwers in his hand. "I think I will take all of the UAACs and the jewelry, and leave."

Shenli shook his head again as Zoxur laughed. "And how do you hope to escape this room? Do you have a key or the command to open the door?"

Occar panicked, the pain of his knee providing more distraction as he attempted to stand. His eyes darted back and forth from Zoxur to Shenli to Chak and missed the thrown knife that ended up in the middle of his chest.

"See, not as smart as a drunk Lumar," Zoxur repeated as he went to retrieve his imbedded knife.

"You are so right, Zoxur." Shenli sighed. "I have a small favor to ask of you. Please carefully remove this Zuparti's head. The pinplant will be much easier to transport then."

* * *

MISSION TIME REMAINING: 31 HOURS

Their search of the HecSha quarters involved more bloodshed. Two HecSha were there, drinking and playing dice. They were taken by surprise and not prepared for the speed or ferocity of Zoxur's knives. Two functioning slates, each with different files, and two UAACs were added to the cache.

"I don't know how either of you feel but my energy is running low. I need time to recharge. This would be a good place to stay, to recover. I know Zoxur is hurt from the bullet wounds. There's some food and drink here. We could take watch shifts," Shenli said, his voice weak.

Zoxur agreed, "I need some time to patch the tiny holes."

"Chak, I need your expertise first, before I can rest. Can you rig up a trickle charge for the pinplant? I can judge the power level and tell when the charge is close. I'm not going to be able to maintain my charge much longer."

"Can do, Shenli. Zoxur and I can cover the early watch shifts and let you recharge."

"Thanks friends, much appreciated."

* * *

MISSION TIME REMAINING: 30 MINUTES

The depleted squad met outside I Spy Consulting Services, took some deep breaths, braced themselves, and entered.

"Welcome to I Spy Consulting Services, do you require our services?" the disembodied voice asked.

Shenli answered emphatically, "No! We're the squad returning from our testing and training mission. We are missing three of our fellow trainees."

"Please wait, someone will attend you shortly."

* * *

MISSION TIME REMAINING: 25 MINUTES

The Jivool they met two days before emerged from the hallway and saw the squad. Not the defeated individuals he had seen two days prior, but a confident team. Straightening up, he motioned for them to follow him, saying, "Please come to the conference room. There are snacks and drinks in the cabinet. The sergeant will be in next. Please make yourselves comfortable." He closed the double doors.

* * *

MISSION TIME REMAINING: 20 MINUTES

The sergeant arrived and assumed her position at the head of the table. Shenli began his report. After the first few sentences, she ordered, "Stop right there. The colonel needs to hear this." She left the room, leaving the doors open.

"Quick, Zoxur, get the best-looking chair to the head of the table for the colonel, then resume your position," Shenli directed. Zoxur moved with speed and efficiency and was back in position before they heard the sergeant and colonel approach.

The sergeant entered the room with the command, "Attention!" Shenli, Zoxur, and Chak stood at attention as the colonel entered, scanning the room. She saw the chair and sat down. "At ease. Now, proceed with your report."

Shenli took a deep breath, then began. "I beg your pardon, Colonel. Could the sergeant close the doors before I begin? The information we've found is more sensitive than you might realize."

The colonel raised an eyebrow. "Sergeant, please indulge the recruits." Turning back to Shenli, she said, "Enlighten me."

"The contract you took and gave to us as a training mission was meant to fail."

"*What!*" the colonel asked, standing up so fast her chair flew back, her face livid.

"Colonel, please, we only found this information out during the mission. You were kept unaware of the subterfuge."

The colonel picked up her chair and sat back down, still fuming. "This better be good!"

"Dream World, through dummy corporations, put out this contract to test their own security. You gave them the information the contract required. They conned all of us. Grey, Carque, and Occar did not survive the mission." Chak and Zoxur indicated agreement. "Through the ingenuity and actions of Zoxur, Chak, and myself, we were able to achieve our freedom and collect the bogus slate we found in the office." Shenli turned to Chak who produced a slate and placed it on the table. "It has no files on it."

The colonel looked puzzled now. "Continue."

"We were captured, placed in race-specific bonds, then questioned by torture, as directed by the Dream World Zuparti leader. Grey, Carque, and Occar died during their capture or questioning. The Dream World Zuparti gloated as he revealed what had happened with the previous contracts they had issued. Those captives either died during questioning or were sold to the HecSha into slavery. On freeing ourselves, Zoxur killed three HecSha, with our limited assistance. We then obtained more information from the overly confident Zuparti.

He revealed the office was a trap. At that point, he began to vent the room to vacuum. Chak tried to find a mechanism to open the door but there was none. The Zuparti pointed to his own head as the air vented. Zoxur killed him. I thought the Zuparti had indicated he had a pinplant and I found he did. I applied a current to keep the pinplant functioning. I found one command routine titled AIR on the pinplant."

Shenli turned to Zoxur and nodded. He placed a travel case on the table and opened it. The head of a Zuparti with wire attachments was inside.

"Chak was able to build a modifiable electric power source to keep the pinplant from shutting down, destroying the encrypted files it contains. We then searched the HecSha, Zuparti, and the remains in their pit."

Turning to Chak again, he nodded. "Here are all the UAACs and jewelry we found. We also went and searched the HecSha living quarters, finding two additional slates. Then we healed, rested, regrouped, and returned here to report," Shenli stopped.

The colonel stood. "Thank you and well done. Each of you will have a personal debrief later today. The three of you had many opportunities to abrogate your responsibilities as honorable mercs, but you did not. You demonstrated initiative, innovation, and integrity. This was meant to be an easy on-the-job testing and training mission and not what you stumbled into. I Spy will be a better unit if you join. We might be playing a bigger role in the future."

Shenli, Chak, and Zoxur looked at each other, nodded, and stood at attention. "Yes, Colonel Ryherd, we're ready to join!"

* * * * *

Kim M. Schoeffel Bio

Kim was taught at an early age how to properly devour books by his mother, a school librarian. He therefore developed a voracious appetite for reading, especially SF and fantasy. After he 'grew up,' graduated osteopathic medical school, and became a pediatrician, he joined the USAF. He hit the jackpot in Las Vegas when he met Sally, a USAF nurse, who later married him. He served as a Flight Surgeon and was awarded a hat, 'Flight Surgeon and Eccentric.' They said going from pediatrics to pilots, the toys only got bigger. They travelled the world with their two children, Geoff and Sarah. When he retired from the USAF, he began a career in academic medicine, tormenting future doctors. Now he wants to try writing. When at conventions, he sometimes treats his friends' musculoskeletal problems.

# # # # #

Redemption Arc by Jon R. Osborne

Karma Station, Karma

"What makes you think anyone will give us the time of day, let alone a contract?" TJ Diller tugged at the black uniform collar, his hand brushing the lieutenant bar. "In case you forgot, we fought on the losing side of the Omega War."

Aldo Alvarez paused to get his bearings. "You mean the wrong side."

"Same difference." TJ pointed. "It's the left passage, then hang a right at the tattoo shop."

"As for why, the mercenary market is flush with contracts thanks to the Phoenix Initiative. Shirazi is throwing credits at mercenary firms, especially new human companies."

"Even us?"

"El Espejo died when Bjorn Tovesson killed Rodrigo Sanchez. Rodrigo founded El Espejo Obscuro to get his revenge and almost got us all killed in the process. The Sun Jaguars may have many of the same personnel—"

"Not to mention the same refurbished CASPers," TJ interjected.

"We have a different purpose; namely to provide for our people on Patoka. Even with the rare earth mine in the north hills, we barely make ends meet. Rodrigo promised them a better life, and we are going to deliver."

TJ stopped, raising his hand. A pair of goat-like Khabar harassed a droop-eared feline H'rang with matted fur. After a minute and an exchange of credits, the H'rang slunk off in one direction while the Khabar shared a bleating laugh before disappearing through a hatch.

"I don't see why you have to repent for everything Sanchez did. He recruited those colonists because he expected Peepo to conquer Earth." Diller led the way to a hatch marked by a hologram of a smiling Besquith. The text under the image morphed into English at their approach: "Mama Wolf's Den."

A wave of noise and odors buffeted them as the hatch slid open. A pair of Torvasi, thuggish, muscular humanoids, flanked the door. One passed Aldo's Yack over a reader, squinted at the display, and nodded. "Sun Jaguars" appeared on the seeking contract lists on displays scattered throughout the establishment. Aldo threaded through the crowd, taking a seat at a huge circular bar. Diller slid onto a stool next to him.

A huge, grey-muzzled Besquith loomed over them. A mottled black and pink tongue wavered as she sampled their scents. "Who is this new unit hunting credits in my pit?"

"Greetings, Rugr'moed. I am Commander Alvarez of the Sun Jaguars. As you astutely observed, we are a new unit, but our warriors come from mercenary firms blooded in the Omega War."

The Besquith grinned, displaying enough teeth to make a great white shark envious. "Welcome, Alvarez. With the Phoenix Initiative, many pups bare their fangs and take up the hunt. If veteran warriors fill your ranks, maybe you shall prevail where the whelps fail."

"That is my hope," Aldo said.

"Good hunting, Alvarez of the Sun Jaguars." Rugr snapped her jaws and turned her attention to another group bellying up to the bar.

"Couldn't she at least take our drink orders?" Diller muttered. "I almost pissed myself when she bared her fangs."

"Use the slate in the bar top." Aldo tapped in his own drink order before raising his gaze to contracts scrolling on a Tri-V display. "Find a contract lucrative enough to cover our costs."

"Don't you mean make a profit?" Diller poked at the menu screen. "We aren't a charity."

"Unvetted mercenary units struggle to break even. We must build our reputation to garner more lucrative contracts." Aldo gestured at the Tri-V scrolling contracts. With mercenaries back in business, contracts abounded, but employers lowballed their offers. "If we can make ends meet, including paying our soldiers, I will thank Dios y Maria."

Diller shrugged. "You're the boss. These contracts are shit, even the shady ones. The achievable ones only want to pay for a platoon or two but will take our entire company to not lose our asses."

"Did you expect to find something in the first fifteen minutes?" Alvarez crunched the numbers in his head for each contract before dismissing them. "But you are right, these are mierda."

"You've got some nerve showing your faces around here."

Aldo turned to face the young woman, Brazilian by her accent. "Do I know you?"

"I'd like to know her," Diller chimed in, appraising the Brazilian. "Let me buy you a drink."

The woman jabbed a finger at Aldo. "You're Espejo Obscuro!"

Aldo spotted the rank insignia and patches on her uniform. "Captain, El Espejo Obscuro died five years ago."

"You bastards worked for Peepo! My entire family died in the Battle of Sao Paolo!"

"Captain... Ruyes. We never fought your mother's unit. It is unfortunate she and others of Ruyes Rebeldes fell in the Omega War, but we all lost loved ones, myself included. Our employment was a matter of business, not personal."

"The Berserkers should have killed you all!" the woman snarled. A large man in a similar uniform positioned himself at the woman's elbow.

"Jefe, I think they're taking it personal," Diller remarked.

"Truly, I share your loss, but we must move on."

"Share my loss?" Ruyes spat on the floor at Aldo's feet. Another man in a Ruyes Rebeldes uniform flanked her. "Move on?"

"This does—" A meaty fist interjected, sending Aldo sprawling against the bar.

"Oh shit!" Diller yelped as the other man yanked him off his bar stool. "Dude! I only work for them!"

"Don't worry. We have your back." While Aldo didn't want to escalate the situation, he admitted relief when Sergeant Pavon and a handful of his troops loomed behind the Rebeldes. Chairs scraped on the floor as more Human mercs joined the Rebeldes.

"Mierda," Aldo muttered as the brawl erupted. He focused on not getting his face caved in, but his men met aggression with aggression. After a few minutes, the melee petered out, with both sides wiping bloody noses and split lips.

Captain Ruyes glared through a blossoming shiner and spat at Aldo's feet again before following her troops toward the door.

"You have impeccable timing, Sergeant Pavon." Aldo leaned on the bar and downed half his drink. Maybe it would dull the pain.

"Hey, can someone give me a hand up? The sonuvabitches knocked my prosthetic loose." One of Diller's legs flopped at an unnatural angle. After several long seconds, one of the Jaguars hauled him upright.

"You okay, captain?" Another trooper slid Aldo a stool. "How many fingers am I holding up?"

"Two, because you would never flip off your captain." Aldo ran his tongue across his teeth. Despite the tang of blood in his mouth, none were broken or loose.

"Here I thought Humans did not fight Humans." Rugr chuffed. "At least you didn't break anything."

"Running a pit, you should know we fight each other all the time." Aldo took a drink. The alcohol burned the split in his lip. "We just do it for free."

"I made a jest." The Besquith laughed and snapped her jaws. She tapped a long talon to a pinport on her temple. "I found your history, Sun Jaguars. Some say wolves can't change their pelts."

"I intend to do exactly that," Aldo said. "The trouble is convincing others, especially Humans, to believe it."

"I may have found the perfect opportunity." The Besquith waved a claw in an intricate pattern over the bar and a Tri-V hologram sprang into view. The text facing Aldo morphed from Besquith to English. The highlighted contract enlarged.

"Split a contract with another unit?" Diller peered over Aldo's shoulder. "I know we're hard up, but we can find a decent gig for a company of CASPers."

Aldo zoomed a paragraph. "Check out the expedition clause. If we can get underway in twelve hours, there's a bonus."

Pavon whistled. "Someone is in a hurry."

"We're going to play second fiddle to a company of tanks?" Diller shook his head. "These Baba's Hammers shouldn't have even squatted on the contract if they didn't have the manpower."

"Armor contracts are as difficult to find as employers willing to gamble on disreputable merc units," a woman stated with a Russian accent.

Aldo turned toward the voice. A pair of women in grey and red uniforms regarded them. One wore a commander's insignia. Her shoulder patch showed a witch riding a tank gun barrel like a broom. "Commander, please join us. I am Captain Aldo Alvarez of the Sun Jaguars."

"I am Commander Alena Zharkova, and this is my second, Lieutenant Valentina Bizenko." Zharkova accepted the offered stool, while Bizenko stood behind her. "Not Commander Alvarez?"

"Once we get a contract under our belt, perhaps I'll update it. I'm in the guild database under captain and putting together a new mercenary firm buried me under digital paperwork."

Zharkova nodded. "Let me buy you a drink, and we can discuss the contract."

Diller nudged Aldo in the back. Aldo could imagine the remark the younger man wanted to make. Both women were striking, tall and athletic with bright blue eyes.

"Gracias. This is my second, Lieutenant Diller."

"Hey. Nice to meet you. Call me TJ." Aldo had witnessed Diller at work with women enough to predict a big beaming smile.

"Quit undressing me with your eyes." Bizenko had the same accent as her captain, though not as husky a voice.

"Thank you, Rugr, for helping us out," Zharkova said when the round of drinks arrived.

The Besquith snorted the equivalent of a chuckle. "Happy to help up-and-coming alphas."

"Valentina, can I buy you a drink?" Diller asked. "We can find a booth and get to know each other."

"It's Bizenko, or better, Lieutenant Bizenko. We prefer to stick to business."

"Ouch; shot down in flames," Pavon whispered from behind Diller. If either of the Hammers overheard, they didn't react.

"Yes, let's talk business." Aldo gestured to the holographic contract. "A Zuparti bank is hiring mercenaries to take possession of a corporation's defaulted assets on Qydenn-3, and they're offering a premium for haste. The contract lists a Zuul firm as the defenders."

"Right. The bank is worried the corporation will reinforce the Zuul if given time, which in turn increases the cost of hiring someone to root them out." Zharkova sipped her beer.

"Plus the bigger the conflict, the greater odds shit will get blown up. I bet there's a steep damage penalty," Diller remarked. Despite his personal shortcomings, Diller had a good head for variables in business and battle.

Aldo scrolled the contract. "He's right. They tacked a hefty charge for 'excessive collateral damage' to the facility and stored inventory."

"Which brings your unit into the mix," Zharkova said. "Our tanks can take out static defenses, but once the fighting gets into the refinery itself, we'd risk destroying our own pay."

Aldo scanned the lines of boiler plate, searching for any of the Zuparti tricks and double-speak typical for their contracts. "What's the landing fee? If we take the starport and move our LZ there, they want to charge us?"

"Those slimy weasels," Zharkova muttered. "I thought we'd caught all their scams in the contract. The Zuparti factor rolled over on the other sneaky charges and fees but remained adamant on the damage clause. If we can't get this revised before departure, we'll have to make sure not to land anything on the tarmac."

"Do you need a ride?" Diller asked. "It could get crowded, but—"

"We have our own landing transports and thrustcore," Bizenko interjected.

"Lieutenant Diller, announce general recall. I want troops ready to depart in eight hours," Aldo said. "Commander Zharkova, you have a deal."

* * *

"Are you sure we can trust them?" Valentina Bizenko asked as they left the merc pit. Two other members of the Hammers joined them, having hung back during business discussions.

"What's not to trust?" Corporal Ksenia Kozlov glanced back at the pit. "The blonde butter bar was cute."

"He thinks he's cute as well," Bizenko retorted. "They formed this unit from the firm who took out several Human mercenary companies at the behest of Peepo to soften Earth for her invasion."

"So, they've skulked around the past five years?" Private Elina Galay kept her hand near her sidearm as they passed a quartet of Goka. "I'm surprised no one put them down."

"Technically, Bjorn's Berserkers put them out of business and killed the commander, Rodrigo Sanchez," Alena replied. "Instead of finishing them off, the Berserkers claimed some spoils and left the

Espejo Obscuro with a bunch of derelict CASPers. The guild delisted the Espejos a year later after the end of the Omega War."

"We're partnering with a bunch of turncoats and traitors." Bizenko scoffed. "How do we know they won't screw us over, given the chance?"

"Lieutenant Diller wanted to screw Bizenko." Kozlov laughed. "I wouldn't mind sharing a bunk with him."

"I served a few years in the Berserkers after the Omega War. It's how I scratched together the funds to build the Hammers," Alena said. "The Espejo commander had a grudge against Tovesson, the Bjorn in Bjorn's Berserkers. He took the whole unit down a dark path on the road to revenge. We all do things we regret."

"Most of them don't involve betraying the Human race," Bizenko snapped.

Alena fought the impulse to call out her second. They needed to present a united front. "My point—they need a path to redemption, and we need to build a rep. Them screwing us over not only means no one will ever trust them again, they won't get paid on the contract."

"I still don't trust them," Bizenko grumbled.

"Which is why you're going with me on their ship. We'll plan the operation while in hyperspace. The platoon sergeants can manage the troops on the voyage."

"What? Captain, do you want me to punch in Diller's veneered smile?" Bizenko shook her head. "With all due respect, I suggest you take my sergeant, Baeva, with you, and leave me to tend our troops during the flight."

At least Lieutenant Bizenko protested with a modicum of decorum. "Noted and rejected."

"This is going to be a long flight," Bizenko muttered.

* * *

"Holy shit. An entire unit of hot Euro babes? This is going to be great!" TJ grinned like a kid in a candy store as he pulled the info on Baba's Hammers into his pinview. "Okay, not all women, but 85% human and of those 70% women. Did you see their LT? She's a smoke show."

"Compose yourself, Diller," Captain Alvarez said. "This is a professional operation, and I expect you to comport yourself as such."

"Leave it to you to take the fun out of it, Captain." Maybe Alvarez would hook up with the Hammer's commander and relax a bit. "My prospects have gotten thin back on Patoka; fresh blood would spice things up."

"You mean you've slept around so much, no chicas will give you a chance." Pavon laughed.

TJ decided against pointing out Sergeant Pavon's sister was on his list of conquests. TJ's reputation as an undercover agent for the previous commander labelled him as untrustworthy, so he struggled for acceptance from the troops.

"I've invited Captain Zharkova and her command element to travel with us on the *Ponce de Leon* so we can formulate a plan of attack and contingencies." Captain Alvarez turned to Diller. "Stay professional. If God favors us, she'll bring only men or aliens."

"An alien might not be a safe bet. Diller would probably hump a shaved Zuul at this point," Pavon said.

Another opportunity to jibe about Pavon's sister—TJ let it pass. "I hope she brings her LT."

* * *

Why did she bring her lieutenant? Aldo didn't let his professional smile falter, but he expected, even hoped, Zharkova would keep her second-in-command with their troops. He'd rather deal with a Pushtal than the sparks certain to erupt between Diller and the Hammer's lieutenant.

"My troops and gear are ready in orbit," Zharkova stated. Her raven-black tresses made her blue eyes brilliant.

Aldo chided himself. He'd spent too much time around Diller. "This shuttle is the last of my assets not in space. As soon as we dock with the *Ponce de Leon*, she can get underway."

"Can I grab your bag?" Diller offered Bizenko. A polite gesture from anyone else, Bizenko snorted and hefted her duffle off the tarmac before clambering up the shuttle's ramp.

"After you." Aldo gestured to the hatch, averting his gaze while Zharkova ascended.

"Captain, are you blushing?" Diller whispered in Spanish.

"Get on board." Last aboard, Aldo hit the control to retract the ladder and secure the hatch. Was he sweating? Aldo welcomed the interruption when the shuttle's engines roared and thrust slammed him into the acceleration couch. He hadn't worried about romantic liaisons since his ill-fated tryst with Commander Sanchez's sister and fellow Espejo, Elena. Five years later, why did it rear its ugly head now?

"I have my own private cabin," Diller bragged despite the high Gs.

"You must enjoy your alone time," Bizenko retorted.

"You and your staff will have access to your command dropship during the voyage," Aldo said. *Stick to business*. "I noticed you use CASVs in your headquarters element instead of tanks."

Zharkova nodded. "Combat Assault Systems-Vehicular, or Casanovas, make a better command and control platform than tanks. While they lack the armor and punch of a tank, they have superior speed and maneuverability as well as space."

Aldo nodded. His only experience with the CASVs stemmed from the battle with the Berserkers, a point best avoided. The attempt at a vehicular version of CASPers never gained popularity, as despite packing heavier weapons than the armored suits they could get swamped by heavy alien infantry and lacked the staying power of full-blown tanks.

"Our Marmaduke tanks provide plenty of firepower. Half field 60mm magnetic accelerator cannons, and the other half A4 heavy lasers," Zharkova recited. "Each have two point-defense lasers as well as the usual assortment of anti-personnel weapons."

The crush of thrust gave way to microgravity. "Five minutes until we dock."

* * *

EMS *Ponce de Leon*, Karma

"Here's your cabin. You can call your ship from the terminal." Diller gestured along the curved corridor and winked at Valentina. "If you need anything, my cabin is 4-A-2."

Commander Zharkova headed off Valentina's biting retort. "Thank you, Lieutenant."

If Valentina's lack of reaction disappointed Diller, he didn't let on. "I'll see you at the pre-jump meeting." With a wave and a pearly smile, he disappeared around the bend.

"Can I please shove him out an airlock?" Valentina asked once she dogged the cabin hatch behind her.

"You don't let men get under your skin. Perhaps you protest a bit too much?" The commander opened her duffle and set to stowing her gear. "He is handsome, in a blonde buff surfer sort of way."

"I don't care about his looks, as long as he can deliver on the battlefield." Bizenko dug into her own duffle. "Besides, if I slept with him, he'd grow even more unsufferable."

"Mmhmm."

"I could say the same for you and Captain Alvarez."

"What-what do you mean? The captain has been a gentleman since we met."

Valentina laughed. The shoe was on the other foot. "Are you blushing?"

"I don't know what you're talking about," the commander protested.

"Here you're about to tell me to get on with it—"

Zharkova shook her head. "I'm a commander, and we're on mission. If you want to play patty-cake with Blondie, scratch your itch. I need to maintain decorum."

"I'm not letting him scratch anything!" Valentina snapped.

"Of course not."

Valentina clambered to the upper bunk. "I'm getting some rack time while we have gravity."

"Are you sure? Lieutenant Blondie is around the corner."

"With all due respect, Commander, bite me."

* * *

ldo rose when the Baba's Hammers officers entered the meeting room. "Captain, Lieutenant."

"Hello, ladies." Diller didn't move from his seat, focusing his toothy smile on Bizenko.

"Gentlemen." Zharkova nodded while Bizenko silently glared at Diller.

Aldo waited for them to settle. Both women moved with the practiced ease of someone accustomed to space travel. His tactical slate projected a Tri-V map of their objective. He tapped a flat portion of the map. "While the contract lists the starport as an objective, calling it a starport or defensible are both exaggerations. Built to serve the refinery, it lacks even domestic security. Once we take the operations tower, the starport falls under our control."

Commander Zharkova crossed her arms. "A shame we can't use it. The factor refused to budge, hoping we'd rather pay the fees than make our troops slog back and forth."

"We'd need to take out the four air defense pillboxes before we could land," Diller stated. "Too bad we lack strike craft."

"How much is the damage fee for the tower?" Bizenko asked.

Diller's eyes flicked back and forth—a sign he was scanning the contract via his pinplants. "They didn't list one. All the charges detail refinery and storage facilities."

"Why don't we laze the tower and knock it over?" Bizenko mimicked a falling tree with her arm. "Our tanks could slag the structural supports from a kilometer away."

Diller's grin grew genuine. "I like how you think. If we can't use the starport, we don't need the tower. They assumed we'd leave it intact for flight operations once we seized it."

Bizenko laughed. "Can you imagine their faces when it goes?"

Diller joined the laughter, parodying someone falling over sideways. "Oh no! What's happening?"

Aldo gave them ten seconds of mirth. "I'd rather not destroy clients' facilities needlessly, even Zuparti clients."

"The starport is the most manageable part of this equation," Commander Zharkova said. "What about the approach to the refinery proper? The main road runs between two low ridge lines. It lets them get closer to our tanks than I'd prefer."

"Could the CASPers jump the defensive wall while the tanks covered them?" Bizenko suggested.

Aldo shook his head. "Until you take out the tower emplacements and clear defenders from the battlements, it would be a suicide run."

"They'd also skeet shoot jumping CASPers with crew-served weapons behind the walls," Diller added.

Zharkova tapped on the holographic interface. Icons appeared on the main road. "If we assault the main gates, can your CASPers keep skirmish units from flanking our tanks?"

Aldo highlighted the ridges. "We send the CASPers below the crest to mitigate fire from the other side of the hills, but any infantry crossing the top would silhouette themselves."

"What's this road? It leads to the south wall." Bizenko poked a wavy line on the map and zoomed in the image. "A maintenance gate."

"It's too narrow. The tanks would never make it through those tight bends unless they crawled single file." Zharkova studied the side gate. "Even a maintenance gate would require serious demolitions charges or heavy weapons."

"A demo team would be sitting ducks as soon as they were spotted. The Zuul could drop rocks on them, but I expect they'd use rockets and grenades," Diller said.

"The Casanovas could make it." Bizenko added four icons to the winding road. "We make a rush for the gate once the assault grabs their attention. A couple of heavy rockets would turn an armored gate into swiss cheese."

Aldo adjusted the map, tilting it horizontally. "Once past this warehouse, they'd have a line of fire on any ground-level emplaced weapons watching for intruders to come over the wall."

Diller's grin faded. "Wait, you want to use your command element to spearhead an attack?"

"He's right. It might take them by surprise, but even once you come out of the last curve, we couldn't get more than two vics abreast," Zharkova stated.

"Not to mention gambling your entire command," Aldo added. He would take the risk himself—few mercenary commanders led from the rear—but he wouldn't throw his whole headquarters team into such a risky gambit.

"I'll take one other CASV with me," Bizenko declared. "You stay with the main body of the attack. Your rumbler only has an A3 laser. We sacrificed heavy firepower for command equipment and a shield node."

"If they sniff you out, you'll be toast." Diller pointed at the map. "It would take CASPers three to five minutes to reinforce you from the south ridge."

"If we come under heavy fire, we can retreat back down the road. Once we reach the curves, we'll break line of sight. You won't have to worry about rescuing me."

Aldo rubbed his chin. No matter the plan, experience taught him it would go off the rails. This risked two vehicles and paid huge dividends if it worked. "If Commander Zharkova agrees, I say let's go with the lieutenant's plan."

Zharkova crossed her arms. Aldo suspected she'd reached the same conclusion. "Fine. We have a Plan A for breaking the perimeter. Once we get inside, we need to locate and capture the command bunker."

* * *

"A whole week, and she didn't thaw," TJ lamented over coffee. The more Bizenko rebuffed him, the more determined he grew. "You'd think she'd want one more roll in the hay before this kamikaze mission."

Alvarez shrugged. "You should have left it alone at the first 'no' and moved on."

"I took a more subtle approach, trying to get to know her, find what we had in common, what she liked—you know, the usual bullshit." His coffee had grown lukewarm. "It paid off back when I hooked up with the tech sergeant in the Berserkers."

The captain shook his head. "Not something I'd brag about. You had a nefarious purpose behind your dalliance with the Berserker woman—I believe you put it 'getting laid was a bonus.'"

A rare twinge of guilt dampened TJ's grin. It was easier to maintain the shallow façade than admit any regrets. "There's nothing wrong with a little bonus, boss. Especially since I don't know if I'll ever see Valentina after this mission. Don't think I haven't noticed you getting chummy with Commander Zharkova."

"We are both professionals, and I have no desire to sour future cooperation by seeking a 'bonus' as you put it."

"If you say so." TJ consulted his pinview. "We have an hour until emergence. We need to go over anything?"

"We've briefed the troops as best we can without simulator runs," the captain stated.

"I mean in regard to Baba's Hammers. If those tanks get swamped by infantry, or the Zuul have a nasty surprise, and we have to cut and run, those rolling slabs need twice as long to get back to the LZ, and their bulky landers can't get closer without landing on the starport tarmac."

"If you're suggesting we abandon our allies—"

TJ held up a hand. "I'm not saying it's Plan A, but I'm pragmatic."

Alvarez glowered at him. "Check on the troops. Once we emerge, we have seventeen hours to orbit. I want them suited with at least sixty minutes to spare. I'll be on the bridge."

"Got it, jefe." TJ floated into the corridor to escape Alvarez's disproving glare. He pushed off toward the vertical passage running parallel to the ship's spine.

As he swung around the bend, TJ almost plowed into Bizenko, her blonde hair damp.

Her blue eyes flashed from surprise to irritation. "Watch where you're going, Diller."

"It's an hour until we drop out of hyperspace, so I have to make the rounds with the other LTs and NCOs. Once I'm done, we have several hours to kill."

"Once we establish communications with our people, the commander and I will have to confer with our leadership and go over the plan." Bizenko ran her hand through her blonde tresses. "Besides, I just showered. I don't want to get hot and sweaty before going into combat."

TJ grinned. "So you want to get hot and sweaty after? I have some quality whiskey we could crack open to heat things up."

She regarded him. "If we win this mission, and you prove your mettle on the battlefield, maybe we can talk celebration."

TJ blanched, the wheels in his head taking a split second to gain traction. "That's not a no."

Bizenko launched toward the cabin she shared with her commander. "It's not a no. Don't forget the whiskey."

* * *

Bizenko slipped through the hatch, a smirk on her lips.

"Something amusing, Valentina?" Alena asked.

"I may have thrown Diller a bone." Bizenko drifted to her bunk, snagging a handhold so she could dig through her kit.

Alena chuckled. "You've shot him down all week, but I suspected you protested too much. Do I need to give you the cabin? If we don't get blown up on emergence, we'll have several hours under thrust to reach the target."

"I tossed him a bone, not a steak. If we live, I may give him a chance."

"You've already decided. I don't blame you—he's a handsome young man—and I appreciate you waiting until after business. I'll be on the bridge for emergence. I want you on our dropship. If a catastrophe happens, don't wait for me. Take the dropships to the thrustcore and make for the stargate."

Bizenko paused halfway through combing through her damp hair. "You'd cut and run on Captain Alvarez? I thought you liked him?"

"Aldo, I mean Captain Alvarez, has nothing to do with my orders. If this ship suffers a calamity, I don't want our people waiting for me. Do you understand?"

"In more ways than one. Did you two sneak a 'command conference' or three when I wasn't looking?" Bizenko's smile brought a flush to Alena's cheeks.

"No, Aldo has remained a consummate professional."

"Consummate?" Bizenko laughed.

"You know what I mean."

"Mmm hmmm." The smile remained as Bizenko finished combing her hair. "All right, boss. I'll grab my gear and get to the dropship."

Alena studied the plan for another thirty minutes before donning her shipboard suit. She descended two levels to the bridge, an armored box nestled against the ship's spine. With ten minutes on the clock, she floated through the hatch and glided to the flag station. Aldo—Captain Alvarez—smiled warmly.

"I hate this part of the mission cycle." Alena wrestled with a harness strap snagged in a gap between her seat and Captain Alvarez's.

Alvarez balked halfway through reaching across her to untwist the strap. "Can I assist?"

Her cheeks grew warm. "I can manage. There!" She clicked the last buckle into place and checked the clock over the tactical Tri-V. Four minutes.

"For the record, I prefer fighting with my feet on the ground. Our ship should emerge moments before your vessel, so any enemy lying in wait should lock onto us first."

Alena laughed. "It's absurd I find that comforting."

"Our cruiser has superior shields, armor, and point defense," Captain Alvarez said. "It stands to reason we lead the charge."

"Not to mention superior facilities. I feel guilty availing myself of your hospitality while the bulk of my people are crammed together on the thrustcore. It's little more than engines, power, shields, and docking clamps."

Captain Alvarez smiled. "You are always welcome to my hospitality. Uh, as a professional courtesy." Despite his swarthy Latin complexion, his cheeks reddened.

"Of course." Alena patted him on the arm, immediately self-conscious of what should be a friendly gesture.

"Emergence in three… two… one!" If the flight officer's call didn't break Alena out of any schoolgirl musings, the lurching and falling sensation did.

"All systems green. Clean emergence."

"Navigational fix confirmed, arrival vector twenty-seven degrees off nominal."

"Comm link established with the other vessel. Telemetry green."

Alena let out her breath as the crew went through their script.

"Bogies bearing three-seven-mark-three-three-two."

Alena sucked her breath back in.

"Shields to full. Ready counter-missile fire. Identify bogies!" the ship's captain barked. "Helm, accelerate to two Gs!"

"Two Gs, aye." A klaxon sounded with the acceleration chime. Alena sank into her couch.

"One Zuul drone corvette and thirteen class-two drones!"

"Missile! Missile! Missile!"

A myriad of icons and lines erupted in the tactical Tri-V.

The captain, a steely eyed woman, leaned forward. "Focus counterfire on missiles and drones tracking toward the Hammers' ship. Weapons, target the corvette with the particle barbette. Fire as soon as you acquire."

Crosshairs drifted through the tactical display toward the largest enemy icon. The lights dimmed when the X intersected the icon.

Aldo's hand clutched the armrest next to hers. "We may only have a merc cruiser, but we pack more punch than they might expect."

The ship shuddered, and a bank of lights went dark. Several yellow lines illuminated in the holographic wireframe of the ship. The largest enemy icon blinked yellow, red, and vanished. Alena's stomach lurched from a twisting sensation—the ship rolled to present fresh shield nodes.

Alena focused on the tactical display. Only seven, now five, enemy icons remained.

"Standby, Cromwell maneuver!' the captain called. "Switch half the lasers to offense and fire the barbette at twenty-five percent."

Multiple stations replied with an affirmative.

"Now!"

The faux gravity of thrust vanished. The Tri-V display spun with Alena's stomach as the ship flipped 180 degrees and reignited its fusion torch, shoving Alena into her couch. A green icon labelled *Iron Cauldron*—Baba Hammers' thrustcore—streaked past.

"All bogies down!" Microgravity returned, along with another gut-wrenching flip. Thrust resumed.

"Reduce to one G once we pass the *Iron Cauldon*," the captain ordered. "Damage report and status of our friend."

"Patching the *Cauldron's* feed to the flag station."

"Minor armor damage, one point-defense turret out, two shield nodes damaged…" the reports faded as Alena focused on the report from her ship.

"Lander Two took a direct hit," Sergeant Dolgava reported. "No casualties, but she'll need repairs before we can risk landing her. They might cobble something together, but even odds she won't lift even if we got her to the ground in one piece."

"*Sukin syn!*" Alena smacked the couch arm opposite Aldo. "We can't risk all those people. Tell them to see if they can come up with anything better by orbit minus two hours."

"Da, commander."

Aldo—Captain Alvarez—glanced from his display. "Bad news?"

"One of our landers took a bad hit. Unless my techs can make repairs on the fly, this takes a tank platoon off the board." Alena cracked her knuckles. "We're down a third in armored firepower."

"If Lieutenant Bizenko's gambit works, it won't matter," Captain Alvarez replied.

"If it doesn't, we might find ourselves hard pressed to crack the front gate."

"Diamonds are lumps of coal which were hard pressed," Alvarez countered. "We will persevere."

"I wish I had your optimism," Alena said.

Captain Alvarez shrugged. "If the glass is only half full, you must fill it the rest of the way yourself."

* * *

"*Holy shit, they lost a third of their tanks?*" Diller cried over the command channel. A few of the sergeants echoed his dismay.

"It doesn't change our component of the plan," Aldo stated. So much for the plan remaining intact until they reached the ground. "We split into two elements of two platoons each. We make sure no one comes over those crests into the valley to hit the tanks from the flank."

"How much longer will it take them to burn the defenses and the main gate?" Sergeant Alhueda asked.

"Longer than before, but they can still achieve their objective," Aldo replied. "If we can keep losses to four tanks or less, we can maintain the timetable, assuming the CASV incursion team doesn't get through the maintenance gate first, in which case we'll rush the defenses and jump the wall."

"*I'm not a fan of the whole 'Valhalla Awaits' business,*" Diller stated. "*You can't spend your paycheck in the afterlife.*"

Aldo flipped to a private channel. "If you can't follow orders, lieutenant, I'll find someone who can! Am I clear?"

The long pause prompted Aldo to check the channel. The indicator remained green. "*Got it, jefe. I'm good to go, I just—*"

"You want to express doubts to me, you do it in private."

"*Sorry, Captain.*"

Aldo switched back to the command channel. "We have fifteen hours until orbit. I want everyone suited up and ready from drop at orbit minus ninety minutes."

Assents preceded the officers and non-comms signing off the channel. Aldo headed for the meeting room. Commander Zharkova already perched in a chair, studying the crude Tri-V tactical simulation of the impending attack. She smiled as Aldo slid through the hatch, but it didn't reach her eyes.

"No luck on getting your third lander back in action?" he asked.

Zharkova shook her head. "I suppose I should count my blessings. We suffered minimal casualties. Even the damage isn't too costly. We tried to figure out if we could float some of the tanks around outside the thrustcore and cram them in intact landers, but it's too risky."

"God was with us. The Zuul commander must lack naval experience, or they would have focused their fire on one of our ships." Aldo gestured to the blue wireframe hologram. "How much firepower does it cost us on the ground?"

"Thirty percent, but only in raw output. The rear platoon can't fire over other tanks at the gate itself, so I relegated them to pouring fire on the walls and any surviving tower emplacements to reduce the risk of a pack of Zuuls with rocket launchers overwhelming our point-defense systems."

Aldo gazed at the image. "It will work."

"We can't fail. Units that lose their first contract rarely get a second, even with the Phoenix Initiative."

"We will prevail, and when we return to Karma, we can celebrate."

"It's a date." Zharkova disentangled herself from the chair and table. "We can talk again before loading for drop, Captain Alvarez."

"When, um, we are in private, feel free to call me Aldo."

Her smile grew genuine. Why did he blush like a schoolboy? "Alena. I'll see you later Aldo."

Aldo's gaze returned to the tactical Tri-V. "This must work."

* * *

Qydenn-3

"All right guys! Everyone ready?" TJ called over the platoon channel.

A few unenthusiastic grunts returned. *"Don't worry, Lieutenant. My boys know what to do,"* Sergeant de Santos said. The gruff platoon sergeant, a survivor of the Battle of Patoka, had the men's respect. TJ knew if the man didn't hate officers save for Alvarez, he would have TJ's job.

"Right. Let's walk away from this with a fat payday, and maybe some of those Slavic tanker chicks will be in the mood for celebrating." This earned TJ a more enthusiastic response.

He checked the tactical display. It showed the two ships braking into orbit, and the landing zone highlighted on the planet's surface. Two Gs of thrust shoved TJ into the padding of his CASPer.

With a lurch, the dropship leapt free of the cruiser, and the tactical display morphed to show their approach to the drop point. He hated drops. At least with his feet on the ground, TJ controlled his destiny.

The dropship shuddered as it bit into the tenuous upper atmosphere. TJ activated another display in his pinview. It showed the two Baba's Hammers dropships. They followed their lander transports, heavy dropships able to handle a platoon of four tanks and support gear. He added their LZ to his tactical map. Terrain and the size of the tank landers meant they would arrive half a kilometer further away than the Sun Jaguars.

A flight of missiles streaked toward the descending craft, but point defense-lasers picked off the incoming threats. The next wave detonated half their number early to confound defensive fire, but the remaining fell to laser pulses or chased countermeasures. The distant shockwaves rattled the dropship, but they lost no craft.

TJ's stomach climbed into his throat as the pilot nosed the dropship into a steep dive. Numbers scrolled by in his pinview—altitude, velocity, G forces, distance to target, and time until drop. He checked his most important number, the twenty-eight troopers in his platoon. All showed ready.

As time to drop approached zero, the back of the dropship opened to the howling sky. Huge holographic numbers counted down, as though every trooper didn't have the timer plastered in the middle of their HUD. At ten seconds, lights in the bay flashed yellow. At zero, they strobed green.

As the platoon lieutenant, TJ was last off the dropship. The rest of the CASPers plummeted toward the hilly terrain below. Nudges of jumpjets grouped squads together. TJ guided his suit toward the remainder of the platoon command element, only four CASPers as opposed to the squads of six.

The altitude warning blinked, and TJ oriented his suit. The disposable jump pack triggered automatically. The G forces hammered TJ toward the feet of his armor. At ten meters, the pack jettisoned and the jets on TJ's suit fired. His armored feet sank several centimeters into the dirt as CASPers thudded to the ground around him.

Twenty-eight—all made it. TJ let Sergeant de Santos muster the troops while he checked the command display. All CASPers survived the drop, and the dropships arched away toward the main LZ.

"*We all made it, a good omen,*" Captain Alvarez announced over the company channel.

"*I have incoming movement, multiple large metallic masses,*" Corporal Lozano called. His CASPer traded its heavy weapon for advanced sensors.

"*Are they the Hammers' tanks?*" Alvarez asked.

TJ's Tri-V HUD updated. The pings approached from the direction of their target. The warbook flashed images over the icons until it settled on the identification: two MD-50 tanks, similar to those used by the Hammers, and a ZF-90, a fusion-powered beast on treads.

"You jinxed us, jefe!" TJ shouted, diving away from the line of the heavy tank's particle beam cannon. He didn't bother shouting the order to spread out and take cover—Sergeant de Santos beat him to it.

Content to let the grizzled NCO handle the troops, TJ focused on surviving the next few minutes.

A searing flash blinded his optics and static sparked over the comm channels as the enormous Zuul tank unleashed artificial lightning from its beam cannon. Smaller lasers added to the chaos, and the other enemy tanks fired their heavy lasers in a crossfire intersecting in the scrambling CASPer formations. Several rockets streaked from CASPers only for point-defense lasers on the tanks to pick them out of the air. CASPer lasers flashed against the ZF-90's shield while MAC rounds sparked off its armor.

TJ's optical sensors polarized, and his visual displays returned in time for him to watch a CASPer shrouded in smoke incandesce as the particle beam lashed out again, leaving a pair of smoldering metal legs and raining debris as the suit's fuel cell, jump juice, and ammo all cooked off.

"Holy shit," TJ uttered.

"*We need to get among them,*" Alvarez commanded.

"*You might want to hold off on tangoing with them,*" Commander Zharkova countered. "*It's about to heat up.*"

A pair of the Hammers' MD-50s fired their siege batteries—clusters of twenty short-ranged rocket launchers. The crew of the fusion tank swung their turret around and fired the particle cannon as forty rockets overwhelmed the tank's point defenses. The shield nudged a few of the outlying rockets off course, but it lacked the strength to stop so many physical projectiles at once. Armor-piercing charges peppered the tank. One struck a crew hatch, blasting molten metal into the driver's compartment, and another caromed off the sloped forward armor to detonate on the underside of the particle cannon's barrel shroud. Fire shot out the end of the barrel before it drooped.

One of the Marmaduke tanks paid the price for their assault. The last particle beam lashed across the armor, leaving a red, molten trail in its wake. The main gun, an A4 laser, shattered, and the remaining volley of rockets in the siege launcher detonated. A half dozen rockets corkscrewed through the air, one striking an unlucky CASPer and blowing through the backside of the mech. A flaming crewmember scrambled from the top turret hatch before an explosion launched the turret skyward.

The two enemy MD-50s reversed in a futile attempt to retreat. One slewed on a damaged tread, but even its quicker partner couldn't escape. More Hammers tanks joined the fight; the fusillade of heavy laser and 60mm MAC rounds chewed the enemy armor into smoking hulks.

* * *

Valentina's gaze bounced between the terrain LIDAR and the tactical display. One Baba tank blinked red and went dark, while two other icons flashed yellow. Her eyes sought the name on the IFF roster for the CASPers. Diller's icon remained green.

The Casanova shuddered as it skidded through a turn. "Don't roll us over, Kiki," Valentina called.

"I'm trying to keep up with Ivanna! The lunatic is taking this road at 90 KPH." The rumbler rocked.

"We're on a tight timetable." Bailing the Sun Jaguars out of the jam with those tanks had slowed the assault, but only by a few minutes. Valentina hoped to take advantage of the extra time to assess the situation at the maintenance gate, plus they needed enemy attention firmly on the frontal assault. "Bizenko to Vladisky. Don't overdo it."

"What's wrong, LT? Can't Kiki keep up?"

"We don't want to break cover too early." Valentina checked the tactical display. The main assault force had regrouped and reached the main road connecting the starport and the refinery. "We have eight minutes until they lay siege to the main gate."

"*Fine, Lieutenant Bizenko. I'll have Ivanna throttle back to seventy-five.*"

Eight kilometers until the last curve, where the road opened from the hills to the quarter kilometer flat. The whine of the rumbler's electric motors slackened from a scream to a wail. Sensors showed nothing metallic or hot. No sensing lasers or active sensors pinged them. Valentina crossed her fingers.

Six minutes later they slowed. Valentina enlarged the video feed from Vladisky's Casanova. The gate remained closed, and two squat metal boxes flanked it. They hadn't appeared in the images used for the tactical simulations.

"*LT, do you see those pillboxes? Dollars to bottles of vodka they're calliopes.*"

"No bet, Sergeant Vladisky." The multi-barreled lasers could turn a CASPer squad into swiss cheese. While the CASVs had heavier armor, Vladisky's rumbler lacked the shield node equipped on Valentina's. "We'll swing around your left when we break cover and fire on the right pillbox. Hopefully they'll focus on us."

"Hopefully?" Kiki called from the driver compartment.

"You take the left pillbox. We'll both fire a bunker buster at the gate. If we can't blow it open, this assault becomes a meat grinder." Valentina watched as her gunner swung the dual minigun turret in anticipation of their emergence from cover.

"Lieutenant, we've got movement at the gate!"

The metal portal ground upward and dark forms milled behind the widening gap. "Please not Tortantulas," she prayed. Over the channel, she ordered, "Don't round the corner yet, but ready to reverse."

"*If we back away, we might not get another crack at the gate,*" Vladisky stated.

A furry mass erupted from the maintenance gate and poured toward the main fight. Many of the creatures lacked armor or weapons, but thick talons tore at the turf in their haste to join the fight. Roughly one in ten wore a harness with dark cylindrical objects—the Zuul equivalent of a K-bomb.

"Shit, shit, shit." Valentina switched channels. "Bizenko to command. You've got Aposa inbound, one hundred plus. Some have explosives. Make it two hundred plus."

"*They haven't seen us yet,*" Vladisky whispered, as though the furry aliens could hear their comms.

"We make our move as soon as they thin out." Valentina switched fire control for the bunker buster rockets to her command console. "We'll need to hit the pillboxes and fire our rockets at the same time. If we wreck the gate tracks or mechanism, we'll jam it."

"*Roger, LT. Give the word.*"

On the video, the swarm diminished to a trickle and the gate inched down. "Now!"

The Casanova shot forward and skidded through a turn, shimmying as it straightened out. Valentina dropped the targeting reticule on the upper corner of the closing gate. Metal covers retracted from the pillboxes, revealing the multi-barreled lasers she feared. As the two rumblers drew abreast, the first laser pulse flashed against her vehicle's shield.

"Fire!" Valentina stabbed the button. The rocket leapt across the 200 meters, hitting the wall above the gate. The gunner peppered the laser emplacement with their miniguns. Sparks showered off the armored shroud, but several bullets found openings and ricocheted inside the pillbox. One or more must have damaged a lasing element, as the weapon fell dark after a staccato of bursts.

Vladisky's rocket soared true. It punched a hole clean through the armored portal, deforming the metal around the impact. The gate's descent ground to a halt. Meanwhile, Vladisky's gunner speared the enemy calliope. A flash of superheated coolant and polymer preceded a gout of flame.

Valentina checked the telemetry displays for both vehicles. Her Casanova showed green. The shields had mitigated most of the laser fire. A couple of yellow spots and one red flashed on Vladisky's rumbler—the latter a fried drive motor. They could limp but not run.

"Sukin syn," Vladisky cursed over the comms. "*Some of those furry psychopaths are doubling back!*"

* * *

"*We nailed the gate, but some Aposa are coming after us. Hammer H4 is damaged, slowing our retreat.*"

TJ checked the battlespace. Two Casanovas—H2 and H4—inched along the winding support road toward the facility. A fuzzy red mass of icons pursued, some swarming into the hills to avoid the back and forth of the road. They'd catch the vehicles in a matter of minutes, well before they reached it.

"Jefe, I'm going to take my platoon and bail them out."

"No, Diller, you're not," Captain Alvarez countered. "*We need to keep the Aposa off the tanks, especially the suicide bombers.*"

TJ flipped to a direct channel. "We can't leave them to die."

"*We can't pull half the left flank to save them. I take no joy in it,*" Alvarez replied. "*You of all people would understand.*"

An icon blinked on TJ's comm display for a private channel. The name "De Santos" glowed over the symbol. TJ isolated his comms to the private channel.

"*I've got this, Lieutenant. Take Squad Delta and save those Hammers,*" Sergeant de Santos said. On the platoon channel, de Santos added, "*Delta, follow the LT.*"

TJ used his pinplants to configure a new comm channel for himself and the squad. Toward the looming defensive wall, weapons fire erupted as the first of the Aposa charged into view. Lasers and rockets from the remaining wall defenders increased their tempo of fire, and the tanks responded while CASPers laid a carpet of destruction into the approaching swarm.

"*LT, what's the plan?*" Sergeant Jimenez called.

"I'm making it up on the fly. First, we need to get there. Follow me!" TJ charged over the crest and turned to intersect the retreating Casanovas. It would take the CASPers two minutes to reach them—roughly the same time the battlefield computer predicted the Aposas would catch the retreating vehicles.

"*Diller! What the hell are you doing?*" Alvarez demanded over a private circuit.

"Something I didn't do before—giving a damn! Fire me or whatever." TJ clicked off the comm.

The CASPers sprinted over the wooded hills, using short bursts of jumpjets to cross the winding gullies. The tactical display showed both vehicles creeping at 20 kph. Staccato gunfire echoed in the hills as the CASPers neared the last ridge.

A flood of muddy brown water chased the vehicles along the curving road. No, not water, but a mass of furry forms pressed in their eagerness to catch their prey. The trailing vehicle fired its miniguns and laser non-stop, but the Aposa boiled over their fallen comrades. An alien in the lead leapt at the vehicle, exploding in a red mist as it made contact with the hull.

When the smoke and mist of viscera cleared, it revealed a deformed dent in the forward armor. More dark brown forms sprinted along the hillside below TJ and his squad. If the aliens intercepted and crippled the trailing vehicle, they'd trap both Casanovas on the narrow service road.

TJ highlighted the scurrying forms in his pinview and passed the targeting data to the squad. "Take these first, then we'll thin out the gang on the road. Light them up!"

TJ didn't wait for confirmation before he fired on the Aposa furthest along the hillside. The rest of the CASPers added laser and MAC fire, each hit slaying or crippling aliens. One of the collapsed forms erupted in a ball of flame and shrapnel. The armored Aposa carried explosives. The armor wasn't to save their lives, but to keep them alive long enough to reach their victims.

Spotting new targets, several Aposa swerved uphill to close on the CASPers. Bombs powerful enough to harm armored vehicles would destroy CASPers.

"Watch out for the ones wearing armor. They're suicide bombers!" TJ called over the comms. Aposa claws grew from an organic carbon-fiber and could dig into CASPer armor, wrecking systems and prying open the canopy to expose the operator to the same deadly talons.

TJ divided his fire between charging Aposa and those closing on the rumblers below. One leapt onto the rear armored vehicle, but TJ's laser punched through its helmet to flash-fry its brains. It slid off the rumbler before it could trigger its payload. The other rumbler ran it over, but fortunately the bombs didn't detonate.

A brown shape sprang over a rock, talons spread to latch onto TJ's mech. TJ flipped out his molybdenum-carbide blade. "I got claws too, asshole."

Another scrambled over the rock only for a CASPer to blast a gory hole in it with a MAC. TJ half clambered, half slid down the slope toward the vehicles. The lead vehicle's miniguns ran dry, the staccato report turning into the whine of empty spinning barrels. TJ snatched a K-bomb off his suit's belt and chucked it into the roiling group of Aposa. The detonation painted the Casanova with a spray of blood and gore. Half a dozen K-bombs arced into dwindling swarm. Thunderous detonations echoed off the hills.

"*That's the last of them,*" Sergeant Jimenez declared after another minute of picking off stragglers. Smoke wafted among the trees and off the two rumblers.

TJ pinged the Casanovas. "What's your status?"

"*The other vic has a wrecked motor, slowing it, and the Aposa ripped off its minigun turret,*" Bizenko reported.

TJ's heart skipped hearing her voice. "How about we hitch a ride on you to give the enemy something else to worry about."

"*I can't believe I'm saying this, but climb on, Lieutenant Diller.*"

TJ grinned.

* * *

"You disobeyed orders!" Aldo yelled. "You could have cost us the contract!"

The thick walls of the bunker ensured no one overheard their conversation. Aldo believed in praising in public, rebuking in private. After the Sun Jaguars and Baba's Hammers penetrated the defenses, the Zuul commander had capitulated.

"Jefe, we won! I called an audible, and it panned out."

"You went rogue because you wanted to get laid!" Aldo paced in the small chamber. "Don't get me wrong. I would understand a humane motivation, not that I expect such from you."

Diller stood. "Every contract is a gamble. Every tactic is a gambit. You can get pissed at me for not following the letter of your orders, but… but have you considered you aren't the only one who needed to prove themselves?"

Aldo blinked. "You? You scoffed at the notion."

Diller shrugged. "I don't know. It was easy to be the asshole everyone expected. Maybe five years of being the guy no one trusted was enough."

"You didn't work hard to dispel the notion before now." Aldo knew the stories. "What changed?"

Diller poked at the table between them. "I grew up. Commander Zharkova's troops respect her; they respect Lieutenant Bizenko. Our guys respect you, but not me. They tolerate me, but only because you make them. For a long time, it was easier to play the part—it's what I'd done my whole life. Join a class, join a team, join a merc unit, and slip into a role so I could fit in. Only the role everyone expected of me was unreliable at best and traitor at worst."

"I should fire you." Aldo sat across from Diller. "In fact, half the sergeants would applaud it."

"I'd wager more than half. Some of them have sisters." Diller half smiled at his joke.

"But if you hadn't saved those rumblers and gotten them into the compound, they wouldn't have taken out those laser batteries behind the walls or warned us about the four ZT-90s waiting for us to blow open the main gate."

Diller chuckled. "I nearly pissed myself when I spotted those fusion tanks. Good thing the CASVs still had a bunker buster each."

"So, as much as it might disappoint a few, I'm not firing you."

Diller set a small box on the table. "Thanks. It might have made giving you this awkward."

Aldo flipped open the lid. A set of mercenary commander insignias nestled on a patch which read "Commander Alvarez."

"You wanted to wait until the Sun Jaguars proved themselves as a legit mercenary unit," Diller said. "They proved it, and so did you."

Aldo picked up the insignia pin. "I guess we both got our redemption arcs."

* * *

Bartertown, Karma

"Diller? You have some brass showing your face around here."

TJ recognized the speaker's German accent. "Gutknecht? Still with the Berserkers, and a platoon sergeant. Good for you."

"What are you doing here, you piece of shit?" Two burly CASPer troopers in Berserker uniforms flanked the young German sergeant.

"It's been five years, Gutknecht." TJ patted an open space at the bar. "Why don't you let me buy you and your friends a drink?"

"What unit would hire a traitorous snake like you?" Gutknecht jabbed his finger at TJ. "You set us up to take the fall on Patoka."

The Berserker on the right cracked his knuckles. If TJ only faced Gutknecht, it would resemble a fair fight, and once he let the kid get a couple of shots in, it would end. However, the other troopers looked eager to use him for a pinata.

"To be fair, I tried to save you, Gutknecht."

The Berserker on the left smacked his fist into his palm. "I lost friends on Patoka."

Shit. "Guys, kicking my ass won't change what happened."

"Maybe it will make us feel better," the trooper on the right snarled.

A quartet of Sun Jaguar NCOs emerged from a booth. Sergeant Jimenez asked, "LT, these guys giving you grief?"

"You want to box, Berserkers?" Corporal Javier added.

Sergeant de Santos crossed his arms. "Diller's our man. You have a beef with him, you've got it with all us Sun Jaguars."

TJ gestured to the bar. "I don't suppose you'll take me up on that drink now?"

Gutknecht spat on the floor. "Fuck you. Let's go, guys."

"Guess I can buy you guys a round for saving my bacon." TJ clapped de Santos on the shoulder. "Thanks."

"Por supuesto. You're one of us," de Santos said.

Javier leaned close. "Just make sure you stay away from my sister."

"No problem. I've got a date with the hot Slavic lieutenant later." TJ grinned. "Bartender! A round for my troops!"

*****

Jon R. Osborne Bio

Jon R. Osborne turned a journalism education and a passion for role-playing games into writing science fiction and fantasy. His second book in The Milesian Accords modern fantasy series, "A Tempered Warrior", was a 2018 Dragon Awards finalist for Best Fantasy Novel. Jon is a core author in the military science fiction Four Horseman Universe, where he was first published in 2017. He now has eight novels and numerous stories published in multiple languages.

Jon resides in Indianapolis, where he plays role-playing games, writes science fiction and fantasy, and extols the virtues of beer. You can find out more at jonrosborne.com and at https://www.facebook.com/jonrosborne.

# # # # #

In the Black by Charli Cox

Danny's Dugout
Astoria, Oregon
Earth

Jameson took a step back as the ledger sailed through the air toward him, narrowly missing his black snout. His brown eyes tracked the trajectory of the paper missile and followed its flight toward the sticky parquet floor, debits and credits landing solidly in the red next to the glowing embers smoldering in the fireplace. Wood smoke permeated the air along with the scent of old leather courtesy of the baseball paraphernalia decorating the bar.

Setting a dingy mop aside, tacky hardwood flooring momentarily forgotten, he reached down for the leather-bound tome and looked at the human who threw it. "Lydia? You might need this—"

His voice broke off when he saw the proprietor slumped on a bar stool, elbows on the polished mahogany surface, head in her hands. Opening his mouth to take a deep breath, the brown Zuul approached his Human boss slowly. "Lydia?"

She turned away from him and underneath the curly blonde tangle, he heard her sniffle. He reached out to place a paw on her shoulder. At his gentle touch, she looked up at him, red-rimmed eyes dripping with exhaustion and desperation.

"Jameson, I don't know what to do. Ever since the mercs stopped taking contracts, there are no credits to go around. Everyone's GiGi stipend is shrinking, and no one is venturing out of their homes. I can't keep this place open with only a handful of customers every night!"

Lydia Price stood and threw her hands into the air in frustration. "What is the point? We haven't shown a profit in the better part of a year. I can barely keep vendors paid, and don't even get me started on the taxes due. With the gravy train from the mercenaries all but dried up, the government is coming after small business owners even harder than usual. If things don't turn around soon, I don't know what I'm going to do."

She collapsed once again with a heaving sigh.

Jameson gave her a consoling pat and worked his way behind the bar. Grabbing a bottle of amber liquid, the liquor responsible for his nickname, he poured two shots. As he placed one of the glasses in front of his boss, he heard a low growl emanate from the front door.

* * *

Lydia looked through the saloon-style doors and saw Benji with his hackles up. He growled again when a loud voice boomed over the rumble.

"Mrs. Price! Call off your mutt!"

Oh jeez, thought Lydia. *If I could only summon customers the way I make the tax collector appear!*

Benji looked back to Lydia who gave him a curt nod. She stood and met Mr. Jericho halfway across the long-deserted dance floor. "How can I help you?"

"You can pay what you owe!" he started.

Lydia took a defensive step back. Compared to the tax man's booming voice and imposing frame, her five feet, five inches were hardly the picture of intimidation. She opened her mouth to respond, but the man continued.

"The balance due on your profits is approaching five figures. Are you ever going to make a payment?"

Lydia let out a haughty laugh. "Profits! What profits? This place hasn't been in the black for months."

Lowering his voice in a conspiratorial tone, Mr. Jericho retorted, "What about prior years' profits? You wouldn't keep this place open if you weren't making money somehow."

Lydia glared at him. "You know full well the reason I keep this place open, and it has nothing to do with money!"

He shrugged and reached out to place a hand on her shoulder. This earned him growls from the Zuul around him.

"I meant no disrespect. Danny seemed like a good man."

"You haven't earned the right to speak his name," Lydia fumed while rolling her shoulder to displace his unwanted physical contact. "All that I have left of him is in this bar. He went out on a contract and never came back. If it wasn't for his death benefits, I wouldn't even have this place."

Mr. Jericho regarded the distraught woman before him. "Speaking of contracts, I might have a way for you to get in the black."

Lydia shook her head. "What?"

"Hear me out. With the end of the Omega War, Earth is in a better position. One of the Four Horsemen managed to sway the Mercenary Council to allow contracts again."

"That's great, but what does that have to do with me?" asked Lydia suspiciously.

"Well, it just so happens that Earth is offering start-up funds for new mercenary companies."

"Now I know you've lost your mind! I lost my husband on a contract. Why the Hell would I follow down that same path?"

"You need money to pay your back taxes, right?"

"So, you're suggesting that I beg the government to bail me out of my predicament in exchange for dying on some far-flung planet so someone or somebeing can control, conquer, or invade for credits? No thanks. I am *not* interested!"

"Lydia, please. Just think about it. For each displaced alien—" he turned to the two Zuul who were listening "—they are offering 100,000 credits to take them off world. You can pay your taxes with just these two." He indicated Jameson and Benji.

The Zuul lowered their hackles in consideration.

"Hmm, maybe the mutts are smarter than I gave them credit for…"

Lydia glared at Mr. Jericho. "That's enough. Get out!"

"Mrs. Price, I will be back tomorrow, and I must either collect payment, in full, for your owed taxes, or I will take the deed of your bar in lieu. I suggest you choose wisely."

He tipped his bowler hat at Lydia, then at the two Zuul as he slowly backed away toward the door.

Once he was well outside earshot, Lydia fumed. "That low life, no good, scheming, conniving, sack of shit!" she roared at the top of her lungs.

Benji and Jameson exchanged a glance. Benji opened his mouth but was cut off abruptly as Lydia turned her glare to him and arched a well-manicured eyebrow.

"I know what you're thinking," she started. "You both have been looking for a way home since you found this place. I knew our arrangement was temporary, but I never thought you would completely abandon me for a few credits!"

Jameson opened his mouth to reply, but Lydia beat him to it. "Don't bother. I'm going to bed. Lock up when you leave."

With that, she stormed up the stairs to her studio apartment and slammed the door behind her.

* * *

Jameson's gaze followed Lydia up the stairs, and he jumped when the door slammed.

Benji just chuckled. "And I thought our females were temperamental…"

Glaring at his friend, Jameson said, "She is just stressed. Moments ago, she almost took my head off with her ledger."

Benji walked over to the bar and picked up the heavy volume of numbered columns. "How could she throw this? It must weigh almost as much as she does!"

Jameson nodded in agreement. "Well, we cannot leave her like this. Perhaps we can persuade her to start a merc company. You and I are both honored warriors. We still have contact with others who were stranded here. Let us do some recruiting and see if we can change her mind."

It was Benji's turn to nod. "Sounds like a plan. You reach out to the other warriors. I will try the pilots, maintenance techs, and weapons experts. Between the two of us, we can scrounge up a few good mercs."

* * *

The next morning, Lydia woke to a cacophony of noise down in the bar. Groaning, she wrapped herself in her favorite purple robe, and slipped into her Ugg booties. Padding down the stairs, she almost fainted at the sight.

Dozens of beings congregated at the various tables in her establishment. On the top of the bar were no other than Benji and Jameson, and it looked as if they were holding court.

If only they could draw this large of a crowd every night, Lydia thought to herself. Running her fingers through her bed-matted hair, she reached the bottom of the stairs and cleared her throat.

Jameson looked at her and jumped down from the bar. "Good morning, Commander Price!" he announced a little too loudly.

"Commander?" she asked.

Benji appeared from behind the bar with a steaming cup of coffee and placed the white ceramic mug into her hands. At her confused expression, he said, "The commander had a late night conducting research on our next mission. Please excuse her disheveled appearance. I assure you; she is a human of unwavering professionalism."

As Lydia's jaw dropped in confusion, one of the beings in the crowd spoke.

"Then why is she dressed in sleeping garments and not in uniform?" asked a palomino Equiri. "Was she up so late, she forgot that she planned this recruiting event?" he continued with a snort.

Lydia looked from Jameson to Benji as a thought crossed her mind. Looking at the assembled snacks and pastries scattered throughout the dining area, she announced with a nervous chuckle, "Thank you all for coming! Please enjoy some refreshments as I confer with my lieutenants for a moment in private." Under her breath, she muttered, "Get upstairs. Now."

The Equiri started to protest when his companion, a dappled gray, placed her hand on his shoulder and whispered into his long ear. He nickered softly and kept his peace.

Once inside her room, Lydia whirled at them and said through gritted teeth, "Just what in the Hell are you two up to? I went to bed last night, cried myself to sleep over the thought of losing Danny's Dugout, and wake up to a merc convention downstairs? What are you thinking?"

Jameson turned to Benji, then spoke. "Lydia, we know how bad things are. After Mr. Jericho left last night, we looked through your ledger."

"You *what?*" fumed Lydia.

Jameson held up a paw to forestall another outburst, and continued, "Your book almost broke my snout when you threw it at me last night; I just had to look to see how bad it is for myself."

Benji continued, "We have a friend who deals with contract payouts for another, um, outfit, and she agrees with Mr. Jericho. There is no way out of the hole you are in, without seriously considering the government's offer."

Lydia turned beet red. "So, let me get this straight. First, you help yourself to my confidential information, then you invite a stranger to peruse through the records of years of my blood, sweat, and tears, and finally, you ask said stranger how bad off I am?" The last was said so quietly that even the Zuul's excellent hearing could barely make out the words.

Benji opened his snout to respond when Jameson punched him in the shoulder.

"How do you know that your 'friend' isn't secretly working for Mr. Jericho? What credentials did she show you to prove that she is just a merc with a knack for numbers? In this day and age, everyone is looking to get ahead at the expense of everyone else around them. For all you know, she snapped photos of my books with her pinplants and sent them to Mr. Jericho's office! You two have seriously crossed a line here." She flounced onto the bed and put her head in her hands.

"Lydia, we were just trying to—"

"Help? Is that what you were going to say, Jameson? Yeah, you sure helped me all right. Right off a—" Her sentence was interrupted by a loud knock at the bedroom door.

Throwing her hands up into the air, Lydia looked up at the ceiling, and uttered, "Now what?"

From the other side of the door came a translated, "Commander? I apologize for my intrusion, but may I enter?"

Jameson and Benji both reached for their holstered sidearms and approached either side of the doorway.

Lydia wiped her face and smoothed her hair before nodding to Benji, who turned the doorknob.

"Enter," said Lydia pleasantly with an air of authority.

A tall, winged being crossed the threshold with its wings folded around its body. "Thank you for seeing me," the sophont said, as it offered a clawed appendage for Lydia to shake.

Lydia stood and grasped the claw of the Sidar with a small smile. "What can I do for you?"

"Actually, ma'am, it is I who can do something for you."

Lydia looked between Jameson and Benji who hadn't moved from their posts at either side of the door. They both avoided her eye contact and ducked their heads like puppies being scolded for soiling the carpet.

"Seems everyone this morning is in a helpful mood," Lydia replied coolly. Both Zuul shivered with the noticeable temperature drop in the crowded room.

The Sidar continued unabashed, "Commander, or do you prefer Mrs. Price?"

"Lydia is fine."

"As you wish. Lydia, my name is Gallinaza, and I represent a being with a bit of a situation."

"Well met," Lydia responded. Then she asked, "What type of a situation?"

"You see, Sozruko holds several off-world facilities and one of them has come under attack. He would like to hire your company to evict the invaders and hold the facility from future incursions until he is able to deploy a security force."

Lydia shook her head and attempted to reply when Jameson cut her off. "Gallinaza here is our 'friend' who reviewed your books."

"Oh, is she now?" Lydia replied.

"I assure you, my peek into your finances had nothing to do with this offer."

"Uh-huh."

"Lydia, my employer considers himself somewhat of a philanthropist and wants to help those in need. He has done exceedingly well for himself and his fellow Zuparti with his many acquisitions over the years.

"He is so generous in fact, that he is willing to finance your entire start-up operation as well as pay all the back taxes on your bar."

"That is indeed generous of him," said Lydia suspiciously.

"Yes, this lost facility is of the utmost importance to him, and he always pays those who assist him handsomely for their time. He even offered bonuses for quick resolution on prior contracts."

"Really?" said Lydia with squinted eyes.

"Absolutely!" replied the Sidar. Leaning closer to Lydia, she whispered, "I took the initiative to look into your background, and I noticed that you do not have any warm feelings for your Earth government. I honestly cannot say I disagree; however, they seem to be trying to do what they can to help humans as well as other beings who find themselves, shall we say, stuck in a tough situation."

Lydia found herself nodding. *'Stuck' pretty well sums up my situation.*

"While I appreciate your employer's generosity, I must admit I am skeptical. No, I do not want to be beholden to the government, but how do I know that your employer won't try to take advantage of the situation?

"As you know from looking through my financials—" she glared at the Zuul who were still standing guard at the door "—I am in a bit of a pickle."

"A fermented and salty vegetable?" asked the Sidar.

Lydia chuckled. "Not exactly. And technically cucumber is a fruit... Anyway, to your point, I am stuck between a rock and a hard place. If I don't take the government handout, I lose my bar. If I accept your boss's offer and fail, I will lose my bar. And if I do nothing, I still lose my bar. So, what do I do?"

The Sidar looked at Lydia for a moment before taking her leave.

As she turned, she said, "I believe you humans have a saying. To 'trust your gut.' Although I am not sure what digestion has to do with decision making..." she trailed off.

Lydia followed her to the door and replied, "We have another saying, too. 'Don't make a deal with the Devil.'" *Although I may not have any other choice...*

* * *

After Gallinaza went back downstairs, Lydia changed into a more professional ensemble. She selected black cargo pants, a leather belt with holster for the Sig P320 Danny had given her as an anniversary gift the year before he died, and an olive-drab blouse with a collar. Donning a black pair of combat boots that she used for hunting, she marched down the stairs with her hair in a French braid.

As she reached the last step, Jameson cleared his throat and announced, "Sophonts and gentle beings, may I present Commander Lydia Price."

The gathered aliens stood and offered polite applause. Lydia waved them off, and Benji cleared his throat. Lydia raised her eyebrows at him as if to say, "What?" and he gave her a look that said, "You have to act the part of a commander, now."

She nodded and announced, "As you were." Everyone sat at the tables with empty plates in front of them.

Lydia stood behind the bar and surveyed the room. The Sidar was still present along with the Equiri couple she'd noticed earlier. At their table, sat two Lumar. In fact, each group of extraterrestrials appeared to have two of their number.

Holy shit! I wonder if this is how Noah felt when he started loading up the Ark, Lydia thought with a smile. She saw elSha, MinSha, and KzSha. Also present were Sirrakan, Pushtal, and Oogar, *oh my!* There in the far corner were two Tortantulas ridden by Flatar. *Nope, I am* not *dealing with giant spiders,* she thought as an involuntary shiver worked its way down her back.

Jameson gave her a "get on with it" gesture, and she addressed the room.

"Thank you all for coming. I apologize for my earlier attire, but I did not think we would receive such a large response to our invitation. For that I am humbled.

"Now that I see so many beings are interested in getting off world, that has made it easier for me to come to a decision. Welcome to the founding meeting of Price's Pilgrims."

Jameson stood and said, "We do not have firm details on our first contract, yet. Those will be finalized later this evening. We will consider whether your skills will be needed for this particular contract as part of our decision-making process. As far as payment, again, that will be determined by your knowledge, skills, and experience."

Benji added, "If you have questions of a more personal nature, please bring them to our attention when we meet with you privately. In the meantime, please help yourselves to the refreshments and let our staff know if you need anything specific." He motioned to the human server who had just entered the bar from the back entrance.

The man approached Lydia and asked, "What is happening?"

She leaned toward him and replied, "It's a long story, but I promise to fill you in later."

He nodded and started clearing empty plates away from the unusual "customers."

Lydia looked out at the crowd and invited them to come forward in two lines. Jameson had the right side of the bar and Benji had the left. Each alien stepped forward and spent about five to ten minutes with the Zuul interviewers.

As the last beings stepped away from the bar, the saloon doors swung open with a slam. "Mrs. Price, your time is up!" announced Mr. Jericho as he sauntered across the room. In his arrogance, he looked past the "clientele" and locked eyes with Lydia. She crossed her arms and stared him down when he was suddenly lifted off his feet by a long black pincer.

Through her translator came, "Ma'am? Would you like me to take care of him for you?"

Lydia's eyes went wide as she looked at the Flatar on the back of a massive Tortantula, whose fangs glistened. "No, thank you. Puh-please, put M-Mr. Jericho down."

"Are you sure?" the Flatar asked. Looking through the sights on her hypervelocity pistol she added, "I have a clean shot."

Catching her breath, Lydia remarked, "If you two can't follow simple instructions, I will be unable to consider you for future employment! Is that clear?"

The Flatar holstered her pistol and tapped the Tort beneath her rear-facing eyes. "Let him down, Ubu."

The Tortantula let out what sounded like a sigh and dropped Mr. Jericho onto the parquet floor. Not missing a beat, Gallinaza approached Mr. Jericho and helped him to his feet.

Lydia dared a glare at the Tortantula who seemingly rolled all ten of her eyes. The Flatar just chuckled in a high-pitched chipmunk-like squeak.

Gallinaza escorted Mr. Jericho to an unoccupied table and gestured to the human server for a drink. Lydia approached the table and sat down. "Sorry about that," she began. "I guess some of the new recruits are looking to score brownie points with the commander."

"Commander?" Jericho asked. After a sip of whiskey, his face reddened while his eyes brightened. "Ah, so you have decided to take me up on the government's offer?"

"Not exactly," said Lydia and she looked toward the Sidar seated next to Mr. Jericho.

Gallinaza continued, "My employer has made Commander Price an offer. If she accepts, he will pay the back taxes on the bar."

Jericho asked Lydia, "So, how do you plan to make the payment?"

Lydia looked to Gallinaza who handed her a slate. "All I need is your thumbprint."

* * *

Aboard the *Speedwell*
Docked at Karma Station

"What do you mean, they went 'AWOL'?" cried Lydia.

Jameson gave her an exasperated look. "Do you want the good news first, or the bad news?"

Lydia sighed, "Just tell me…"

Benji came to Jameson's rescue. "Well, we told you coming to Karma first was a mistake."

Lydia glared at him, but he continued anyway, "Yes, we know that is what you were instructed to do, but it was a stupid idea."

Jameson jumped in as Lydia fixed them both with a look that would wilt flowers.

"Yes, not your idea, we know. Anyway, coming to Karma was not the problem. We needed fuel and other supplies, so we had to come here. The problem was allowing our mercs to have liberty on the station."

Lydia was about to open her mouth, but Benji held his forepaw out to stop her. "The Pushtal and Jivool do not have the same sense of honor as us Zuul. Most of the marooned beings were looking for any excuse to get back home. By giving them a free ride to Karma, the most well-traveled and closest station to Earth, they bailed." He shrugged his furry shoulders.

It was Jameson's turn to glare at Benji. "I did say there was good news, remember?"

Lydia's eyes shrank from their saucer size, and she slowly nodded.

"OK, so we lost some heavy muscle. Like I said, the Jivool and Pushtal left and have not returned. We picked up some new recruits while here, though."

"New recruits?" asked Lydia hopefully.

"Yes," continued Jameson. "It turns out there were a number of humans who were stranded on Karma, and they want to get back to the fight."

"When we offered them another chance to 'Kill Aliens and Get Paid,' they were all too eager to join us," said Benji with a grin.

"So, who are these humans? Do they have training? Are they experienced? Do they have any of their own equipment? Sozruko only gave us enough CASPers for the people we hired back on Earth," Lydia advised.

"We remember," said Benji and Jameson in unison.

"Only one of the humans is an experienced CASPer driver," Jameson said. When Lydia looked like she was about to pull more of her blonde hair out, he quickly added, "But he has his own Mk 7 CASPer, *and* he said it has a special add-on that he upgraded himself."

"With the loss of some of our fighting force, beggars can't be choosers," Lydia sighed. "Have him bring his CASPer to the dock and we will get one of the elSha to perform a diagnostic on it. Whatever his 'special add-on' is, I don't want it to blow any of us up during the trip through hyperspace.

"Let's round everyone else up and get ready to leave. I don't want to run the risk of losing any more of our crew who are enjoying their 'liberty.'"

"About that," said Jameson.

"Now what?" whined Lydia.

"The Equiri are not back, yet."

"What?"

"You recall they are a mated pair, yes?"

"Yes, that was one of their stipulations for me hiring them. I had to take them both or neither of them. Since they both have ground combat experience, I didn't mind agreeing to those terms."

"Well, they mentioned something about having private time while on liberty."

"OK? We have been on station for 48 hours. How much alone time do Equiri need?"

Jameson shuddered. "I do not want to know."

A knock on the door prevented Lydia from saying anything further. "Enter," she announced, and then took an involuntary step back when the Tortantula and Flatar squeezed through the hatch.

I will never get used to those things. Taking a deep breath to compose herself, Lydia asked, "Ubu, Roz, what can I do for you?"

Roz spoke for the pair, which was common with Tortantula/Flatar teams. "We couldn't help but notice that you are missing a sizable chunk of your company."

Lydia's face reddened, but she nodded for Roz to continue.

"I just thought you should know that despite this adventure promising to be a complete and utter failure, we are in it for the duration."

"How kind of you," remarked Lydia.

"Do not misunderstand. Kindness has nothing to do with it."

"Think of the slaughter," Ubu said reverently while a trickle of venom dripped off her fangs and singed the rug covering the metal plate floor.

Roz waved the comment away. "Yeah, yeah, you are here for the slaughter. I am here purely for the entertainment value. No offense lady," she said looking at Lydia. "You have no idea what you're getting all of us into…"

"Now, wait a minute," Lydia fumed while Benji and Jameson's hackles started to rise.

Ubu stared them down, and they thought better about confronting the tank-sized spider inside such a confined space.

"No, seriously, I mean no disrespect," Roz continued while polishing the barrel of her hypervelocity pistol. "I am just stating a fact. One way or another we are all gonna die. Ubu and I are good with that, that is why we're still here. I just wanted to let you know that you do not need to worry about scouring Karma Station to find us.

"Besides, those lovebirds you were looking for just came back from their rendezvous. They look a little out of breath, but it is nothing some time in hyperspace can't cure."

With that, Ubu backed out of the doorway and the duo sauntered off down the corridor.

Lydia shook her head. "I don't know whether to be insulted, honored, or impressed. Who talks to their commander like that?"

Benji answered, "When you have your own personal death-dealing machine as a bodyguard, I guess you feel like you can say whatever you want to whomever you want any time you want."

* * *

Aboard the *Speedwell*
Hyperspace, En Route to Nommos

"Dude, your CASPer is cherry!" remarked the elSha technician.

"You need to stop watching twentieth century Earth Tri-Vs. It's corrupting your vocabulary," teased Lydia.

"No way," protested the elSha. "If anything, it is helping us to blend with the rest of the humans here."

William Finn agreed, "Yeah, these blokes really know their way around a CASPer. I can't remember the last time my baby purred like a kitten after a full body massage." His words affected an accent Lydia was unfamiliar with.

Lydia shook her head. "Where did you say you were from again?" she asked their new recruit.

"I come from the land down under, you know, Oz."

Lydia gave him a confused expression.

"No offense, ma'am, but you need to get out more. Aust-ra-li-a," he sounded out each syllable like he was pronouncing it for a preschool child.

Lydia retorted, "I'm not sure how to get more 'out' than off planet."

He chuckled and said, "Too right."

The elSha tugged on Lydia's sleeve and led her over to the waiting CASPer. It was eight feet of alloy steel with weapons mounted all over it. Peering at a box off to the side, Lydia asked, "What is that?"

"Oh, right. This is my 'special add-on.'" He beamed while his bright green eyes gleamed in appreciation. "Let me introduce you to 'Golly.'"

"What is it?"

"Well, my great-great-grandpa served in the United States Air Force. He flew the A-10 Warthog. When he retired, he and one of his buddies in maintenance 'acquired' some spare parts as mementos. One of those souvenirs stayed in our family for generations.

"When Pa heard I was joining a merc company, he wanted to make sure I had every advantage to complete the contract and get back home in one piece."

Lydia glanced at the deck plating and thought, *I wish Danny would have had that opportunity. If so, maybe he would still be alive, and I wouldn't have to be doing this to save his bar.*

Sniffing, she asked, "So, what does it do?"

He chuckled and opened the box. Inside was the largest crew-served weapon she had ever seen. Its seven barrels were thirty millimeters in diameter and 2.3 meters long.

Lydia whistled in appreciation.

"She's a beaut, right? Been with me ever since my first contract. She's a GAU-8 and once I rain fire on the enemy, they start wondering what is happening to them; right before they explode into a cloud of pink mist, that is." His eyes gleamed when he said that last.

Lydia shivered at his open display of bloodlust.

"So, you enjoy killing aliens?"

"Enjoy killing? No. I'm not a monster. I do what I must to continue living, so I can fight, and get paid, another day. You know what I mean?"

I can't say that I do, thought Lydia. Instead of voicing her inner opinion, she said, "That's the plan!"

The elSha from earlier interrupted them to ask, "Ma'am, I need some type of counterweight for Mr. Finn's CASPer."

"Why?" asked Lydia.

"His weapon is too heavy for the CASPer to fire unassisted. I need something to compensate for the weight of the weapon, otherwise it will fall backward before it even fires."

Finn waved the elSha away. "Don't worry, love. I haven't needed a counterweight before, and I won't need one now. As long as I can lean against a dropship, me and Golly will be just fine."

* * *

Approaching the Facility
Nommos

Their tanks rolled along the muddy path as the twilight of dawn lit up the southeastern horizon. Behind them, the CASPers would flank and keep an eye out for enemies on their backtrail. Out front, the Equiri and Oogar duos would act as force recon, relaying imagery from their slates and pinplants to the battlemap available to everyone else's HUDs.

Since she did not have "pins" and swore to never get them, Lydia would keep track of the battle on her slate. She had no combat experience but knew enough about combat to know that her company was better off with her out of the way.

They were the professionals; she just had to make sure they defeated the occupying force of Selroth and took back control of the facility for Sozruko. Once that was done, she could go home, and never think about the merc life again, or so she hoped.

"Godspeed and good hunting!" she announced from the crew compartment.

Lydia wore body armor at the insistence of Finn and her Zuul lieutenants. She was also armed with her trusty Sig P320 in a drop holster at her right thigh.

As they approached the opening to the facility, one that had been hidden from them on their initial recon of the structure, the hatch irised open. A lone Selroth emerged wearing a rebreather helmet. Through a translator, they heard, "Greetings honored warriors. To what do we owe the pleasure of your visit?"

"Ma'am, he doesn't appear hostile," observed Finn on their private channel.

"I concur, but it could be a trap. Be careful."

Finn walked his CASPer to the outside of their formation as another CASPer driver, Sia, did the same. From their vantage points, they could see inside the facility as well as any potential hostiles attempting to flank their company.

From inside her tank, Lydia broadcast, "Greetings. We are Price's Pilgrims on a contract to retake this facility for Sozruko, its rightful owner. Lay down your weapons and we can negotiate peacefully."

The Selroth looked behind him and more of his kind approached, all doubled over in what appeared to be laughter. Bubbles emerged inside their helmets and the tentacles on their faces spasmed as they tried to compose themselves.

Once the laughing fit subsided, the lead Selroth said, "You must be mistaken. This facility has belonged to my clan for generations. Whom did you say you represent?"

Lydia answered, "Sozruko. He hired us to evict those who infiltrated his facility. Are you one of the infiltrators?"

"Hardly. I invite you to come inside and see for yourselves."

Lydia cautiously climbed out of the tank and walked toward the facility entrance. Cabal and his Equiri mate flanked her along with Jameson and Benji.

The CASPers could not fit inside the opening, so Finn and Sia moved up to cover their boss from the entrance. On comms, Lydia heard, *"Ma'am, we're right outside. If you need anything, give us a shout and we'll blast our way in."*

"Copy that; thanks Finn."

As the Pilgrims followed the Selroth, he gave them a brief history of the structure while they descended toward the heart of the facility.

"I still do not understand why you have come," he began without preamble. "This facility has been ours for generations. How dare he call us infiltrators?"

His voice was free of emotion; however, that could have been due to the translator. If he spoke the truth and Lydia were in his fins, she would be fuming.

She responded, "I only know what my employer said: This facility was stolen from him, and you and your clan infiltrated it. He wants it back, so he hired me and my company to evict you."

Once again, the Selroth bent over in laughter. "You are welcome to try; however, our number is much larger than appearances would indicate. This facility is our home, and we will fight to keep it."

He stopped and turned around to face Lydia, staring down at her from an armlength away. Cabal stepped between them and let out a low growl in warning.

The Selroth continued, "I mean you no harm as long as you do not intend to bring any to my clan. As I said before, your employer is mistaken. Perhaps he lied to you."

Lydia took a deep breath while allowing herself time to think. After gathering her thoughts, she replied, "Do you have any way to prove your claim?"

The Selroth nodded like a human. "Indeed, I do. Follow me."

Cabal led the way, intent on keeping himself between Lydia and any potential threats. Jameson and Benji followed behind. The three made a triangle with Lydia securely in the center of their protective detail. Cabal's mate trailed them to cover any threats from behind.

They walked deeper into the tunnel, and Lydia noticed its lighting for the first time. It wasn't particularly bright, but it was more than enough to see by. Lining the walls of the tunnel were murals that looked remarkably like cave drawings from human history on Earth.

She saw depictions of celebrations and wars, hunts and gatherings. She even noticed a drawing of this very facility as it was constructed who knew how long ago. Stopping to admire the drawn depictions of their history, she felt the Selroth standing behind her. Her entourage tensed, but she waved them away.

Turning around, she met the Selroth's eyes and said, "If you had only been here a couple months, I doubt you would have had time to create these murals. Some of them are so faded, they are difficult to decipher what is being shown."

Again, the Selroth nodded.

Lydia continued, "I do not understand why Sozruko would lie about being the owner of this place. What does he have to gain?"

The Selroth looked deeper down the tunnel and Lydia followed his gaze. From the shadows another Selroth appeared. He was wizened with age, and instead of stepping lightly on the stone floor, he shuffled unsteadily. The younger Selroth approached him and offered an arm to assist in his locomotion.

As the elder approached Lydia, her bodyguards moved to defend her.

The elder waved his hand. "That will not be necessary. Our clan is peaceful. We do not harm others. Our only acts of violence are in defense of ourselves."

Looking again at Lydia he asked, "Will violence be necessary today?"

She shook her head. "No, you do not need to defend yourselves from us, but I wonder what will happen next.

"Gallinaza made it sound like this facility was important to Sozruko, so I doubt he will give up just because we fail in our contract."

Cabal looked gob smacked. "What do you mean 'fail our contract'?"

Lydia waved her arms at the cave drawings. "Look around Cabal! Obviously, we were duped! I was duped!

"This facility doesn't belong to him, and it never did! How can we evict this sentient civilization from the only home they have ever known? And for what? A Zuparti's greed?"

Flustered, Lydia muttered, "I'm going to lose everything…"

Jameson and Benji exchanged a glance and moved along the stone floor to her side. Cabal stared at her, jaw working furiously, but no words escaped from his long face.

Benji put an arm around Lydia and said, "Let's get you back to the ship before we make any hasty decisions, okay?"

She sniffled and nodded.

Jameson turned to the Selroth and said, "We have a few things to discuss amongst ourselves. Thank you for the hospitality. We will be in touch tomorrow."

"Very well," said the elder Selroth. "Until tomorrow."

The Pilgrims walked out toward the exit where Finn and Sia were waiting.

"Well, how did it go?" asked Sia.

* * *

Finn took one look at Lydia's pained expression and lightly punched Sia in the arm of her CASPer. "What was that for?" she protested.

On their private channel, he admonished, "You are great with tech, but not so great with people. By the expression on her face, things didn't go very well. Let's follow them back to the dropship. I have a feeling a change in mission will be forthcoming."

* * *

Back at the Dropship
Nommos

Lydia walked aboard the dropship and flopped into the co-pilot's chair. "Stupid, stupid, stupid," she muttered as she banged the heel of her hand on her forehead in rhythm to her outburst.

Jameson brought her a cup of tea, and she smirked at him. "Got anything stronger?"

"No offense, but now is not the time. We will all need clear heads to get out of this one."

Lydia nodded and ceased the self-deprecating mantra. She accepted the tea with a sigh. "OK, what do you suggest we do?"

Benji appeared from behind her and said, "Nuke them from orbit? It's the only way to be sure."

Lydia chortled at the old Tri-V reference. "Nuke who? It's not the Selroth's fault. They are as much a victim of Sozruko's scheming as we are."

"So, what do we do now?" asked Jameson.

"I wish I knew," Lydia muttered and stared out the canopy at the jungle surrounding them. "Do we know anyone with experience in these types of situations?"

Just then Finn entered the conversation. "I don't know what pissed in your Cheerios, love, but whoever it is will get a piece of my mind."

Lydia chuckled and said, "Let's just say our illustrious employer wasn't exactly straight with us."

"Are they ever?" asked Finn. "Seriously, I've seen more cranked shite since being a merc, than anything Oz could throw at me."

Lydia looked to Jameson for guidance, and he just shrugged. "Sorry, Lydia, but we did not have any dealings with the contract holders in our previous company. Or job was just to break shit and kill beings." He shrugged again.

Benji started to pant. "We were really good at it, too."

Just then, Ubu and Roz made an appearance. Lydia wondered how exactly Ubu had managed to squeeze herself into the overflowing cockpit, but here she was. Roz asked, "Did someone say 'break shit and kill beings?' We are in!"

Ubu added, "So much slaughter."

"Not yet, ladies," Lydia chided. "We need a plan first."

Just then, Sia pinged Lydia's slate, "*Ma'am? The* Speedwell *has been trying to reach you.*"

Lydia sighed. "I guess I can't hide in here forever. Can you connect all of us?"

Sia worked her magic and from the dropship speakers came, "Commander, we have a situation. Another ship dropped out of hyperspace and is headed to the planet. What are your orders?"

"Did you try hailing them?"

"They are not responding to our hails. If they have a transponder, it is not broadcasting."

Under her breath, Lydia muttered, "Great…" Her slate chimed with an incoming message. "Stand by," she ordered.

On her slate, the smug visage of her employer appeared. "Commander Price, are you successful already? It has only been a few days since you arrived."

"What are you doing here Sozruko?"

"I wanted to check in on my investments," he said with a sneer. "If the Selroth have already been evicted, and you are departing the planet already, I may have to give you a bonus."

"That won't be necessary," she replied.

"No?" Confusion covered the Zuparti's face. "Why would you refuse a bonus for a job well done?"

Lydia sighed. "Because the job isn't done."

"What do you mean?" the Zuparti raged.

Lydia took a deep breath and yelled, "You lied to us, you furry bastard!"

Sozruko stared at her with beady black eyes. "Lied to you?" he asked incredulously. "I paid you handsomely for a simple task and you failed." The last word dripped out of his snout with menace.

"You told us the Selroth took control of your facility, but it wasn't your facility at all! It has been their home for generations. You expected me to kick them out of their home?"

"You had one job," Sozruko argued. "Evict the Selroth and take control of the facility. I should have known better than to place my trust in a has-been bar wench!"

Lydia stared daggers through the screen. "Now listen here you little—"

"*NO!* You listen. I had a feeling you would fail to perform to my expectations. I am sending you a video and suggest you watch it. Now!"

Lydia's slate chimed again, and she selected the notification to open a video file. On her screen, a satellite image of the west coast of Earth appeared. As the view zoomed in, it condensed to Astoria, Oregon and a bird's eye view of Danny's Dugout.

She looked up from the screen in confusion. "What is this?"

"Keep watching," Sozruko instructed.

From the side of the screen, a cylindrical object zoomed toward the bar at breakneck speed. Vapor trails reached across the view as it drew closer and closer. Lydia let out a gasp as the missile collided with the roof, sending sparks and smoke high up into the chilly Oregon sky.

"What did you do?" Lydia asked breathlessly.

Sozruko's face reappeared on the screen. "You need additional motivation to complete your task. Consider yourself properly motivated. Now, kick out the Selroth before I do to their facility what I did to your precious bar."

Her slate went blank and dropped out of her numb fingers. In shock, she opened her mouth to speak with no success. Sia picked up the slate and set it on the seat next to Lydia just as she slumped bonelessly to the floor.

"She's in shock." Finn's voice came through the fog as many hands hoisted her from the floor and into the cargo hold.

"Lydia?" Jameson tried to rouse her. As her company milled around her, all she could think was that it was a good time to take a little rest. She had been through a lot lately and could use a nap. A prick on her arm brought her out of the mist, but then everything went dark around her.

* * *

"What did you give her?" Jameson asked the Jeha medic.

"Just a little something to help her relax."

"Relax! We need our commander to lead, not take a nap!" Finn protested.

"I'm okay, boys," Lydia said as she looked to Jameson and Finn. "Call a company meeting. I want everyone's input before we decide what to do next."

"Ma'am," asked Benji, "are you sure that's a good idea? Your home was just destroyed while you watched. Besides, you're the commander. You tell us what to do, remember?"

Lydia hung her head. "It's time to stop pretending. I'm a business owner, or I was; I know how to manage inventory, mix drinks, and run payroll. When it comes to being a merc, I am completely out of my depth.

"No more leading without advisement from my beings in the trenches. It's time I learn from the wisdom of others. Call the meeting."

"Yes, ma'am!" Both Jameson and Benji sketched a salute, while Finn and Sia stood at attention. Roz just backed Ubu out of Lydia's way so she could make her way off the cramped dropship.

"Give everyone five mikes, then meet me outside."

* * *

After Lydia splashed some water on her face and ran a brush through her unruly blonde hair, she felt ready to hear what her company had to say. She'd known this was a stupid idea from the beginning, but what choice did she have?

Sozruko had given her everything she needed to save Danny's Dugout, and all he asked in return was for them to make a few Selroth leave his facility.

But it wasn't his facility. He had lied to her, and to make matters worse, he destroyed her home and the only tangible connection to her deceased husband just to make a point.

How could she do what Sozruko wanted? The Selroth were the rightful owners of the facility. It had been their home for generations. Their history was literally drawn on the walls!

She looked up at the ceiling and thought, *Danny, I could really use your guidance about now. How did you always talk me off the ledge when everything went to shit? God, you would know exactly what to do in this situation!*

She fiddled with the wedding band on her left hand and imagined her husband in the room with her. His green eyes, his dimples, his scruffy beard that tickled every time he nuzzled her neck. *God, I miss you.*

A knock at the door brought Lydia back to the present. "Enter," she responded.

Cabal opened the door. "Everyone is assembled, ma'am."

"Thank you."

She followed the Equiri down the dropship ramp and into the crowd of assembled mercs waiting for her leadership. As she scanned over them, she felt a sense of calm she hadn't known in years.

These beings followed her to a no-name planet at the ass end of the galaxy. They were experienced mercs, surely they knew what a joke she was when they signed on to join the Pilgrims? What was it that made them follow her here? Why didn't these beings go AWOL at Karma like the Pushtal and the Jivool had? She looked over the group again and caught Roz's gaze.

Thinking back to what Roz had said before they departed for Nommos, she laughed. *I'm here purely for the entertainment value.* Maybe that was it. These mercs had seen death, and defeat. They were all stranded on Earth before Jameson and Benji had sent out the invitation to join up and go off world. Perhaps, they just needed a laugh. Or they needed hope. Hope that one day, they would get back home to their families and loved ones who were scattered across the galaxy just like them.

Now Lydia's home was destroyed; her entire reason for taking this godforsaken contract in the first place was a burning pile of rubble. What did she have left to fight for?

These thoughts raced through Lydia's mind. Steeling herself, she addressed her company, "As most of you may know, this contract is not what I thought it was. It was supposed to be simple: evict the Selroth and take back the facility for Sozruko. As we now know, Sozruko isn't the rightful owner. The Selroth have lived here for generations. This is their home.

"If someone were to try to take your home from you, what would you do? You would fight, right?"

"Too right!" yelled Finn from somewhere in the back of the crowd.

Lydia nodded. "My home was just taken from me by our employer. I can't in good conscious allow my company, *our* company, to do the same to the Selroth.

"I have literally *nothing* to offer you. Without Sozruko's credits, I am bankrupt. My bar is gone, demolished at his hands. The only thing I have left is my word that I will do whatever I can to make this right.

"Do we do what Sozruko wants, evict the Selroth and complete the contract? Or do we stand with them and defend their home from the very being who paid us to assault it?

"I am asking *you*. This is your company as much as it is mine. What would you have me do?"

Cabal was the first to speak. "Any merc company worth their salt completes the contract. If we don't, we lose our status with the Merc Guild, and we can never take another contract again. We are mercs. We do this for the credits." He snorted the last.

Roz was next to speak. "Speaking for Ubu, we are simply here for the slaughter. Whether we kill the Selroth or Sozruko, it makes no difference to us."

Jameson spoke next. "Zuul have honor. Yes, we should complete the contracts we take; however, if there is no honor, what is the point? Is it better to finish a dishonorable contract for the credits? Or do we do what is right, consequences be damned?"

"Zuul are not the only beings among you with honor," said the Oogar. "We may be known as 'big purple don't care bears' to Humans, but in reality, we have large hearts."

Lydia looked to see if anyone else had something to say. Seeing none, she announced, "I have made my decision. We will not fight.

"Anyone who wants to stay here and evict the Selroth, you have one hour to disembark. Everyone else, we will lift off and head back to Karma."

Cabal snorted again. "You mean to say you are going back to Karma?"

"Yes. If we are not going to complete the contract, I have to go to Karma to register the contract as uncompleted."

"Why didn't you say that from the beginning? Let us go to Karma and put this blasted contract behind us."

Lydia nodded. "Okay, everyone load up. I need to tell the Selroth we are leaving."

* * *

Dropship Cargo Bay
Nommos

As Lydia and her protective detail made their way to the Selroth facility, the rest of the company got to work preparing for their departure.

Finn looked longingly at Golly while stroking the arm of his CASPer. "Too bad we didn't have a chance to show 'em what we got, eh love."

The dropship speakers crackled to life, "Incoming!"

Finn ran the length of the hold and looked up in time to see three dropships scream across the sky in the direction of the Selroth facility. He keyed his comm, "Ma'am! Do you copy?"

"*Go ahead, Finn.*"

"We've got three bandits heading right for you!"

"*WHAT?*"

"Get as far away from the facility as you can. Golly and I got this! Finn, OUT!"

"*Wait, Finn?*"

He ignored Lydia and climbed inside his CASPer.

Once inside, he raced through the start-up sequence. Just as he was about to run down the ramp, Sia exclaimed, "Not without me, you don't!"

"You have to catch me first," Finn responded with a crooked grin.

He bounded down the ramp and engaged his jumpjets as he leaped through the dense foliage of the jungle canopy.

"*You couldn't wait for back up,*" complained Sia as she bounded toward him in her own mech.

"Like I told the boss, Golly and I got this."

His expression changed as a missile arced above them and into the mountain atop the facility.

"*Get down,*" yelled Sia as she dropped into the prone. Centering the sights of her MAC on the nearest dropship, she squeezed her hand into a fist to fire. Rounds spit out of the barrels, but only impacted trees in between them and her target.

"Let me," offered Finn, as his CASPer took a knee. Leaning back against a stout tree trunk, he aimed Golly into the air and fired. 30mm shells screamed across the sky and punched holes into the fuselage. Smoke billowed behind it. Before it could erupt into a fireball, the pilot banked hard toward the ocean, where it plummeted into the sea.

"*One down, two to go,*" observed Sia.

The other two ships came back around for another pass at the facility, but instead of a gun run, they orbited near the entrance.

"*Finn, what are they doing?*"

"Looks like making a delivery," he remarked as beings wearing battle armor slid down ropes from the sides of the craft. "Sia, you engage the new arrivals. We can't let them take out the Selroth."

"*Copy,*" she acknowledged as she aimed her laser at the armored fighters.

Finn took a deep breath, let it halfway out, then held it. As he waited for a space in between heartbeats, he lightly pressed Golly's trigger and was rewarded with another *BRRRRRT*. The projectiles struck true, and the dropship landed in a heap, right on top of the beings who had just disembarked.

From out of nowhere Roz and Ubu pounced on the wounded survivors and cleaned up the aftermath of the crash.

"*I think I'm gonna puke,*" remarked Sia as she watched the giant spider eat her way across the clearing.

Finn ignored her and said, "That's two. Where's the other one?"

A shadow loomed over the pair, and Finn looked up to see a small weasel leaning out of the dropship. Before he could speak, Sia turned her MAC on the Zuparti's craft and blasted a hole through one of the wings. The dropship fled before the Humans could inflict any further damage to it.

Sia helped Finn to his feet, and he pretended to blow the smoke from the end of Golly's barrels. "See love, we got our chance after all," he said with a proud smile.

"*Do you always talk to inanimate objects?*" asked Sia.

"Only when they keep me alive."

* * *

On the Trail
Nommos

Lydia's entourage met up with the CASpers shortly after Sozruko fled and started back to their dropship.

"Well, that's enough excitement for the next… forever," remarked Lydia.

"That was nothing," said Finn. "Just wait. The longer you stay in the merc business, the more drawn-out fights you'll experience."

"What makes you think I want to stay a merc?" she asked with a raised eyebrow.

Jameson and Benji held their breath waiting for her to explode.

Finn held his hands up in front of him and answered, "Let's just say that I don't know of any other person who could wrangle a ragtag group of oddball aliens and convince them to take a contract under a commander with zero experience, on a backwater planet, with the only payment being their honor remaining intact."

Cabal snorted, "We are mercs. We don't have any honor!"

Lydia chuckled and everyone else joined in.

After a moment, Sia said over her speakers, "I hate to ruin the mood, but what do we do now? Sozruko doesn't seem the type of being to give up. If we go back to Karma, who is to stop him from trying to retake the facility again, with a different company?"

"Good point," Lydia said. "I wonder…"

As she turned around to head back to the Selroth home, she saw a group of aquatics walking in their direction. She waved and waited for them to reach her group.

"Commander," the Selroth from earlier spoke, "are you still planning to leave?"

She was about to answer when Benji stepped in front of her. "That depends. Our business here is concluded… unless you have something to discuss with us?"

Lydia held her breath and waited.

"It would seem that we are not as well protected as we thought. Yes, we have numbers; however, your mechs and weapons are much more effective than our own. Would you consider staying here at least until we can find another company to relieve you?"

Lydia was about to speak when Jameson shook his head. "What are you offering?"

The Selroth looked at the ground while he thought. "We have plenty of room for you to live comfortably underground, all the food you could need, fresh water, it really is paradise."

Benji cocked his head to the side and remarked, "Uh huh. A vacation sounds great, but once we are done, how do we afford a ride home?"

"Speaking of home—" Lydia started to say, but Cabal cut her off.

"We are mercs, and for us to consider another contract, first any prospective employer would have to buy us out of the current one. Then, and only then, would we be able to consider a new opportunity. There is a code you know…"

Lydia raised her hand to her face in astonishment, but kept her mouth shut while she waited for the Selroth to respond.

After what felt like an eternity, he asked, "How many credits was your contract?"

Lydia gave him a number and bubbles erupted within his rebreather helmet. She turned back toward the dropship and quietly remarked, "I understand—"

"Wait!" the Selroth exclaimed. "You defended us when you did not have to and helped protect our home with no loss of life. We would be honored to agree to your terms."

Lydia pulled out her slate and typed up a new contract; this time to defend instead of assault the Selroth facility. After it was reviewed both by her mercs and the Selroth, they each placed their thumbs on the screen. A soft beep indicated it was complete and the funds that

Sozruko had given Lydia at the start of this experience were returned to him.

As they marched back to the dropship to tell the others, Lydia said, "It will be nice to get that weasel off my tail."

Jameson chuckled. "And to think, the whole reason you originally took this contract was to get in the black."

"So much black," remarked Lydia with a chuckle. "So. Much. Black."

* * * * *

Charli Cox Bio

Charli Cox is a fledgling author who has written quite a few short stories. Her professional experience had been as a Realtor, HVAC Business Manager, IT Office Manager, and freelance bookkeeper. She volunteers as the Legacy Media Director for SetOregonFree.com and is working to create an affiliate for The Libertarian Party of Oregon in Douglas County. An animal lover and #boymom, she lives in SW Oregon with her husband, two sons, an Arabian mare, and a Shepsky who thinks he is hooman. This is her first published work.

# # # # #

Chip by Mark Wandrey

Astrid Amunson struggled to sit calmly and wait as one after another applicant entered the office. A varying time later they would exit. Most were straight faced upon exit while some showed obvious disappointment or excitement. Of course, most were men. Her appointment had been for 13:30 hours but had mentioned there might be a wait, as applications were more extensive than anticipated. Yeah, it was already 15:00 and her stomach was growling.

She was searching her pockets for a protein bar when another woman came out of the meeting room, tears glistening on her cheeks. Astrid couldn't tell what kind of tears they were before the woman turned and hurried out of the waiting room, and her slate chimed.

"Astrid Amunson—the committee is waiting for your testimony."

So much for a bite, she thought and stood, putting her slate into its holder on her belt. She straightened her shirt and strode to the door. It opened as she approached, and she entered a security corridor. A voice spoke, "Please present your Yack."

A plate glowed red. She took her universal account access card, UAAC or Yack for short, and pushed it against the plate. "Recognized, Amunson, Astrid, Mercenary Guild registration..." and it rattled off the long numeric sequence. The plate turned green and the inside doors opened. After a calming breath, she walked through.

The meeting room was what she expected. A long table at the other end was set with nine chairs. The panoramic window behind the chairs showed a spectacular view of the Houston skyline, the starport with its startown to the left, and downtown to the right.

Each chair held a man or woman. It looked like six men and three women, all dressed in either military uniforms or business suits. None looked familiar except one. At the far left was a man in his thirties, though with worry lines making him look older. He appeared overweight but his Terran Federation military uniform had three stars on it. *I should know who that is,* she thought. There hadn't been time to keep up with current events, so she couldn't place him.

A single chair was placed in the center of the room, about three meters from the long table and facing it. The meaning was obvious. She walked smartly to stand next to the chair. Everyone at the table was concerned with their slates at the moment, so she waited patiently. Finally, the man in the center of the table spoke.

"Miss Amondson?"

"Amunson," she corrected. "Astrid Amunson."

"Ah, I see. Sorry about that. Ma'am. I am Dean Horowitz, the Director of Mercenary Affairs for the Terran Federation, and I was appointed chairman of the Phoenix Initiative Committee, sponsored by the Federation through a joint grant of private donors as well as the Council for Development and the Ministry of War. By presenting yourself here you have been accepted as a finalist for our grant competition. The purpose of these grants are to provide seed money for deserving mercenaries who wish to start their own company."

Astrid remained standing, waiting not so patiently while Horowitz ran down. Now that she was finally here, she just wanted it all over with.

"Ms. Amunson, do you have any questions before we begin?"

"No, sir."

"Very good, please have a seat." She did. "I'll briefly explain the process. As you're in the final stage, your proposal has been through three levels of review and gotten to this part. Sadly, we don't have the funds to give grants to all the remaining applicants at this point. Your review is one of the last, and we still have one grant remaining.

"Each of us are allowed to ask you up to two questions, which you can either answer or choose not to; it's up to you. If you don't believe you have the information you need to answer the question, you can have a few minutes to access the answers, but you cannot defer to a later date, as explained in your invitation.

"Please keep in mind these questions aren't for the purpose of deciding any special qualifications or assigning any guilt. Their purpose is merely to help us, the committee, evaluate on a case-by-case basis the most deserving of a grant. Do you understand?"

"Yes, sir."

"Normally you'll get the committee's decision within forty-eight hours unless we make a negative determination here and now. You shouldn't feel like you've failed if we do not choose you. Considering your age and experience, compared to many other applicants, just being in this room is an impressive accomplishment. Are you ready to begin?"

"Yes, sir." She swallowed, trying to work up some spit in a dry mouth.

"Very good. Okay, the first question will be from Ms. Cheng, who is the assistant director of the MST, the Mercenary Service Track."

An Asian woman cleared her throat and consulted her slate before speaking. "Good afternoon, Ms. Amunson. As you might or might not realize, because you're rather young, the MST is a legacy, or carryover program from the old Earth Republic, and was responsible for many thousands of young people entering the merc profession. Unfortunately, it was rather haphazard in its methods. We've endeavored to make them more effective."

"I was on the MST in school, ma'am."

"I see that. Your VOWs score was exemplary, in the top five percent. Overall, the new VOWs pay a little more attention to critical thinking. New CASPers aren't quite as reliant on muscles and more so on brain power. Are you hoping for the funds to help cover pinplants?"

"No ma'am." She brushed her medium length hair back to reveal the pinlink above her right ear. "I paid for my own as soon as I had enough credits."

Cheng nodded and made a note, but Astrid didn't know if that was good or bad. The woman continued.

"Very well. I see here you went straight into cadre after just a two-year associate's program at Idaho State University in…" Her eyes narrowed as she looked at a name she didn't know how to pronounce.

"Pocatello Idaho, ma'am. It's not a big town, just east of Twin Falls."

"Oh, interesting. Anyway, that is an MST-accredited program, though apparently not too popular."

"Idaho grows more farmers than mercs, ma'am."

"May I ask what drew you to mercenary service?"

* * *

"You got your homework done yet?"

"Almost, mom," Astrid said, stashing her slate in its backpack and pretending she'd been working on the school provided laptop all along. Her mother stuck a head in her room and saw exactly what Astrid wanted her to see, her daughter working hard on the crappy computer the school loaned her.

"You aren't playing with that slate your dad sent you, are you?"

"No mom," she said, a tiny smile on her face.

"You have a final in algebra tomorrow, if you blow that you won't make AP."

"I *know*, mom."

"Take a break for an hour and play a game, then get back to studying for the test."

Astrid's grin was ear to ear. Her mom chuckled and left her alone. The slate was a present from her dad. He was off somewhere fighting aliens. The slate would have cost her mom more than she made in a year; dad said it was "snack money." It was the coolest gift she'd ever gotten. Only the snooty rich kid who'd moved to Twin Falls from Seattle had one, and his was way older and way smaller. She happily pulled it back out of her bag and used the Tri-V projector to go back to fighting invading aliens.

It was less than an hour later when the doorbell rang. Glancing at her watch it was nearly 10pm. *Who would come by at this hour?* Her grandparents lived in Pocatello; there was no way they'd pop in uninvited. She got up and went to her door, popping it open gave a perfect, if sidelong, view of the front door. It opened toward her so all she saw was her mom.

"Yes?" her mom asked. Something made her take a step back from the door. For some reason Astrid felt dread. She couldn't hear the other person's voice, so she crept quietly into the hall.

"May I come in?"

Her mom nodded and backed up. The person who came in was dressed in a uniform, black with gold. A woman, tall and ramrod straight, hair in a ponytail. The logo on her shoulder was a person on horseback, firing a bow over their shoulder. Almost nobody on Earth would fail to recognize it, even a 14-year-old girl in Twin Falls, Idaho. Her mom was crying now, and Astrid's blood ran cold.

"Is he gone?" her mom gasped, shaking her head.

"I'm afraid so, in an act of extreme valor. I don't know if he ever told you, but his callsign was Snuffle Bear. He'd wanted Honey Badger, but it just didn't stick." She shook her head. "He said you'd want to know." She held out an envelope which her mom took with shaking hands. "With my condolences and the planet's thanks. He saved many lives."

Astrid's mother sank to her knees and wept, hands over her eyes. The woman turned and saw Astrid, dark gaze taking her in. "Your father was a hero," she said. "I'm sorry." The grief would take days to sink in. At that moment all she could think about was the look of calm concern on the face of Sansar Enkh just before she left.

* * *

"That was the end of the Omega War, wasn't it?" Cheng asked.

"Yes, ma'am."

"We lost a lot of good mercs. I don't remember seeing your family name among the lost."

"I'm not here for any favors."

"That's good, because your family won't get you any on this board. Meeting the commander of the Golden Horde made quite an impression on you, then?"

"She took the time herself to come to our house. The honor for a fallen soldier, it got me thinking. I pushed into the MST as soon as I began high school."

"The Republic Government took it out of pre-high school curriculum," Cheng said. "We've fixed that." She consulted her slate. "So, after graduating from the two-year program at Idaho State, you went straight into cadre with…"

* * *

"Welcome to Tom's Total Terrors," the drill instructor said, marching down the isle of double bunks. Astrid was the only woman in the rank of forty-four prospective mercs, but she wasn't the shortest. She'd gotten her dad's height, if not his build. He'd been a fireplug of a man; she was thin and carved taut muscle. "Or Triple T, as we prefer."

"We only accept fifty new recruits into cadre each year," another DI said. "Triple T goes back to just twenty years after the Alpha Contracts. We aren't one of the Horsemen, but we have just as storied a history."

"Dump your shit on your cots, get into PT gear, and be on the parade ground in five minutes!"

Astrid dumped the rucksack full of gear she'd been given and looked around for the locker room. It took a full second to realize everyone around her was stripping right where they stood.

"What are you looking for, little lady?"

It was the first DI who'd spoken. Astrid swallowed and looked for the bathroom. "You got four minutes now, girly. You gonna get to it or make an EEOC claim? Your daddy ain't here to get you out of this."

"Leave my father out of this," she snarled.

"Oh, daddy important to you?"

The punch she threw was aimed perfectly at his nose. An instant later she was bent over double, held in an armbar, her shoulder screaming in agony.

"You take a punch at your DI an hour in? Where you think that'll getcha?"

"Leave… my… dad… out… of… this," she gasped between spasms of pain.

"Who's you father?" he asked, sounding curious. She told him.

He released her arm, adding a little push that would have landed most people on their ass. She'd taken hundreds of hours of gymnastics, and instead was facing him immediately, arms at her side, fists clenched so hard her nails were drawing blood from the palms of her hands.

He looked her up and down, his face a study of lines and intensity. Slowly, oh so slowly, a tiny smile crept across his face. "Okay," he said. The DI turned and pointed to a door. "That's the women's head, there's a small shower in there too. Boys don't give a shit who sees their peckers, no matter how small they are." Laughter rippled through the barracks.

"Why didn't you say that at first?" Astrid demanded, massaging her shoulder.

"If you quit over that, you'd never make a merc. Many deployments have no head at all. You'll get over your shyness sooner or later." He leaned closer. "And once these guys are your battle buddies, they'd fuck up *anyone* who so much as looked at you sideways."

She was too shocked to answer. He just nodded and hooked a thumb toward the indicated door.

"I knew your old man," he admitted and gave her a respectful nod. "You're gonna take some shit for it, but now I get it. You've got a chip on your shoulder."

"And?"

"And now you only got three minutes. *Move, boot!*" he roared, and she moved.

"You've got a lot to learn before you're ready for anything."

* * *

Astrid gave a cry of exhilaration as she pushed the aging Mk 6 CASPer to the very edge of its endurance. Metal legs pounded against the muddy ground as tracers flew behind her.

"*Jesus Fucking Christ, Amunson, wait for the rest of the squad!*"

"Hurry up, slowpokes!" She laughed at them over the radio.

"*You can't push a Mk 6 that hard,*" one of the other boots in her squad complained.

Astrid grinned and she continued to push just as hard, reaching the cover provided by a crumbled dropship wreck before the tracers had done more than scratch her paint. "Bravo Six, in position," she commed, and raised the top of her CASPer high enough to get sensor data. The turret was visible.

"Bravo Six standby for backup."

Astrid checked the rest of her squad, which was pinned down next to a building as bullets bounced off the brickwork. "Taking the shot," she said under her breath, popping out from behind the wreck. Her shoulder-mounted MAC was still coming down when the rocket hit her square in the chest, splattering her with paint.

"*Amunson, you are* dead!"

An hour later she stood in her haptic suit, dripping sweat because the barracks wasn't air conditioned, the rest of her squad lined up with her.

"Why are you dead?" Nobody responded to the DI. "I said, *why are you dead?!* Nobody? You're dead because you didn't act as a squad." He walked to within an inch of Astrid's nose. It took everything she had to not flinch back. "Nobody?"

"My squad didn't keep up," she said quietly, instantly realizing it was a mistake.

"You didn't wait for them! A CASPer squad is no more powerful than its parts. As squad leader, you were the lynch pin that held it together. Why did you run ahead of them?"

"I knew what my CASPer was capable of. I went over every millimeter of it."

"You did? That's outstanding! Did the rest of your squad?" She blinked in confusion. "Did you go over their suits with them?"

"No," she said, casting her eyes down. "No."

"No, you didn't. Those suits are old, by modern standards positively ancient. We have you work with them because if you can push a Mk 6 into combat, you'll do better in a Mk 7, or even a Mk 8. But no, you didn't hold that squad together, you left them. You were killed before taking the objective. The rest of your squad then tried to rescue your dead ass and died as well."

"They shouldn't have come after me."

"You couldn't tell them that, because you were *dead*, Private Amunson."

The grilling went on for another twenty minutes in the oppressive Mississippi heat. To her squad's credit, none of them said a word afterwards. Their surreptitious looks were worse than accusations. Later, after chow, the DI caught up with her again.

Astrid jumped to attention, but he made a gesture. "At ease, I just wanted a word."

"Yes, drill instructor?"

"That was some of the best driving I've seen from this class of boots, and with you rattling around inside a Mk 6 like the last pea in a tin can."

"Why didn't you say that before?"

"Because it was the worst leadership I've seen. God damn it, Amunson, you've got the makings of a real leader. But, because of your old man, you've got a chip on your shoulder the size of a *Phoenix*-class dropship. If you don't learn to balance that chip, use it as fuel instead of letting it burn you, you'll end up dead and you'll take more men with you." He didn't ask if she understood or not; he just left.

The next morning at equipment check-out, the cockpit of her Mk 6 had new paint. "Astrid "Chip" Amunson.

* * *

"What did you learn in your time with Triple T, Ms. Amunson?" Director Cheng asked.

"I learned if a leader doesn't act with the interest of their team foremost then she's not worth her stripes, ma'am."

Cheng nodded and made some notes. "Thank you," she said and went back to her notes. The portly man on the end in uniform hadn't looked up the whole time. He was either looking down at a slate in his lap or had nodded off. He didn't look old enough to Astrid for him to nod off in the early afternoon.

Horowitz cleared his throat and spoke. "Thank you, Director Cheng. Next up is Commander Grayson Boyer. He's a former merc and is now the Federation Mercenary Guild Liaison reporting to Speaker Shirazi."

"Good afternoon, Ms. Amunson."

"Sir," she replied.

He consulted his slate. "You were with Triple T for a year, is that correct?" She nodded. "You didn't see your first combat there, though."

"No sir. We were deployed on two missions, both garrison contracts that went without major incident."

"You did command a section, though?"

"First contract as a sergeant, with a squad. Second contract I was a provisional second lieutenant with a platoon."

"Good marks by your commanders," he said, nodding as he read. "I know Benjamin, the owner of Triple T. He said you had platoon leader qualities."

"They're not a combat unit," Amunson said, cutting him off. "After the Omega War they concentrated on garrison. The opportunities to advance were through retirement, not attrition."

"I see. What would you say was the most difficult situation you faced as a provisional officer?"

* * *

Astrid rode her jumpjets down to a solid landing. The parking structure shuddered but took her Mk 7's weight. Eleven more CASPers thundered down behind her as she deployed her suit's sensors, reaching out to the twenty-odd remotes flying around the east side of town. A moment later one of Triple T's rare Mk 8s flew in. 500kg lighter than the Mk 7s, this one was equipped as a scout with more powerful jumpjets and sensors.

"*Lieutenant,*" the scout reported as he grounded.

"Corporal, what did you find?"

"*Nine companies have disembarked from their landing on the western ridge.*"

"Are they advancing?"

"*Negative.*"

Astrid chewed her lower lip. They only had two companies of Triple T on Bastrada. More than enough to hold the factory complex, but not nearly enough to face over four times their number in a standup fight. "Why aren't they advancing?"

"*They're Aposa, Lieutenant Amunson.*"

"Aposa?" Her worry turned to amusement. Aposa were about half the size of a Human. "Heavy equipment? Tanks, missiles, or arty?"

"*Nothing lieutenant, just ground forces. I spotted some squad-supported weapons, but right now they're just bivouacking around their dropships.*" A feed from his CASPer came to hers. On the Tri-V built into her CASPer's cockpit she noted their deployment. The only cover they had was their own ships.

"Captain Stanley?" she called over the command frequency.

"*Go, Amunson.*"

"Recon report is in," she said even as she was punching in details to the file going to her commander.

"*Noted, if they haven't advanced toward our position, fall back.*"

She finished punching keys and transmitted. "If we use Company B, we can hit them from two sides and keep Company A at the complex."

"*That's a solid plan, Lieutenant.*"

"Shall I coordinate with the other platoon leaders?"

"*Negative, fall back as ordered.*"

She gaped. "But sir, they're wide open."

"*Again, noted. We're on garrison for this industrial complex. Our contract is clear.*"

"The Aposa are rabid. Once they realize we're thoroughly defended against light attack, they'll turn on the civilians."

"*Not our problem.*"

"But Captain, look at the—"

"*Return to the perimeter, provisional Lieutenant Amunson!*" The last words were a hiss.

"*Lieutenant?*" her platoon sergeant asked on their private channel. "*I know what you're thinking, but we can't do it without support. They might be a soft target, but there are over a thousand of them.*"

"Eric," she said to her sergeant, unable to keep the pleading note out of her voice. "The civilians?"

"*I know,*" he said. "*I know. Orders?*"

The following seconds seemed to stretch out to days, then a voice came out of her mouth which didn't seem like her own. "Form up, RTB."

"*Roger that,*" Eric said. "*Everyone, return to base.*"

* * *

"What happened the next morning?" Boyer asked.

"You've got the reports, you know. The Aposa sent a platoon to scout our position. After we mauled them, they returned to the rest of their forces and took it out on the city. Sacked, burned most of it, and then left in their ships unopposed."

"Did you complain?"

"Formally, to Commander Benjamin. He noted my tactical decisions as sound but supported Captain Stanley's field command decision. A favorable review was entered in my contract, and I was affirmed at the rank of Lieutenant."

"Didn't sit well with you, did it?" Boyer asked.

"No," she said, the memory of the burning town and screams of the natives echoing in her mind. "It damned well didn't. I resigned from Triple T as soon as we got back."

"That's all," Boyer said, nodding to Horowitz.

"Thank you," Horowitz said and looked down the table. "Next up is Mr. Valter Stenström, managing director of Binnig North American. He was the lead engineer who helped develop the Mk 6 CASPer.

Astrid's eyes widened. The little man didn't fit the Scandinavian Viking image in her head. He was no more than 50 kilograms and maybe 130 centimeters tall. His completely white hair fell to his shoulders, and he had a little pointy Van Dyke beard. Yet his eyes held vast knowledge and intensity the likes of which she remembered from that horrible night when Sansar Enkh visited her home.

"Guut aftarnuun, miz Amunson," he said in a thick accent. "It iz a pleasure to meets you." His head gave a little bow.

"Same here," she said. "I've spent a lot of hours in Mk 6 CASPers."

"And how do yoo finds zem?"

"Roomy," she said with a smile.

"Yez, of course. You moost understood, vin vee developed dem, the driverz ver all kvite large, yez?" She nodded. "Gut, gut. So, Mizz

Amunson, can you tell me your next assignment? Vuz not dis du firs time yu vuz injuud?"

Astrid blinked and shook her head. "I'm sorry, what? Injuud?"

"Yu knoz, injuud? Hoort?"

"Oh, injured!" A hand unconsciously ran down her left leg and she nodded.

* * *

"Sergeant, are you okay?"

Astrid shook her head and instantly regretted it. A man in medic armor swam into view, the weird double-headed eagle thing of the Varangian Guard for his unit patch was prominent, if a little chipped.

"Yeah," she said. "What the fuck happened?" Then she remembered. A wave of light rockets from a rooftop 250 meters away hitting her like a sledgehammer over and over again. "How's my ride?"

"Your CASPer? It's swiss cheese. I'd be more worried about you."

"What do you—*yeaa!*" Sitting up was a huge mistake. Her left leg was agony. She immediately checked; it was still attached, but wrapped in a quick-curing cast from below the knee to her ankle. "How bad?"

"No penetration," the medtech said. "Spalling from the armor. Those CASPers are tanks."

"Give me something for the leg so I can get up."

"Not standard procedure, sergeant. We wait for a medical evac."

"In case you didn't notice, we're in house-to-house cleaning. The Tsar ain't sending in a VTOL to get a sergeant with a busted leg. So, you either give me a shot so I can contribute, or I'll crawl over to my fucking ride, dig out a handful of CASPer candy, and self-medicate the shit out of myself."

"Well, if you put it that way," the man said and dug into his kit. "Sorry, you know the Tsar's rule on medical nanites."

"Yeah, only for life-saving intervention," she said, repeating the order verbatim.

He came back to her with a disposable syringe. "Show me some ass."

"Pervert," she said and tugged down the side of her BDU pants. "You already cut up a perfectly good pair."

"They were shredded by the spalling, quit being a baby." A needle pierced her buttock, and the sting became a wave of fire.

"Ouch." The pain in her leg began to wane with surprising speed. "Hmm, that's better."

"No problem."

Astrid found a piece of metal debris the right length to use as a crutch and with the medtech's help leveraged herself to her feet.

"You good, Sergeant?"

"Yeah," she said, looking over her mangled CASPer. "Go help someone who's hurt."

"Take it easy," he said and grabbed his kit. "Oh, hey?"

"Yeah?"

"Nice ass."

* * *

"Yoo handled dat vell," Stenström said.

"Thank you, sir."

"Vut I am moor interest in vut happen immediate after da injury."

"What do you mean, sir?"

"Your lef leg, it iz hurt bad? What did you den du?"

* * *

Astrid verified for herself, her trusty Mk 7 CASPer was well and truly fucked. One of the MinSha rockets had tagged her right in the mech's brainbox. The cute medic had to use the emergency explosive bolts to pry her out. The central torso and left leg were drenched in her blood. She swallowed and realized she might have died from such an injury.

"Not looking forward to writing Mom about this," she mumbled and dropped onto the CASPer's chest. Pain shot up her leg, and she cursed. She'd been jacked with some good stuff, definitely. But drugs still had their limit if you remained upright and at all coherent.

"Sergeant Amunson?" A CASPer was slouching into the alley, smoke rising from several joints.

"Private Ivanov, you look like shit!"

"Dah," the private said. His Mk 6 came to a stuttering stop, just managing not to fall over. The cockpit hissed and rotated up to expose the driver, a young Russian man maybe a year older than her.

"What happened?" she asked.

"The bugs, they had a weapon I haven't seen. The lieutenant thought it was a laser, but the beam was more like a flashlight, dispersed blue light…"

"EMP," Astrid said. "We've started to see them sometimes. The Mk 8s are immune, but our older CASPers get wrecked by them." She nodded slowly. "Makes sense the MinSha have them."

"We are mostly Mk 6 and Mk 7," Ivanov said, then cursed in Russian too quickly for her to follow. A few months with the Varangian hadn't been enough time to absorb *that* much Russian. "We need to call the Tsar, order a withdrawal."

Astrid accessed her pinplants, purchased after the last contract bonus. The few weeks of practice had yet to make her an expert with the brain implants. Hardly basic proficiency, truth be told. She had at least mastered using them to link with the battlespace. Luckily Private Ivanov's CASPer was still full up, so she used his link. As a sergeant, she had access.

"Jesus," she hissed after a moment.

"What?"

"We're behind the lines. The Tsar already pulled back Third Platoon. It was stored in the message buffer, but comms are down now. We're hanging out in the open." No sooner had she spoken than the rest of Ivanov's platoon came straggling in, most in as bad a shape as he was. Her squad was safely behind the lines; the lieutenant had verified she was okay then bugged out. She didn't know if he'd been aware they were about to be overrun, but it was sure as shit going to come up in the debrief.

"What da fuck are we going to do?" Ivanov demanded.

Corporal Campbell, one of the few non-Russians like Astrid, in a still operating CASPer, had popped his cockpit open and was using pinplants to analyze his ride's systems. "Take the two most functional CASPers and the rest go on foot?"

"If we get in a pitched battle, we're dead," Astrid said, then pointed to the three-man medical team waiting nearby. They had a flyer, but if it took off behind enemy lines the MinSha would turn it into confetti.

"You're senior, Sarge," Ivanov said to her. "Your call."

She knew the smart move would be to find somewhere for the medics and wounded to hunker down while she took one of the two remaining operational CASPers along with Ivanov, who wasn't injured, and went for reinforcements. Once outside the MinSha jamming they could relay the situation.

The problem was the probability the bugs would backtrack her escape route and find those left behind. With no more CASPers and several others injured, it would be a slaughter.

"I'm not leaving anyone here for the bugs," she said and hobbled over to the medic's flyer. First she thought maybe everyone could climb on and the troopers could provide fire against anything. It only took a minute for her to be sure it wouldn't work. The flyer could handle six people, maximum. With the medics they were nine.

The medic who'd treated her, the one who'd complimented her butt, came over. "What are you doing with our MEDEVAC?"

"Thinking about a plan." Not on her back in pain, now she could focus on his uniform. "Private Chen? Most medics don't have rank."

"I used to be a CASPer driver, like you."

"What happened?"

He pointed at his temple where a pinlink was visible. "Didn't go well. Damage wasn't too bad, but I have a hard time processing threats. I get all jammed up." He gestured at all the medical equipment. "Funny enough, not this kind of stuff. I'm fine doing medical, so here I am." He put a hand on the sidearm on his hip. "I still carry, though."

"Only smart," she agreed, then opened the main control access panel. "This is all V-tech systems?"

"Yeah, they did all the flight avionics for these flyers. Why?"

"Because the Mk 6 uses V-tech avionics. The Mk 7 I'm driving doesn't, but it's chewed to shit anyway."

He stared at his flyer in alarm. "What are you going to do?"

"Improvise," Astrid said, pulling control modules. She ignored his howls of protest about how he'd signed the flyer out of the motor pool. "Hey, if you want to wait here for backup, or for the MinSha to show up and deal with you, be my guest. Since you don't have a lot of direct combat experience, you might not know what MinSha do with captured enemies."

"If they're not officers, they usually just kill them," Chen said, looking a little green.

"Bingo. So, you helping, or not?"

He grabbed the control bus to disconnect its various connections with a vigor.

Two hours later, under the protection of four "nominally" functional Mk 6 CASPers, Sergeant Astrid "Chip" Amunson led five people out on foot, with another on a stretcher. A single squad of MinSha had tried to flank them. Astrid and Campbell turned their assault at great personal risk to their lives. At least, that's what the Tsar put on her official commendation.

Private Chen utilized a more personal method of expressing his gratitude for getting him out alive. She enjoyed his gratitude several more times before leaving the Varangian Guard, but that never went into the official logs given to the Phoenix Initiative board members.

* * *

"Dat is de firs time you were given a commendation, yes?" Stenström asked.

"Correct, sir."

"Yu also were writ up fer de fryer, yes?"

Astrid nodded.

"Du yu regret dis?"

"No in the least," she said, looking him square in his pale blue eyes.

"I haz no moa qvestion," Stenström said and made a note in his slate.

Astrid fumed. She'd saved that squad *and* the medics, but all he was worried about was being written up for the fucking flyer? She could see the way this was going. No grants for people who take risks or are worried about people's lives, both innocents or in her unit.

The next two questioners were quick and unmemorable. One was a bank person and asked about her prospective TO&E. She answered his questions, and the next one, a lawyer specialized in mercenary law. Stenström's question rattled her enough to lose track of where she was, and what she was doing. It only made her madder.

Horowitz was speaking again, and she almost missed it. "The next to last speaker is Tracy Copp, owner of Arizona Aerospace."

Astrid was a little surprised to see an older woman in the group. The lady had blended into the background and somehow avoided Astrid's notice, which was interesting. The name tickled the back of her mind.

"I'm actually just the chief engineer," the older woman said. "I hold majority share, but I haven't run the company for almost twenty years." Astrid merely nodded, confused. "Ms. Amunson, for a young merc you've had an interesting career."

"I'm just getting started."

Copp's eyes narrowed.

"Ma'am."

A hint of a smile crossed the woman's lips. "So, up till now all the questions have revolved around your creativity, leadership, and planning. What I want to know is how you handled your first HALD drop."

Astrid felt her blood run cold. "I'd rather not, ma'am."

"Are you refusing to answer my question?"

She hesitated, instantly uncertain, as now everyone at the long table were no longer working on their slates, they were all watching her. "Mr. Horowitz did say that was my right."

"It absolutely is." Copp made a note in her slate and then raised an eyebrow. "Is that what you're doing here?"

Astrid didn't know why she was surprised her first orbital drop came up. It was all in her merc file. The good, the bad, and her first HALD drop.

* * *

"This is what you trained for!"

"Yes sir!" the squad roared. The dropship was so loud they could barely hear each other. The lieutenant went on.

"High Altitude, Low Deploy is the signature operation here at Simpson's Smashers. Commander Eric Simpson helped pioneer the HALD operation. Many brave troopers have crashed and burned developing all the knowledge you've been given. Your squad are all rookies, which is why I am in command." His eyes found Astrid. "Follow your sergeant, Chip, and she'll see you safe to the ground." The five men around her all roared, pumping their armored fists in the cramped space. "See you on the ground." A second later Astrid's command comm channel beeped. *"You good?"*

"Yes, Lieutenant," Astrid responded.

"I know it sucks to put you in charge of all these kids, but we don't have a choice. Renova is a hard target, and the Skipper has every swinging dick… shit, every trooper we have, in a suit ready to drop in."

"It's okay, sir. I've done nine drops, just never under fire." Her regular uniform had a HALD tag, silver. After this, she'd get a gold one. The ridiculous, stylized CASPer, hanging under a parachute was the most coveted pin a CASPer driver could wear. It's the main reason she'd joined Simpson's Smashers. Next to Cartwright's Cavaliers, they were the second best HALD unit out there. With any luck, this was her springboard to the Four Horsemen.

Multiple G's slammed into them, compressing Astrid into her CASPer's padding. The Mk 7 she wore now was much newer than anything she'd ever driven; it had been built a few years ago as part of Binnig's comeback after the damage they'd suffered during the Omega War. The internal controls and computer were brand new, upgraded to work with her pinplants.

"You'll do fine," the lieutenant said, smacking her shoulder with an armored hand. *"Two minutes to drop."*

"Roger that, sir."

Another heavy G shock as the dropship pilot maneuvered with its squadron, trading off energy for a more ideal drop orbit. She'd dropped from as high as 800 km, and as low as 450 km. The dropships were using a parabolic course, dropping their CASPers at the bottom of the arc for more initial velocity. Her briefing said they'd get the green light somewhere around 250 km, just a hair's breadth above Renova's atmosphere.

As an NCO on the drop, Astrid was tuned into the dropship-linked operations channel, so she knew the instant everything went sideways.

"Slamdunk Three, I've got active seekers!"

"Slamdunk Four, confirmed. Smoke in the air!"

Astrid blinked. Did that mean what she thought it meant?

"*Slamdunk One; abort, abort, abort!*"

Before the first instance of abort was out of the flight leader's lips the dropship's engines roared, slamming the suited mercs against the pads in their cockpits with brutal force. Because the CASPer was configured for HALD, Astrid's suit had G-meters and other flight instruments. In less than a second they went from 2.4 Gs to over 8 Gs. This was bad. This was *very* bad.

She clenched her abdominal muscles and spoke. "Wellness... check," she grunted to her squad.

"*Nielson... ok.*"

"*Baker... ok.*"

"*Reed... ok.*"

"*Chu... ok.*"

One hadn't called. "Booker... respond." Her pinplant link to the squadnet showed Booker as his telltale went from green to amber. "Lieutenant?"

"*Driver says... nothing... just... hang on!*"

In another second, the G forces increased slightly, and Booker's vitals began flashing yellow. *Damn it,* she silently cursed.

"*Drones!*" one of the dropship pilots screamed.

Astrid was just wondering if that was her pilot's voice when they were hit.

* * *

"How many of you were hit?" Copp asked.

Astrid swallowed. "Out of the ten dropships Simpson's Smashers had, eight were hit. Two of those limped back to orbit." She fought to keep her voice even as her emotions roiled.

"And yours?"

"It's in the logs, ma'am."

"Indulge me."

"Is that your second question?" The old woman nodded slowly, and Astrid hissed in annoyance. The hiss turned to a sigh, and she continued.

* * *

Dropping through the atmosphere in an out-of-control dropship turned out to be much worse than in the protective heatshield/cocoon of a CASPer drop pod. Much, much worse. A straight-in HALD drop was brutal G forces from your feet up. You had some extra padding in your CASPer, and the drop pod let you hold a somewhat-reclining position. As the dropship spun wildly, she grew to understand how an ice cube in a blender felt.

"We're trying to level our descent!" the pilot yelled over the PA.

"*Can you drop us?*" the lieutenant asked.

"Negative," the pilot said. "We already tried." The dropship shuddered. "We're below their fighter and drone screen. Prepare for a hasty landing."

"*You heard them, squad. Set drop controls for landing!*"

She didn't need any more prompting and instantly used her pinplants to override the CASPer drop pod's own sensors and tell it they were about to land. Hopefully the gyros would help.

"This is it," the pilot said a heartbeat before they hit. The world went black.

She didn't know how long she had been unconscious. Probably not too long. Amazingly, she wasn't in extreme pain, but then realization set in. Her left arm was numb. The pinplants were no longer linked with her CASPer, so Astrid used her right-hand palm controls to access the suit. It was on battery power only, none of the main features were working. Her beautiful new suit was DOA.

"You in there, Chip?" a gruff voice asked.

"Yeah!" she yelled to her lieutenant. "Suit's dead!"

She felt someone leaning on the suit and tried to wait patiently. Not an easy thing with her arm numb.

"I'm popping the emergency release," he said. "Watch your eyes."

She did the best she could to turn her head as the explosive bolts blew. Flecks of hot metal peppered her, a few burning through her haptic suit. Luckily none got her face or set anything on fire. He pulled the disabled cockpit up and away revealing the interior of the wreck that had been a dropship only minutes ago. Surprisingly, it was in one piece. The lieutenant was out of his CASPer and had blood flowing down the right side of his face. Other than that, he seemed fine.

The crew section was *bent*, and they were lying on their side. Broken electrical conduits sparked and flashed like some kind of crazy photoshoot. Hydraulic fluid was running from severed lines, and everything smelled like blood and burned insulation.

Her squad was strewn around the bay of the dropship. She couldn't tell who most of them were; the crew was too new to have customized their CASPers. However, one suit was impaled on a strut, the metal protruding out of the center of the cockpit, the titanium dripping red. Unit number on the suit was 2091, Private Booker. It was his first HALD, and his last.

"How bad?" she asked the lieutenant.

"Just you and me, Sergeant. Everyone else is flatline."

"Oh my God."

"Let's worry about getting you out of that suit first."

She'd extracted her right arm and was releasing the suit's harness. He finished it for her and grabbed her right hand and pulled. The numbness in her left was gone, replaced by brilliant agony. She screamed and her vision swam.

"Jesus," he said, leaning over to her left side. "Your CASPer's arm is folded into the bulkhead. I need to find the medkit," he said. Before he could find it, an explosion shook the dropship making the lieutenant fall sideways and flooding the bay with dark red light from Renova's star.

Astrid was considering another attempt to free her hand when she heard growling hisses and froze as her translator worked. "Do not move, Humans." Her pinplants informed her the language was HecSha.

The lieutenant didn't seem interested in following reptilian orders. He dove sideways and came up with a heavy machinegun blazing. In an instant he was gone, engulfed in white-hot lasers. Tears rolled down her dirt-covered cheeks as she listened helplessly to the HecSha digging through the remnants of her squad until they found her. "You want fight too, Human?"

"I'm pinned," she said, or she would have tried. Her sidearm was secured in the thigh compartment of her disabled CASPer. It might as well have been a light year away.

"Pin? How pin?" The blunt, flattened head of the HecSha trooper came into view. They looked a lot like some Earth dinosaurs, even with stubby spines around their flattened heads. Those dinosaurs had been herbivores. The HecSha were merciless killers, one of the most feared merc races because of those traits.

The trooper moved around her, examining her CASPer and how she was trapped. Then it spoke. "You pain?"

"Yes," she said.

Lips pulled back over razor-sharp teeth. "Good." It grabbed her and pulled. Her screams were mercifully short.

* * *

"That's the first time you ever lost anyone in your command?"

Astrid nodded, unable to keep a couple tears from rolling down her cheek. She flexed her left hand against the memories, metallic muscles moving under the nearly perfect synthetic skin. The cutting, the screaming, the completely senseless violence.

"You were ransomed from the HecSha two month later?" She nodded.

"And the Slammers were wiped out."

"Not completely," she said, then shrugged. "I think they still do small-scale ops. They lost most of their gear and the insurance payouts almost bankrupted them."

Ms. Copp nodded at her and gestured to Horowitz that she was done.

Astrid raised her hand. "Ms. Copp?"

"Yes?"

"May I ask why you asked about that mission?"

"Certainly. There were two reasons. First, it was the most trying moment of your life, and I was curious if it damaged your ability to lead."

"To lead, or to have men and women die under my command?"

"Both," Copp said.

"Then why didn't you just ask?"

"I wanted a response to the situation, directly based on the events, not a canned response."

"Are you happy?" Astrid asked, her teeth clenched.

"It wasn't about making me happy; it was about satisfying the requirements of the grant."

Her dark gray eyes, carrying years of experience, felt like they were boring into her.

Copp stood and cocked her head. "But as you brought it back up, I'm wondering. Can you live with more blood on your hands?"

Astrid swallowed, the tears drying on her cheeks reminding her she'd just given an emotional response. She decided it might as well play out. "I say their names every night as I go to sleep. Nielson, Baker, Reed, Booker, Chu, and my LT, Hernandez. Every single night, and I suspect I'll add more to that list before I'm done. But I'll add as few as I can, because that's what a commander does."

"Fair enough," Copp said and slowly started to sit.

"Wait, the second reason?"

The elderly woman finished sitting with a grunt. "Thirty-five years ago, I was the lead aeronautical engineer on the *Phoenix*-class dropship. That mission on Renova was the last large-scale use of the *Phoenix*. There are dozens still flying, but Renova with the Smasher's was their swansong. I'd never seen the mission details until I saw your mission log. You might want to know that airframe survivability was a key aspect in the design philosophy. Their day might be past, but I'm glad to know they brought a few of you home alive."

"When I got back to Earth and saw the flight profile, I couldn't believe we'd survived the crash, or that any of the others made it out," Astrid said, and bowed her head. "Hell of a bird, ma'am. Thank you."

Copp nodded back and sighed, a not-quite-smile playing across her face. Astrid would have called it bittersweet. She waited for the last series of questions only to have Horowitz surprise her.

"That's all we have, Ms. Amunson." All the members at the table glanced at their slates, then around at each other. "It seems we've already made our determination."

Astrid felt like she'd been gut shot. Horowitz had said back at the beginning that if they made an immediate determination with no deliberation she'd been denied. It was over, and she was back to struggling to find a slot in whatever shit company would hire her. Disappointment morphed into anger, which quickly kindled into rage.

Horowitz had stood up and started to speak. "It is the determination of this committee that Astrid Amunson—"

"Don't bother," she growled and leaped to her feet. "I don't need your consolation or your pity!"

"Ms. Amunson, really—"

She marched up to the table and aimed a knife hand at his chest. "I've been told all my life I wasn't good enough. Too short, too young, too rash, too… *everything!*" The man gaped at her. "You know what? I'm going to catch on somewhere. I'm going to save every credit I can make. Eventually I'll have enough to stand up my own company, and every mission we do I'll send you an email telling every one of you what fucking idiots you are!"

Horowitz's lips narrowed; his eyes boring into her. After a moment he nodded. "I understand," he said.

Everyone at the table got up and walked to the door to the right and exited. Copp glanced back at her, a grin on her face, then she shook her head and walked out.

"What the fuck was that all about?" she said aloud, staring after them.

"I was thinking the same thing."

Astrid's head spun around in surprise. The somewhat portly man in Federation uniform hadn't gotten up with the others. He was still in his seat, staring at her with intense eyes.

"Uhm, sir?"

"I'm not your commander," he said and rose to his feet.

The sound of mechanical actuators drew her attention. He was wearing a support exoskeleton on his lower torso. As he straightened, the name tape on his uniform came into focus and she swallowed. *I should have known better,* she chastised herself. *There's only one three-star in the Federation military, for fuck's sake!* She came to attention.

"Didn't I just say I'm not your commander?"

"Sir, you're—"

"I know who I am, Sergeant Amunson. I'm a little surprised you didn't know who I was before now."

"I was a bit overwhelmed," she admitted, staying at attention.

He walked around the table, coming right up to her. "That was quite the speech, young lady. What do you have to say for yourself?"

"I don't like losing, sir."

"Yeah, I know that. Neither do I. But what was that episode about?"

"I didn't see any reason to sit there and be told I'd failed."

"I can understand that." He held out a slate to her. "Take it."

Astrid accepted the slate and glanced at it. Her eyes bugged out.

"Congratulations, Commander Amunson."

She took a step back, her eyes still wide as she read. "It is the honor and privilege of the Phoenix Initiative Committee to present Astrid

Amunson with a full grant to establish a new mercenary unit, under complete authority and authorized by The Mercenary Guild and its council." There were pages and pages of writing that followed, and a sum of credits. An astounding sum of credits.

"I don't know what to say," she said, numb with shock and still coming down from her rage of a minute earlier.

"Thank you would be enough."

"Thank you?"

He chuckled and nodded. "It was yours to lose when you walked in here. You already had my vote, which is why I didn't ask any questions. I've followed your career from the day you took your VOWs. I couldn't leave you in the hands of the HecSha, either."

"You paid the ransom?"

He nodded, then shrugged. "It wasn't as much as you thought. I owed your commander a favor. He didn't have to twist my arm too much."

Astrid gestured with the slate and shook her head. "I'm overwhelmed, sir."

He nodded his head and spread his hands. "What you do from here is up to you."

The door opposite the one the other members had departed through opened and a short being entered. Less than half the height of a Human and in a red uniform that somehow contrasted with the long furry ears and tail. The new arrival said something in a sing-song language Astrid's translator didn't recognize. No surprise, very few Humans would know how to speak Dusman.

"Yeah, I'll be there in a few minutes." The alien nodded and left through the same door. "I have a meeting. Good luck, and I'll keep an eye on you. As Minister of War, I have quite a few jobs that come up, and my good friend Nigel Shirazi can sometimes toss a prime contract or two. I'll be seeing you around."

"Minister Cartwright?"

"Call me Jim," he replied, and put a hand on her shoulder. "I knew your dad, Lieutenant Chris Sommerkorn, Chip. One of the bravest guys I ever knew, but he was shit at logistics." Jim Cartwright turned and exited after the Dusman, leaving her alone with her surprising success.

* * *

The office was hard worn. The paint was peeling, and it smelled like cigar smoke and stale beer. But it came with plenty of room, a warehouse next door she'd rented at a discount, and direct access to Houston starport. Real estate was getting hard to find in Startown, so when the email came from the office of the Minister of War, she'd acted fast and got a shockingly low price.

The last two months had been long days and short nights, but she was ready. The warehouse was full of equipment and more arrived every day. Only one major task remained.

She stretched inside the new uniform, checking herself in the mirror. A single gold eagle insignia rode on each epaulet, her brand-new company logo on the shoulder patch. The nametape was, for some reason, the most jarring. It would take some getting used to.

"They're waiting, Commander," her XO said, leaning his head into the office. "You look fine."

"I suddenly feel like I'm in grade school playing dress up."

Her XO snorted. "Jim Cartwright was only twenty when he led his first mission as CO of the Cavaliers. Nigel Shirazi was twenty-two. You're twenty-three."

"Not helping."

"Changing your mind?"

"Fuck no."

Her XO laughed. "Then get your shit together and let's start the game."

"Very well, Major Stanley. Just remember, this isn't Triple T; I'm never walking away from helpless civvies."

"Never liked that one, but I followed orders."

"You were a fair CO. You wrote that commendation even when you were told not to."

"That's part of being a fair CO. Glad to be your executive officer, Commander."

Astrid straightened her new uniform tunic and went to the door. "Let's go."

Stanley walked into the conference room first. "Attention!" There was a rustle of commotion as everyone came to attention. "Your Commander, Colonel Astrid "Chip" Sommerkorn."

"Thank you, XO. I'm not big on barracks formality, so ease up on the discipline. As long as the job gets done, that's all I'm worried about. This is Major Reginald "Rex" Stanley, my XO. Over there is Lieutenant Benjamin Chen, our chief medical officer." The smile she got was just a tad more familiar than appropriate, as was the one she returned. "I'd like to welcome you all to your first day with the Honey Badgers. We have a lot to go over, so let's get to work."

* * * * *

Mark Wandrey Bio

Mark Wandrey has been creating new worlds since he was old enough to write. A four-time Dragon Award finalist, Mark has authored over 25 books with more on the way. He has a lifetime of diverse jobs, extensive travels, and living in many areas of the country which he uses to color his stories in ways many find engaging and thought provoking. Now living full-time traveling in an RV with his wife Joy and their chihuahua Pollo, Mark writes while fighting an addiction to dash cam videos.

# # # # #

About the Editors

A Webster Award winner and three-time Dragon Award finalist, Chris Kennedy is a Science Fiction/Fantasy/Young Adult author, speaker, and small-press publisher who has written over 25 books and published more than 100 others. Chris' stories include the "Occupied Seattle" military fiction duology, "The Theogony" and "Codex Regius" science fiction trilogies, stories in the "Four Horsemen," "Fallen World," and "In Revolution Born" universes and the "War for Dominance" fantasy trilogy. Get his free book, "Shattered Crucible," at his website, https://chriskennedypublishing.com.

Called "fantastic" and "a great speaker," he has coached hundreds of beginning authors and budding novelists on how to self-publish their stories at a variety of conferences, conventions and writing guild presentations. He is the author of the award-winning #1 bestseller, "Self-Publishing for Profit: How to Get Your Book Out of Your Head and Into the Stores," as well as the leadership training book, "Leadership from the Darkside."

Chris lives in Virginia Beach, Virginia, with his wife, and is the holder of a doctorate in educational leadership and master's degrees in both business and public administration. Follow Chris on Facebook at https://www.facebook.com/ckpublishing/.

Mark Wandrey has been creating new worlds since he was old enough to write. A four-time Dragon Award finalist, Mark has authored over 25 books with more on the way. He has a lifetime of diverse jobs, extensive travels, and living in many areas of the country which he uses to color his stories in ways many find engaging and thought provoking. Now living full-time traveling in an RV with his wife Joy and their chihuahua Pollo, Mark writes while fighting an addiction to dash cam videos.

* * * * *

Get the **free** Four Horsemen prelude story "**Shattered Crucible**"

and discover other titles by Theogony Books at:

http://chriskennedypublishing.com/

* * * * *

Meet the author and other CKP authors on the Factory Floor:

https://www.facebook.com/groups/461794864654198

* * * * *

Did you like this book?
Please write a review!

* * * * *

The following is an
Excerpt from Book One of The Prince of Britannia Saga:

The Prince Awakens

Fred Hughes

Available from Theogony Books

eBook, Paperback, and Audio

Excerpt from "The Prince Awakens:"

Sixth Fleet was in chaos. Fortunately, all the heavy units were deployed forward toward the attacking fleet and were directing all the defensive fire they had downrange at the enemy. More than thirteen thousand Swarm attack ships were bearing down on a fleet of twenty-six heavy escorts and the single monitor. The monitor crew had faith in their shields and guns, but could they survive against this many? They would soon find out.

Luckily, they didn't have to face all the Swarm ships. Historically, Swarm forces engaged major threats first, then went after the escorts. Which was why the monitor had to be considered the biggest threat in the battle.

Then the Swarm forces deviated from their usual pattern. The Imperial plan was suddenly irrelevant as the Swarm attack ships divided into fifteen groups and attacked the escorts, which didn't last long. When the last dreadnought died in a nuclear fireball, the Swarm attack ships turned and moved toward the next fleet in the column, Fourth Fleet, leaving the monitor behind.

The entire plan was in shambles. But, more importantly, the whole fleet was at risk of being defeated. The admiral's only option now was to save as many as he could.

"Signal to the Third, Fifth, and Seventh Fleets. The monitors are to execute Withdrawal Plan Beta."

The huge monitors had eight fleet tugs that were magnetically attached to the hull when not in use. Together, the eight tugs could get the monitors into hyperspace. However, this process took time, due to the time it took for the eight tugs to generate a warp field large enough to encompass the enormous ship. It could take up to an hour to accomplish, and they didn't have an hour.

Plan Bravo would use six heavy cruisers to accomplish the same thing. The cruisers' larger fusion engines meant the field could be generated within ten minutes, assuming no one was shooting at them. "The remaining fleet units will move to join First Fleet. Admiral

Mason in First Fleet will take command of the combined force and deploy it for combat."

The fleet admiral continued giving orders.

"I want Second Fleet to do the same, but I want heavy cruiser Squadron Twenty-Three to merge with First Fleet. Admiral Conyers, I want you to coordinate with the Eighth, Ninth, and Tenth Fleets. I want their monitors to perform a normal Alpha Withdrawal. As they're preparing to do that, have their escorts combine into a single fleet. Figure out which admiral is senior and assign him local command to organize them." He pointed at the single icon indicating the only ship left in Sixth Fleet. "Signal *Prometheus* to move at best speed to join First Fleet. That covers everything for now. I fear there's not much we can do for Fourth Fleet."

The icons were already moving on the tactical display as orders were transmitted and implemented.

"I've given the fleets in the planet's orbit their orders, Admiral," the chief of staff informed him. "The other fleets are on the move now. The Swarm should contact Fourth Fleet in approximately ten minutes. Based on their attack of Sixth Fleet, the battle will last about twenty minutes. With fifteen minutes for them to reorganize and travel to First Fleet, we're looking at forty-five minutes to engagement with the Swarm."

"What are the estimates on the rest of the fleets moving to join up with First?"

"Twenty minutes, Admiral. However, *Prometheus* is going to take at least forty-five and will arrive about the same time as the enemy."

"Organize six heavies from Seventh Fleet and have them coordinate a rendezvous with *Prometheus*, earliest possible timing," the admiral ordered. "Then execute a Beta jump. Unless the Swarm forces divert, they should have enough time. Then find out how many ships have the upgraded forty-millimeter rail gun systems and form them into a single force. O'Riley said that converting the guns to barrage fire was a simple program update. Brevet Commodore O'Riley will be in command of the newly created Task Force Twenty-Three. They are to form a wall of steel which the fleet will form behind. I am not sure if we can win this, but we need to bleed these bastards if we can't. If they win, they'll still have to make up those losses, and that will delay the next attack."

* * * * *

Get "The Prince Awakens" here: https://www.amazon.com/dp/B0BK232YT2.

Find out more about Fred Hughes at: https://chriskennedypublishing.com.

* * * * *

The following is an
Excerpt from Book One of The Last Marines:

Gods of War

William S. Frisbee, Jr.

Available from Theogony Books

eBook, Audio, and Paperback

Excerpt from "Gods of War:"

"Yes, sir," Mathison said. Sometimes it was worth arguing, sometimes it wasn't. Stevenson wasn't a butter bar. He was a veteran from a line infantry platoon that had made it through Critical Skills Operator School and earned his Raider pin. He was also on the short list for captain. Major Beckett might pin the railroad tracks on Stevenson's collar before they left for space.

"Well, enough chatting," Stevenson said, the smile in his voice grating on Mathison's nerves. "Gotta go check our boys."

"Yes, sir," Mathison said, and later he would check on the men while the lieutenant rested. "Please keep your head down, sir. Don't leave me in charge of this cluster fuck. I would be tempted to tell that company commander to go fuck a duck."

"No, you won't. You will do your job and take care of our Marines, but I'll keep my head down," Stevenson said. "Asian socialists aren't good enough to kill me. It's going to have to be some green alien bastard that kills me."

"Yes, sir," Mathison said as the lieutenant tapped on Jennings' shoulder and pointed up. The lance corporal understood and cupped his hands together to boost the lieutenant out of the hole. He launched the lieutenant out of the hole and went back to digging as Mathison went back to looking at the spy eyes scrutinizing the distant jungle.

A shot rang out. On Mathison's heads-up display, the icon for Lieutenant Stevenson flashed and went red, indicating death.

"You are now acting platoon commander," Freya reported.

* * * * *

Get "Gods of War" now at: https://www.amazon.com/dp/B0B5WJB2MY.

Find out more about William S. Frisbee, Jr. at: https://chriskennedypublishing.com.

* * * * *

Made in United States
Troutdale, OR
06/16/2023

10633812R00355